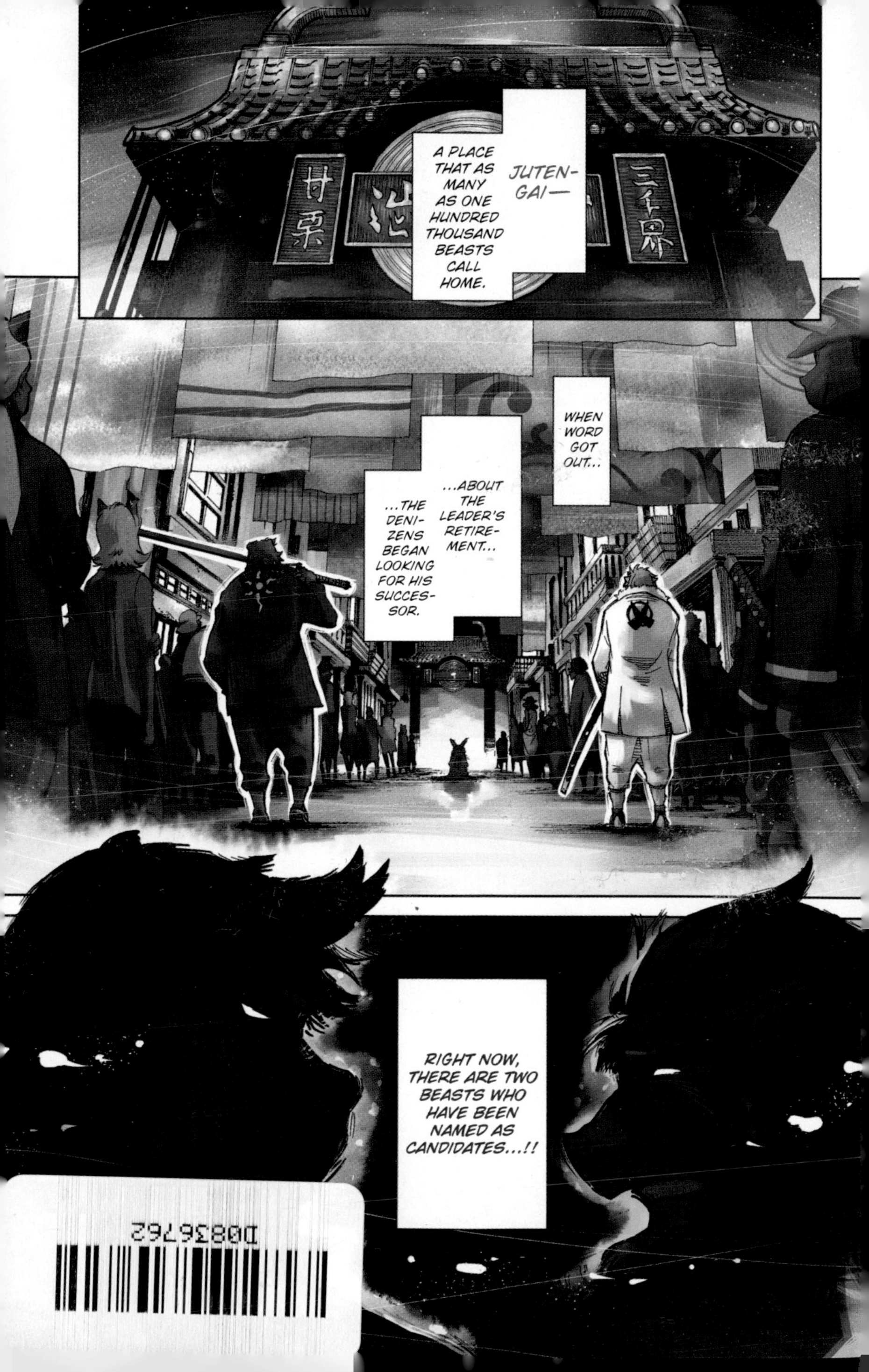
JUTEN-GAI—
A PLACE THAT AS MANY AS ONE HUNDRED THOUSAND BEASTS CALL HOME.
WHEN WORD GOT OUT...
...ABOUT THE LEADER'S RETIRE-MENT...
...THE DENI-ZENS BEGAN LOOKING FOR HIS SUCCES-SOR.
RIGHT NOW, THERE ARE TWO BEASTS WHO HAVE BEEN NAMED AS CANDIDATES...!!

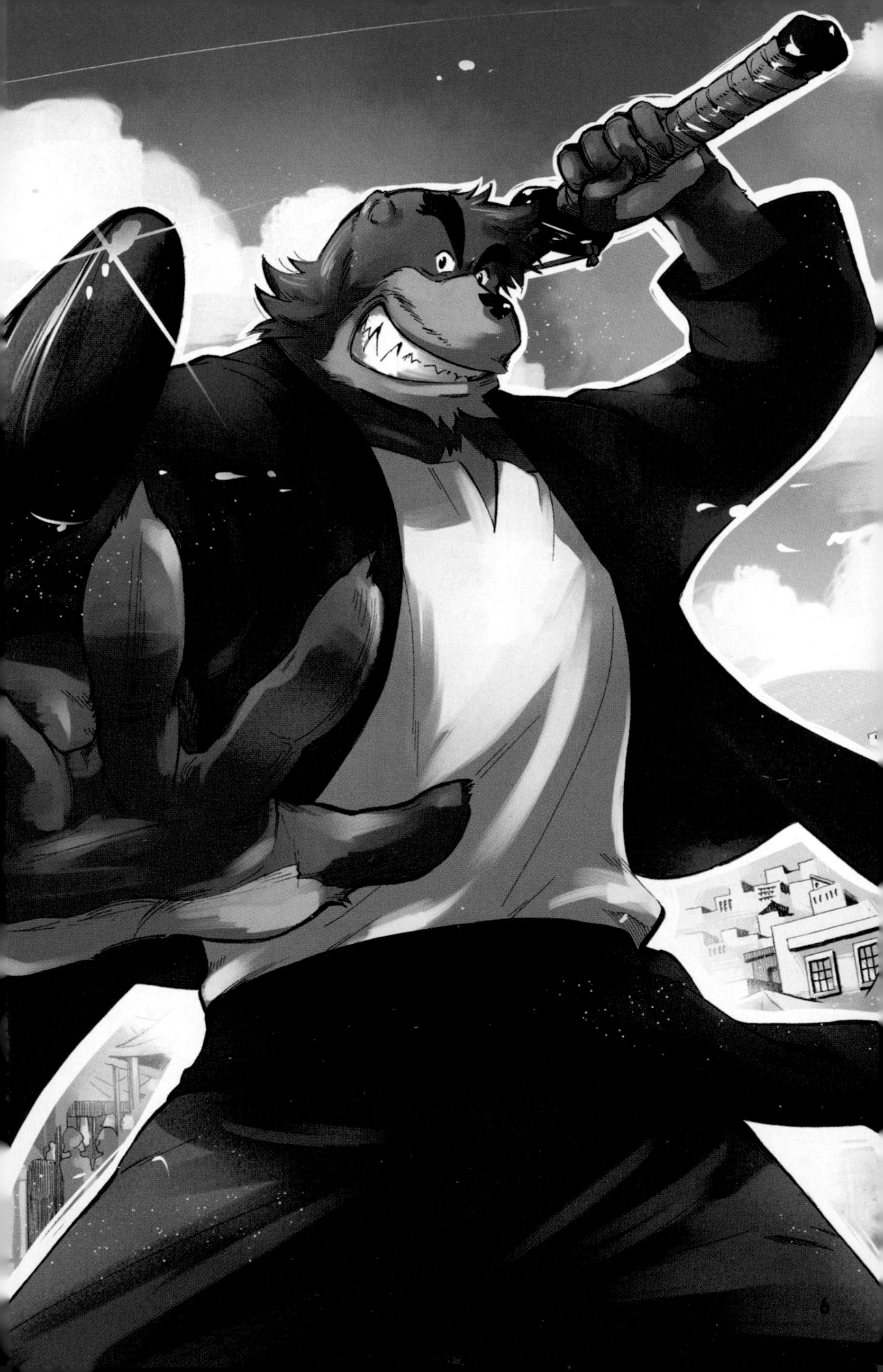

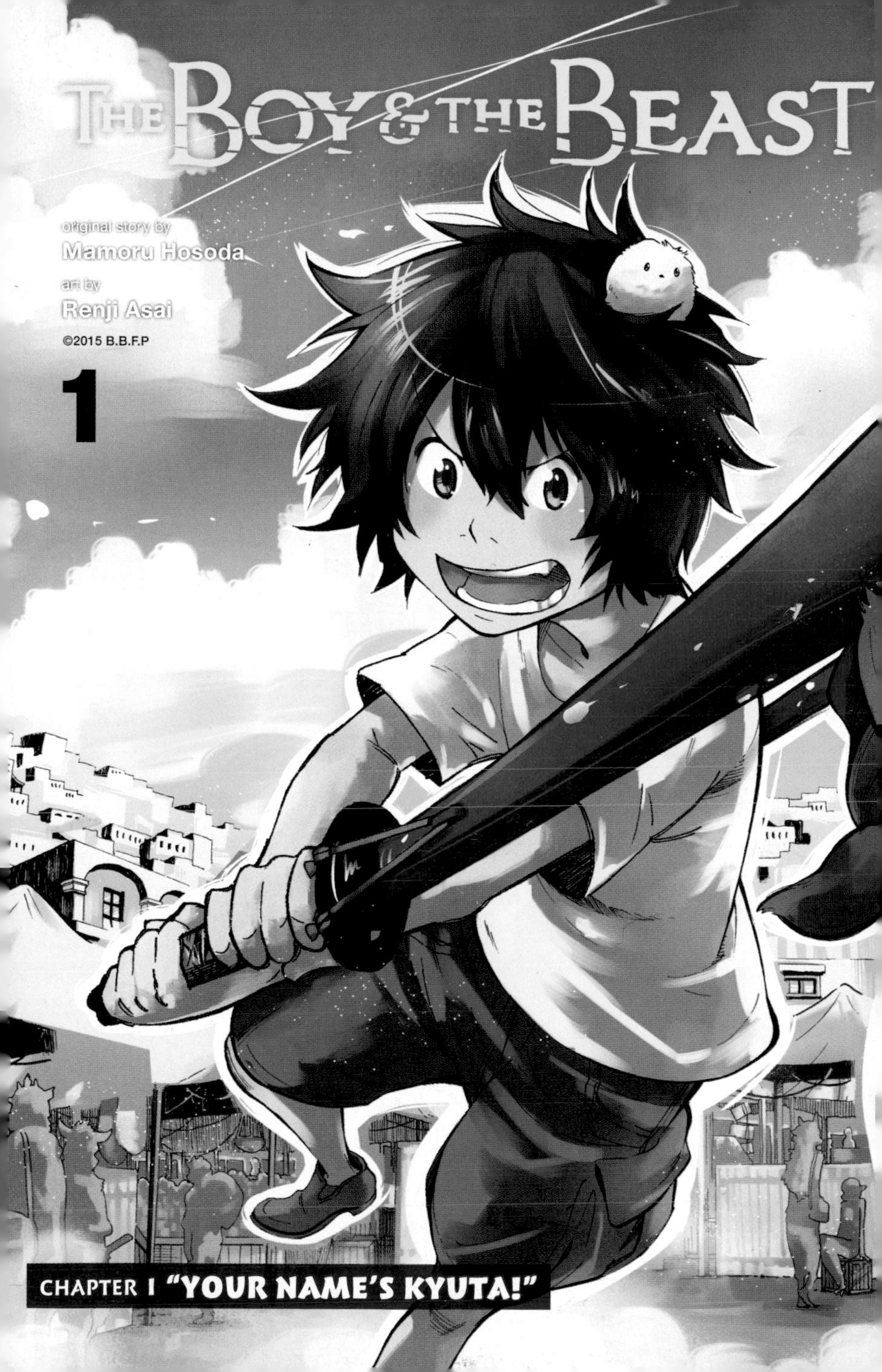
THE BOY & THE BEAST
original story by
Mamoru Hosoda
art by
Renji Asai
©2015 B.B.F.P
1
CHAPTER 1 "YOUR NAME'S KYUTA!"

THE BOY & THE BEAST

original story by
Mamoru Hosoda
art by
Renji Asai

1

CONTENTS

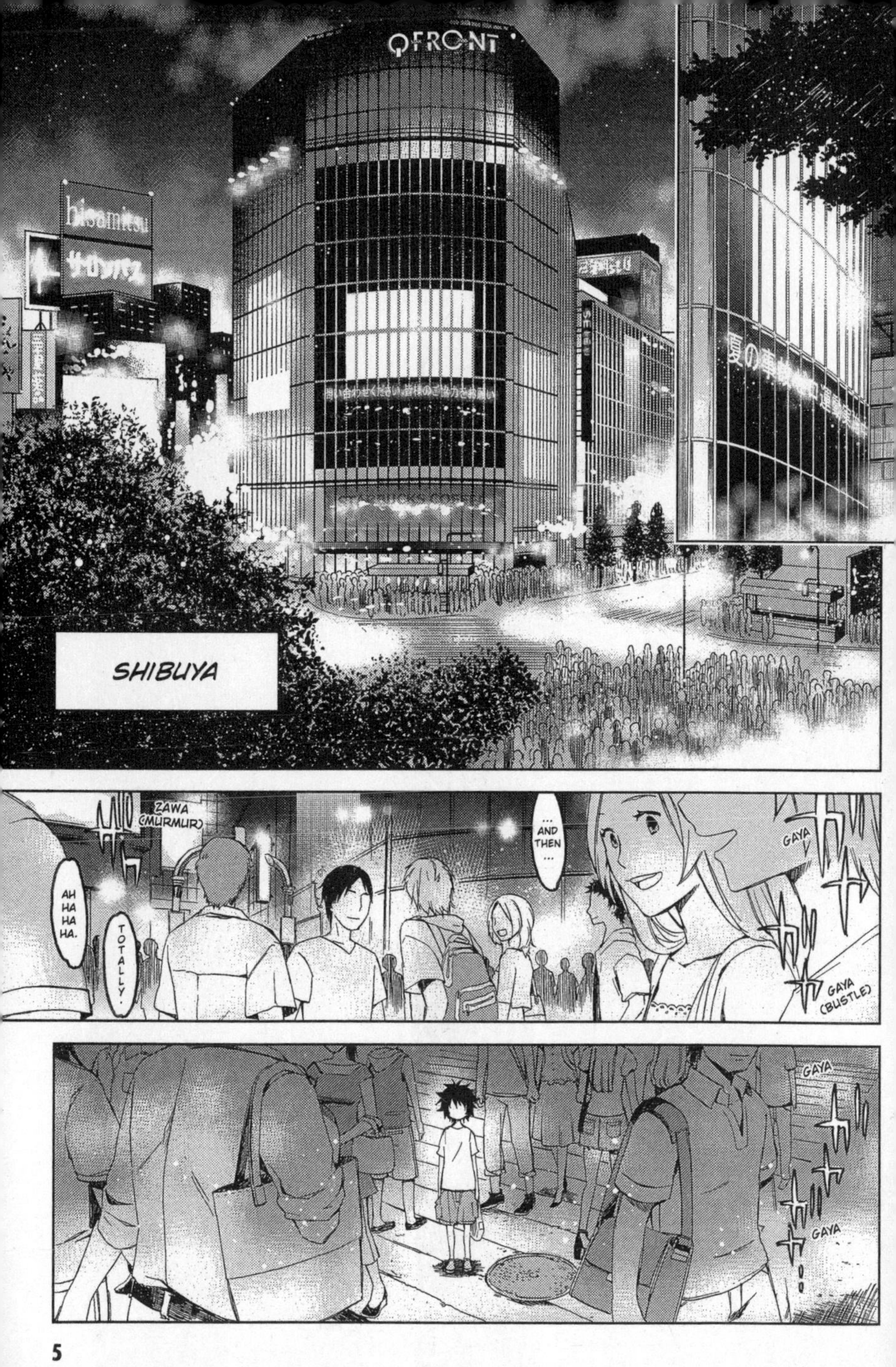
QFRONT
hisamitsu
SHIBUYA
GAYA
GAYA (BUSTLE)
...AND THEN...
ZAWA (MURMUR)
TOTALLY.
AH HA HA HA.
GAYA
GAYA

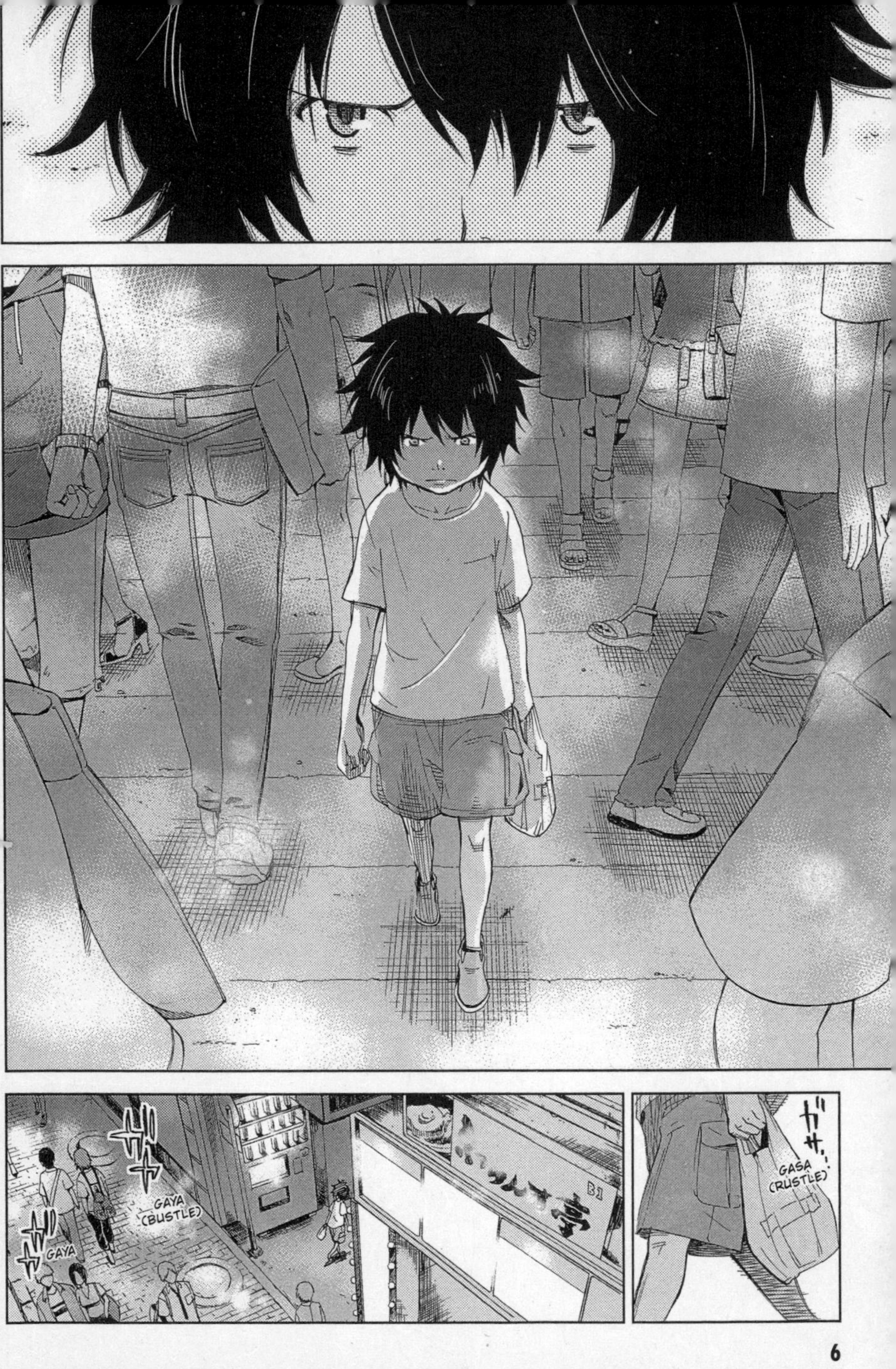
ガサ…
GASA (RUSTLE)
ガヤ
GAYA (BUSTLE)
ガヤ
GAYA

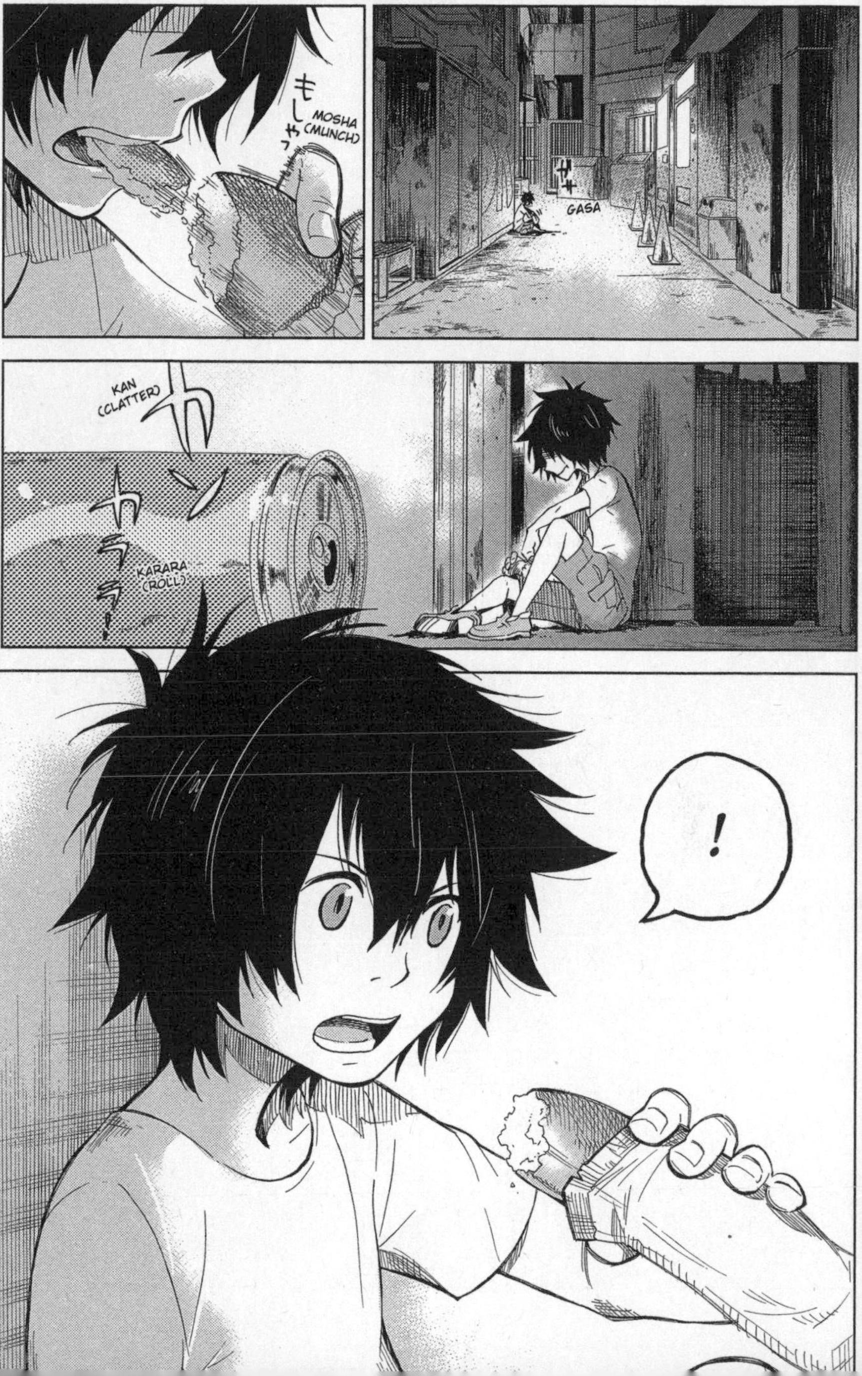
ガサ
GASA
もしゃっ
MOSHA (MUNCH)
カン
KAN (CLATTER)
カラララ!
KARARA (ROLL)
!

A BABY RAT?

......

じ (STARE)

OR MAYBE ...

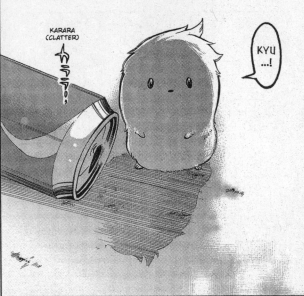

KARARA (CLATTER)

KYU ...!

!

KORO (ROLL)

BIKU (TWITCH)

HYO (TOSS)

SASA (DASH)

KARA

KARA

URU (TEARY)

GO ON, EAT.

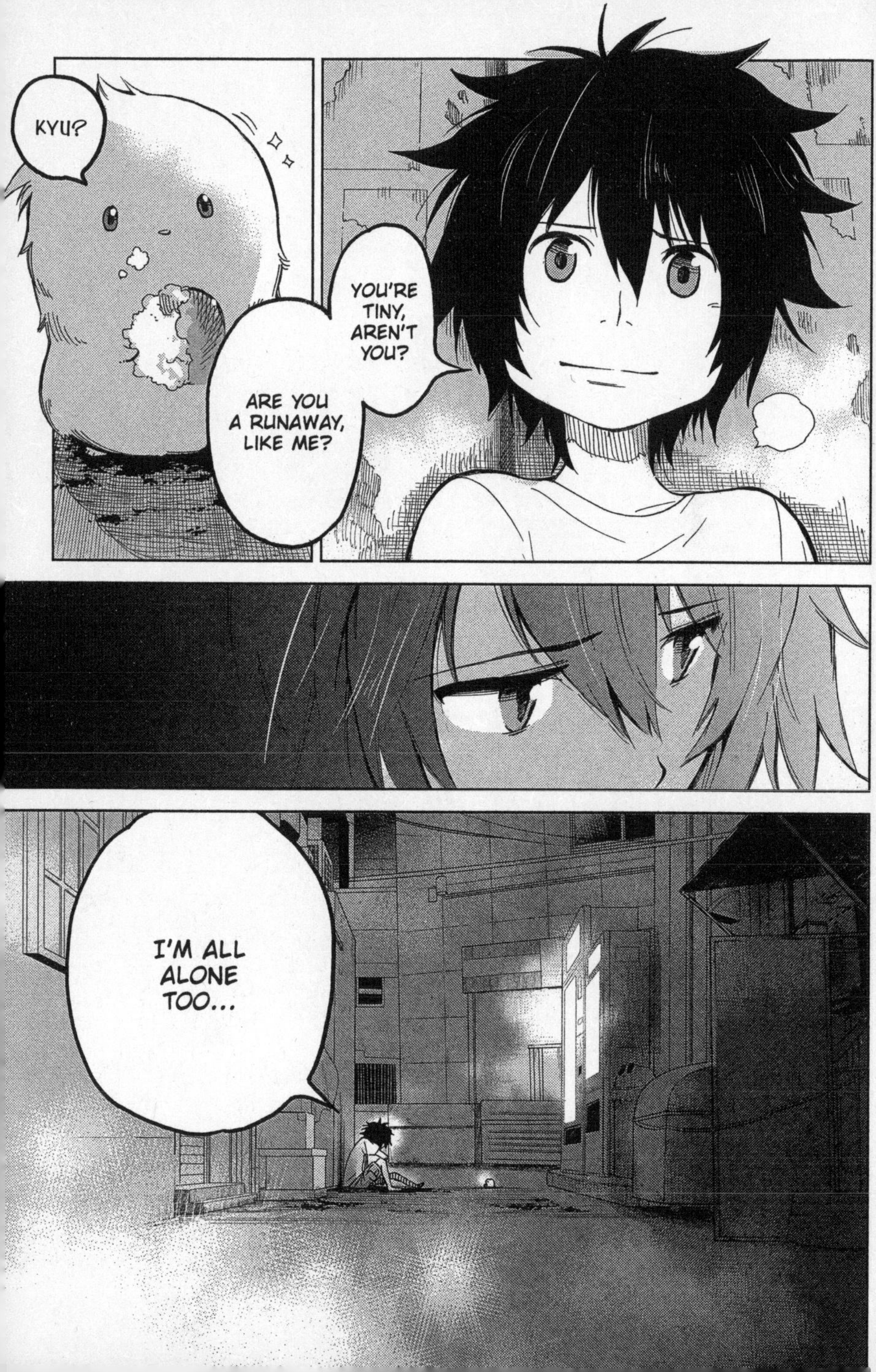
YOU'RE TINY, AREN'T YOU?
ARE YOU A RUNAWAY, LIKE ME?
KYU?
I'M ALL ALONE TOO...

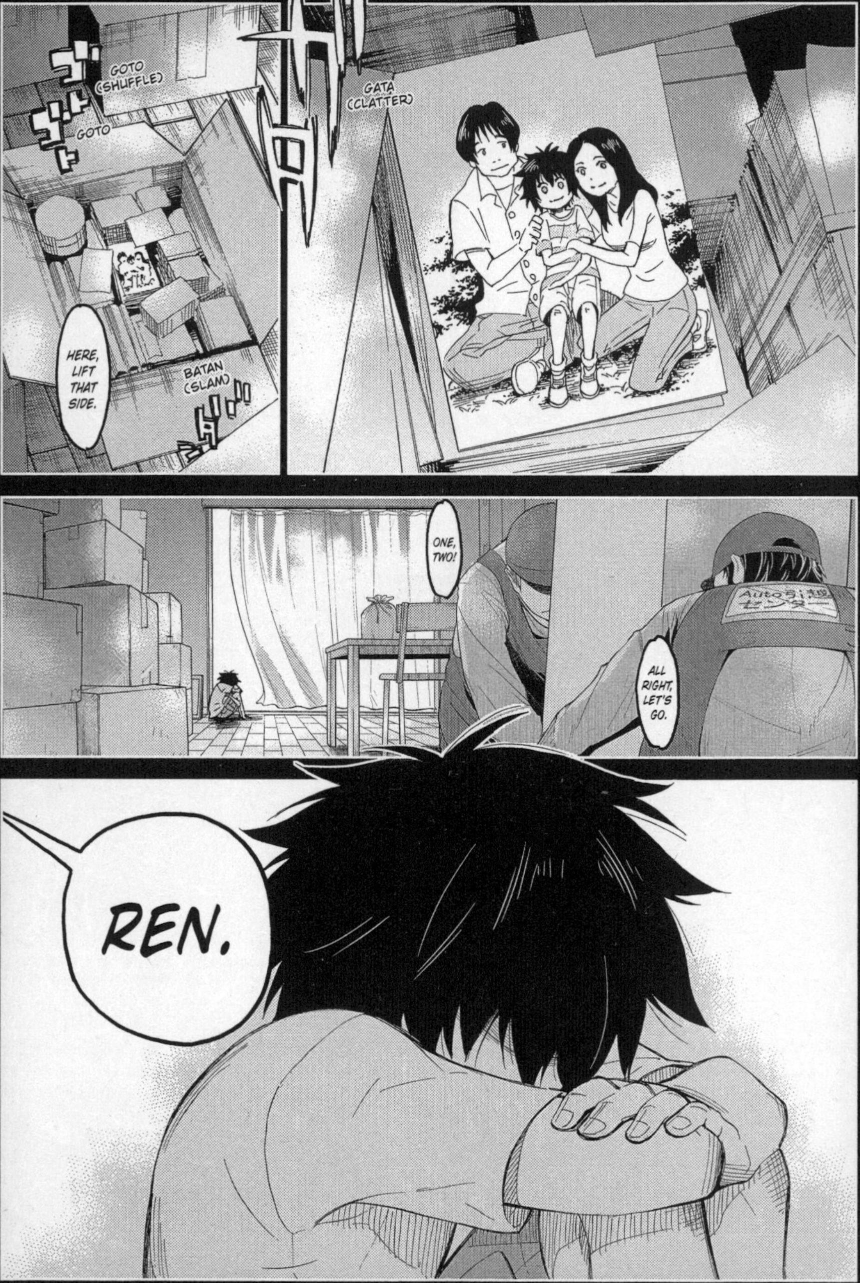
GATA (CLATTER)
GOTO (SHUFFLE)
GOTO
HERE, LIFT THAT SIDE.
BATAN (SLAM)
ALL RIGHT, LET'S GO.
Auto引越センター
ONE, TWO!
REN.

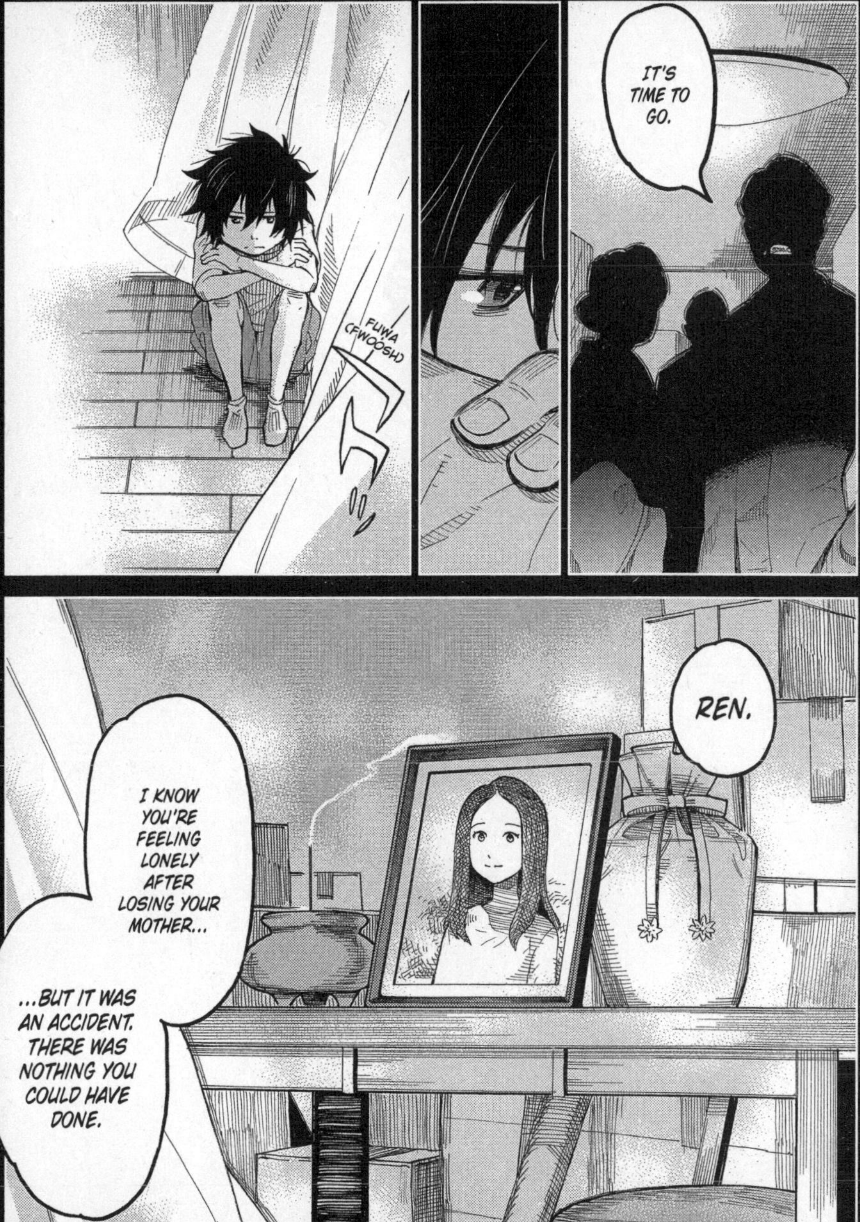
IT'S TIME TO GO.
FUWA (FWOOSH)
REN.
I KNOW YOU'RE FEELING LONELY AFTER LOSING YOUR MOTHER...
...BUT IT WAS AN ACCIDENT. THERE WAS NOTHING YOU COULD HAVE DONE.

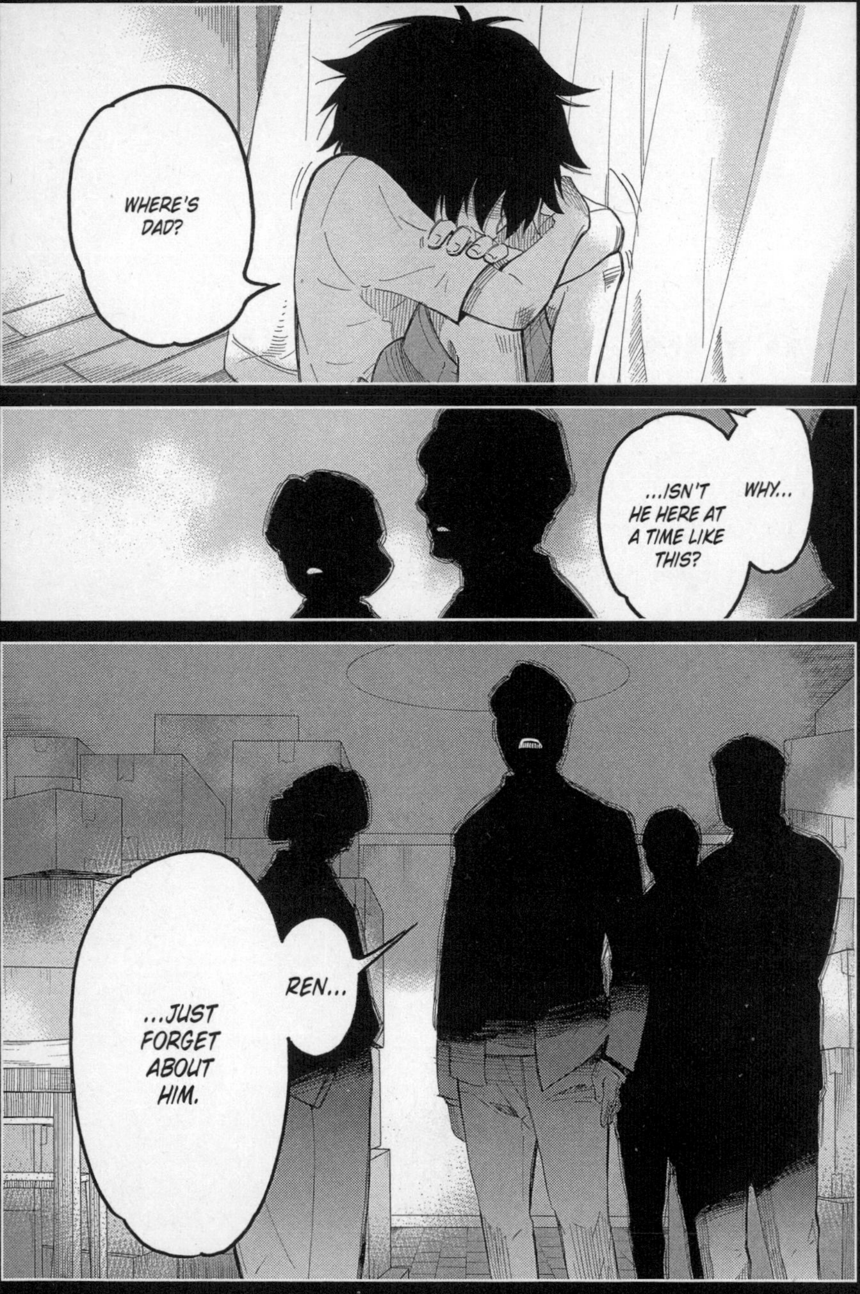
WHERE'S DAD?
WHY...
...ISN'T HE HERE AT A TIME LIKE THIS?
REN...
...JUST FORGET ABOUT HIM.

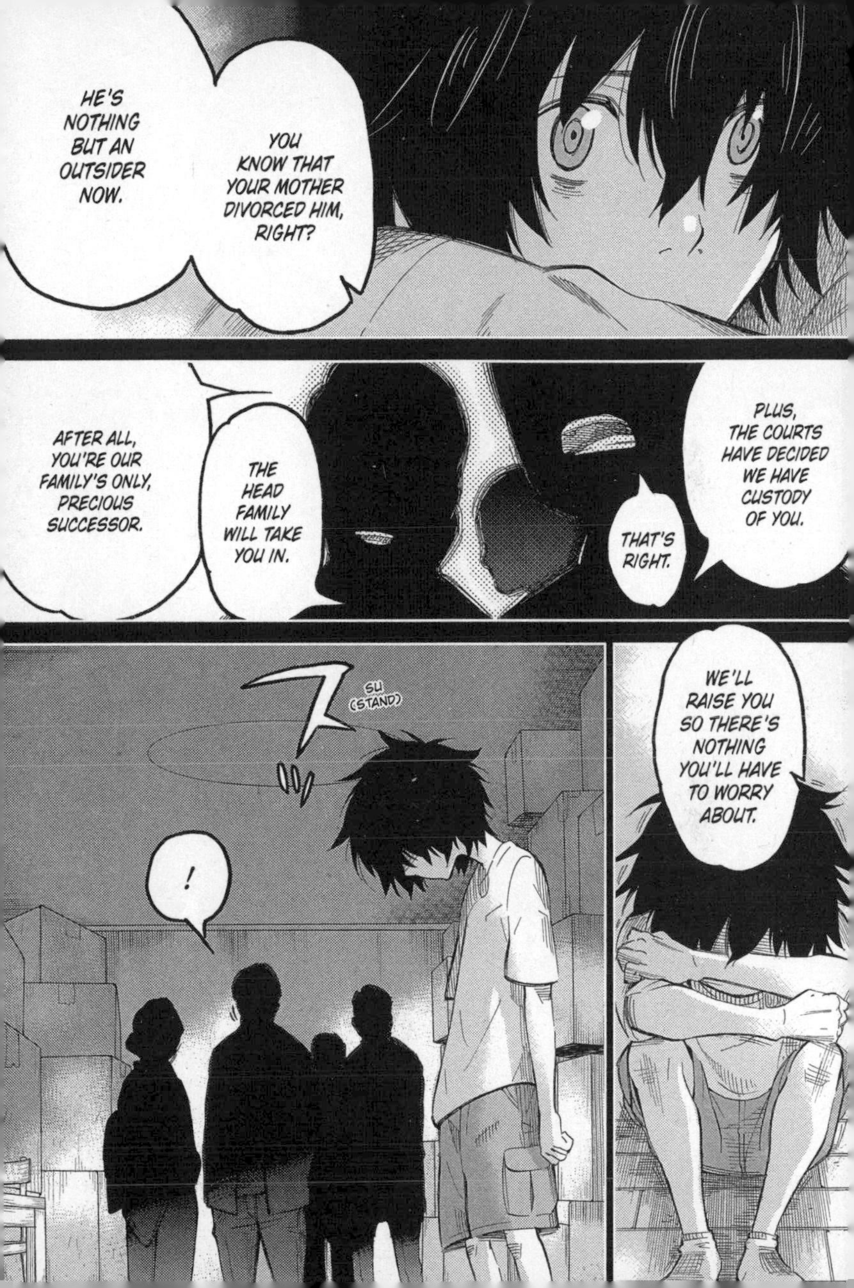
YOU KNOW THAT YOUR MOTHER DIVORCED HIM, RIGHT?
HE'S NOTHING BUT AN OUTSIDER NOW.
PLUS, THE COURTS HAVE DECIDED WE HAVE CUSTODY OF YOU.
THAT'S RIGHT.
THE HEAD FAMILY WILL TAKE YOU IN.
AFTER ALL, YOU'RE OUR FAMILY'S ONLY, PRECIOUS SUCCESSOR.
WE'LL RAISE YOU SO THERE'S NOTHING YOU'LL HAVE TO WORRY ABOUT.
SU (STAND)
!

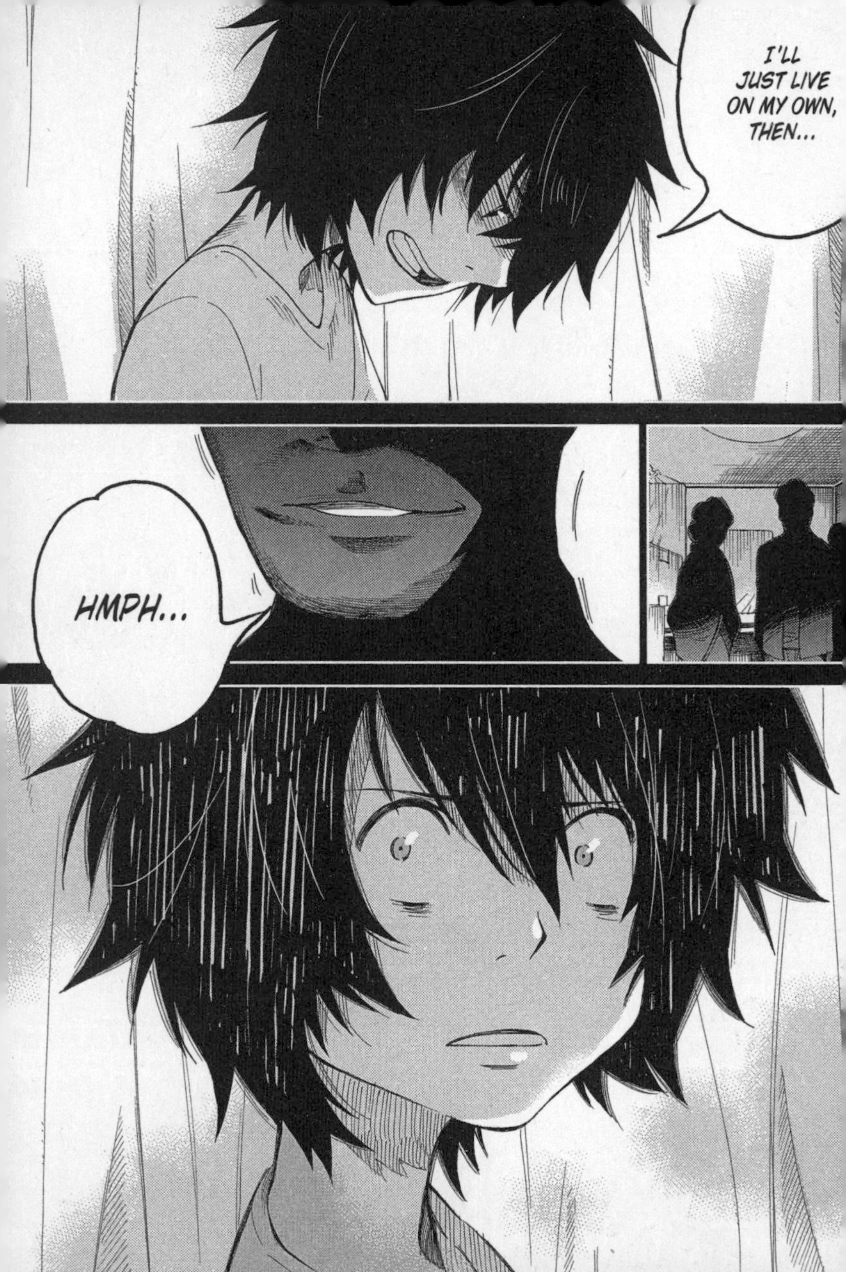
I'LL JUST LIVE ON MY OWN, THEN...
HMPH...

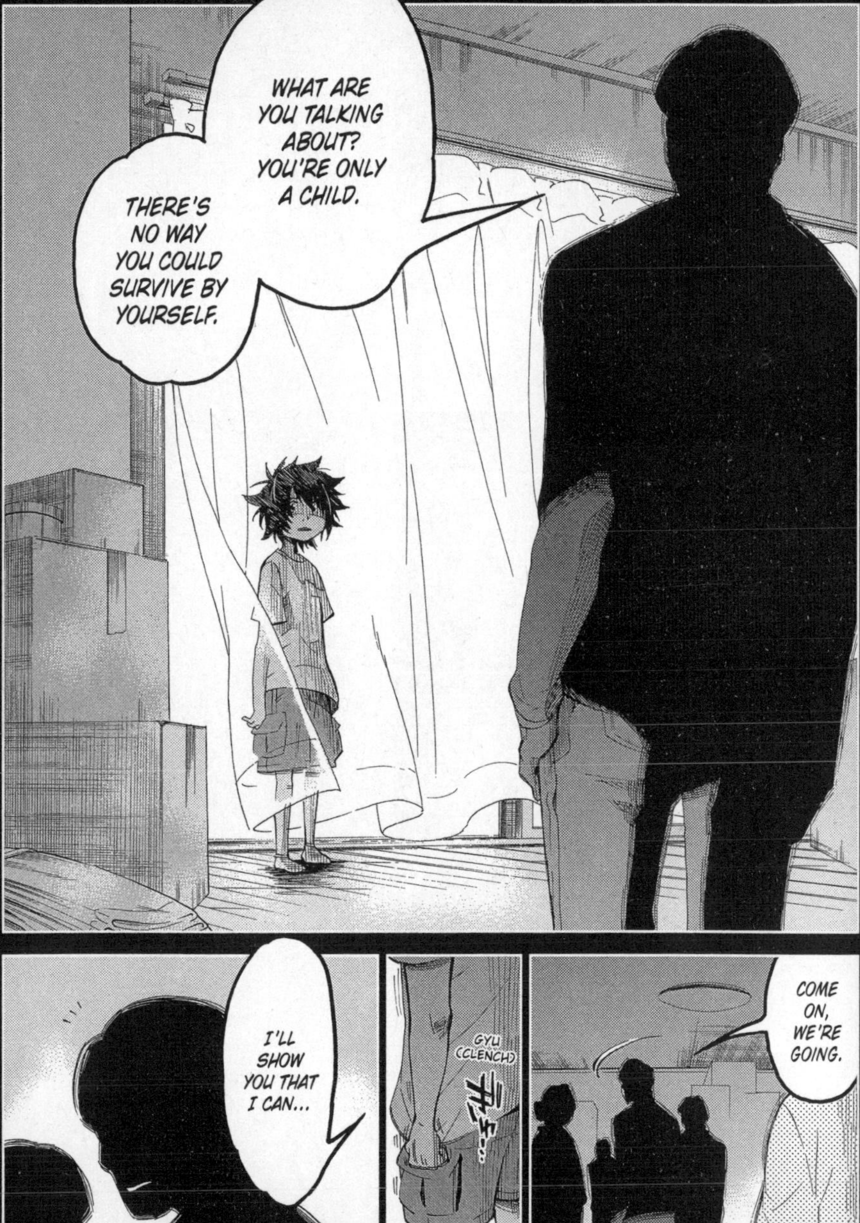
WHAT ARE YOU TALKING ABOUT? YOU'RE ONLY A CHILD.
THERE'S NO WAY YOU COULD SURVIVE BY YOURSELF.
COME ON, WE'RE GOING.
GYU (CLENCH)
I'LL SHOW YOU THAT I CAN...

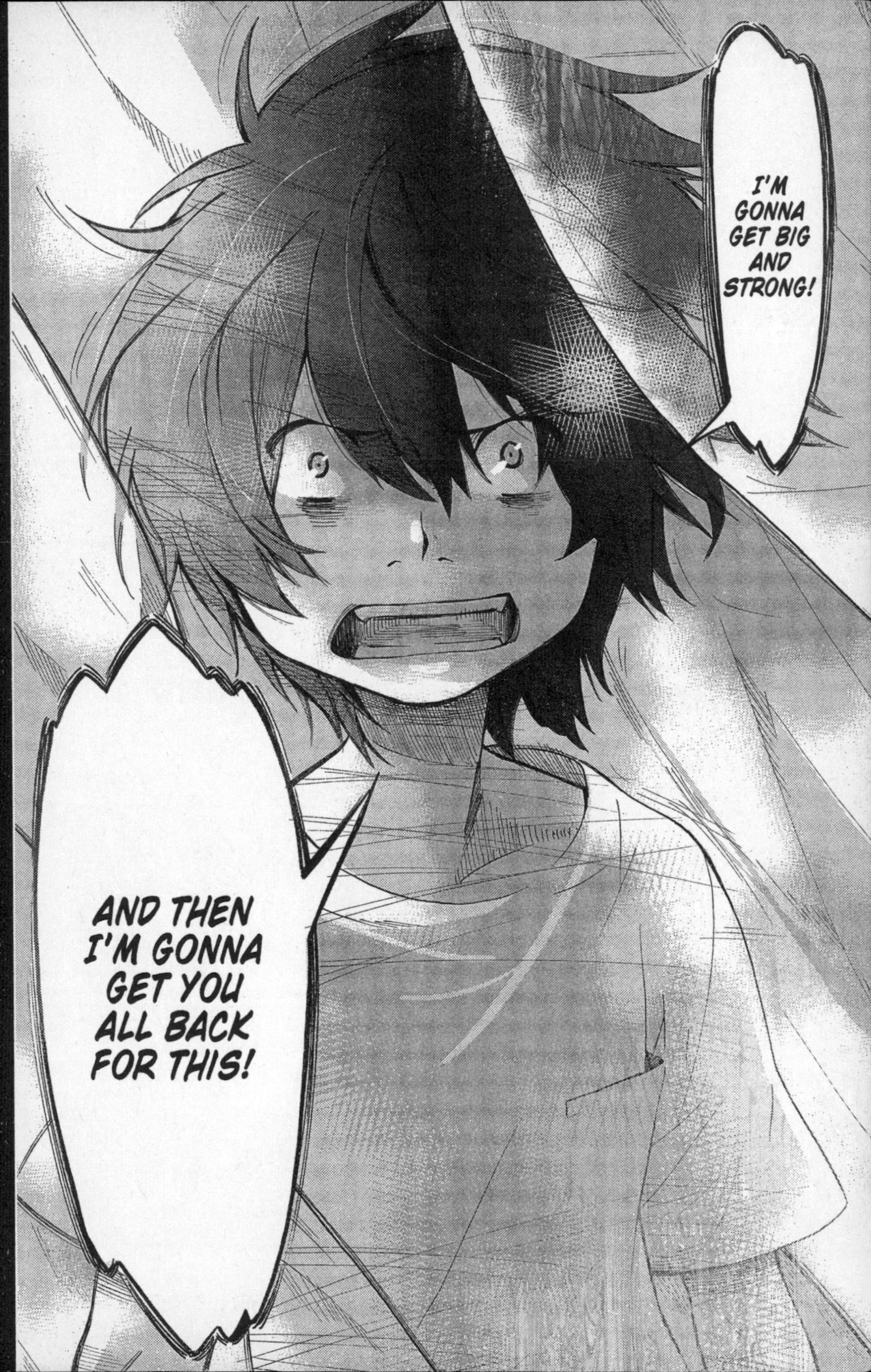
I'M GONNA GET BIG AND STRONG!
AND THEN I'M GONNA GET YOU ALL BACK FOR THIS!

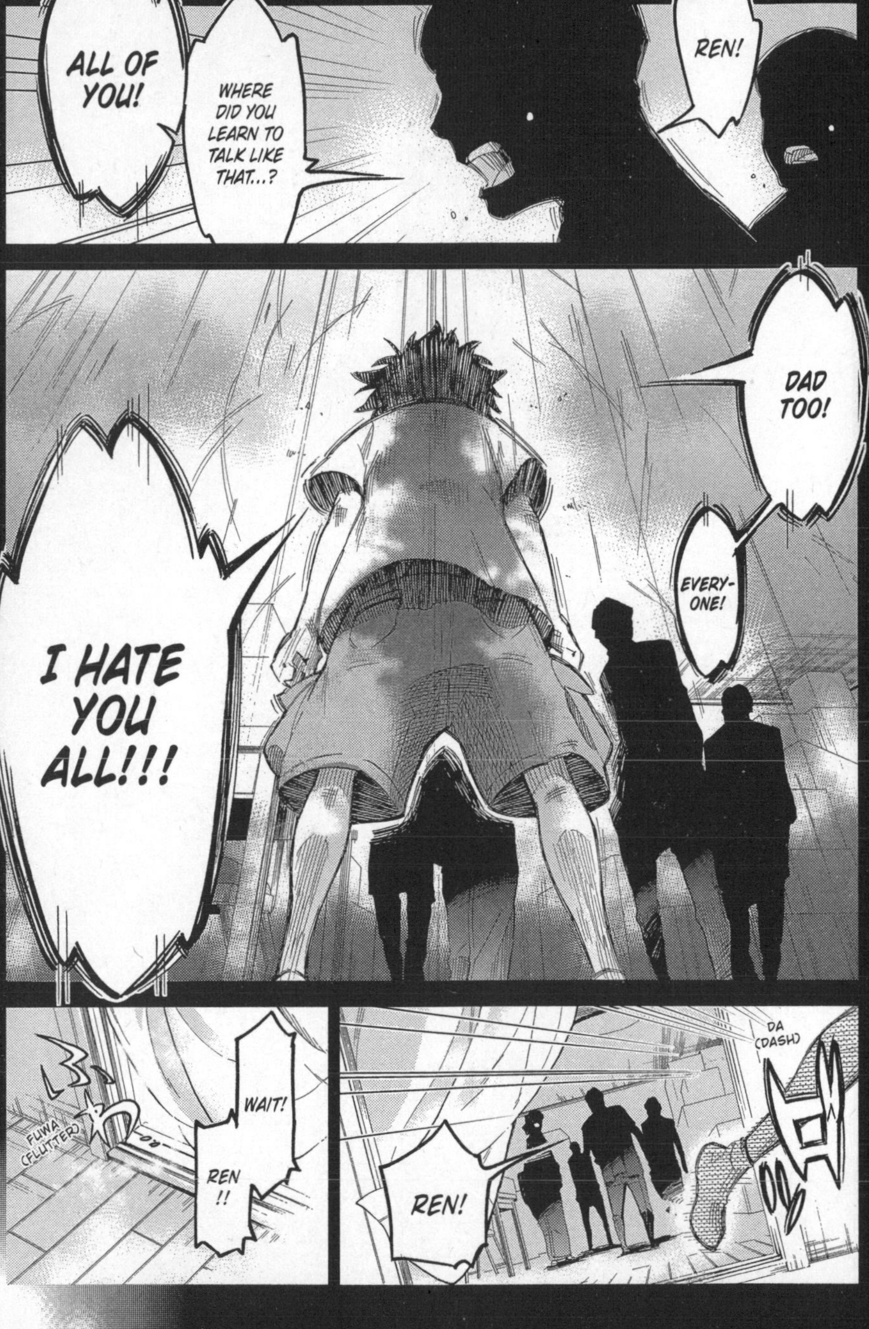
REN!
WHERE DID YOU LEARN TO TALK LIKE THAT...?
ALL OF YOU!
DAD TOO!
EVERY-ONE!
I HATE YOU ALL!!!
DA (DASH)
REN!
WAIT!
REN !!
FUWA (FLUTTER)

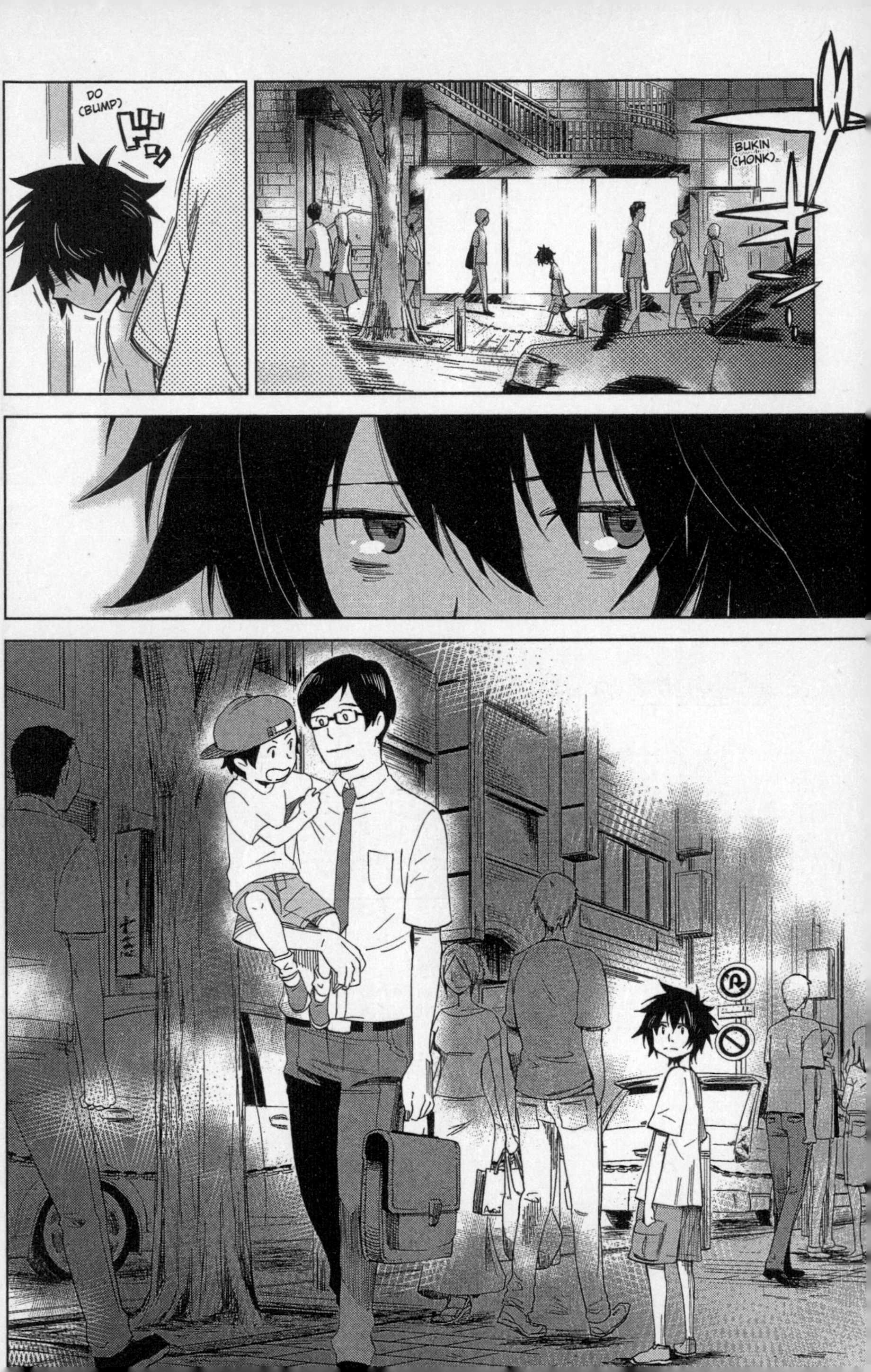
BUKIN (CHONK)
DO (BUMP)

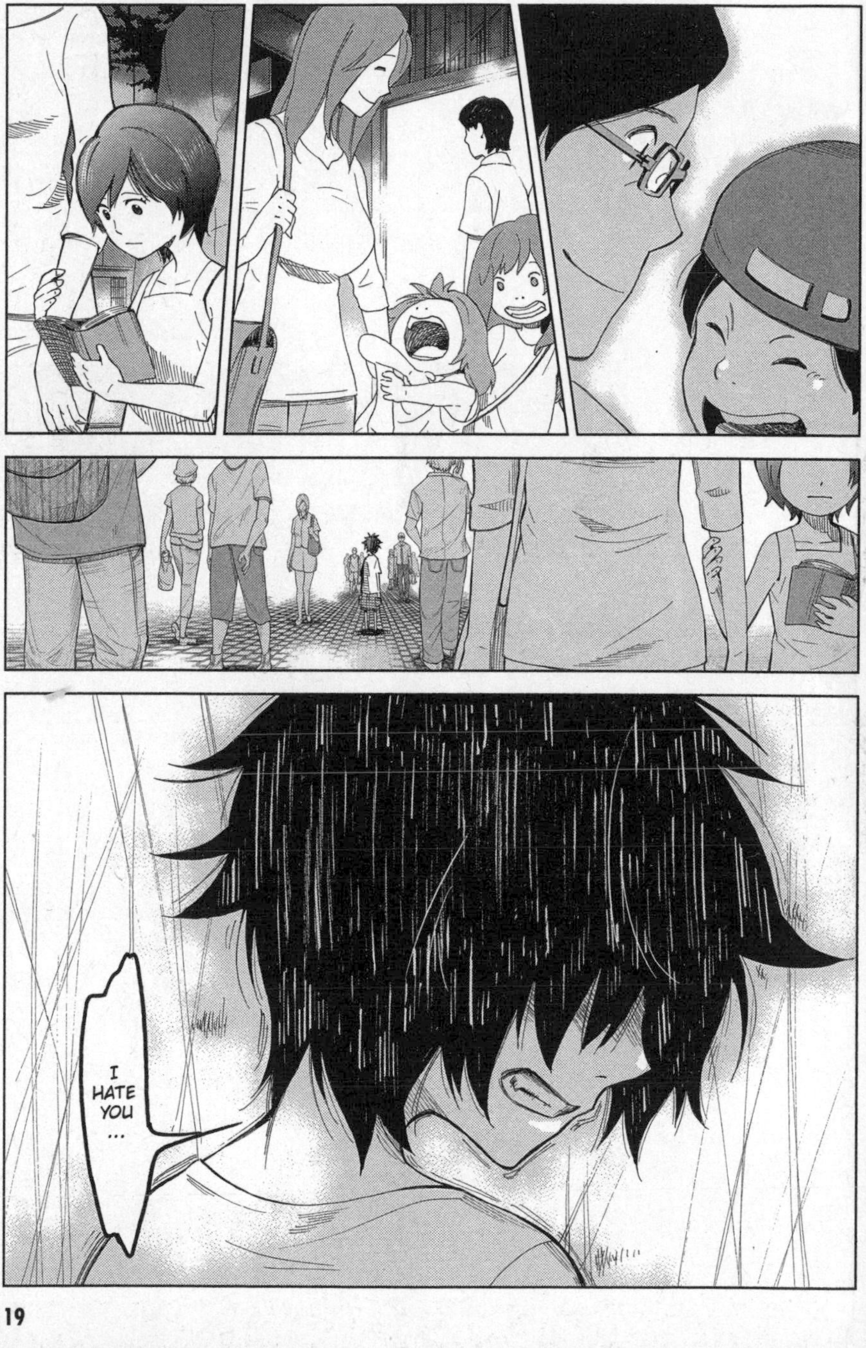
I HATE YOU ...

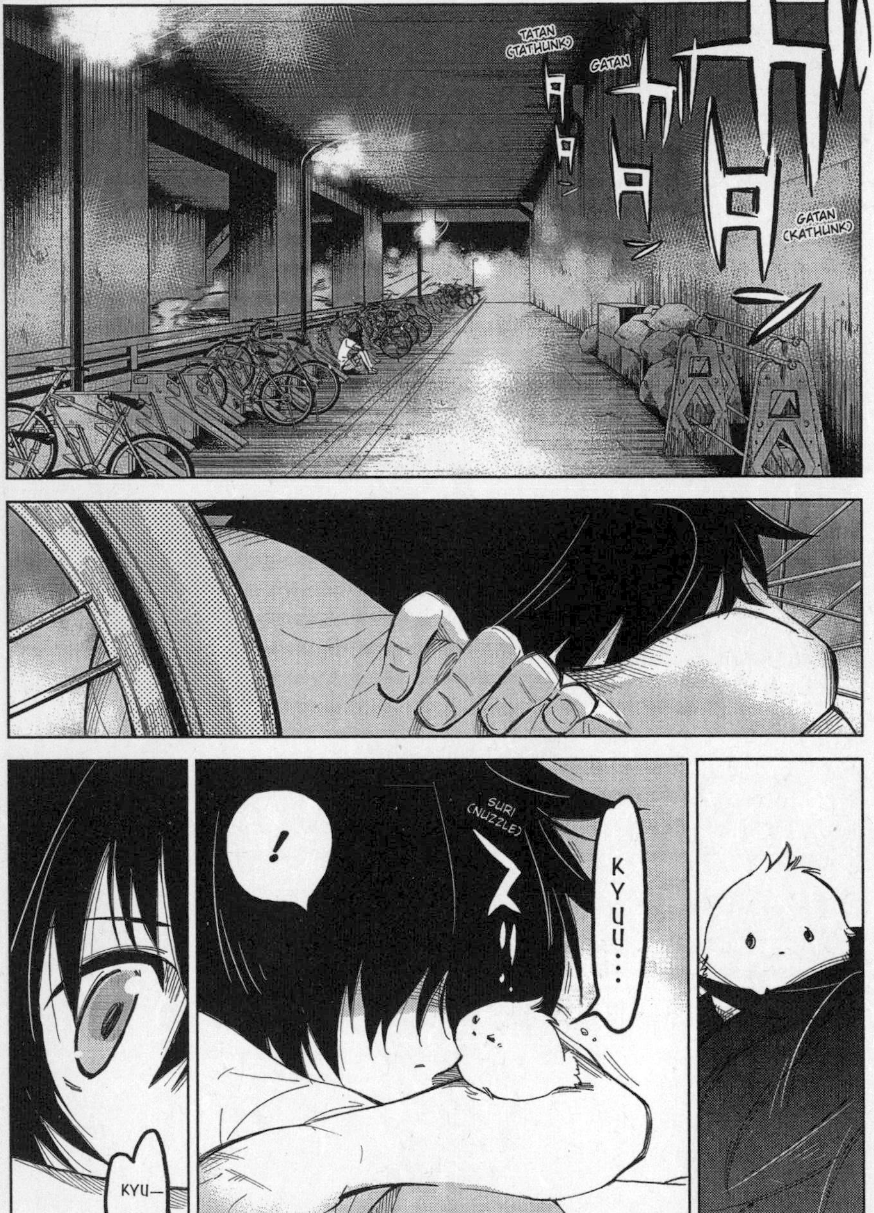
GATAN (KATHUNK)
GATAN
TATAN (TATHUNK)
KYUU...
SURI (NUZZLE)
!
KYU— KYU—

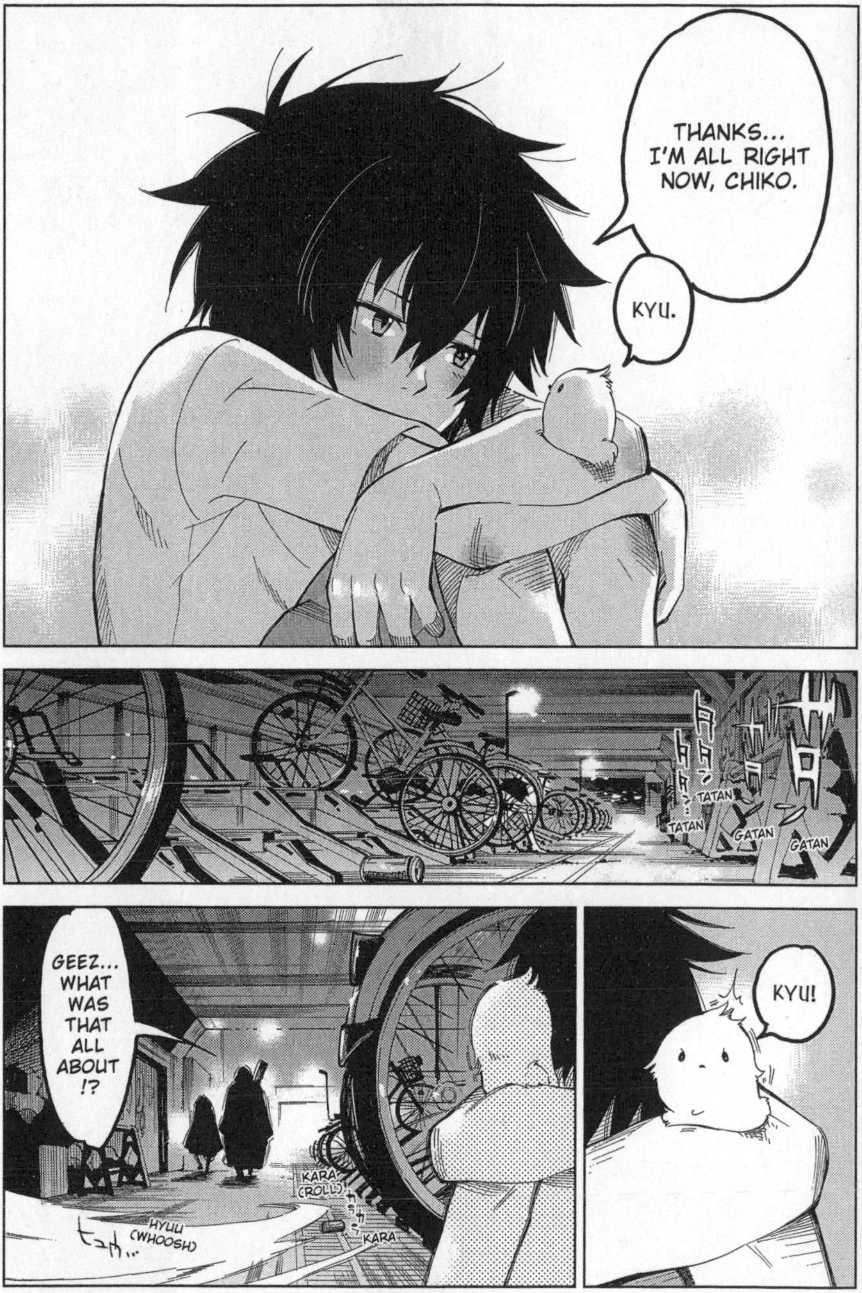
THANKS... I'M ALL RIGHT NOW, CHIKO.
KYU.
TATAN
TATAN
GATAN
GATAN
KYU!
GEEZ... WHAT WAS THAT ALL ABOUT!?
KARA (ROLL)
KARA
HYUU (WHOOSH)

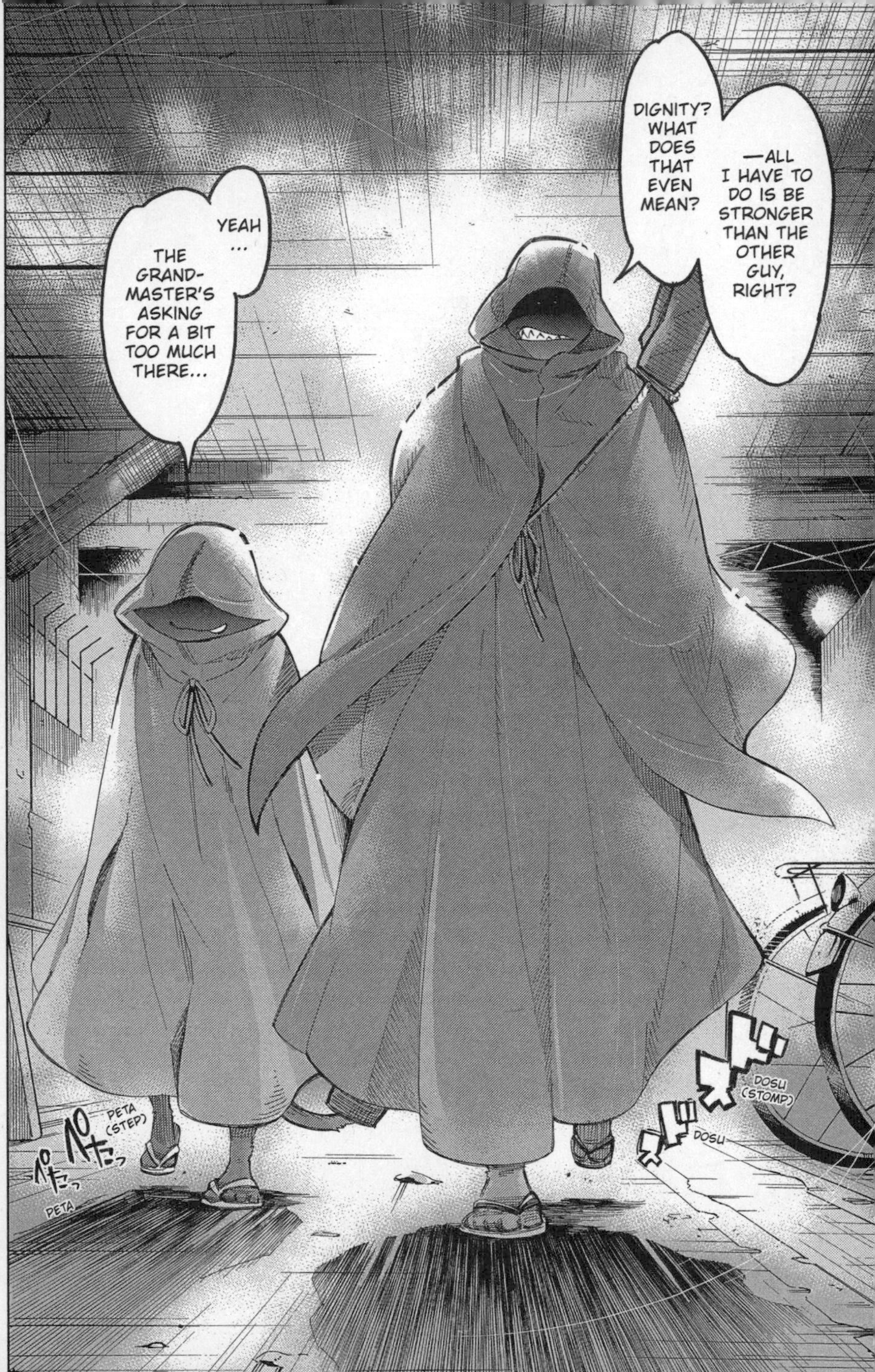
DIGNITY? WHAT DOES THAT EVEN MEAN?
—ALL I HAVE TO DO IS BE STRONGER THAN THE OTHER GUY, RIGHT?
YEAH ...
THE GRAND-MASTER'S ASKING FOR A BIT TOO MUCH THERE...
DOSU (STOMP)
DOSU
PETA (STEP)
PETA

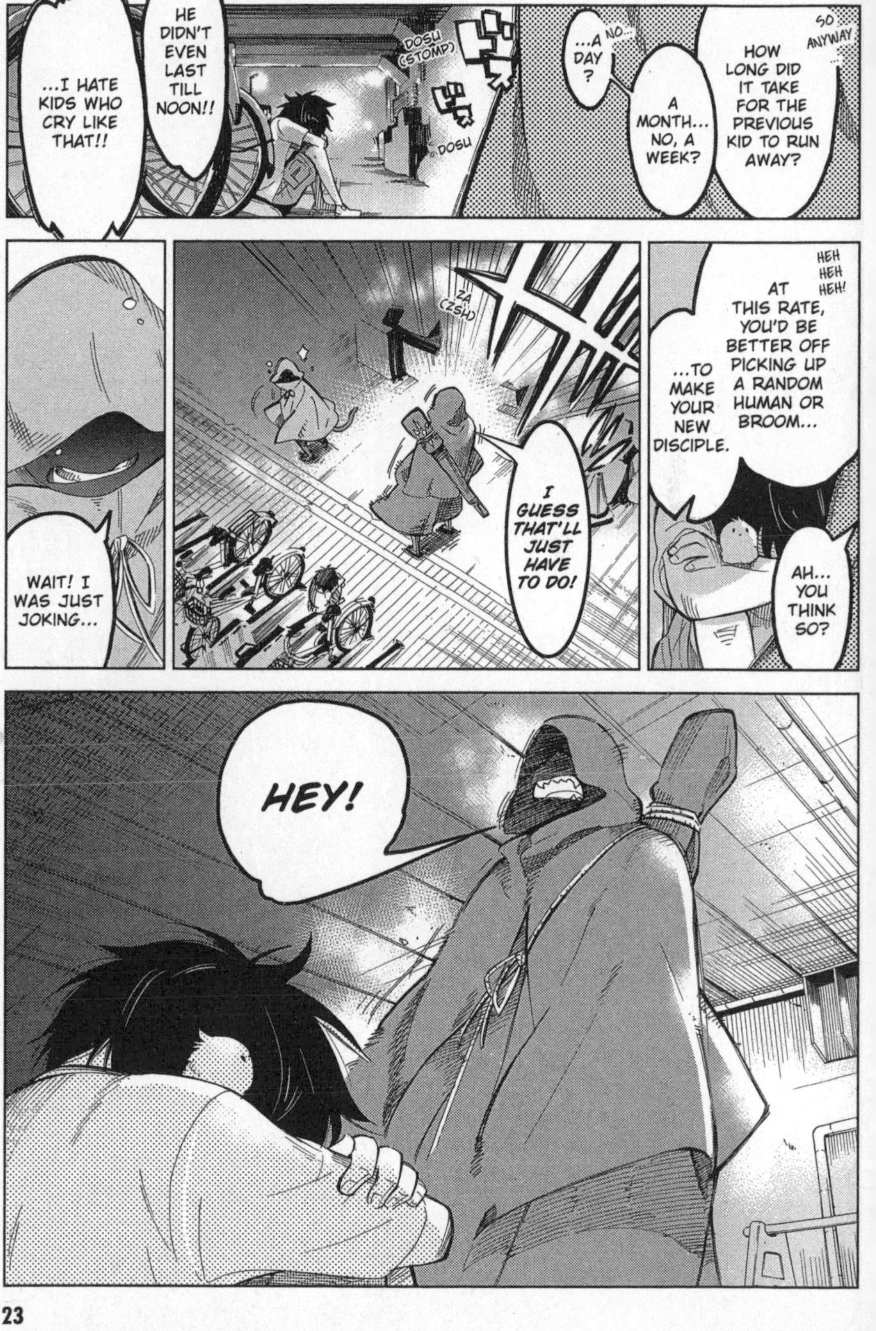
SO ANYWAY...
HOW LONG DID IT TAKE FOR THE PREVIOUS KID TO RUN AWAY?
A MONTH... NO, A WEEK?
...A DAY?
NO...
DOSU (STOMP)
DOSU
HE DIDN'T EVEN LAST TILL NOON!!
...I HATE KIDS WHO CRY LIKE THAT!!
HEH HEH HEH!
AT THIS RATE, YOU'D BE BETTER OFF PICKING UP A RANDOM HUMAN OR BROOM...
...TO MAKE YOUR NEW DISCIPLE.
AH... YOU THINK SO?
ZA (ZSH)
I GUESS THAT'LL JUST HAVE TO DO!
WAIT! I WAS JUST JOKING...
HEY!

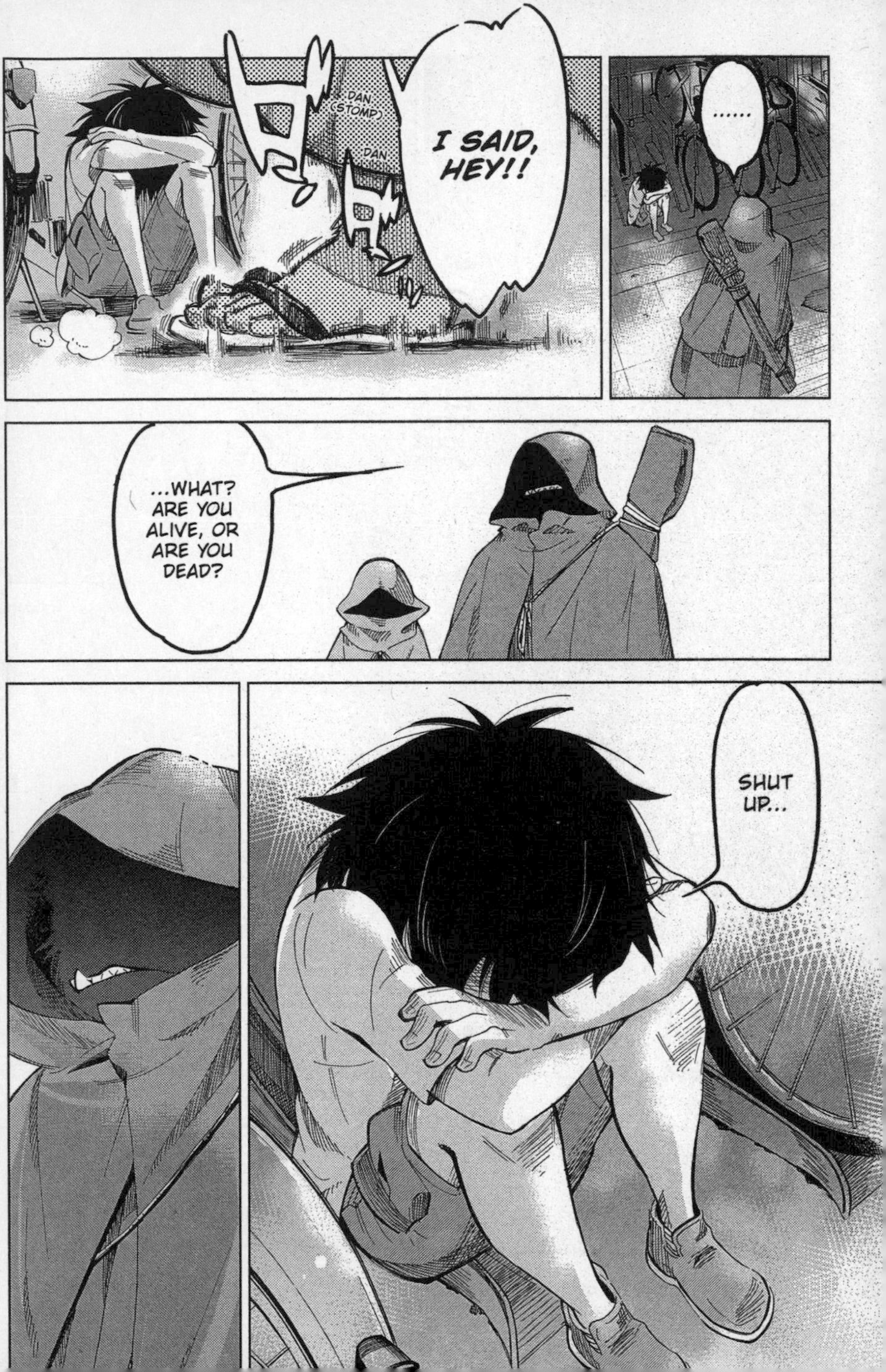
......
I SAID, HEY!!
DAN (STOMP)
DAN
...WHAT? ARE YOU ALIVE, OR ARE YOU DEAD?
SHUT UP...

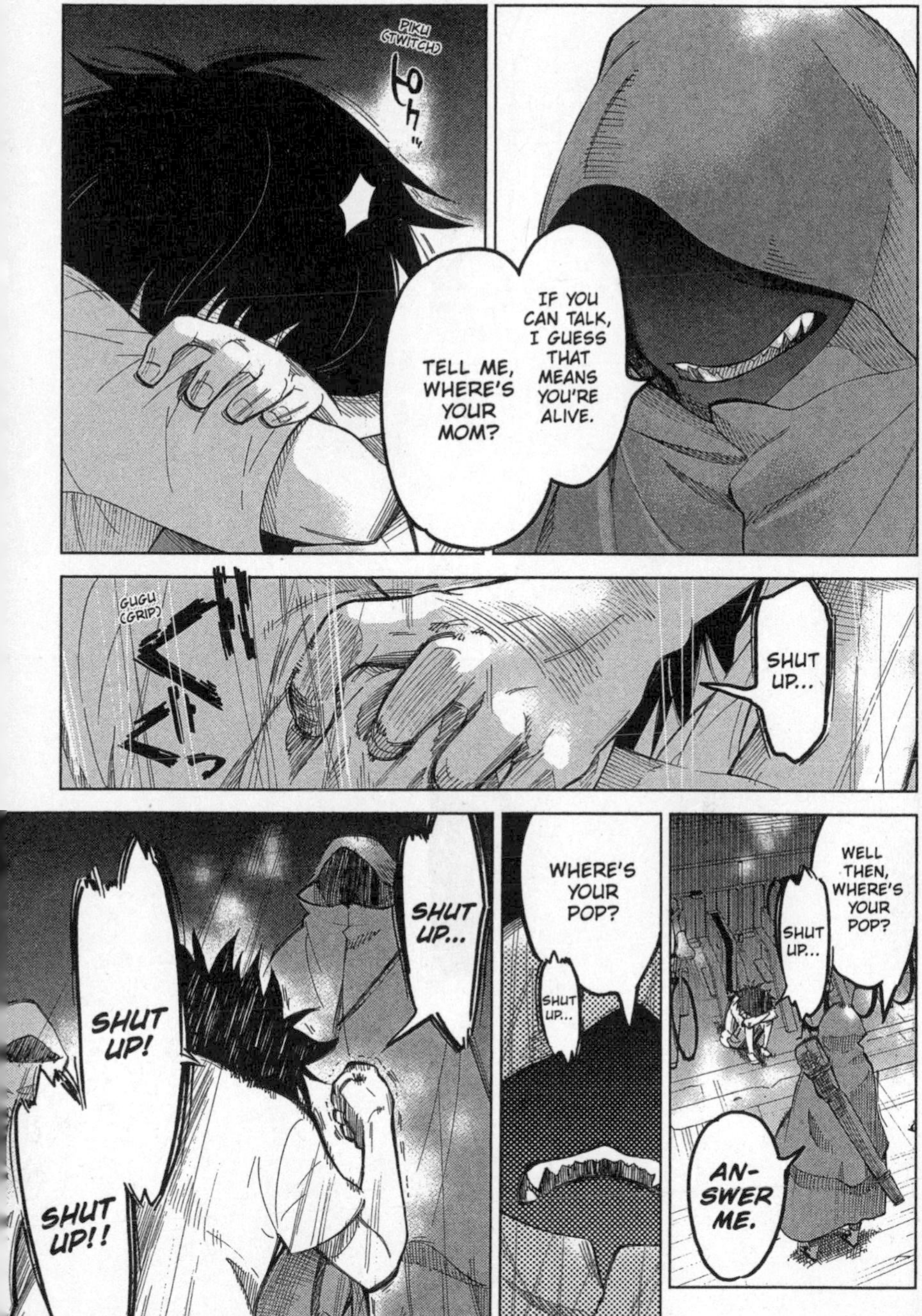
IF YOU CAN TALK, I GUESS THAT MEANS YOU'RE ALIVE.
TELL ME, WHERE'S YOUR MOM?
PIKU (TWITCH)
SHUT UP...
GUGU (GRIP)
WELL THEN, WHERE'S YOUR POP?
SHUT UP...
AN-SWER ME.
WHERE'S YOUR POP?
SHUT UP...
SHUT UP...
SHUT UP!
SHUT UP!!

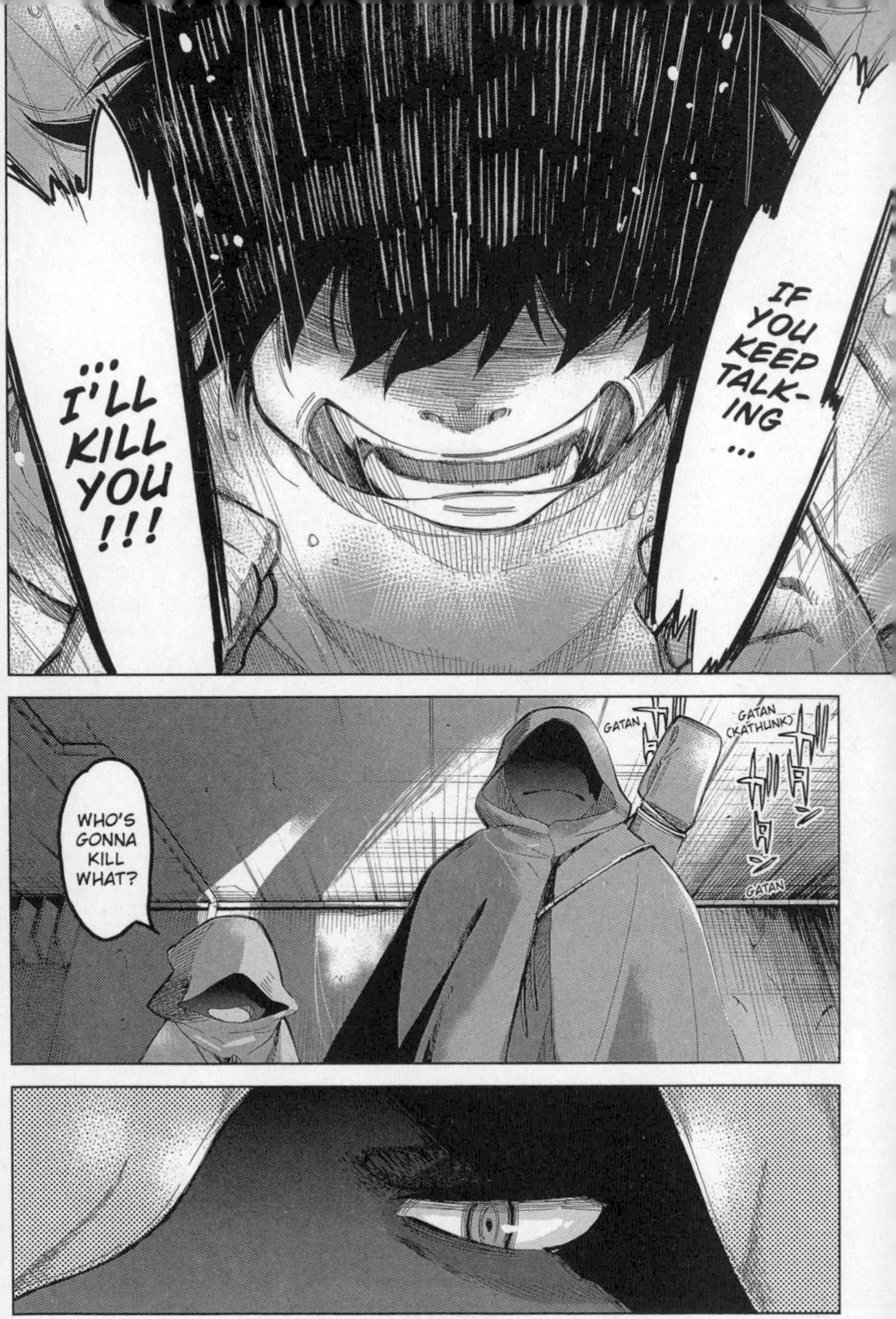
IF YOU KEEP TALKING...
...I'LL KILL YOU!!!
GATAN (KATHUNK)
GATAN
GATAN
WHO'S GONNA KILL WHAT?

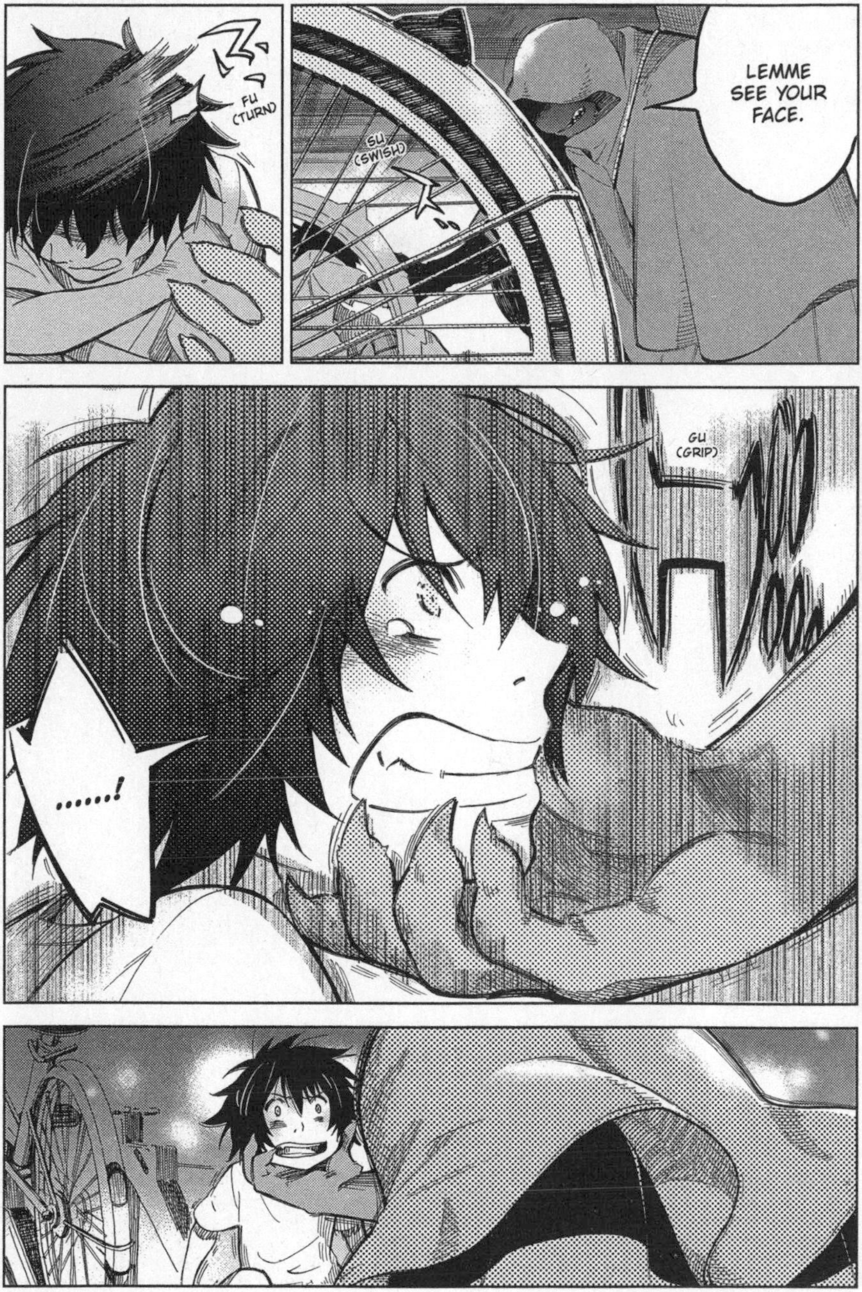
LEMME SEE YOUR FACE.
SU (SWISH)
FU (TURN)
GU (GRIP)
......!

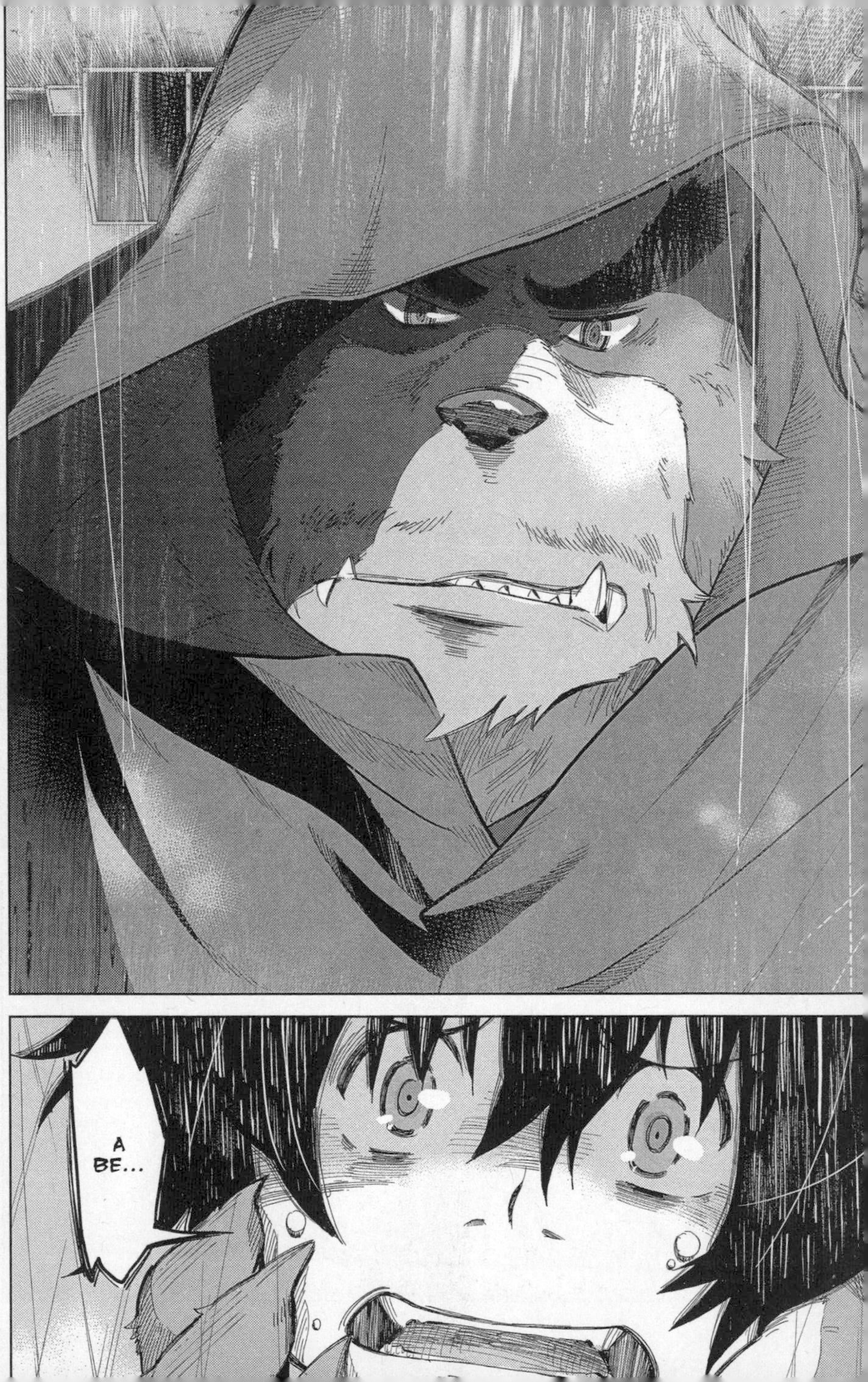
A BE...

GATAN

GATAN
(KATHLINK)

ZASHA
(ZSH)

GUN
(SHOVE)

A
BEAST
...!

...NOT
BAD.

THAT'S
PLENTY,
DON'T
YOU
THINK?

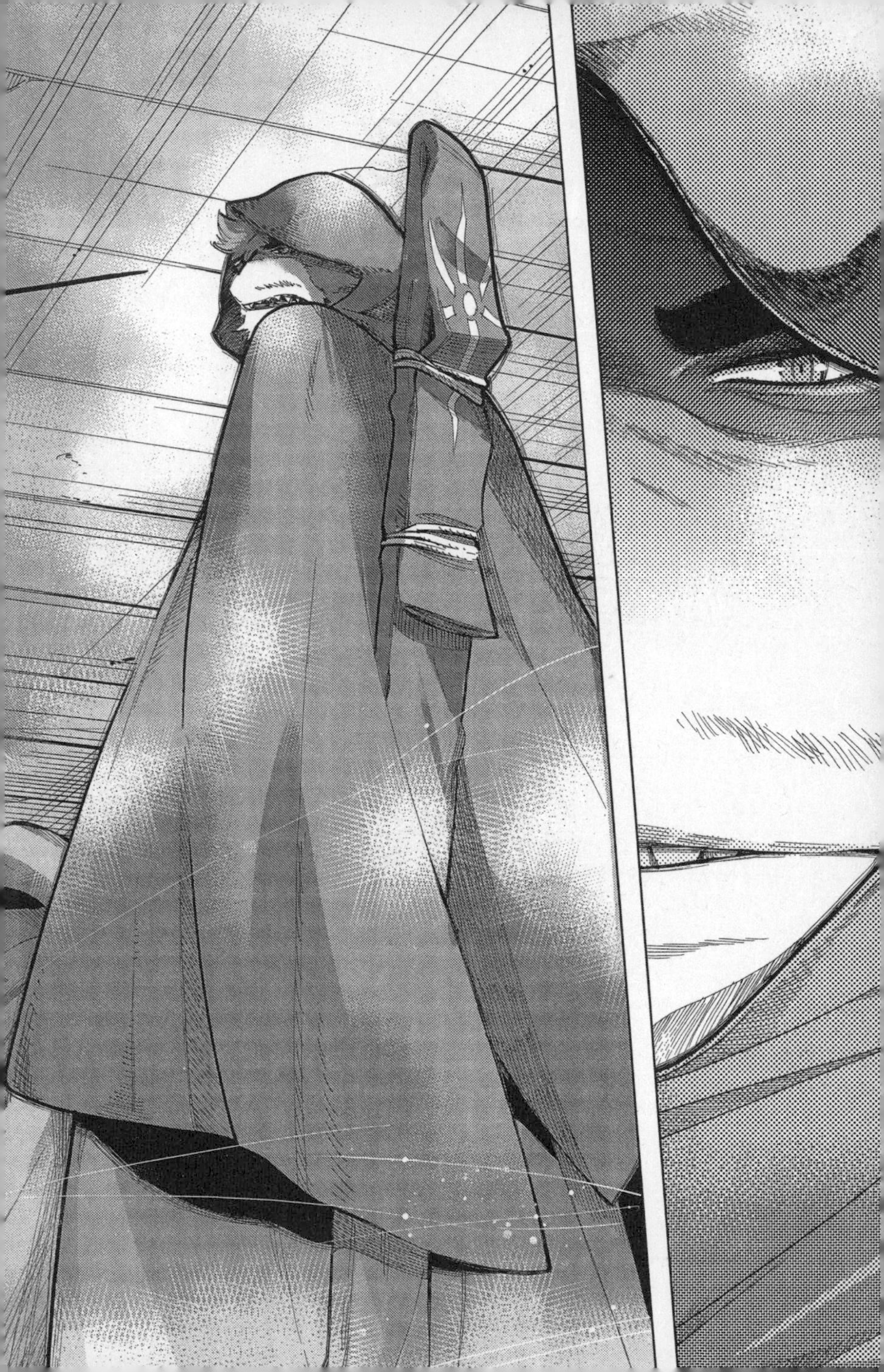

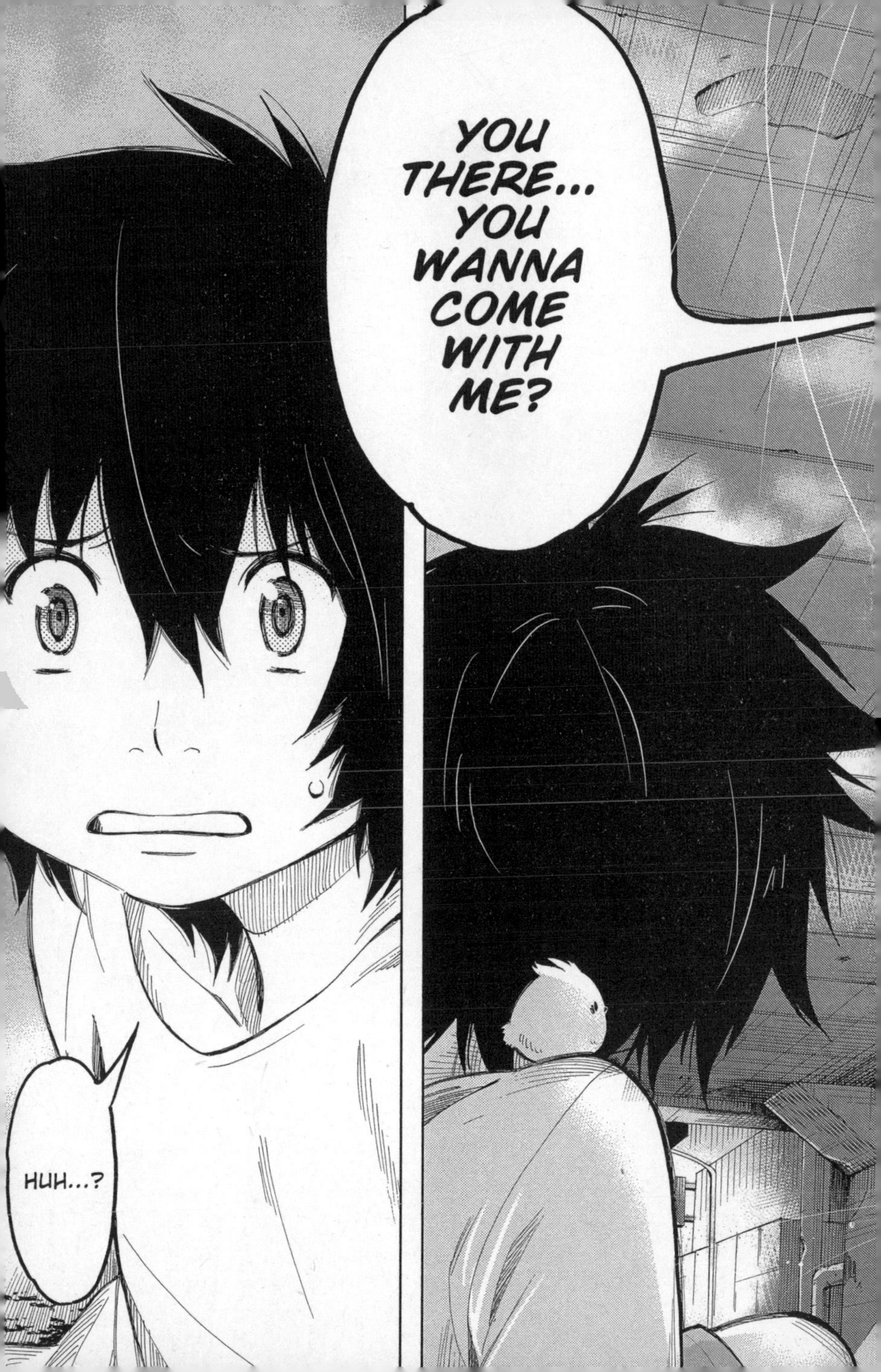
YOU THERE... YOU WANNA COME WITH ME?
HUH...?

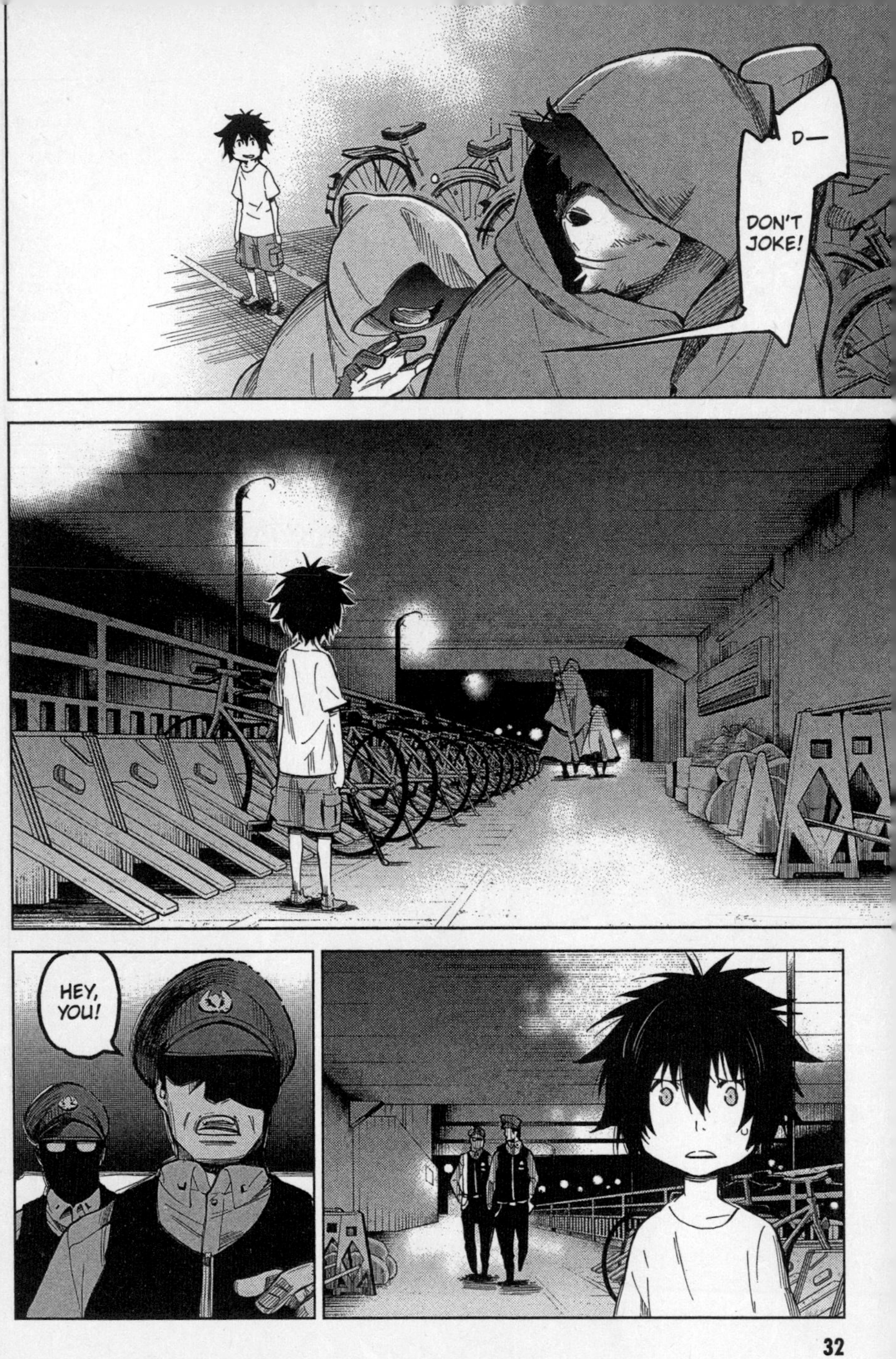
D—
DON'T JOKE!
HEY, YOU!

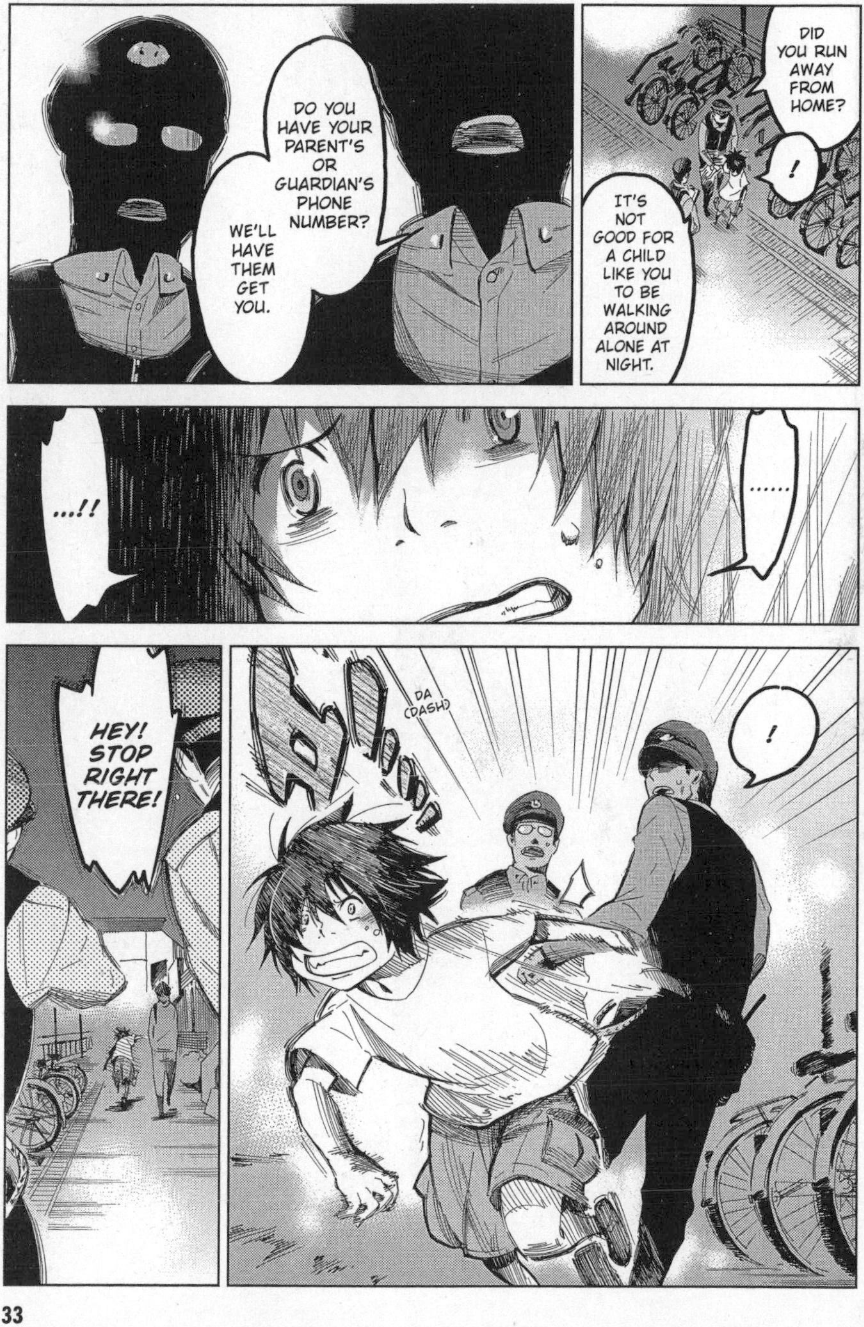
DID YOU RUN AWAY FROM HOME?
!
IT'S NOT GOOD FOR A CHILD LIKE YOU TO BE WALKING AROUND ALONE AT NIGHT.
DO YOU HAVE YOUR PARENT'S OR GUARDIAN'S PHONE NUMBER?
WE'LL HAVE THEM GET YOU.
......
...!!
!
DA (DASH)
HEY! STOP RIGHT THERE!

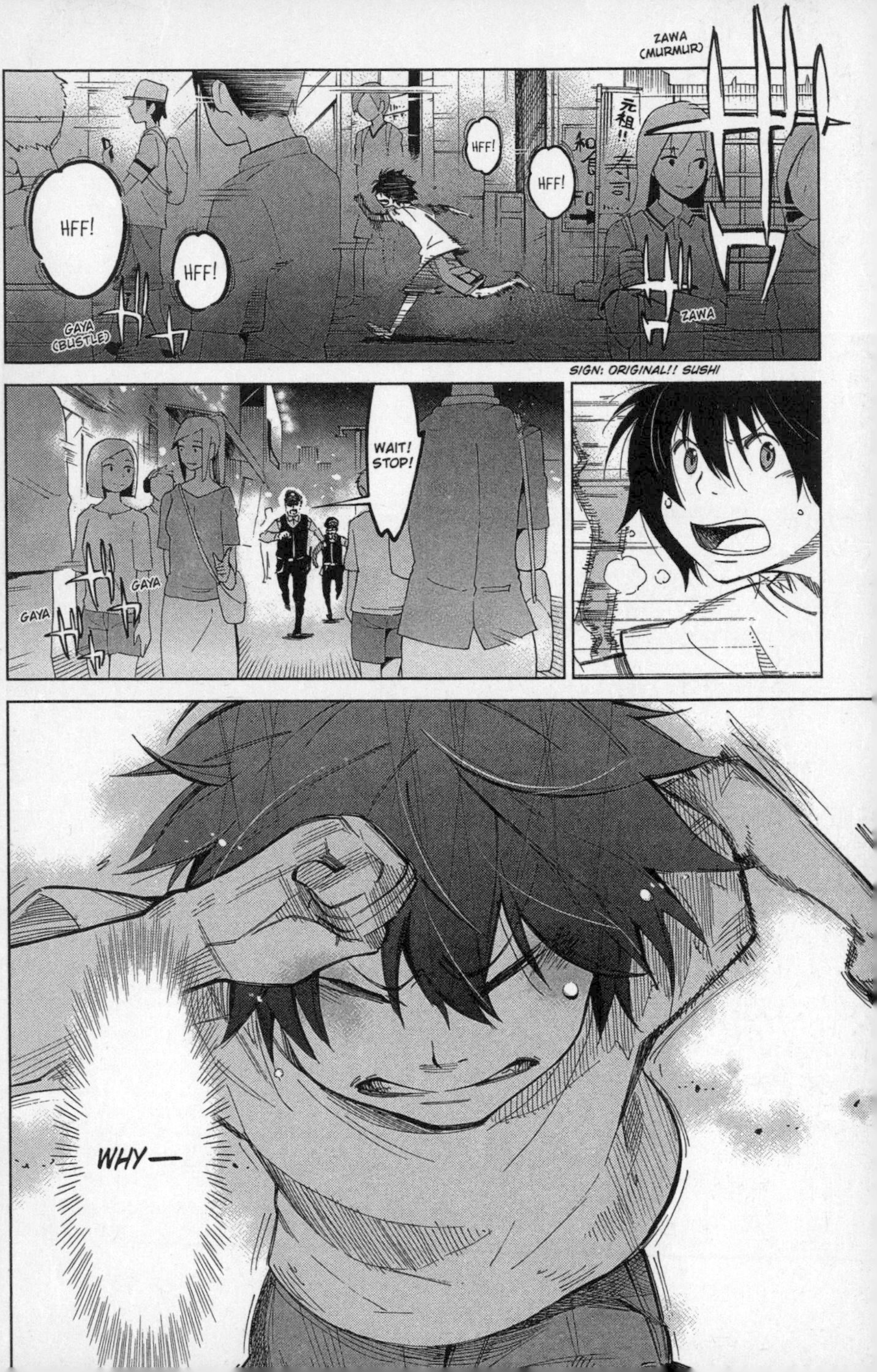
ZAWA (MURMUR)
元祖!!
寿司
SIGN: ORIGINAL!! SUSHI
ZAWA
HFF!
HFF!
HFF!
HFF!
GAYA (BUSTLE)
WAIT! STOP!
GAYA
GAYA
WHY—

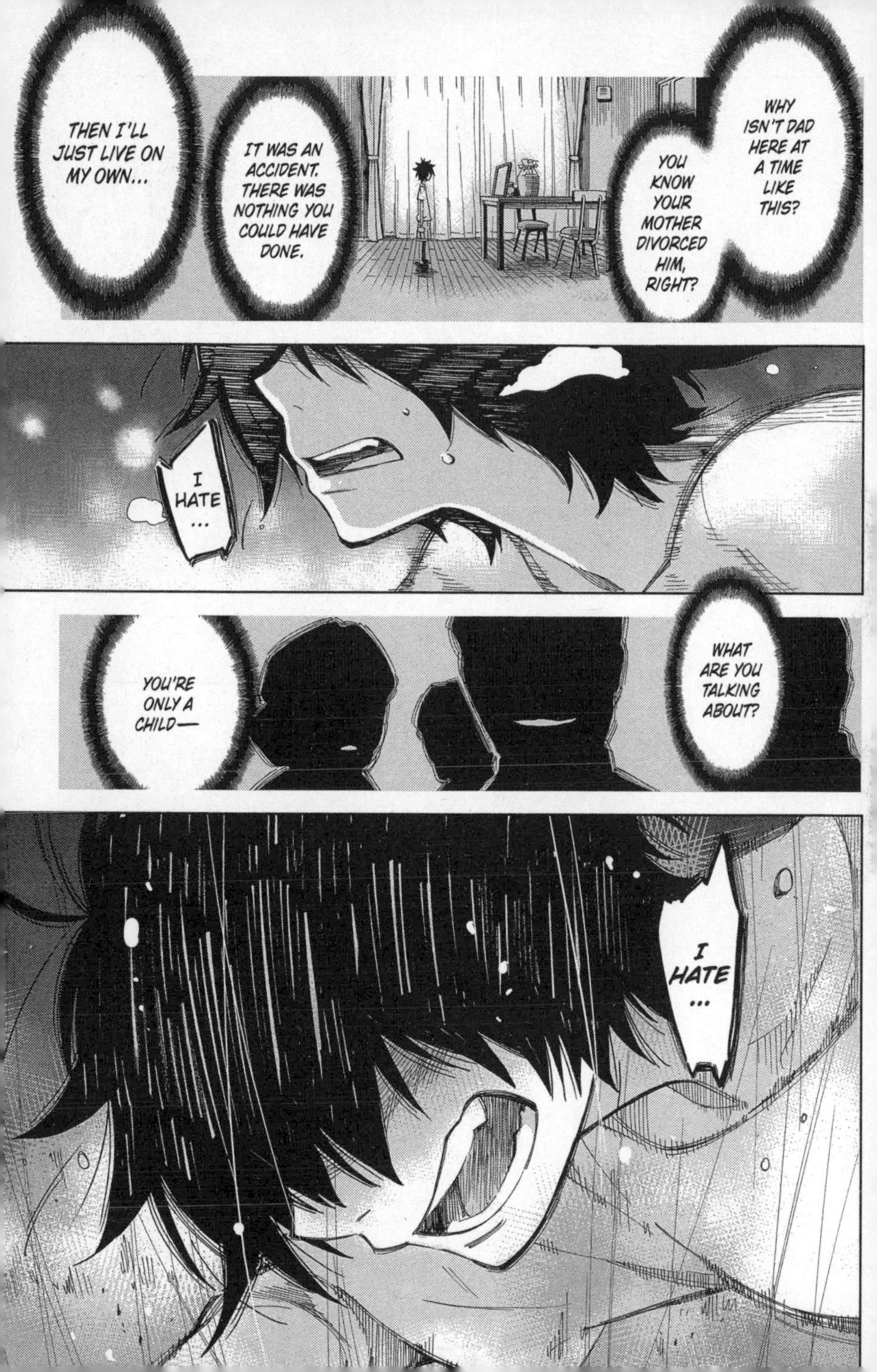
WHY ISN'T DAD HERE AT A TIME LIKE THIS?
YOU KNOW YOUR MOTHER DIVORCED HIM, RIGHT?
IT WAS AN ACCIDENT. THERE WAS NOTHING YOU COULD HAVE DONE.
THEN I'LL JUST LIVE ON MY OWN...
I HATE ...
WHAT ARE YOU TALKING ABOUT?
YOU'RE ONLY A CHILD—
I HATE ...

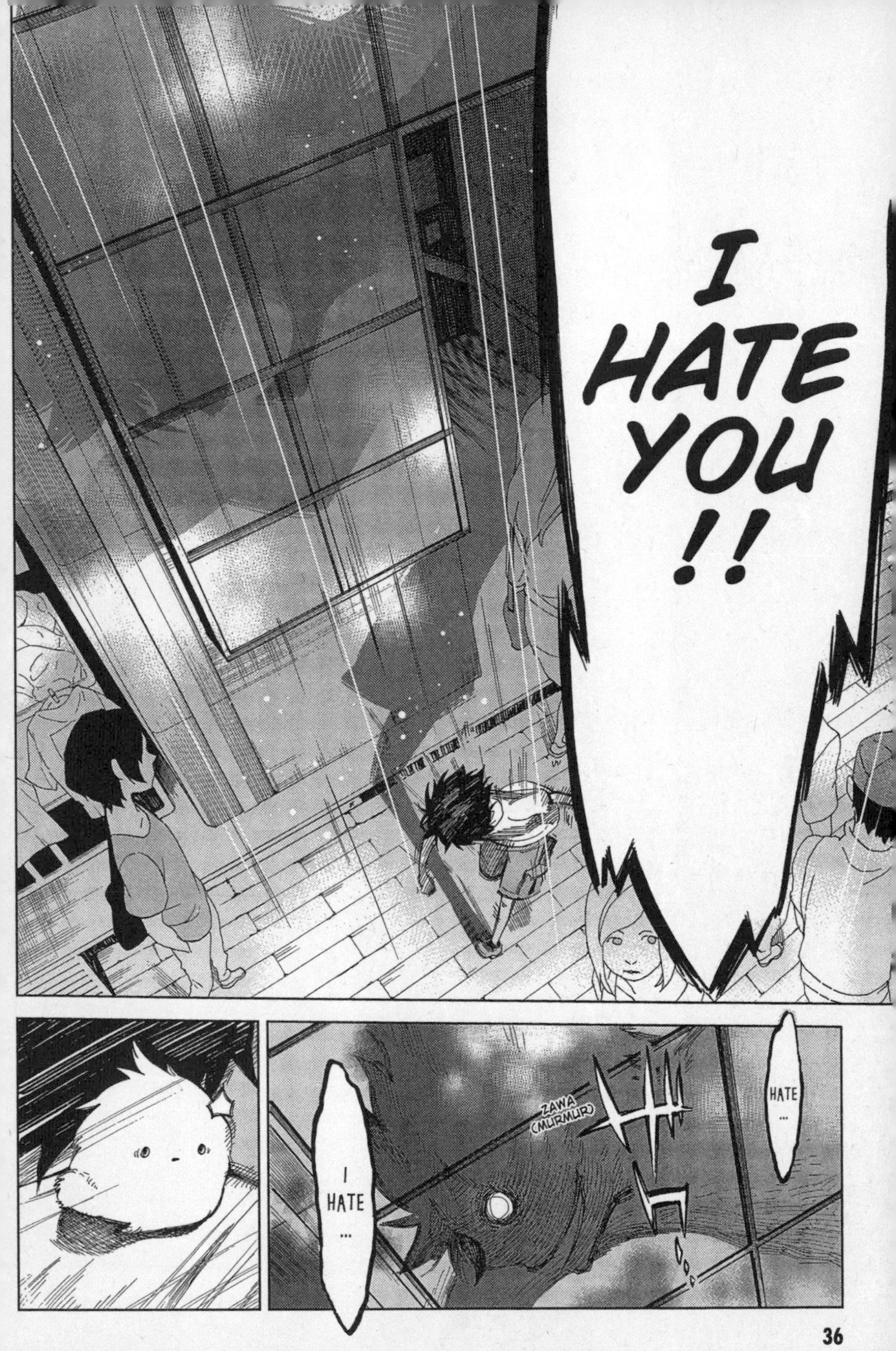
I HATE YOU!!
HATE...
ZAWA (MURMUR)
I HATE...

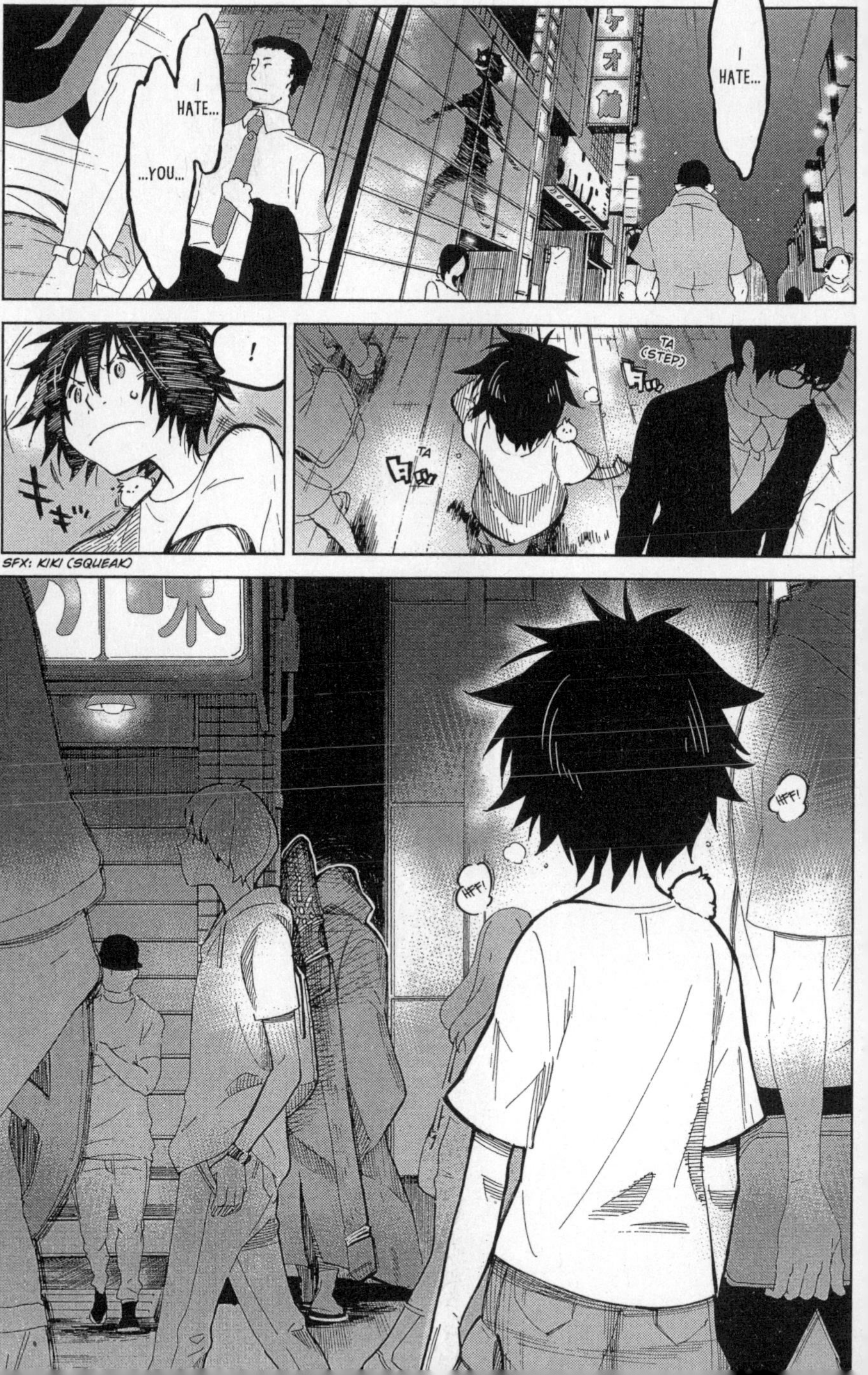
I HATE...
I HATE...
...YOU...
TA (STEP)
TA
!
SFX: KIKI (SQUEAK)
HFF!
HFF!

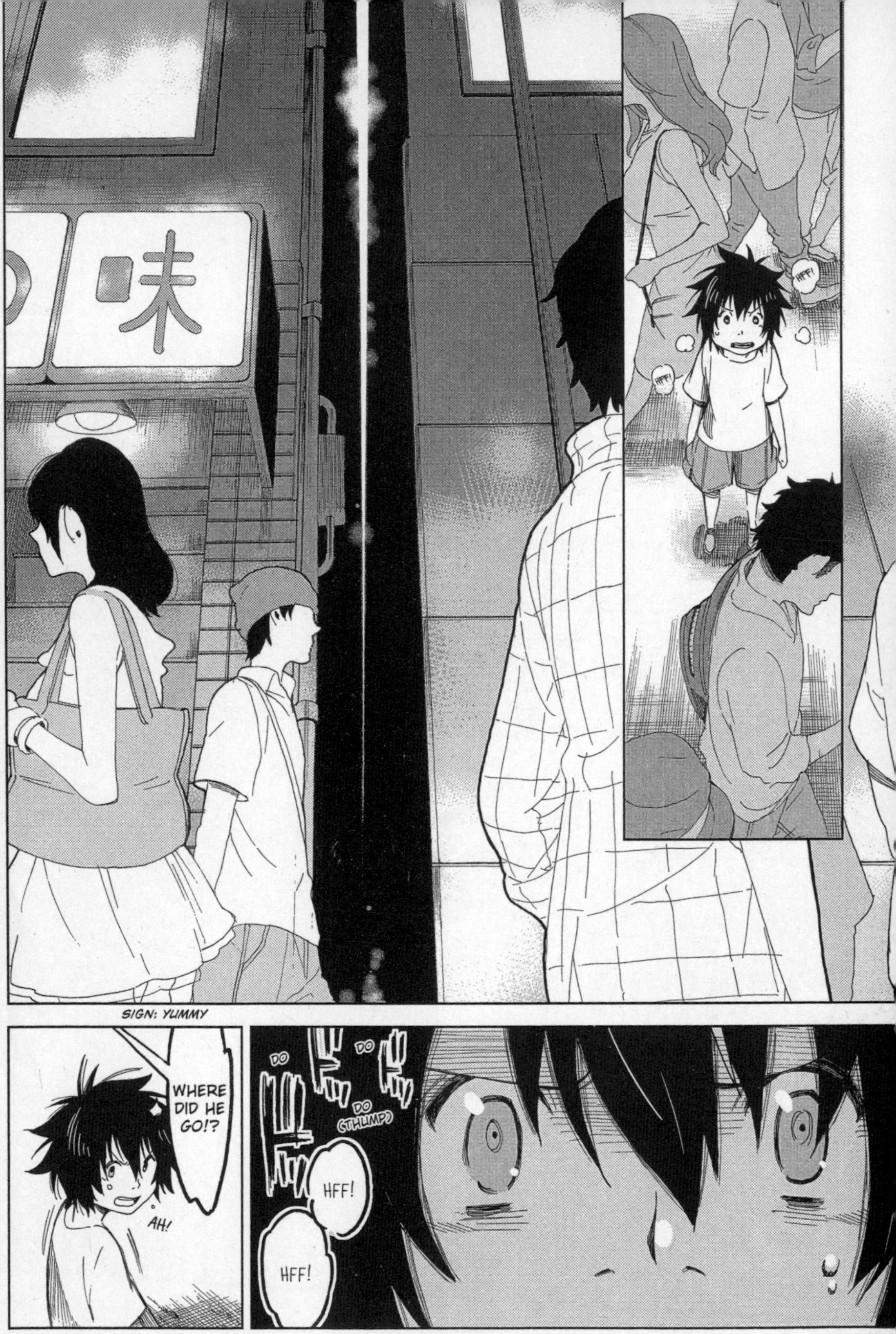
HFF!
HFF!
SIGN: YUMMY
DO
DO
DO
(THUMP)
HFF!
HFF!
WHERE DID HE GO!?
AH!

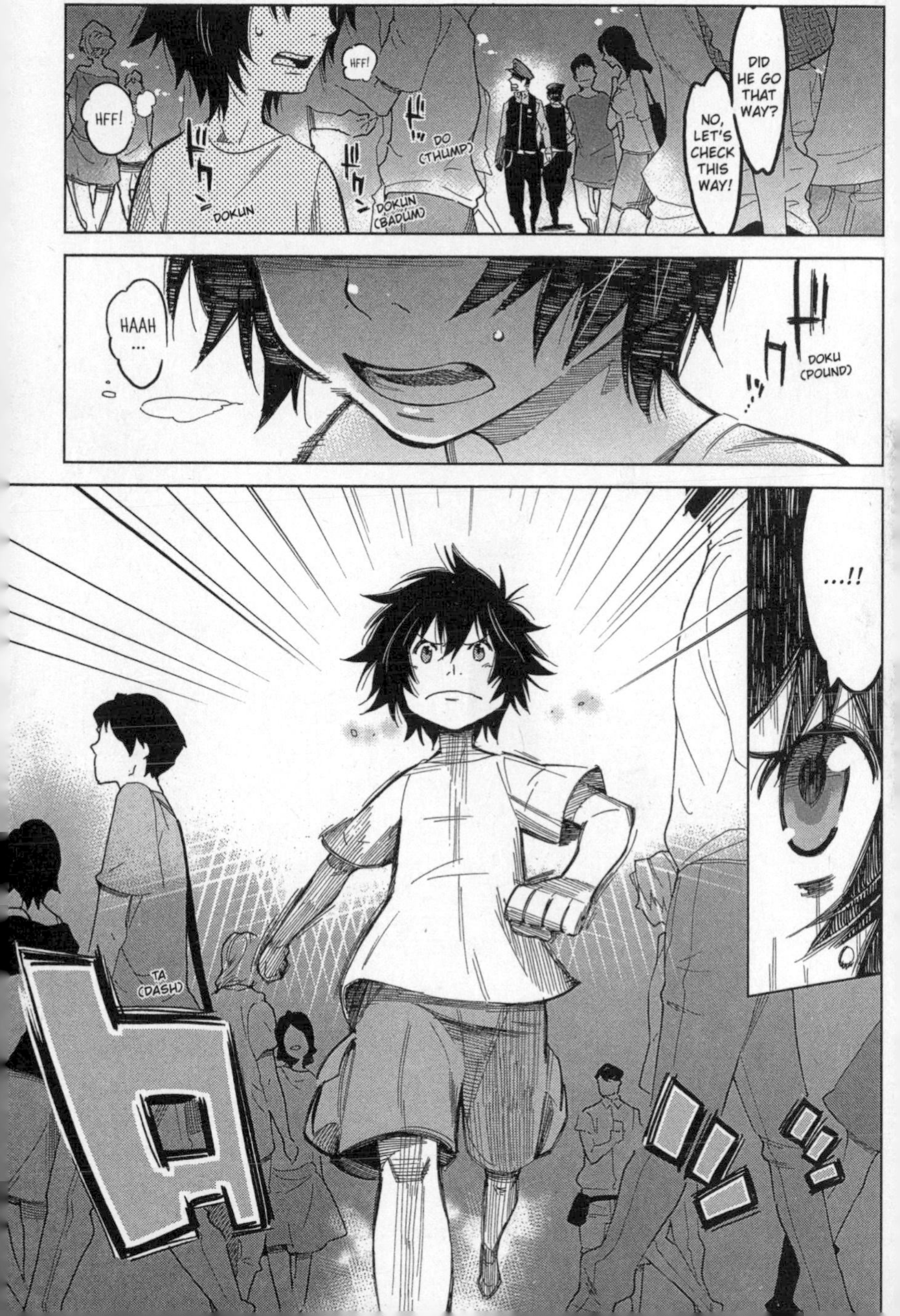
DID HE GO THAT WAY?
NO, LET'S CHECK THIS WAY!
DO (THUMP)
HFF!
DOKUN (BADUM)
HFF!
DOKUN
DOKU (POUND)
HAAH ...
...!!
TA (DASH)

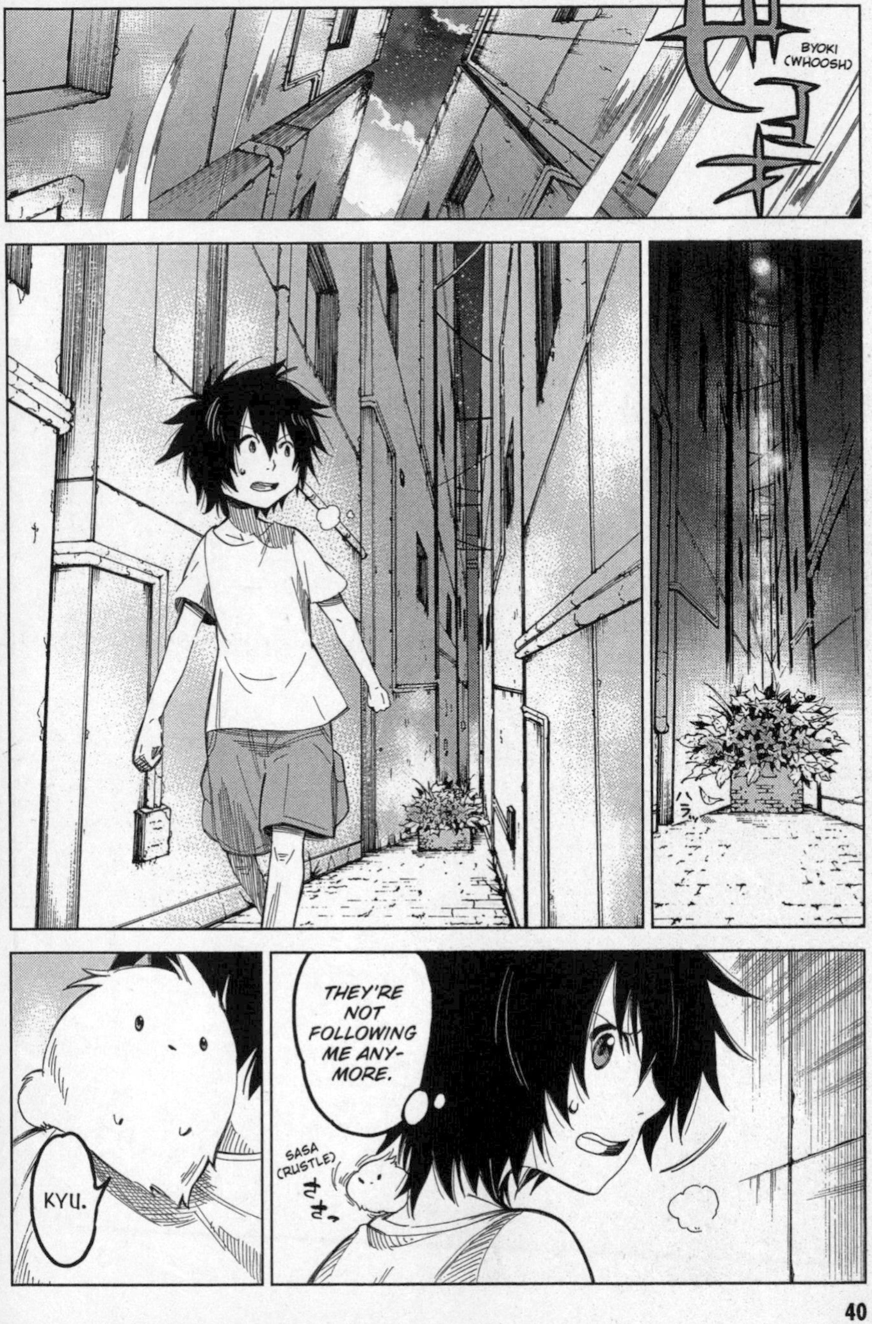
BYOKI (WHOOSH)
THEY'RE NOT FOLLOWING ME ANYMORE.
SASA (RUSTLE)
KYU.

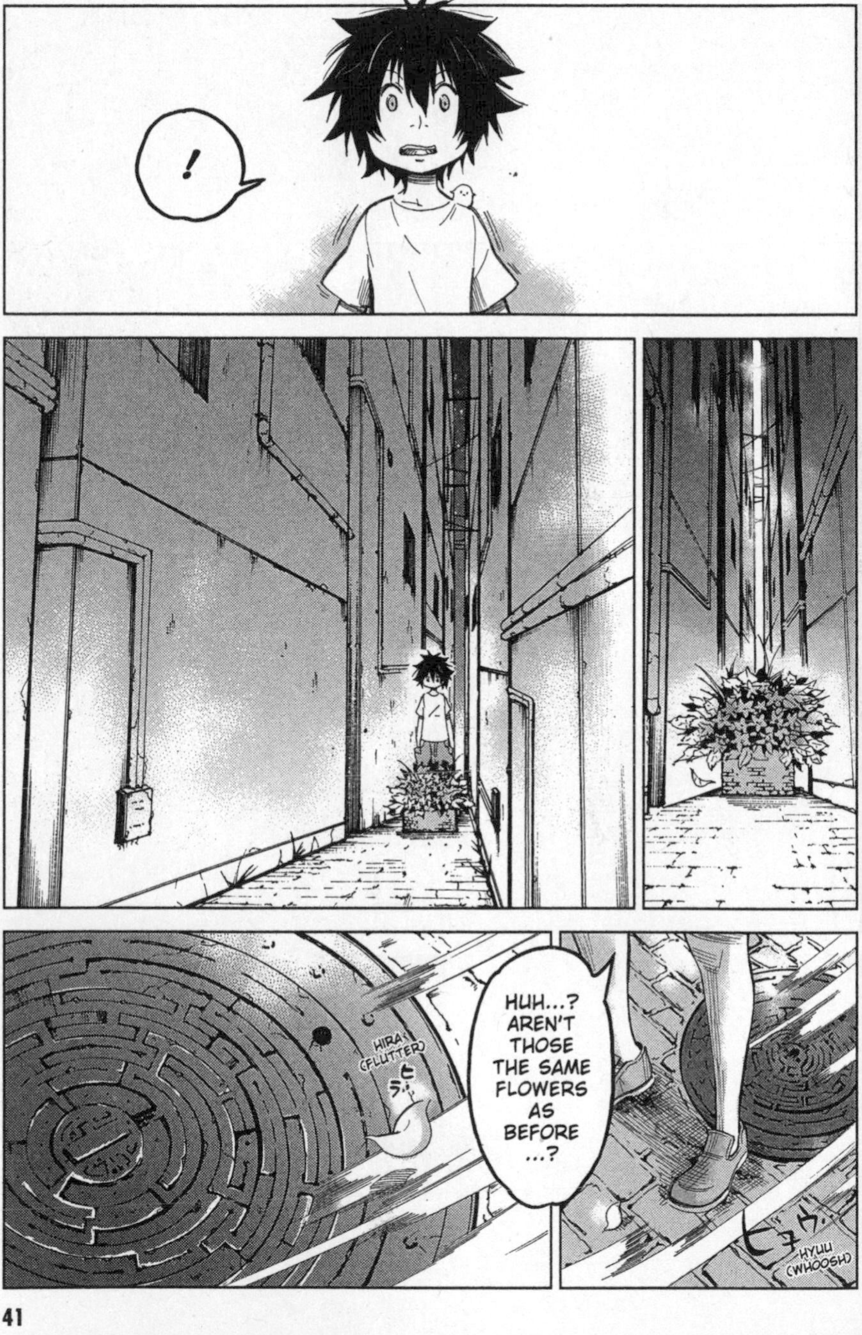
!
HUH...? AREN'T THOSE THE SAME FLOWERS AS BEFORE ...?
HYUU (WHOOSH)
HIRA (FLUTTER)

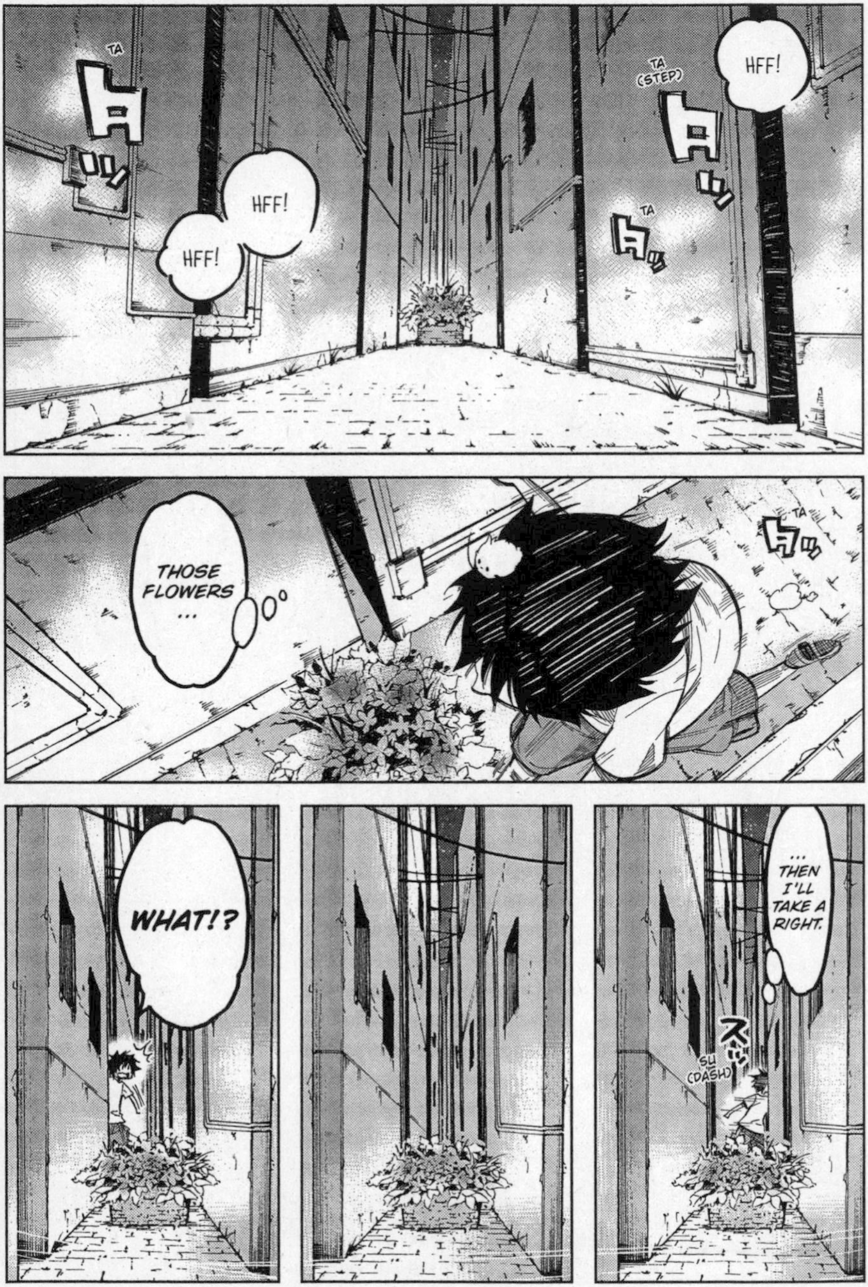
HFF!
TA (STEP)
TA
TA
HFF!
HFF!
TA
THOSE FLOWERS ...
... THEN I'LL TAKE A RIGHT.
SU (DASH)
WHAT!?

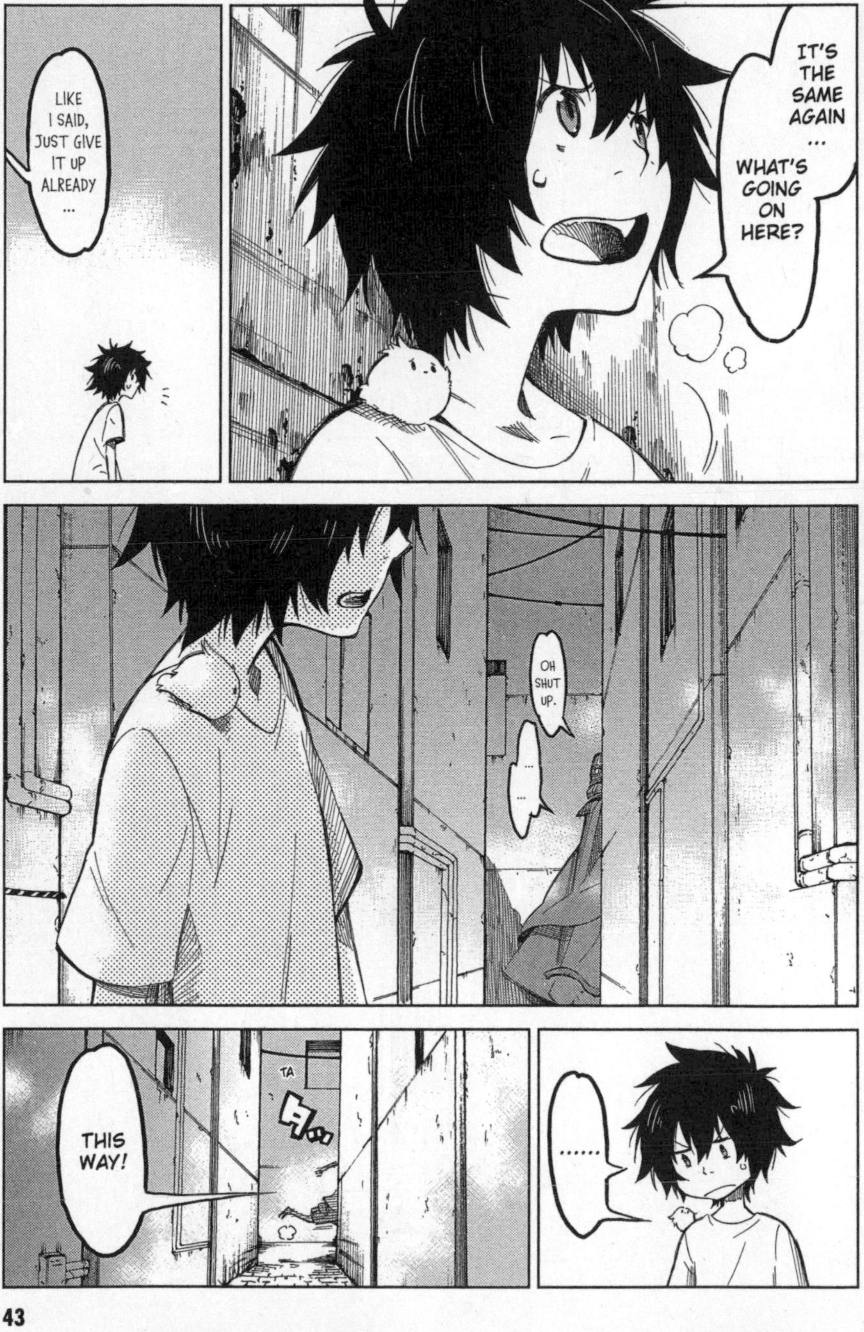
IT'S THE SAME AGAIN ... WHAT'S GOING ON HERE?
LIKE I SAID, JUST GIVE IT UP ALREADY ...
OH SHUT UP.
... ...
....
TA
THIS WAY!

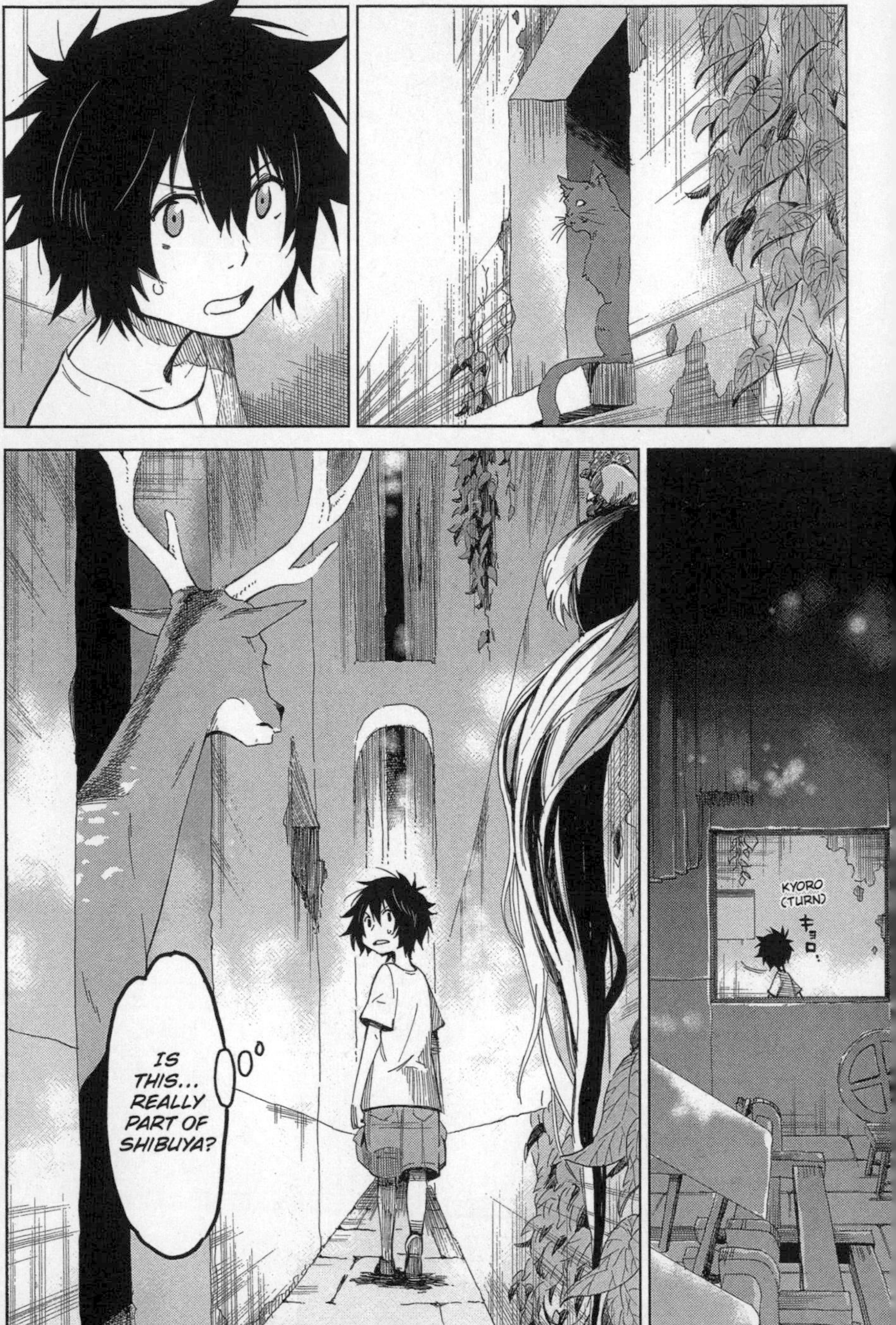
KYORO (TURN)
キョロ
IS THIS... REALLY PART OF SHIBUYA?

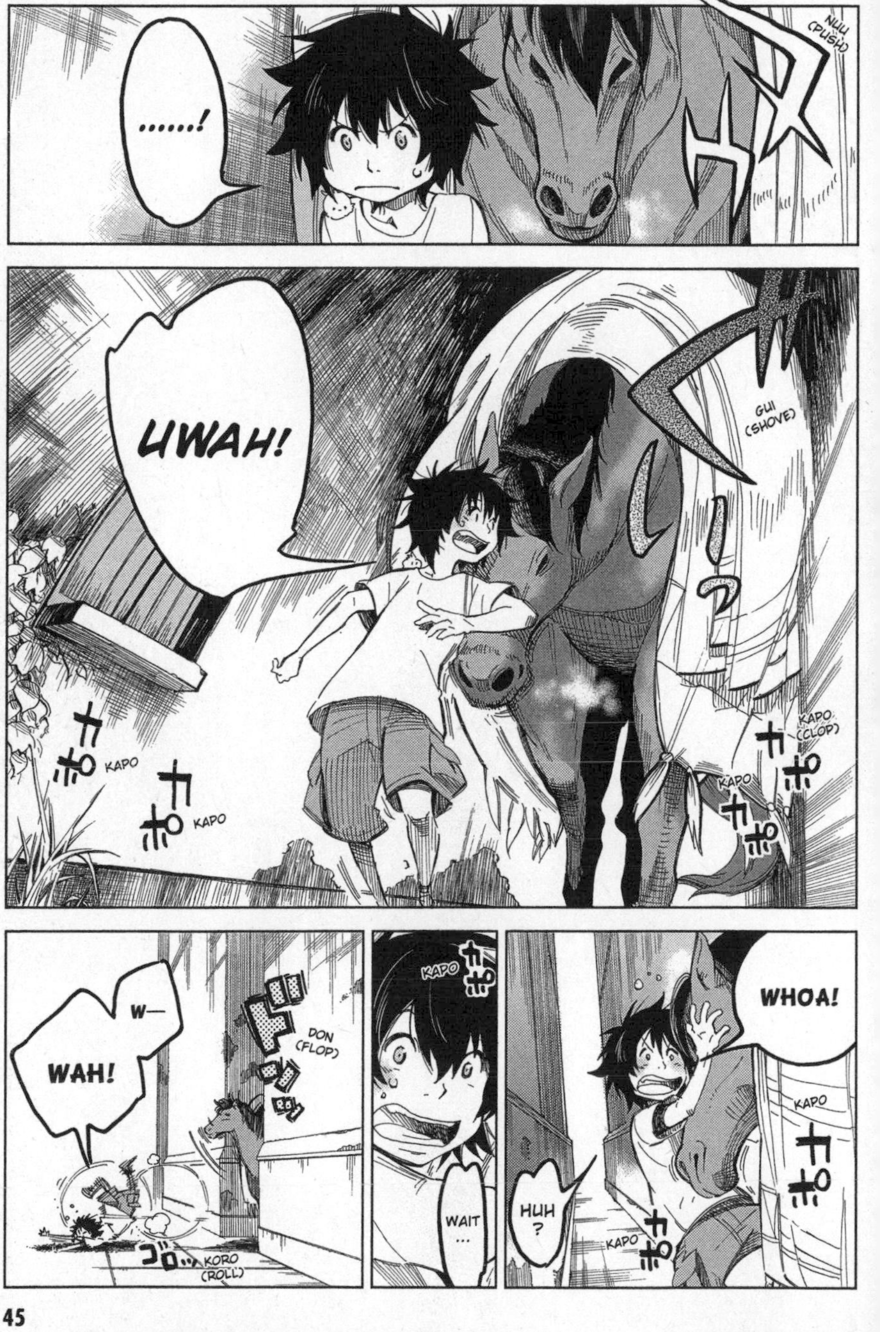
NUU (PUSH)
......!
GUI (SHOVE)
UWAH!
KAPO (CLOP)
KAPO
KAPO
KAPO
WHOA!
KAPO
HUH ?
KAPO
KAPO
WAIT ...
DON (FLOP)
W— WAH!
KORO (ROLL)

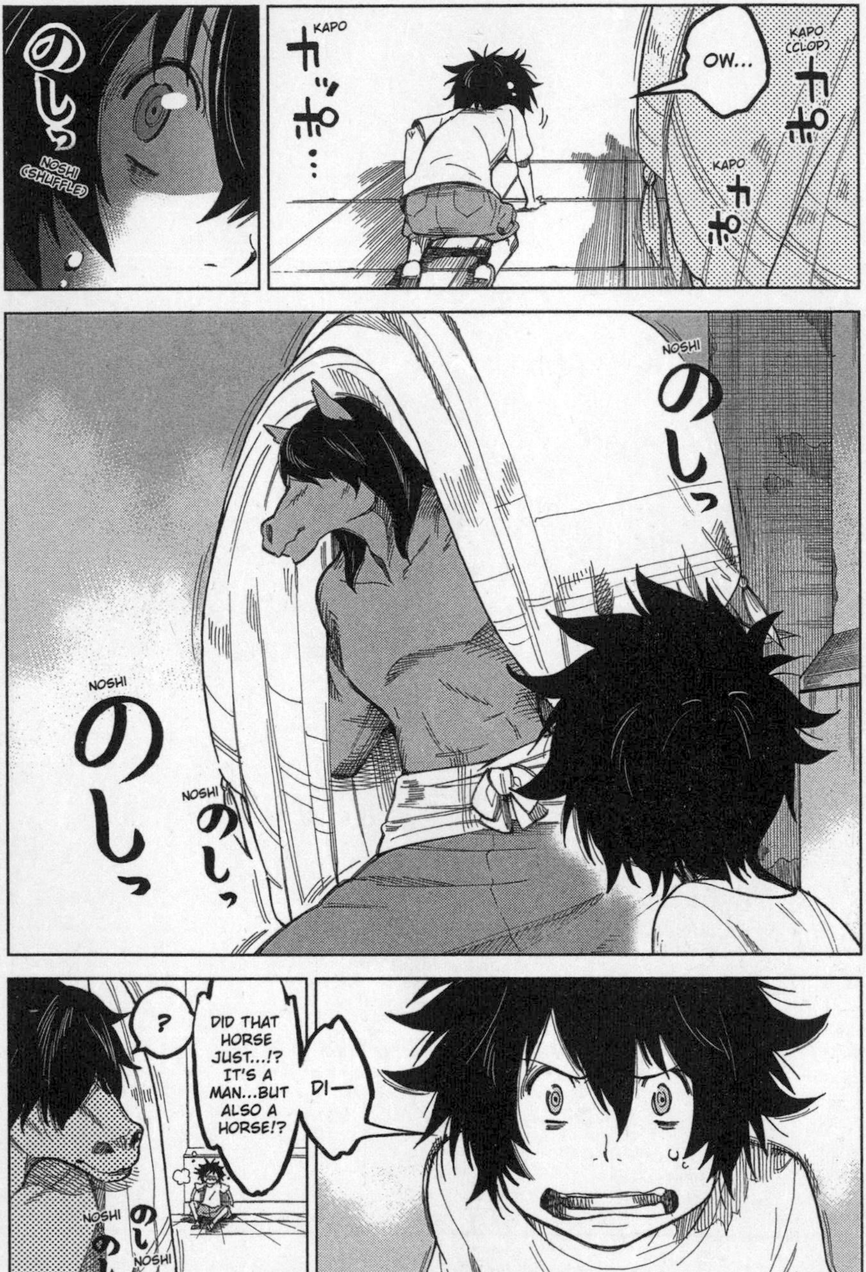
KAPO (CLOP)
カポ
OW...
KAPO
カポ
KAPO
カッポ…
NOSHI (SHUFFLE)
のしっ
NOSHI
のしっ
NOSHI
のしっ
NOSHI
のしっ
DI—
DID THAT HORSE JUST...!? IT'S A MAN...BUT ALSO A HORSE!?
?
NOSHI
のし
のし
NOSHI

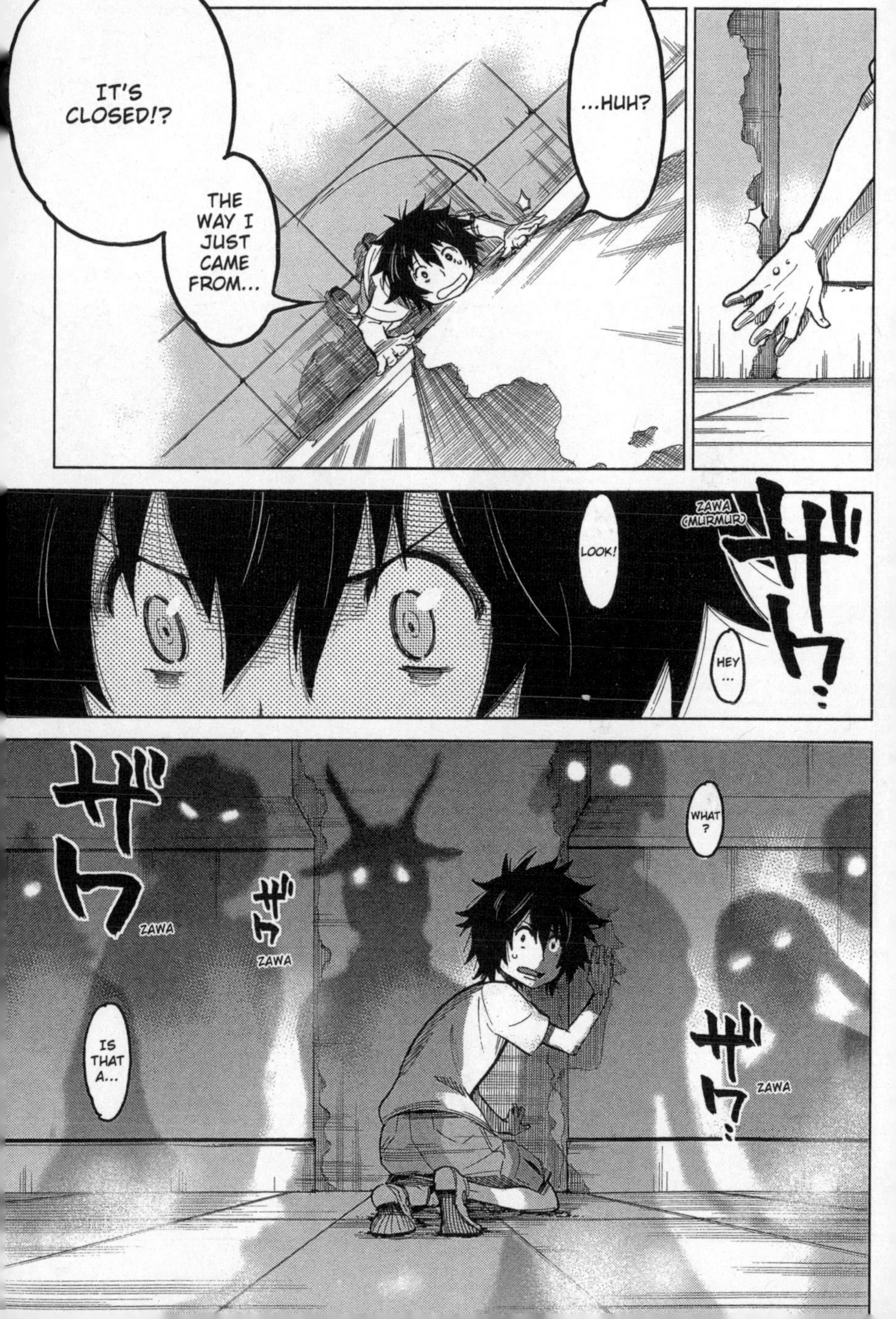
...HUH?
IT'S CLOSED!?
THE WAY I JUST CAME FROM...
ザワ
ZAWA (MURMUR)
LOOK!
HEY ...
WHAT ?
ザワ
ZAWA
ザワ
ZAWA
ザワ
ZAWA
IS THAT A...

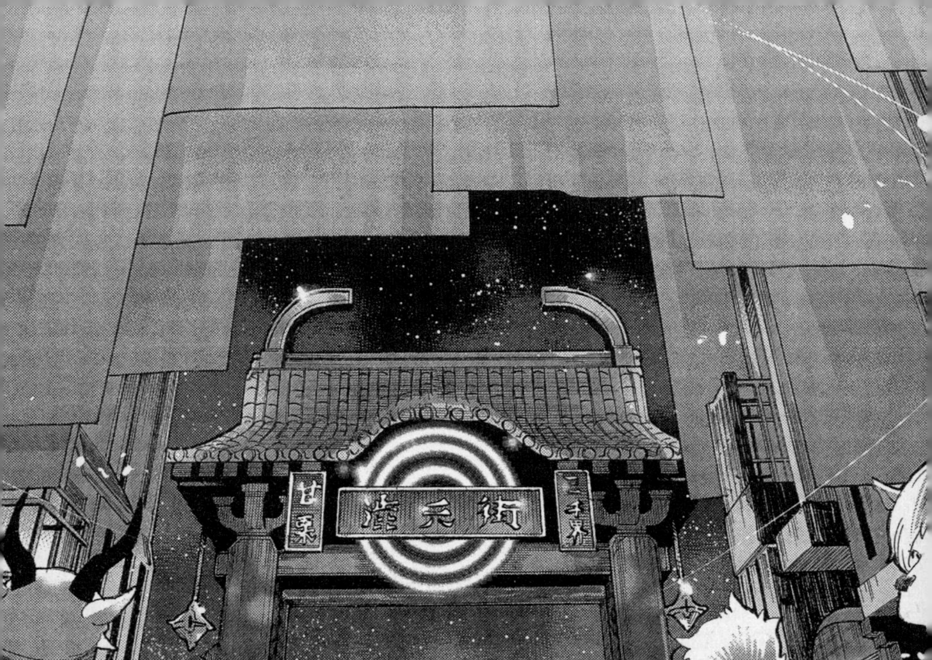
SIGNS (RIGHT TO LEFT): PARADISE, JUTENGAI, SWEET CHESTNUTS

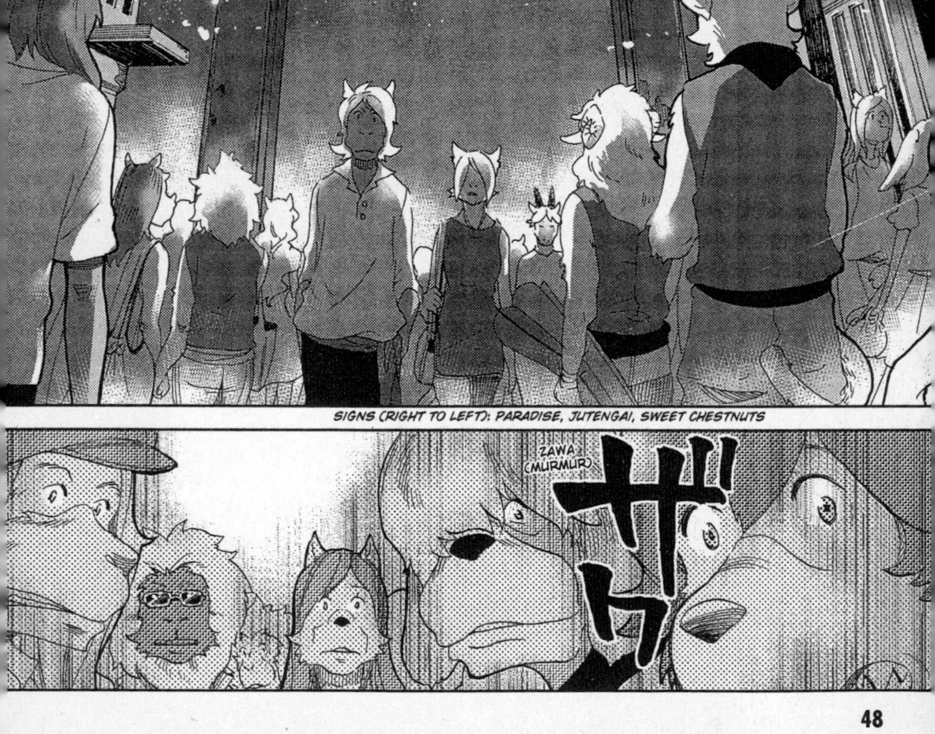
ZAWA
(MURMUR)

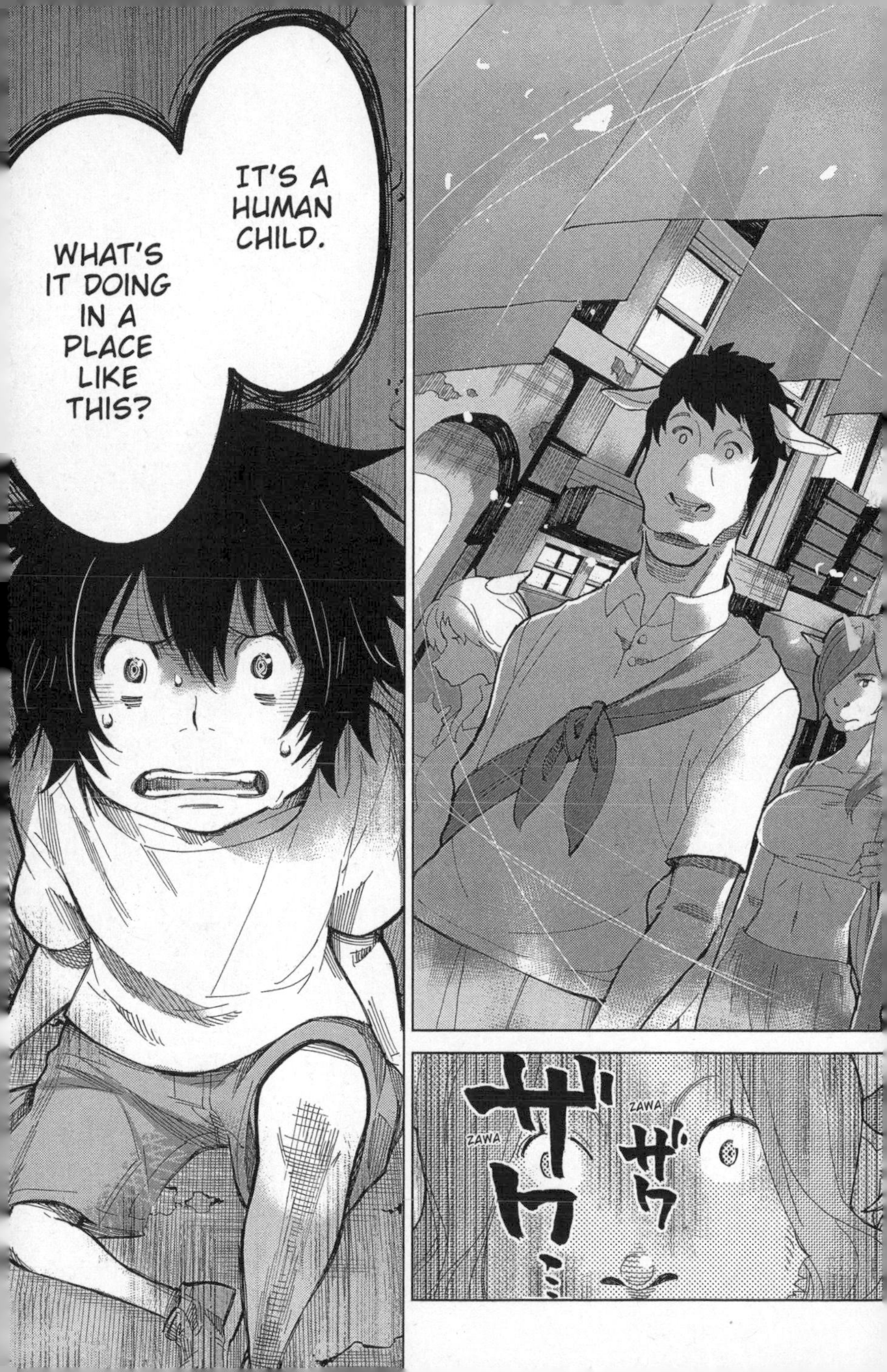
ザワ
ZAWA
ザワ
ZAWA
IT'S A HUMAN CHILD.
WHAT'S IT DOING IN A PLACE LIKE THIS?

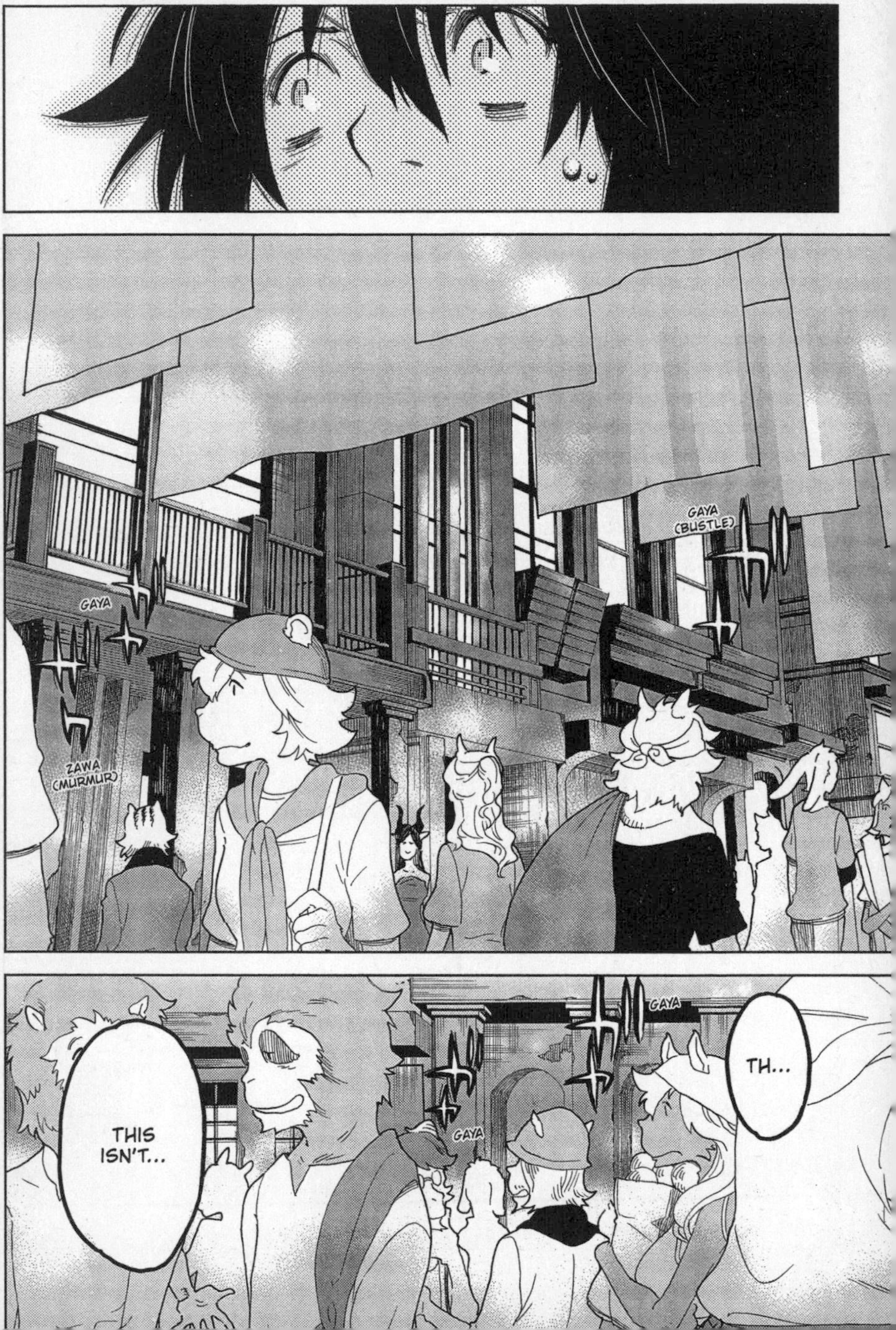
GAYA (BUSTLE)
GAYA
ZAWA (MURMUR)
GAYA
TH...
GAYA
THIS ISN'T...

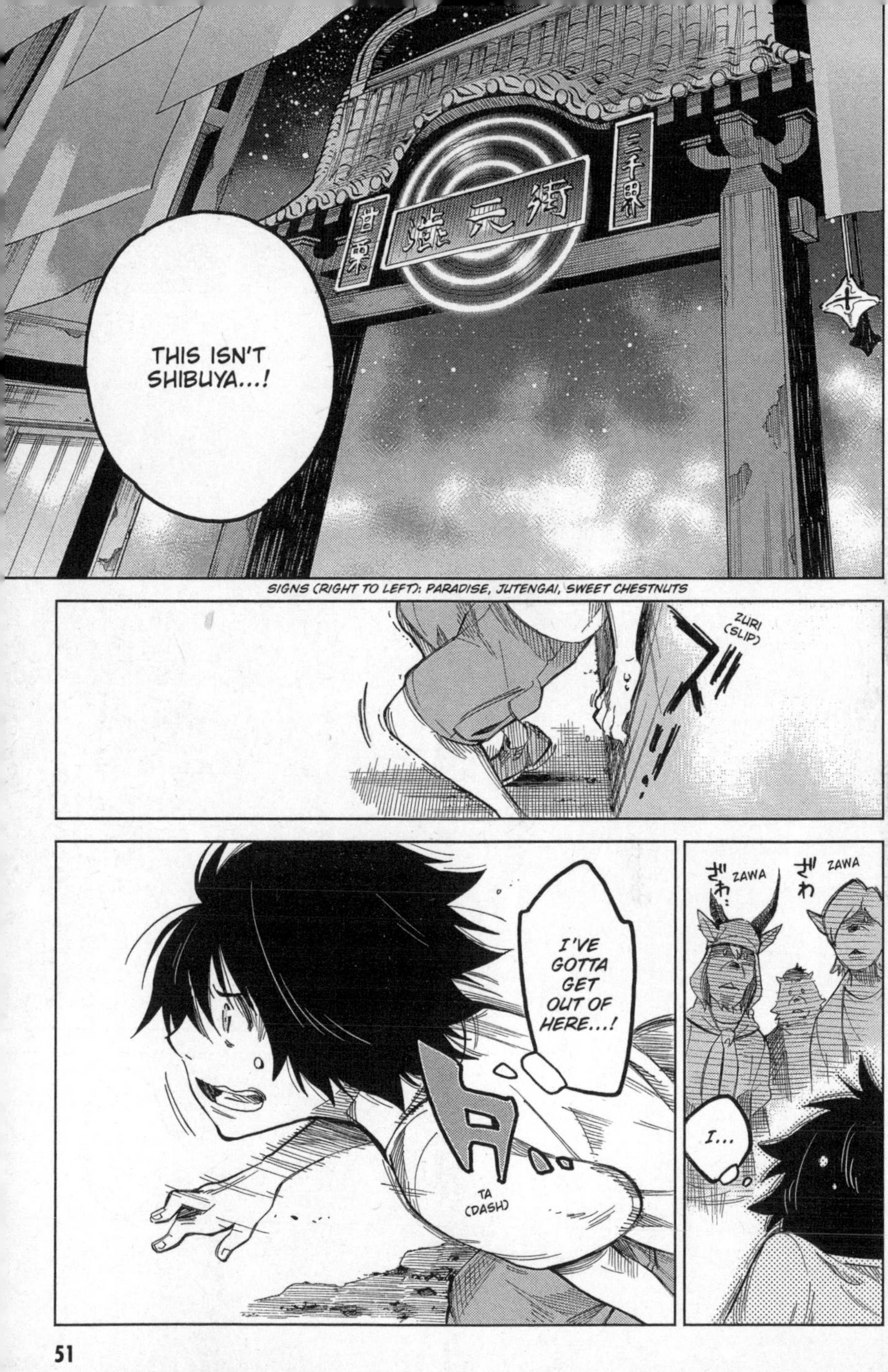
THIS ISN'T SHIBUYA...!
SIGNS (RIGHT TO LEFT): PARADISE, JUTENGAI, SWEET CHESTNUTS
ZURI (SLIP)
ざわ
ZAWA
ざわ…
ZAWA
I...
I'VE GOTTA GET OUT OF HERE...!
TA (DASH)

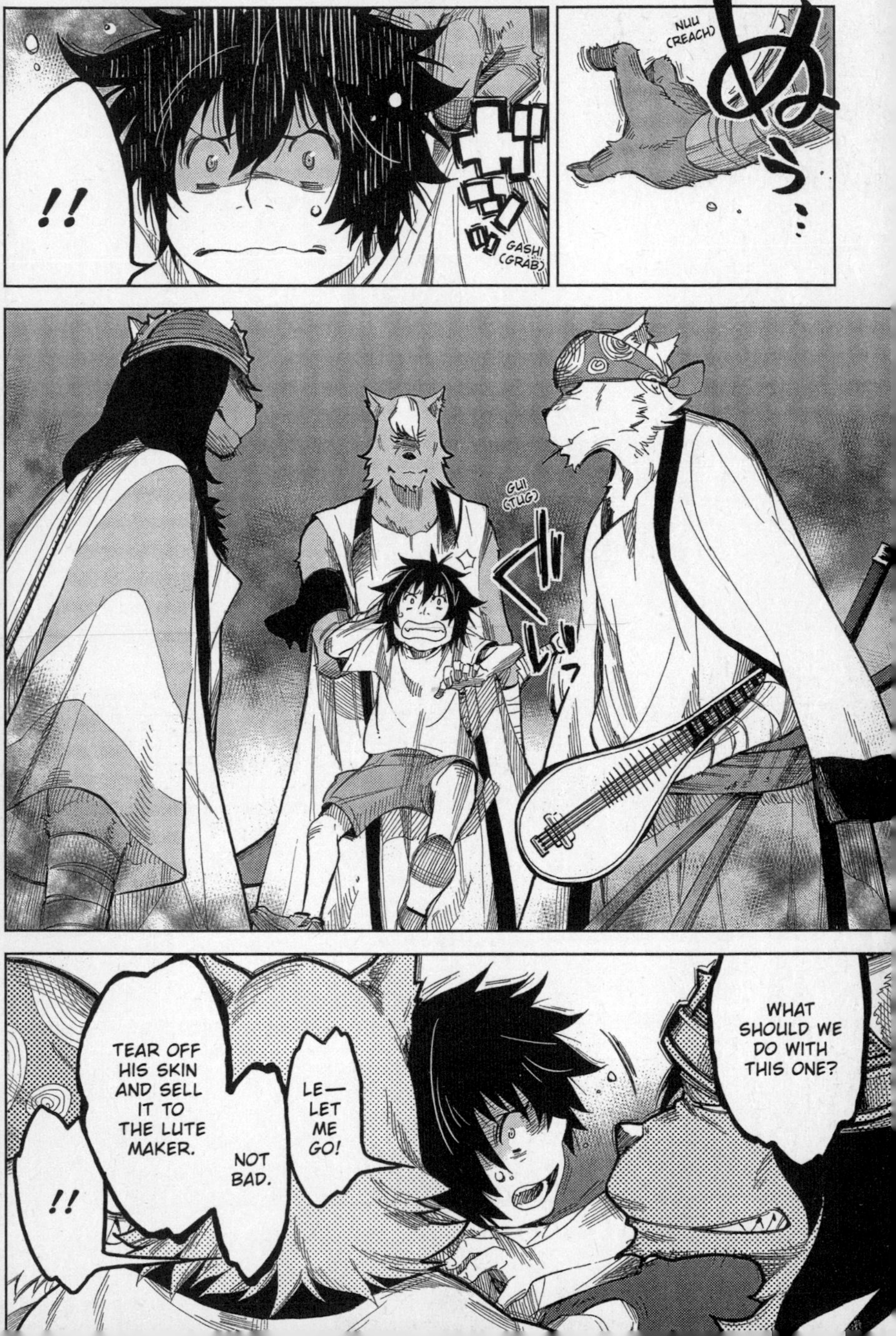
NUU (REACH)
GASHI (GRAB)
!!
GUI (TUG)
WHAT SHOULD WE DO WITH THIS ONE?
LE— LET ME GO!
TEAR OFF HIS SKIN AND SELL IT TO THE LUTE MAKER.
NOT BAD.
!!

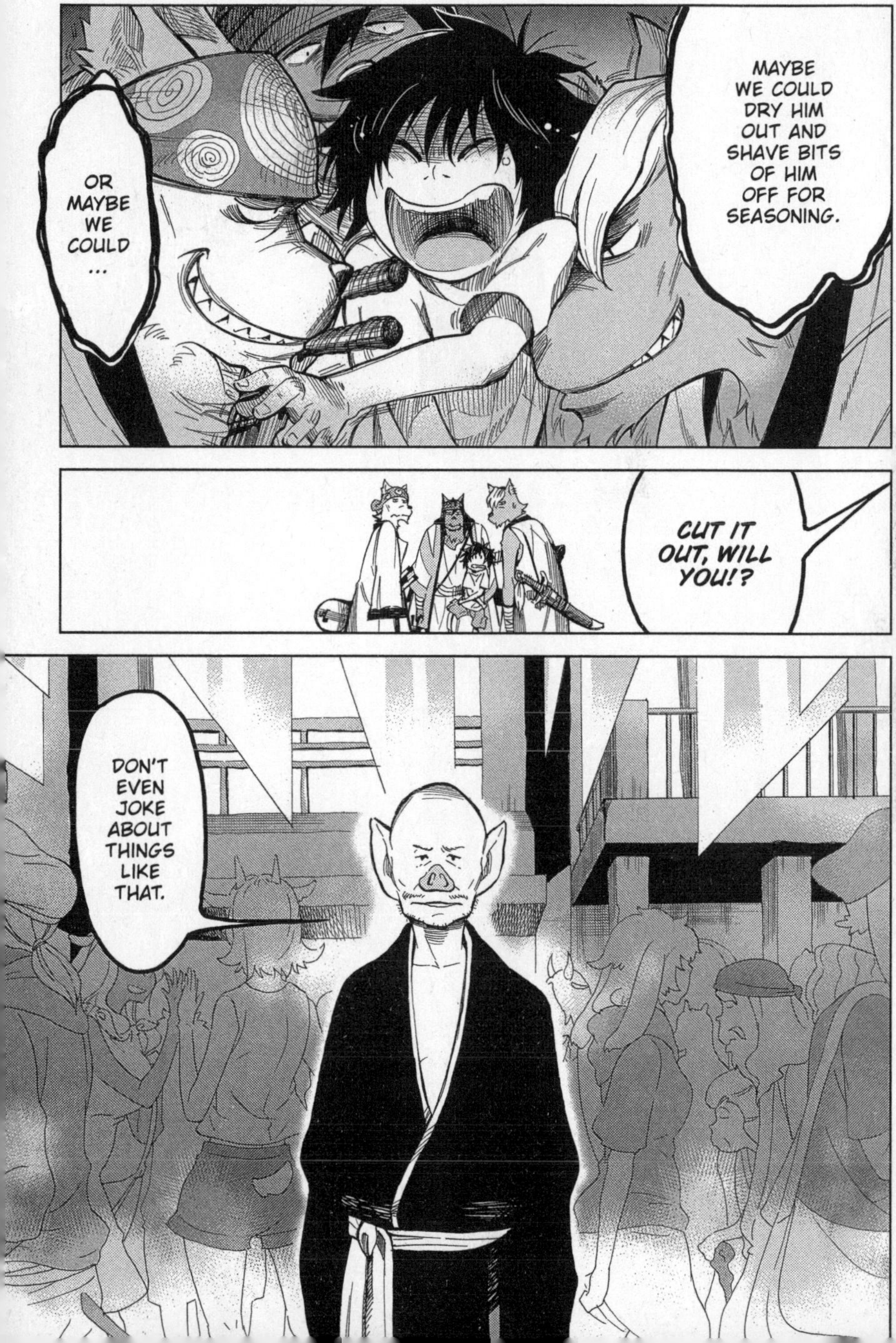
MAYBE WE COULD DRY HIM OUT AND SHAVE BITS OF HIM OFF FOR SEASONING.
OR MAYBE WE COULD ...
CUT IT OUT, WILL YOU!?
DON'T EVEN JOKE ABOUT THINGS LIKE THAT.

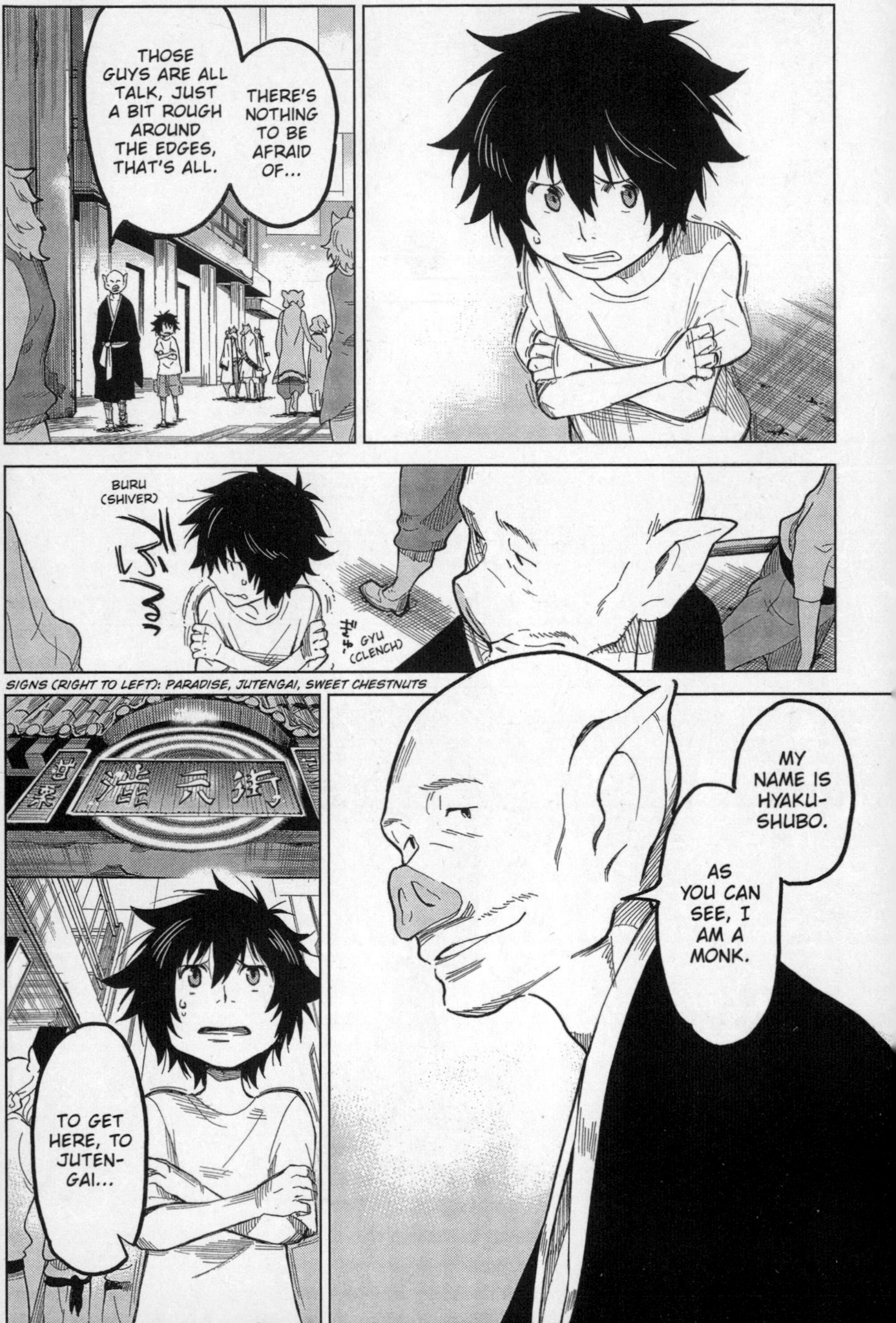
THOSE GUYS ARE ALL TALK, JUST A BIT ROUGH AROUND THE EDGES, THAT'S ALL.
THERE'S NOTHING TO BE AFRAID OF...
BURU (SHIVER)
GYU (CLENCH)
SIGNS (RIGHT TO LEFT): PARADISE, JUTENGAI, SWEET CHESTNUTS
MY NAME IS HYAKU-SHUBO.
AS YOU CAN SEE, I AM A MONK.
TO GET HERE, TO JUTEN-GAI...

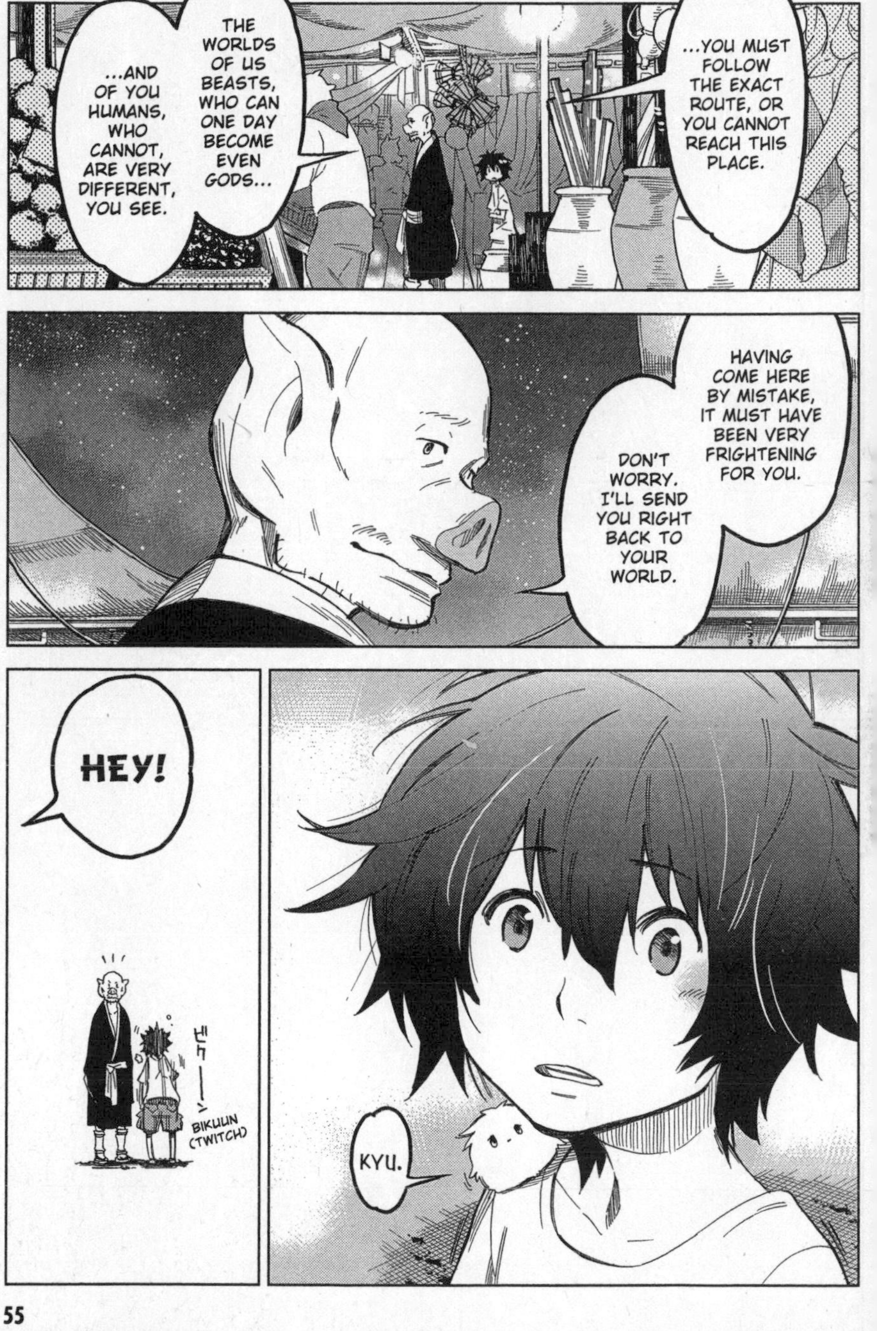
...YOU MUST FOLLOW THE EXACT ROUTE, OR YOU CANNOT REACH THIS PLACE.
THE WORLDS OF US BEASTS, WHO CAN ONE DAY BECOME EVEN GODS...
...AND OF YOU HUMANS, WHO CANNOT, ARE VERY DIFFERENT, YOU SEE.
HAVING COME HERE BY MISTAKE, IT MUST HAVE BEEN VERY FRIGHTENING FOR YOU.
DON'T WORRY. I'LL SEND YOU RIGHT BACK TO YOUR WORLD.
KYU.
HEY!
ビクーン
BIKUUN (TWITCH)

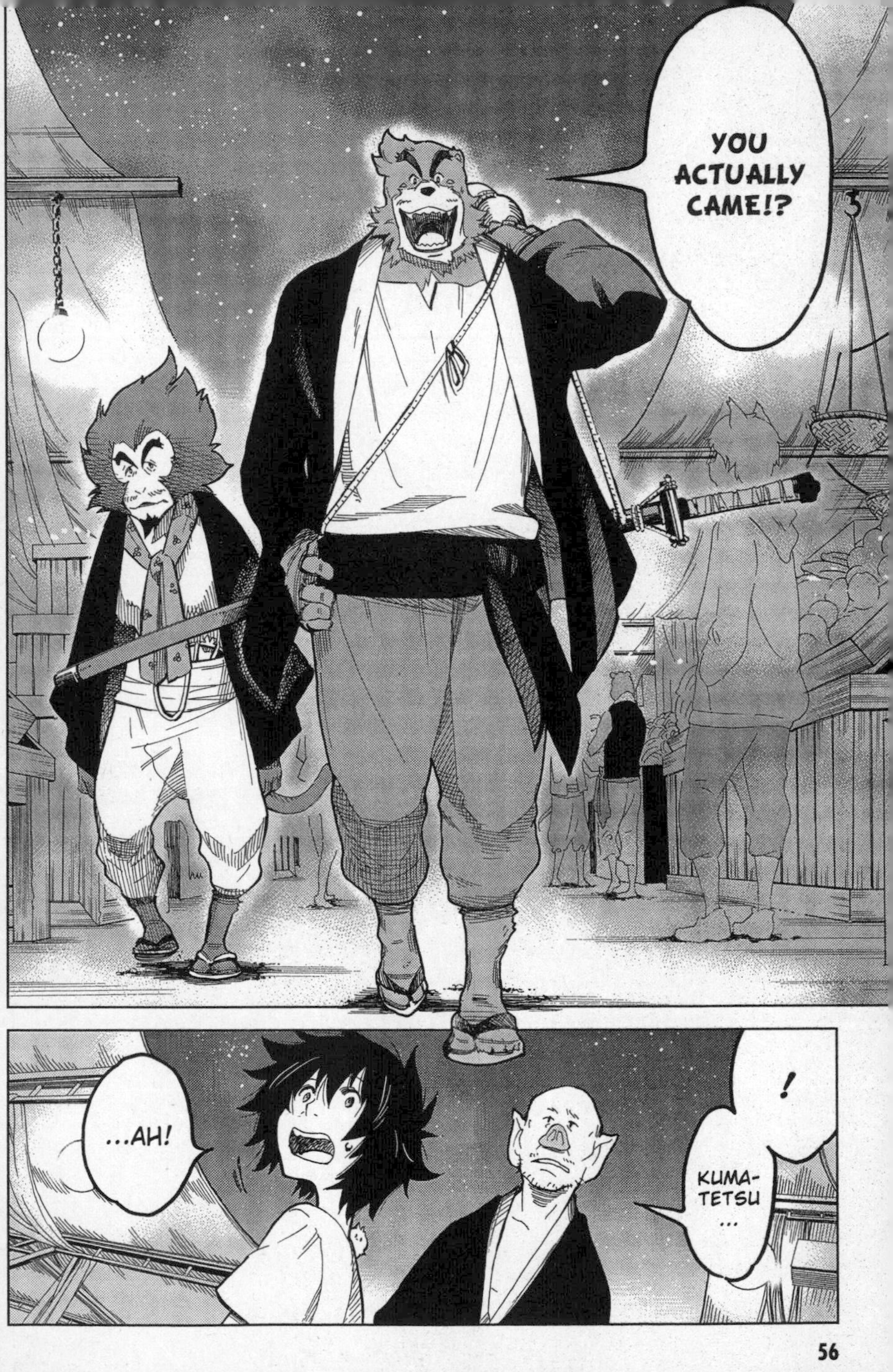
YOU ACTUALLY CAME!?
!
KUMA-TETSU...
...AH!

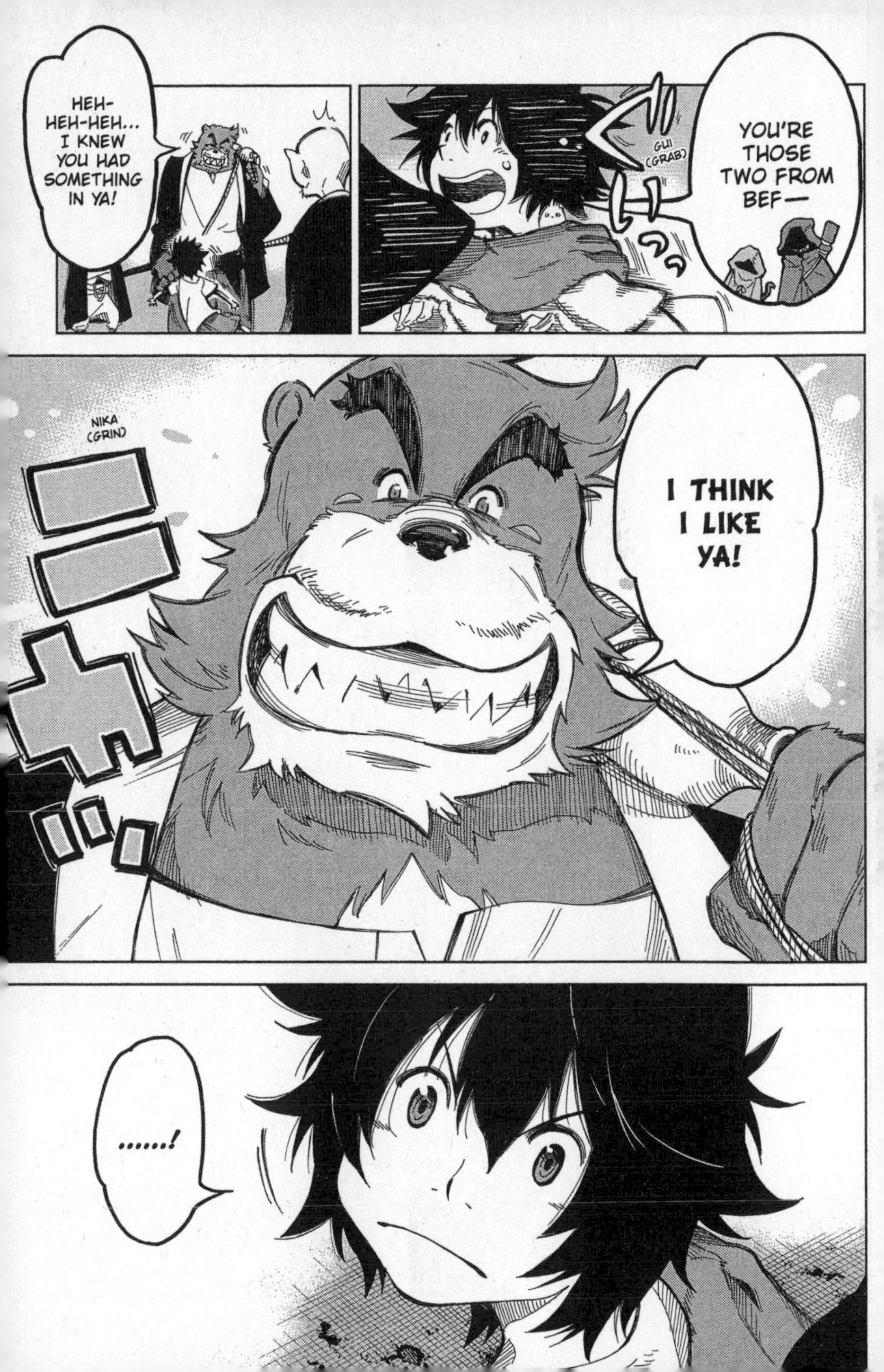
YOU'RE THOSE TWO FROM BEF—
GUI (GRAB)
HEH-HEH-HEH... I KNEW YOU HAD SOMETHING IN YA!
I THINK I LIKE YA!
NIKA (GRIN)
......!

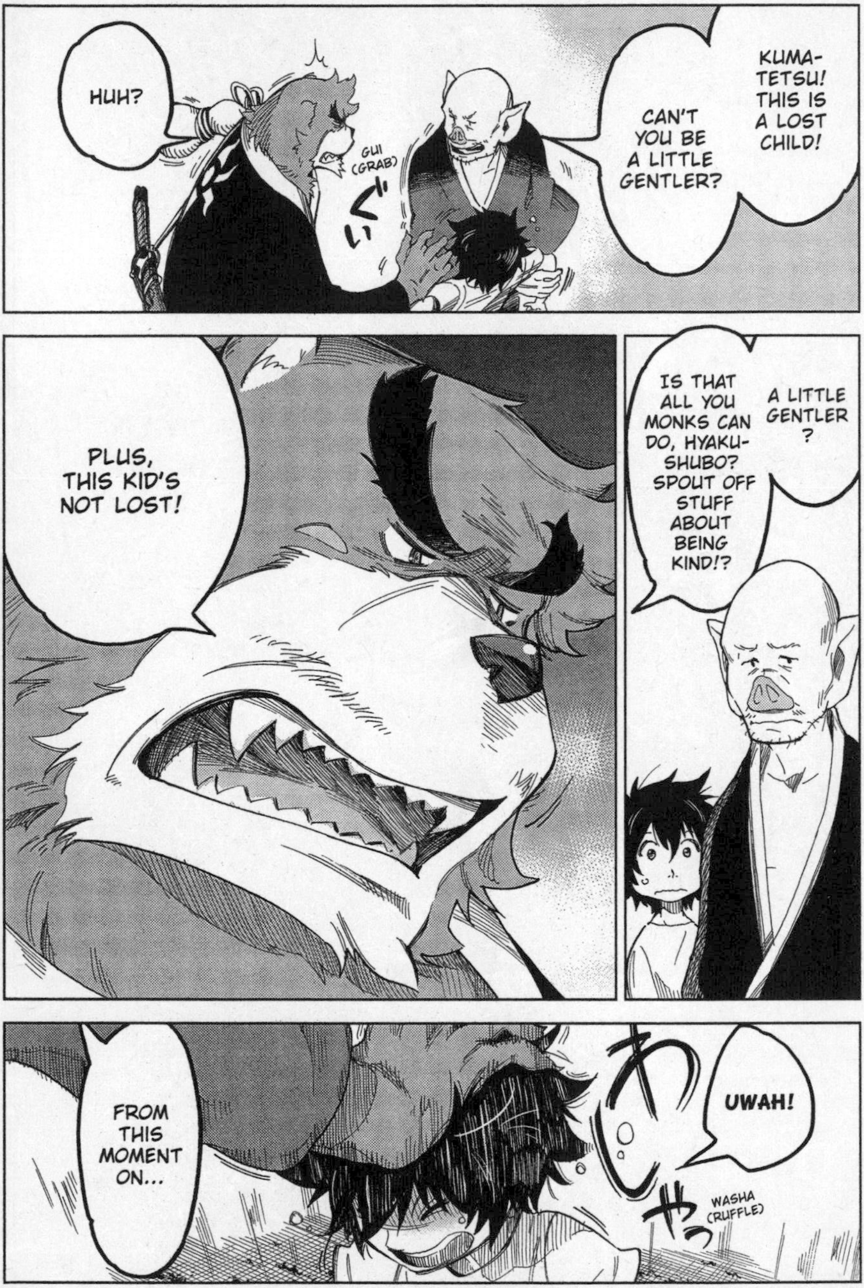
KUMA-TETSU! THIS IS A LOST CHILD!
CAN'T YOU BE A LITTLE GENTLER?
GUI (GRAB)
HUH?
A LITTLE GENTLER?
IS THAT ALL YOU MONKS CAN DO, HYAKU-SHUBO? SPOUT OFF STUFF ABOUT BEING KIND!?
PLUS, THIS KID'S NOT LOST!
UWAH!
WASHA (RUFFLE)
FROM THIS MOMENT ON...

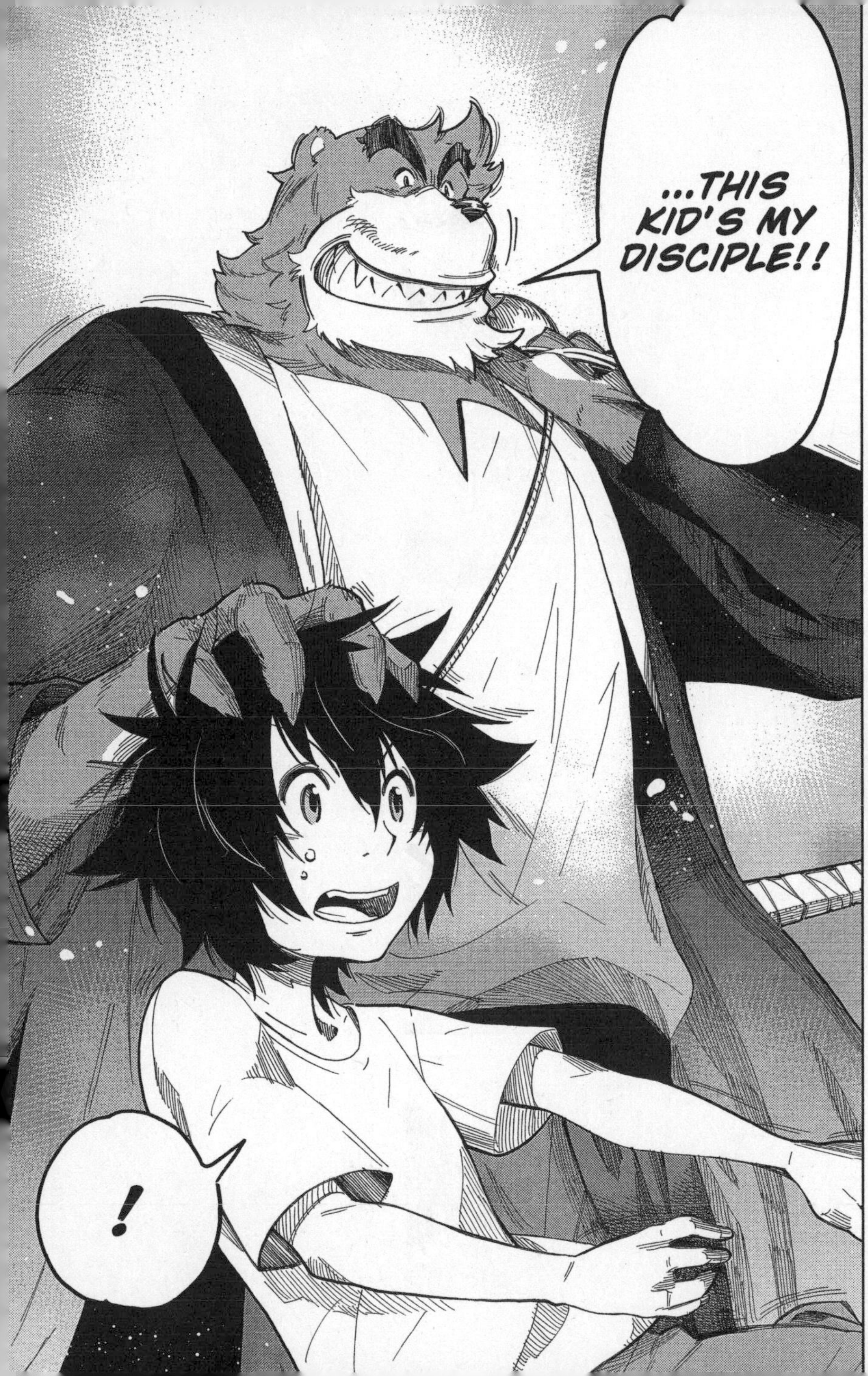
...THIS KID'S MY DISCIPLE!!
!

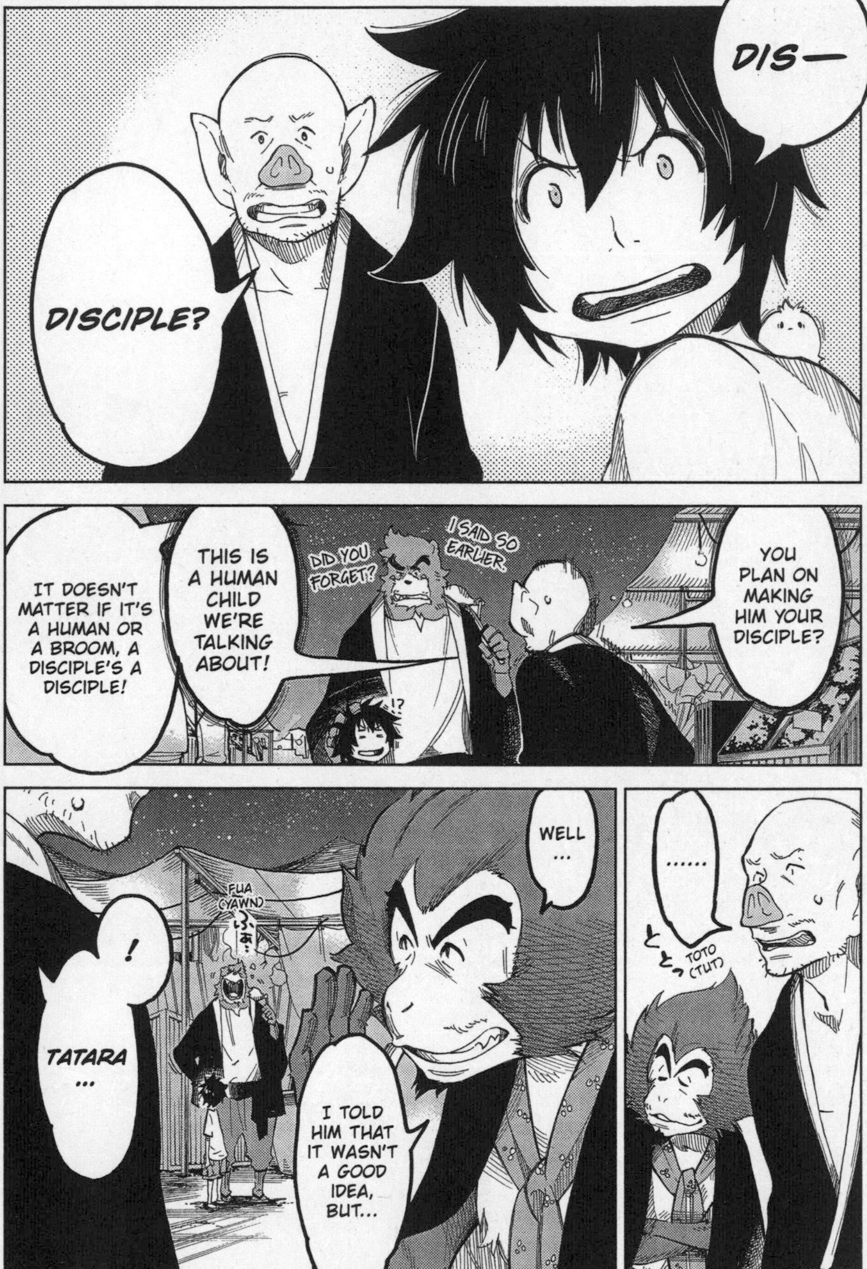
DIS—
DISCIPLE?
YOU PLAN ON MAKING HIM YOUR DISCIPLE?
I SAID SO EARLIER.
DID YOU FORGET?
THIS IS A HUMAN CHILD WE'RE TALKING ABOUT!
!?
IT DOESN'T MATTER IF IT'S A HUMAN OR A BROOM, A DISCIPLE'S A DISCIPLE!
......
とと
TOTO (TUT)
WELL ...
I TOLD HIM THAT IT WASN'T A GOOD IDEA, BUT...
ふぁ…
FUA (YAWN)
!
TATARA ...

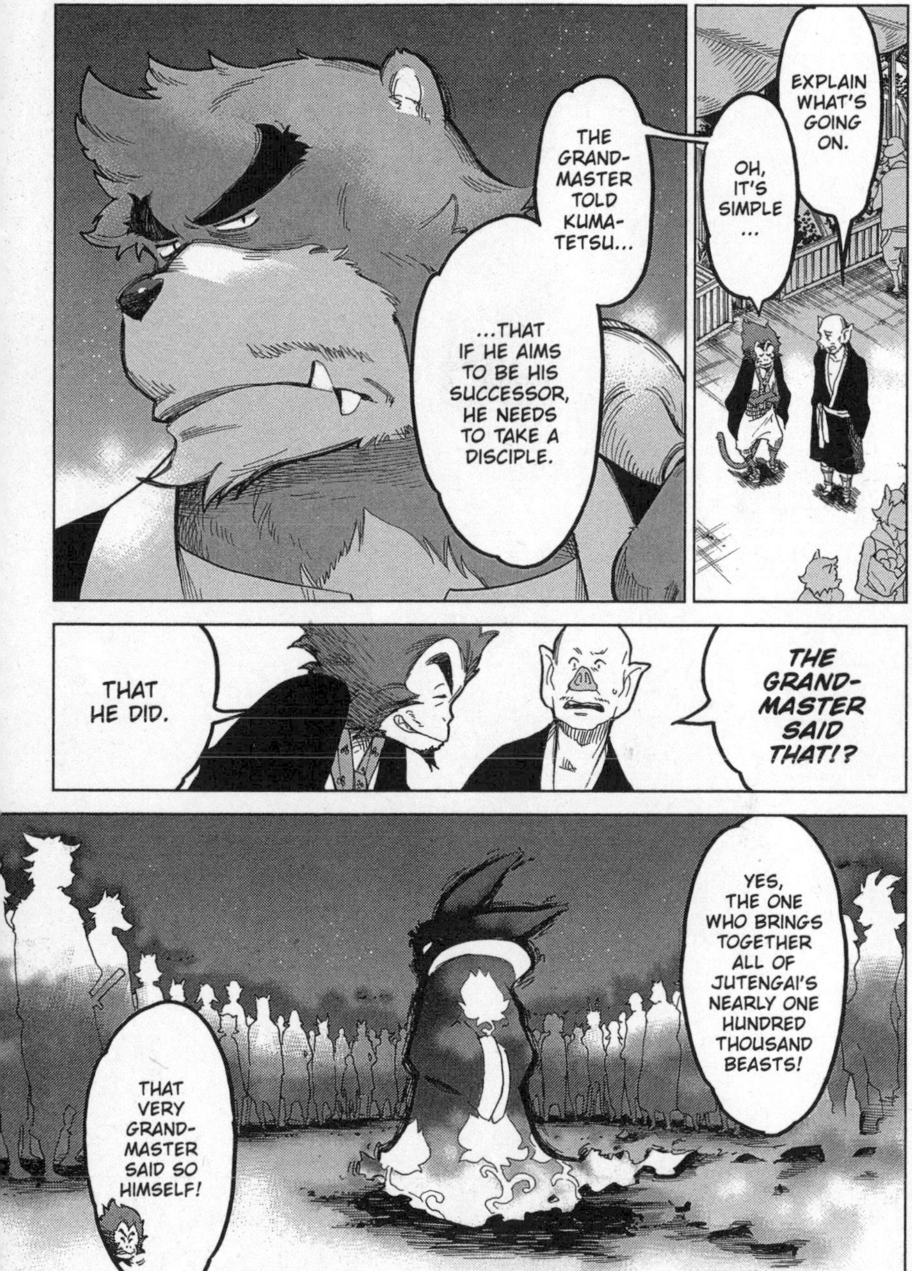
EXPLAIN WHAT'S GOING ON.
OH, IT'S SIMPLE...
THE GRAND-MASTER TOLD KUMA-TETSU...
...THAT IF HE AIMS TO BE HIS SUCCESSOR, HE NEEDS TO TAKE A DISCIPLE.
THE GRAND-MASTER SAID THAT!?
THAT HE DID.
YES, THE ONE WHO BRINGS TOGETHER ALL OF JUTENGAI'S NEARLY ONE HUNDRED THOUSAND BEASTS!
THAT VERY GRAND-MASTER SAID SO HIMSELF!

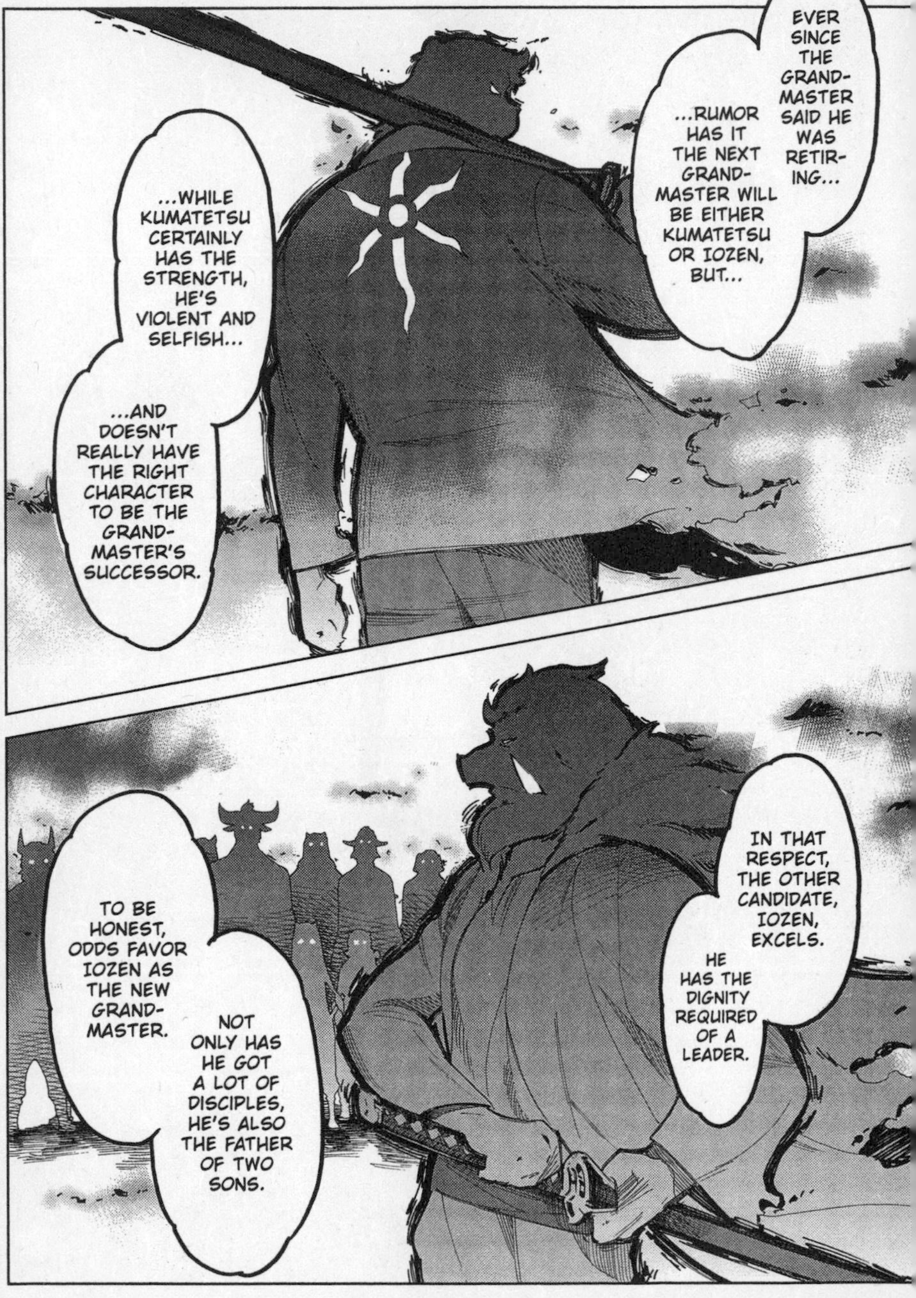
EVER SINCE THE GRAND-MASTER SAID HE WAS RETIR-ING...
...RUMOR HAS IT THE NEXT GRAND-MASTER WILL BE EITHER KUMATETSU OR IOZEN, BUT...
...WHILE KUMATETSU CERTAINLY HAS THE STRENGTH, HE'S VIOLENT AND SELFISH...
...AND DOESN'T REALLY HAVE THE RIGHT CHARACTER TO BE THE GRAND-MASTER'S SUCCESSOR.
IN THAT RESPECT, THE OTHER CANDIDATE, IOZEN, EXCELS.
HE HAS THE DIGNITY REQUIRED OF A LEADER.
TO BE HONEST, ODDS FAVOR IOZEN AS THE NEW GRAND-MASTER.
NOT ONLY HAS HE GOT A LOT OF DISCIPLES, HE'S ALSO THE FATHER OF TWO SONS.

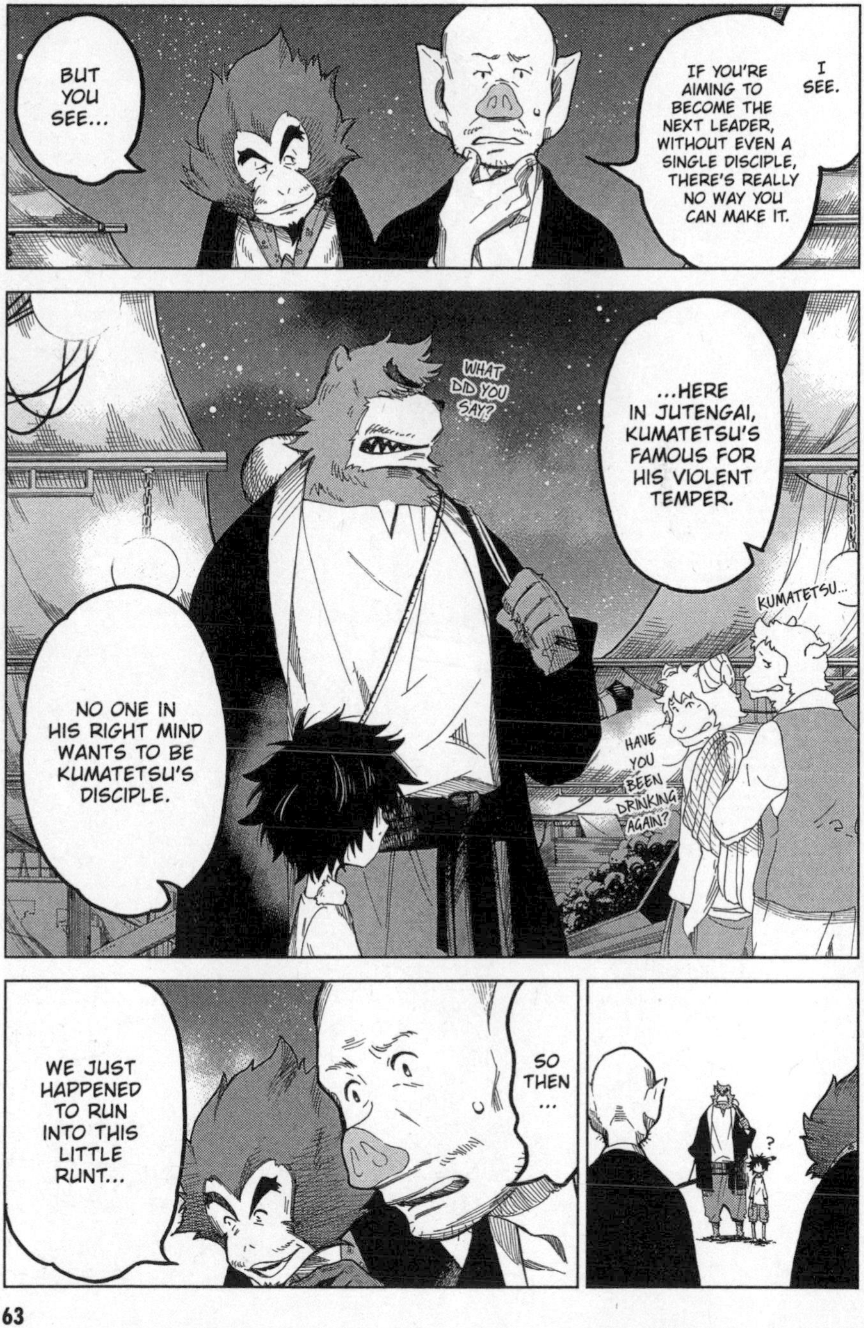
I SEE.
IF YOU'RE AIMING TO BECOME THE NEXT LEADER, WITHOUT EVEN A SINGLE DISCIPLE, THERE'S REALLY NO WAY YOU CAN MAKE IT.
BUT YOU SEE...
...HERE IN JUTENGAI, KUMATETSU'S FAMOUS FOR HIS VIOLENT TEMPER.
WHAT DID YOU SAY?
KUMATETSU...
HAVE YOU BEEN DRINKING AGAIN?
NO ONE IN HIS RIGHT MIND WANTS TO BE KUMATETSU'S DISCIPLE.
?
SO THEN...
WE JUST HAPPENED TO RUN INTO THIS LITTLE RUNT...

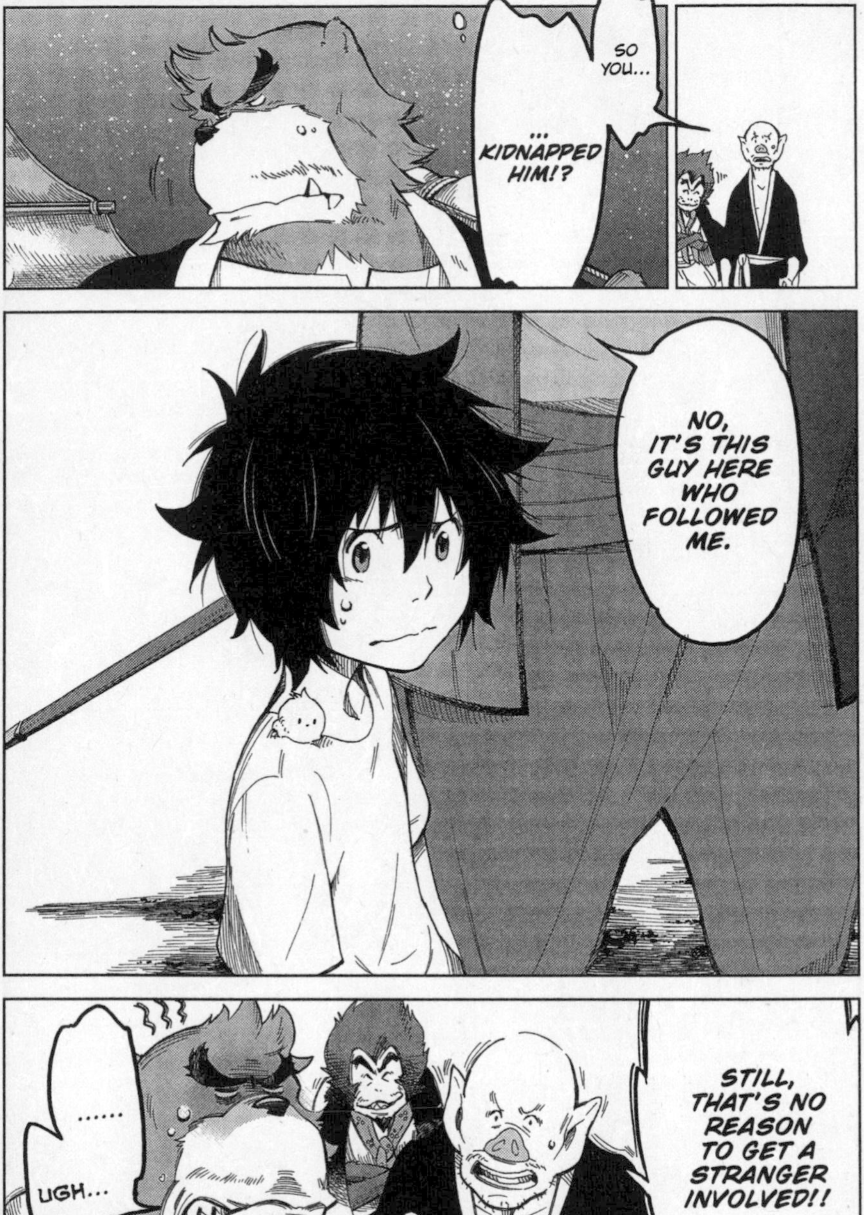
SO YOU...
...KIDNAPPED HIM!?
NO, IT'S THIS GUY HERE WHO FOLLOWED ME.
STILL, THAT'S NO REASON TO GET A STRANGER INVOLVED!!
......
UGH...

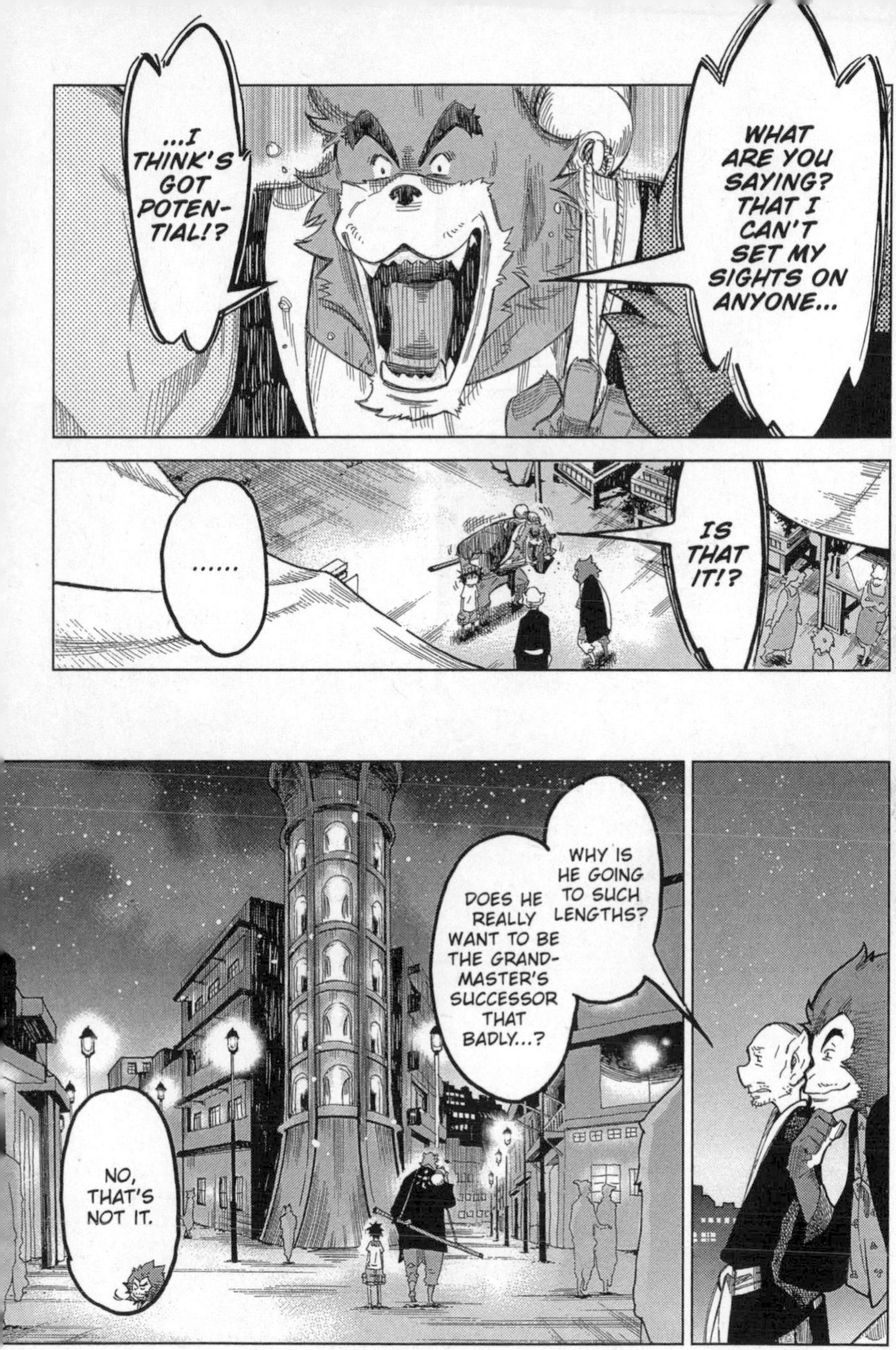
WHAT ARE YOU SAYING? THAT I CAN'T SET MY SIGHTS ON ANYONE...
...I THINK'S GOT POTEN-TIAL!?
IS THAT IT!?
......
WHY IS HE GOING TO SUCH LENGTHS?
DOES HE REALLY WANT TO BE THE GRAND-MASTER'S SUCCESSOR THAT BADLY...?
NO, THAT'S NOT IT.

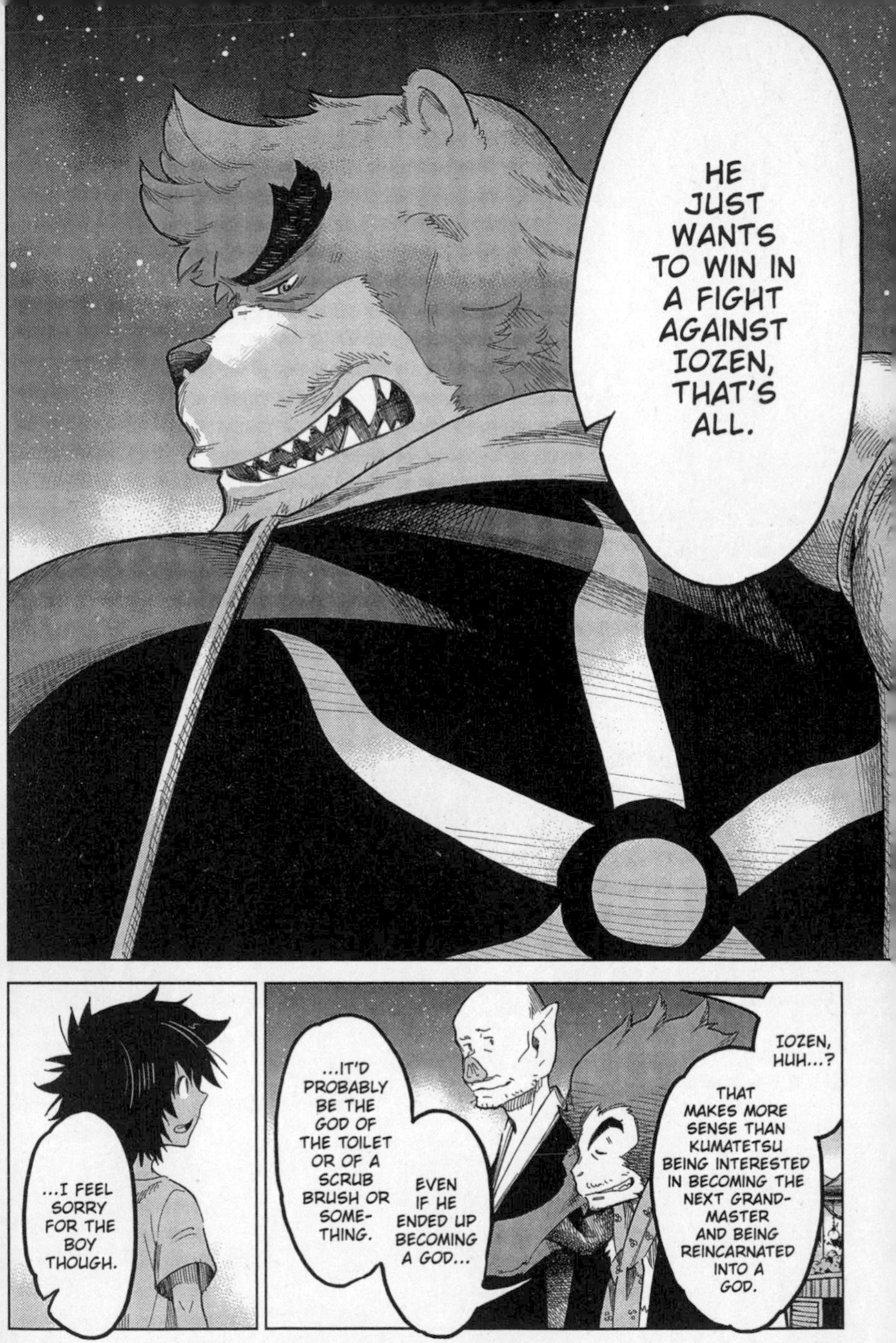
HE JUST WANTS TO WIN IN A FIGHT AGAINST IOZEN, THAT'S ALL.
IOZEN, HUH...?
THAT MAKES MORE SENSE THAN KUMATETSU BEING INTERESTED IN BECOMING THE NEXT GRAND-MASTER AND BEING REINCARNATED INTO A GOD.
EVEN IF HE ENDED UP BECOMING A GOD...
...IT'D PROBABLY BE THE GOD OF THE TOILET OR OF A SCRUB BRUSH OR SOME-THING.
...I FEEL SORRY FOR THE BOY THOUGH.

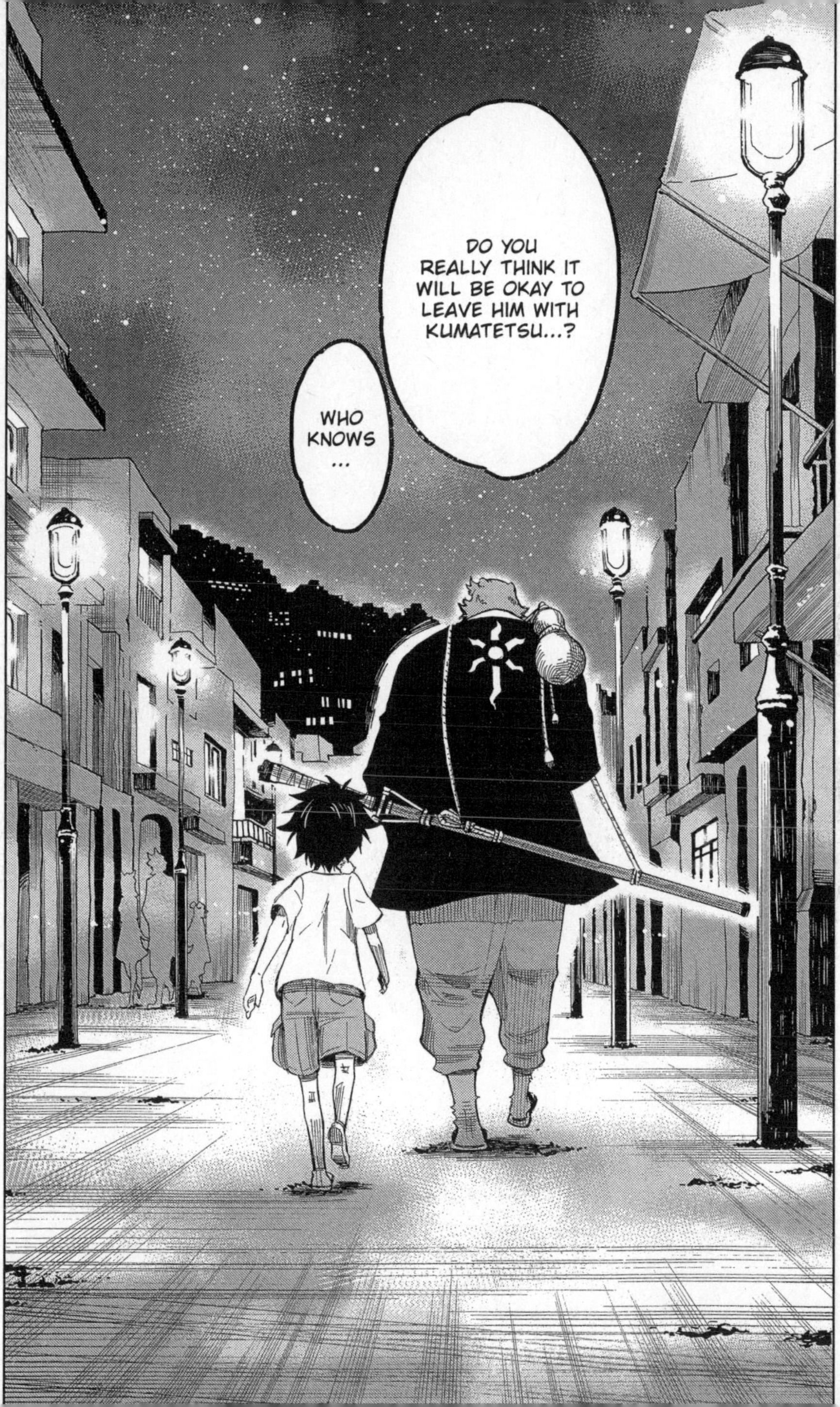
DO YOU REALLY THINK IT WILL BE OKAY TO LEAVE HIM WITH KUMATETSU...?
WHO KNOWS ...

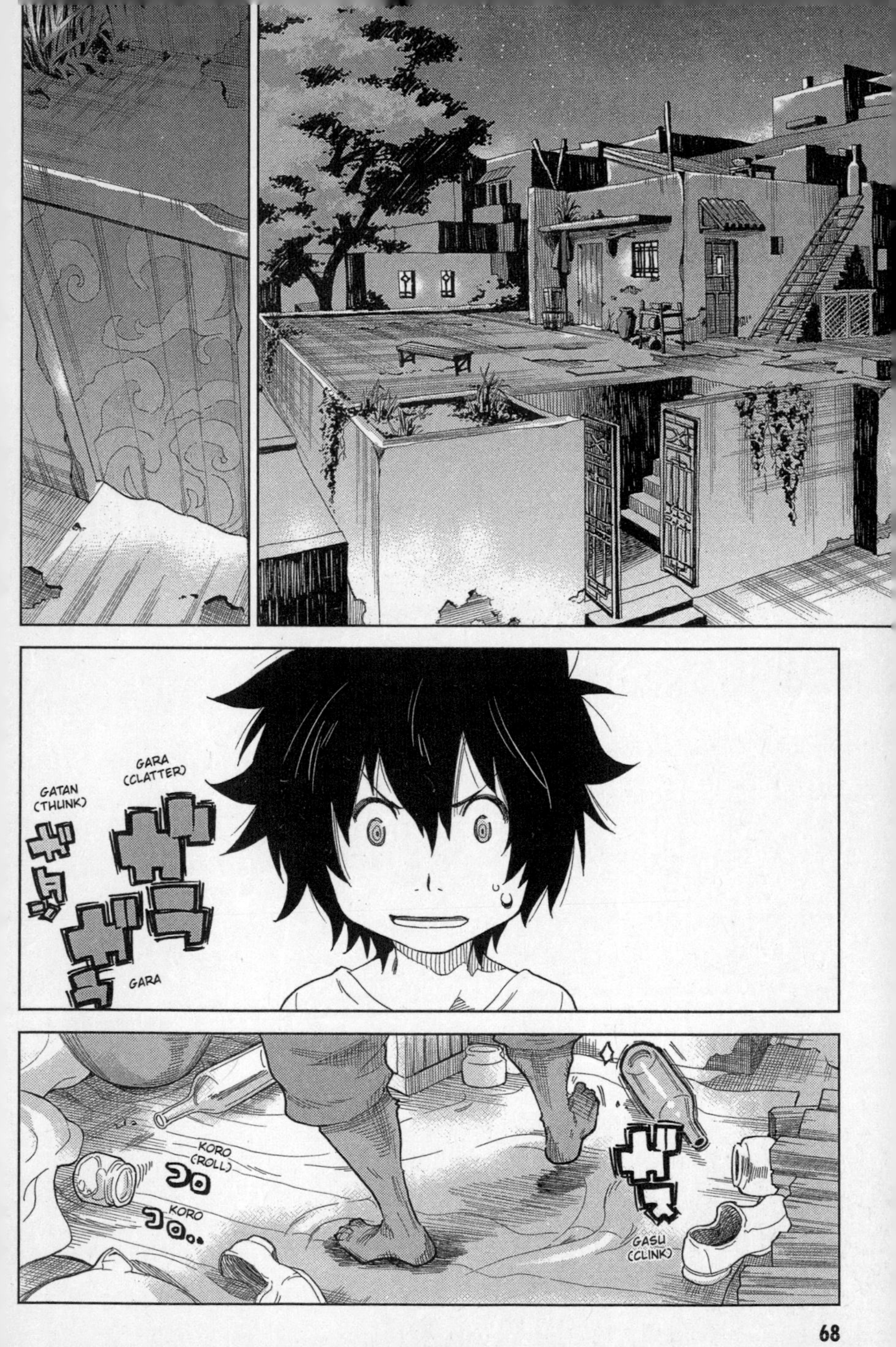
GARA (CLATTER)
GATAN (THUNK)
GARA
GASU (CLINK)
KORO (ROLL)
KORO

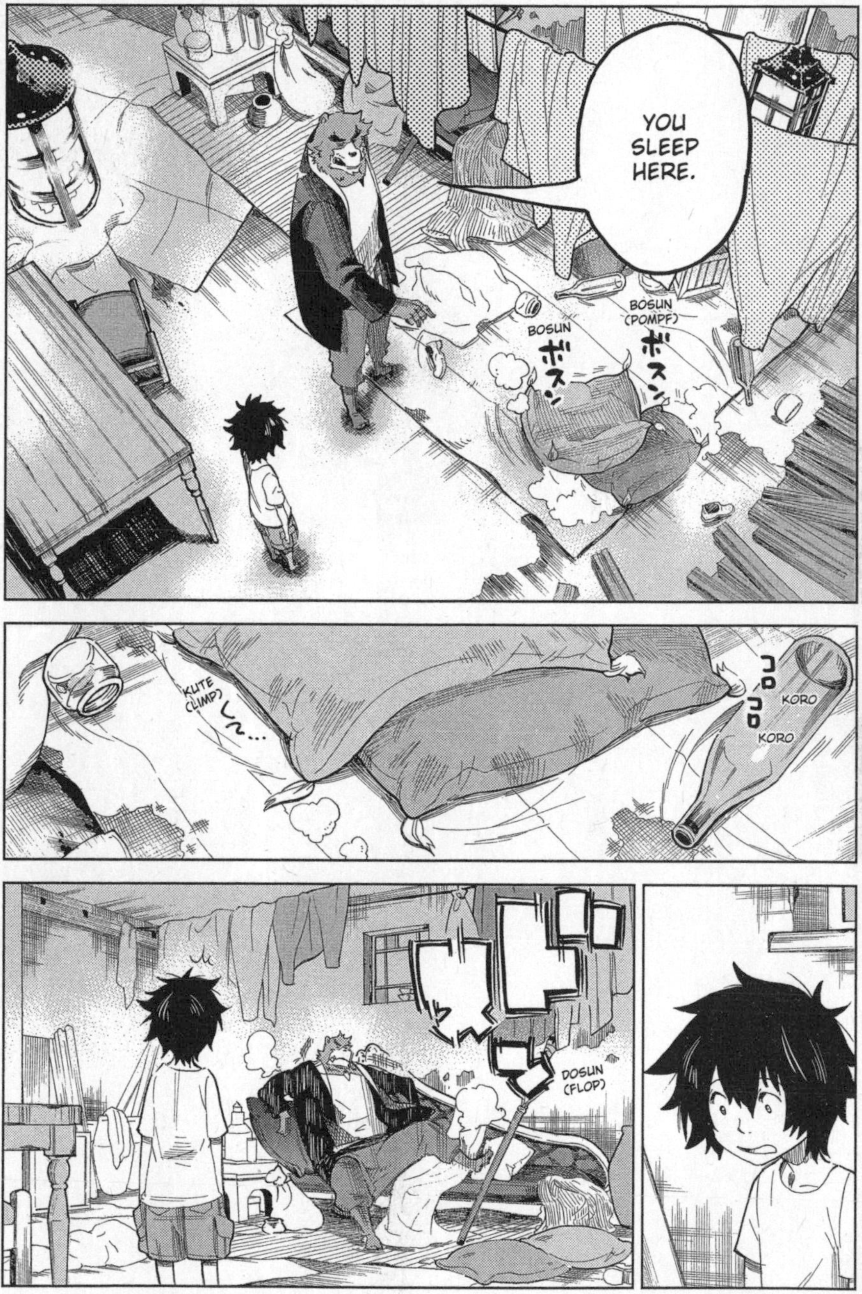
YOU SLEEP HERE.
BOSUN (POMPF)
ボスン
BOSUN
ボスン
コロ
KORO
コロ
KORO
KUTE (LIMP)
DOSUN (FLOP)

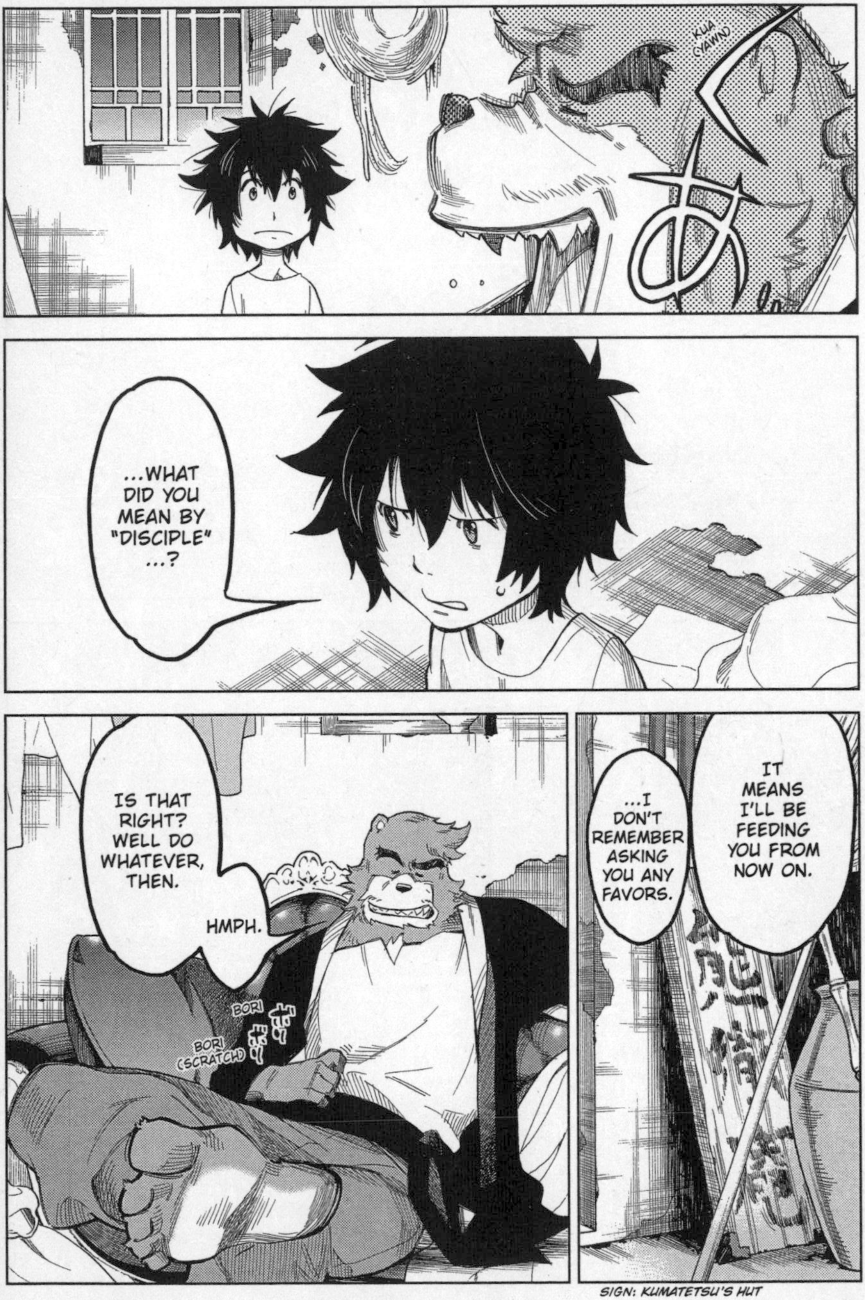
KUA (YAWN)
...WHAT DID YOU MEAN BY "DISCIPLE" ...?
IT MEANS I'LL BE FEEDING YOU FROM NOW ON.
...I DON'T REMEMBER ASKING YOU ANY FAVORS.
IS THAT RIGHT? WELL DO WHATEVER, THEN.
HMPH.
BORI BORI (SCRATCH)
SIGN: KUMATETSU'S HUT

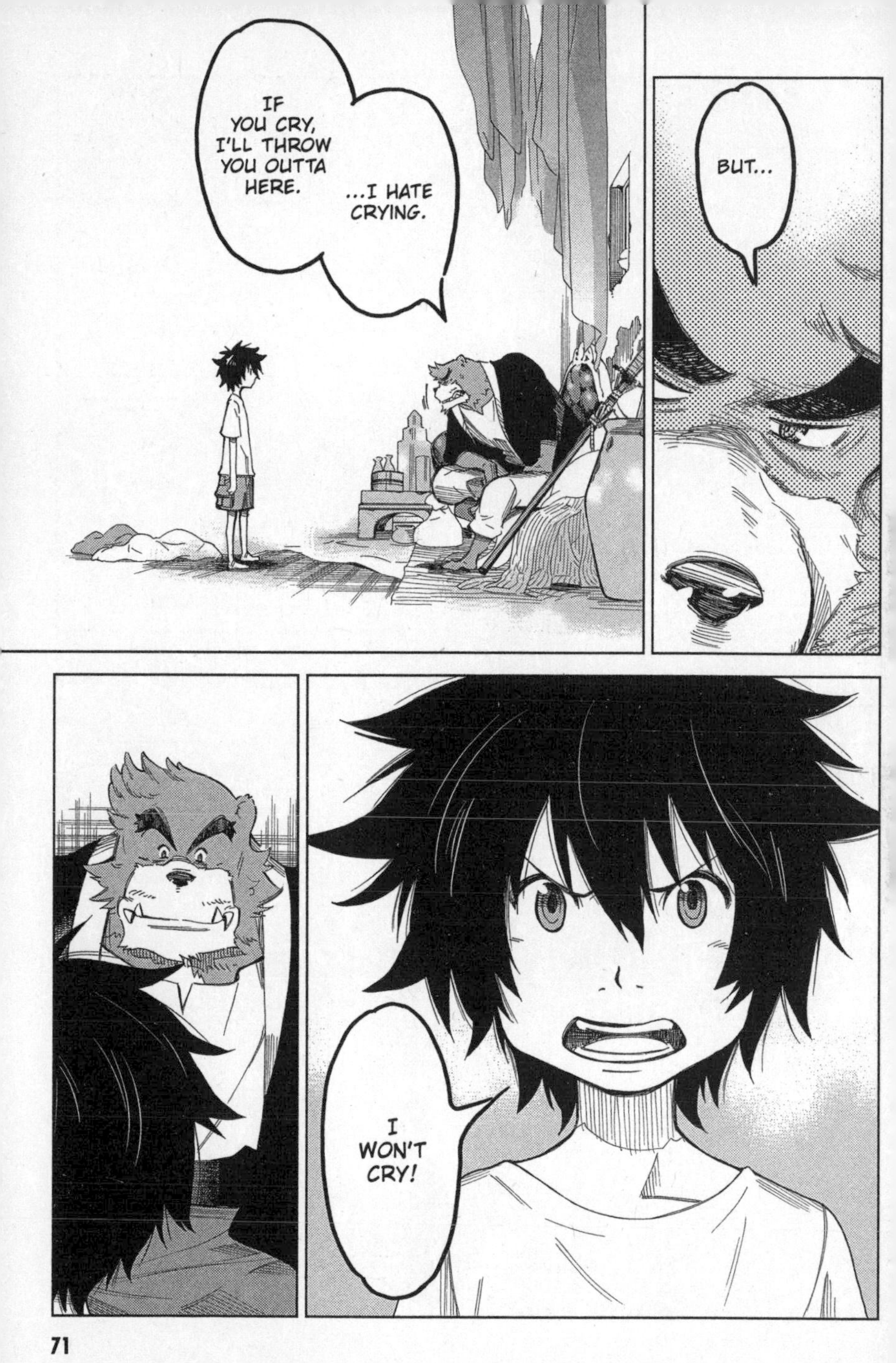
BUT...
...I HATE CRYING.
IF YOU CRY, I'LL THROW YOU OUTTA HERE.
I WON'T CRY!

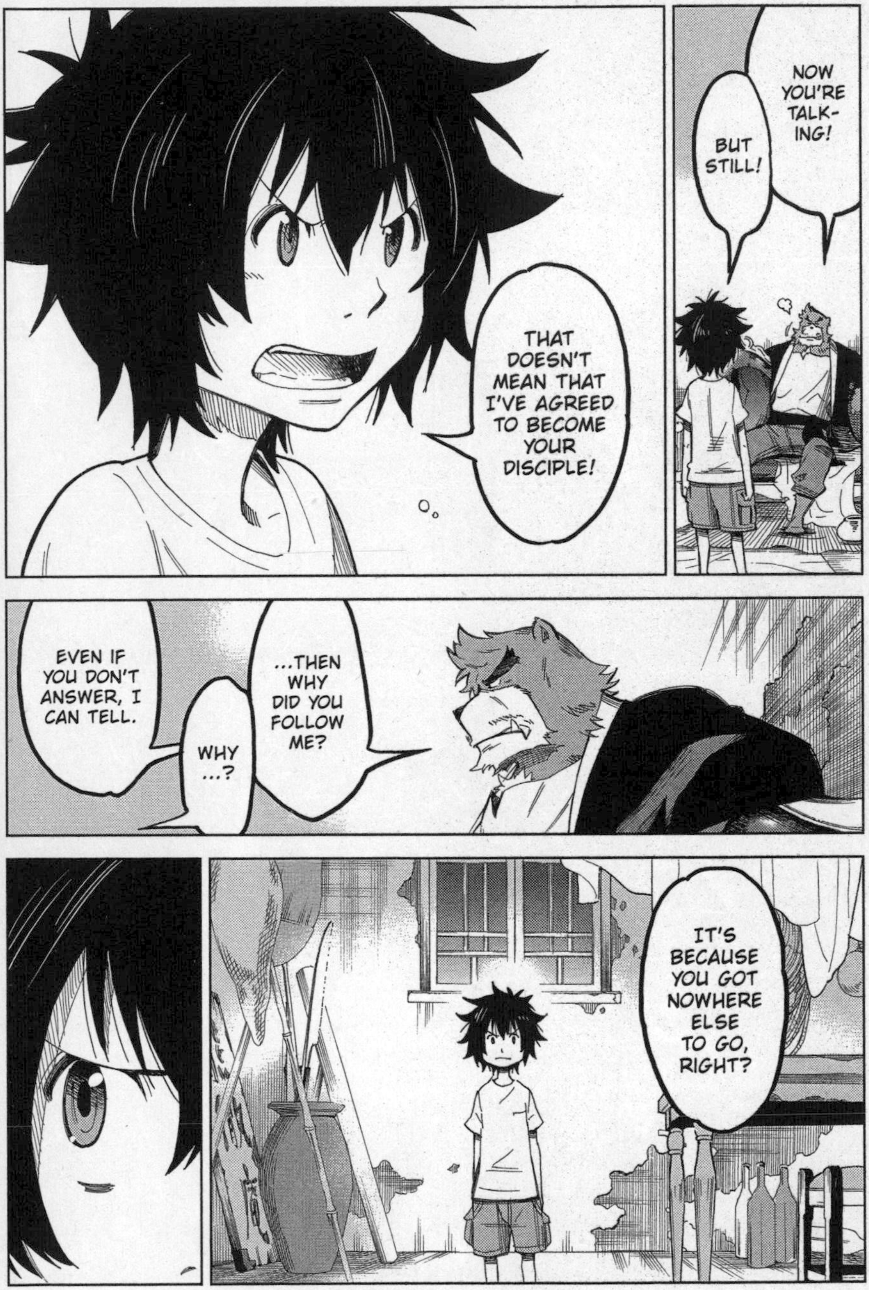
NOW YOU'RE TALKING!
BUT STILL!
THAT DOESN'T MEAN THAT I'VE AGREED TO BECOME YOUR DISCIPLE!
...THEN WHY DID YOU FOLLOW ME?
WHY ...?
EVEN IF YOU DON'T ANSWER, I CAN TELL.
IT'S BECAUSE YOU GOT NOWHERE ELSE TO GO, RIGHT?

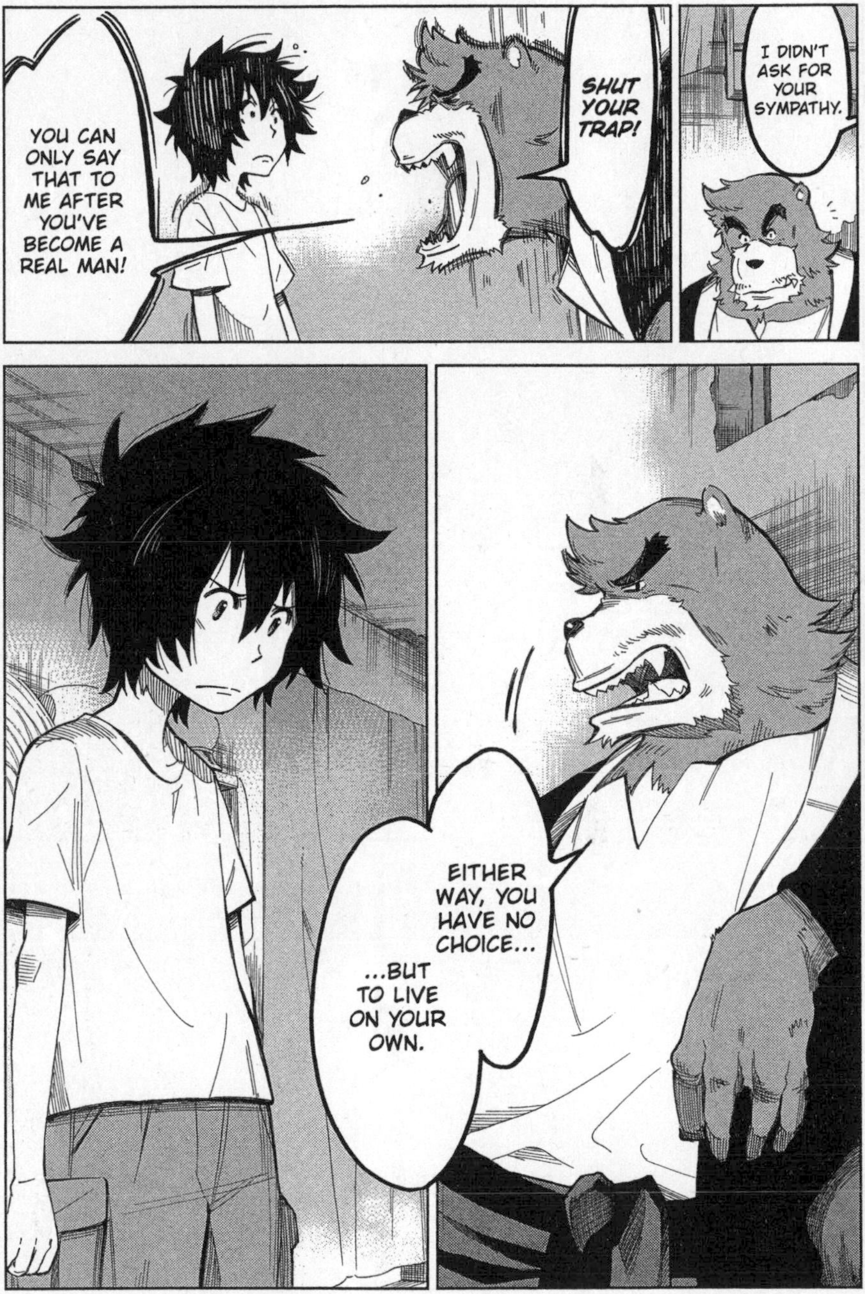
I DIDN'T ASK FOR YOUR SYMPATHY.
SHUT YOUR TRAP!
YOU CAN ONLY SAY THAT TO ME AFTER YOU'VE BECOME A REAL MAN!
EITHER WAY, YOU HAVE NO CHOICE...
...BUT TO LIVE ON YOUR OWN.

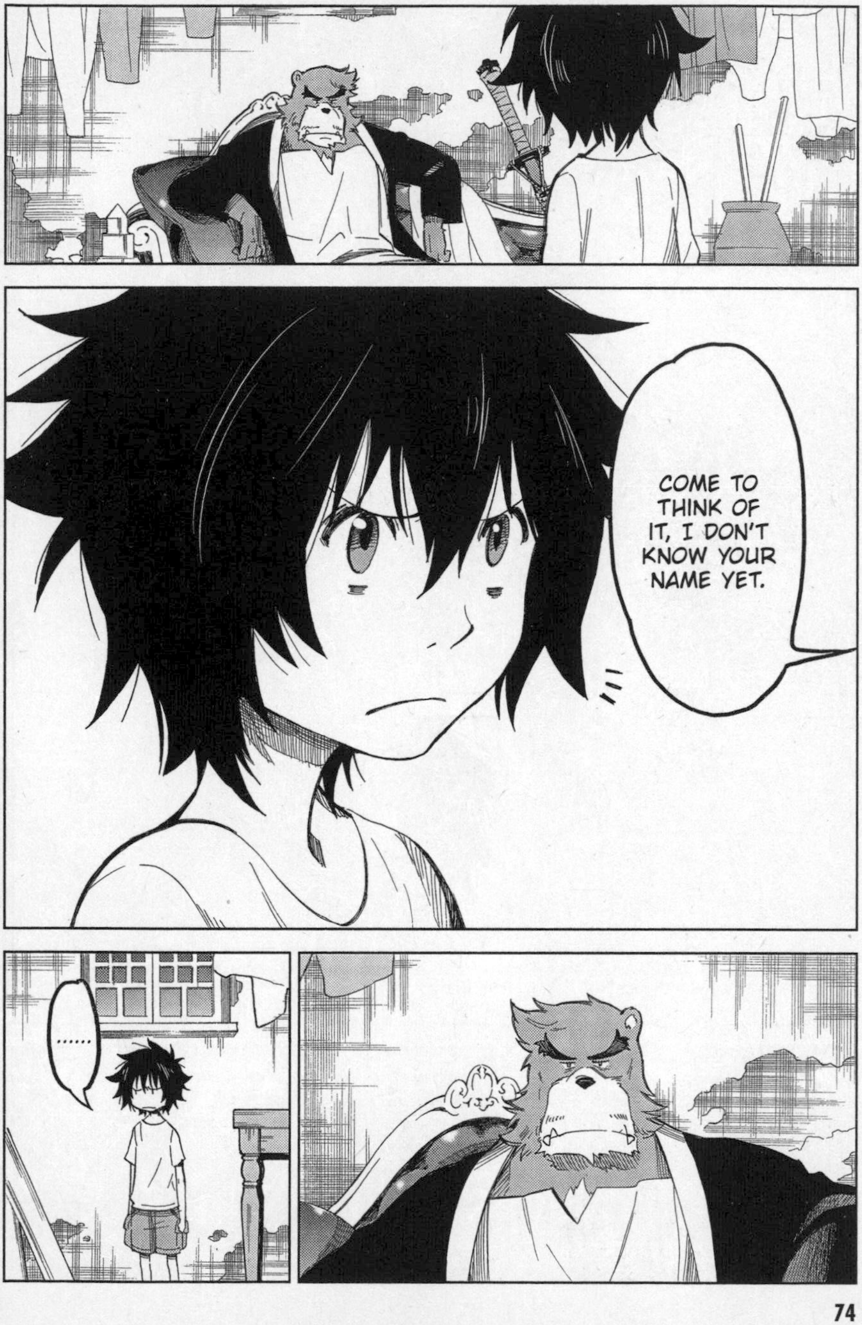
COME TO THINK OF IT, I DON'T KNOW YOUR NAME YET.
......

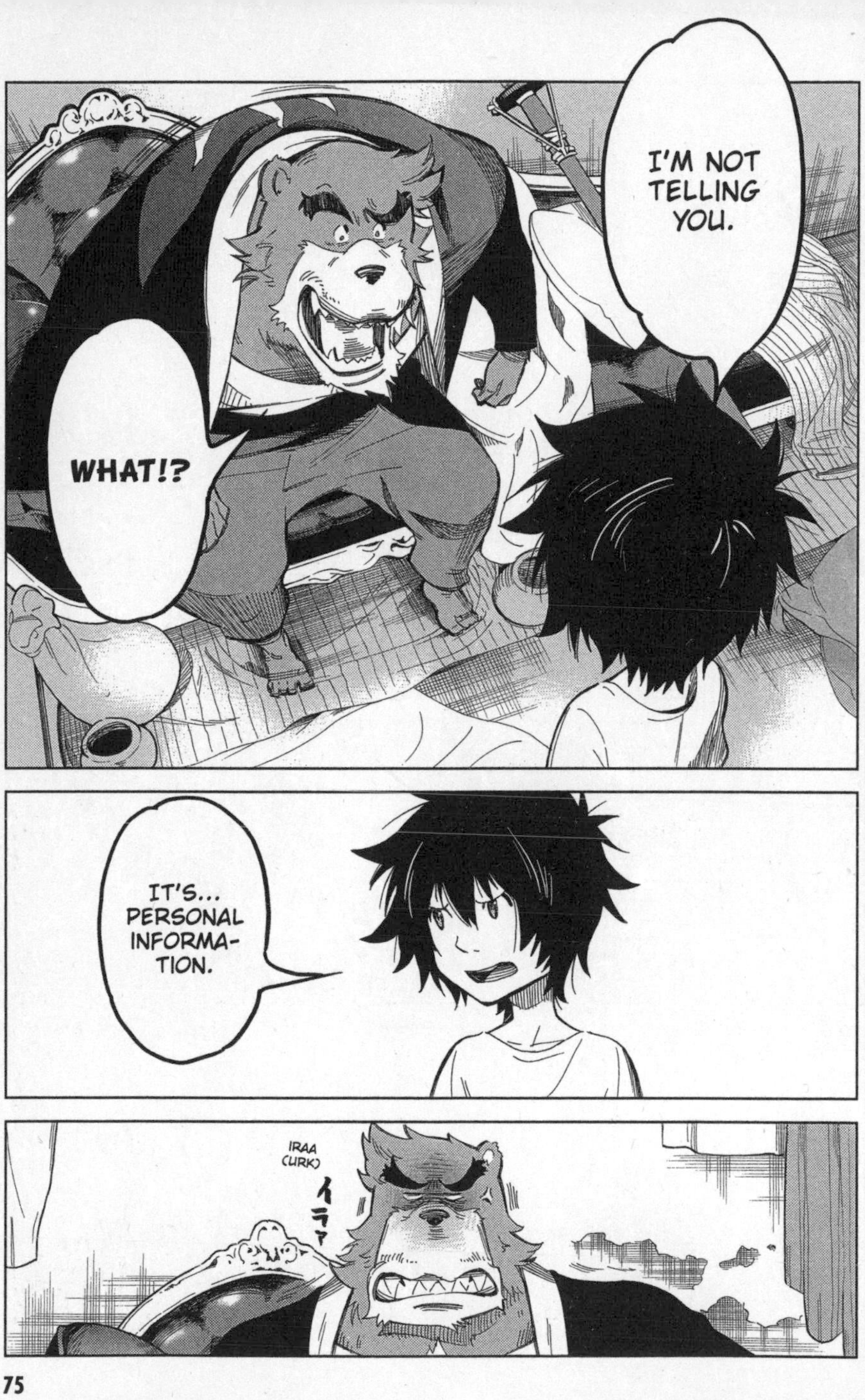

I'M NOT TELLING YOU.
WHAT!?
IT'S... PERSONAL INFORMA-TION.
IRAA (URK)
イラァ

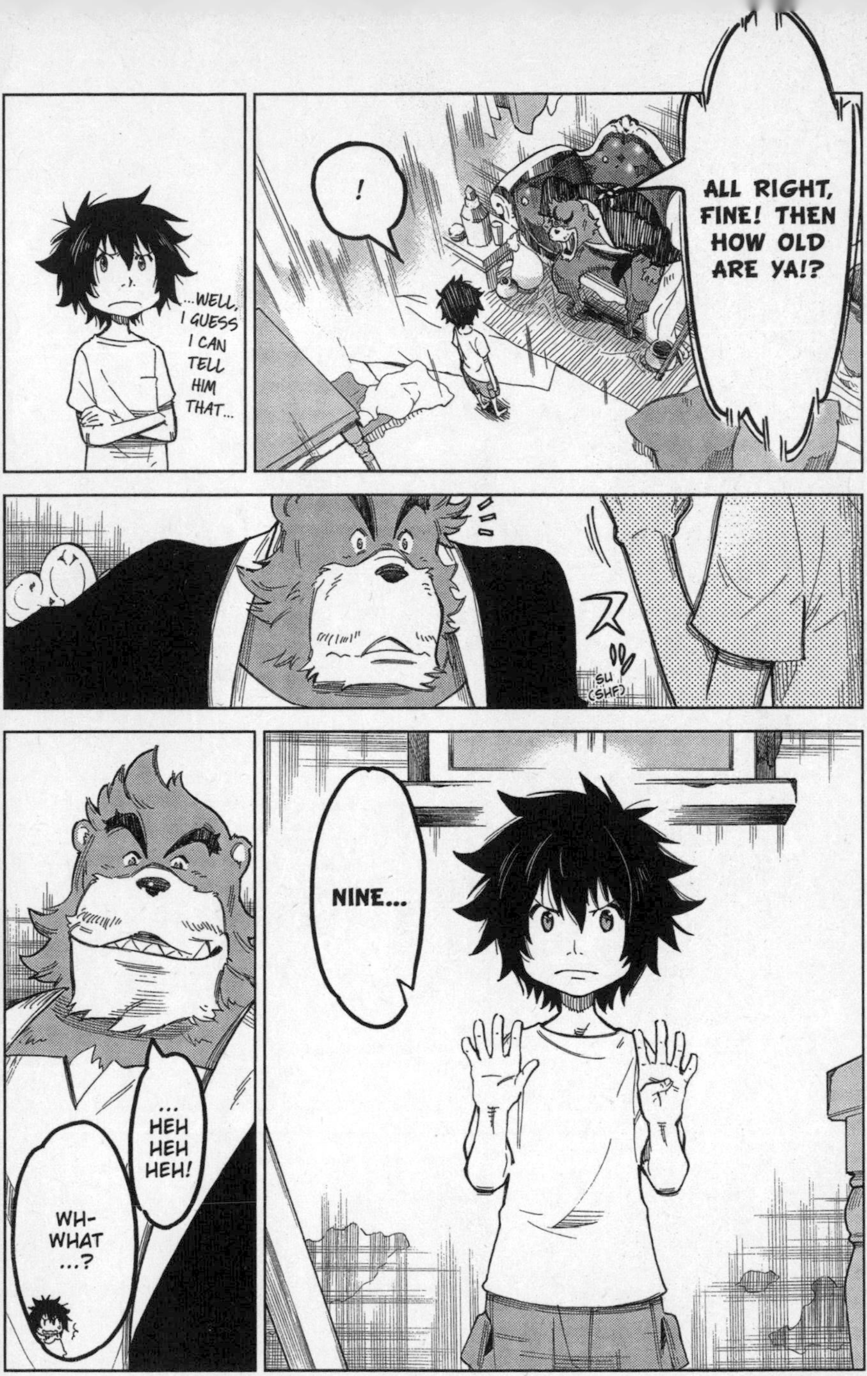
ALL RIGHT, FINE! THEN HOW OLD ARE YA!?
!
...WELL, I GUESS I CAN TELL HIM THAT...
SU (SHF)
NINE...
... HEH HEH HEH!
WH-WHAT ...?

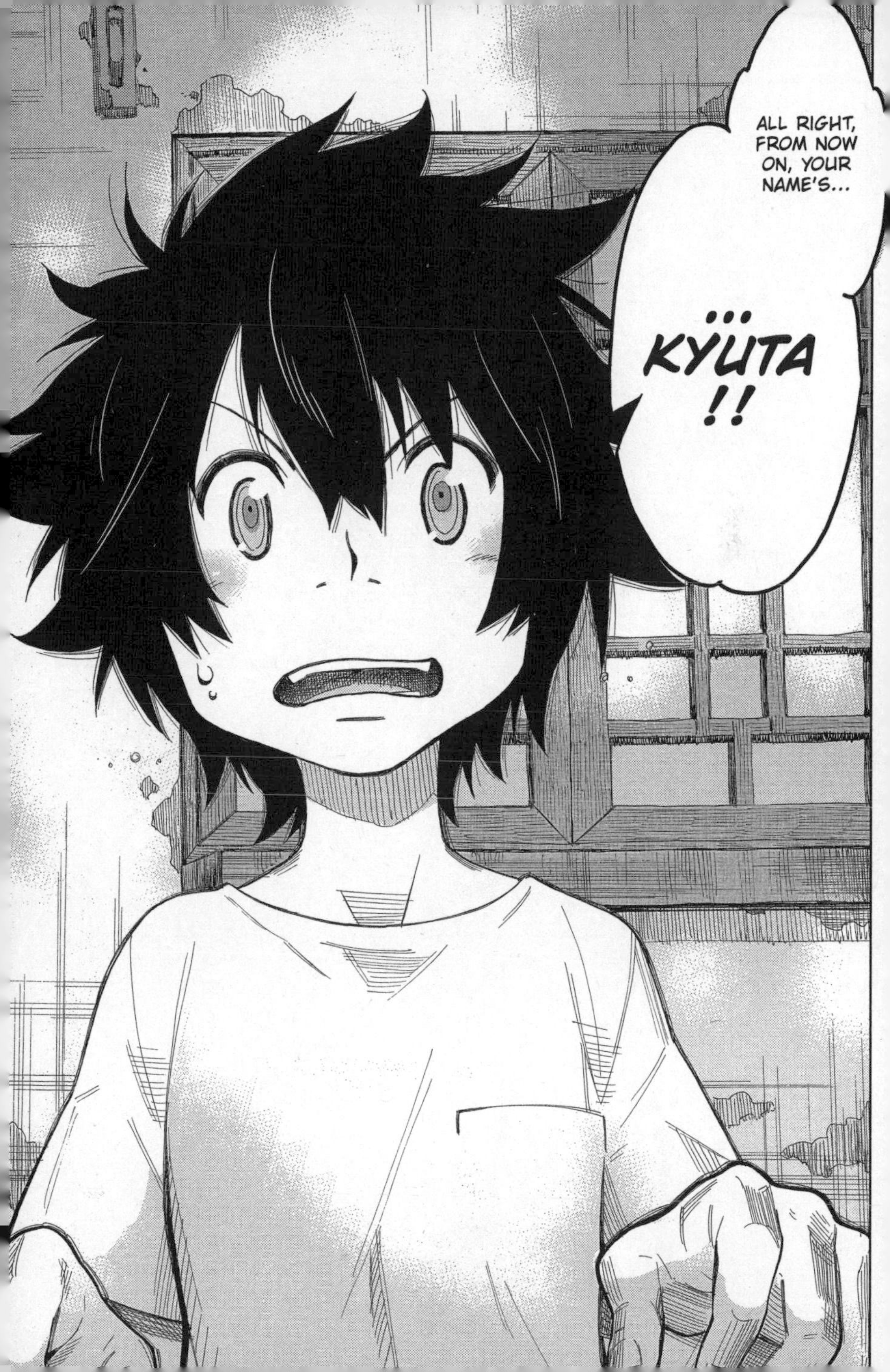
ALL RIGHT, FROM NOW ON, YOUR NAME'S...
...KYŪTA!!

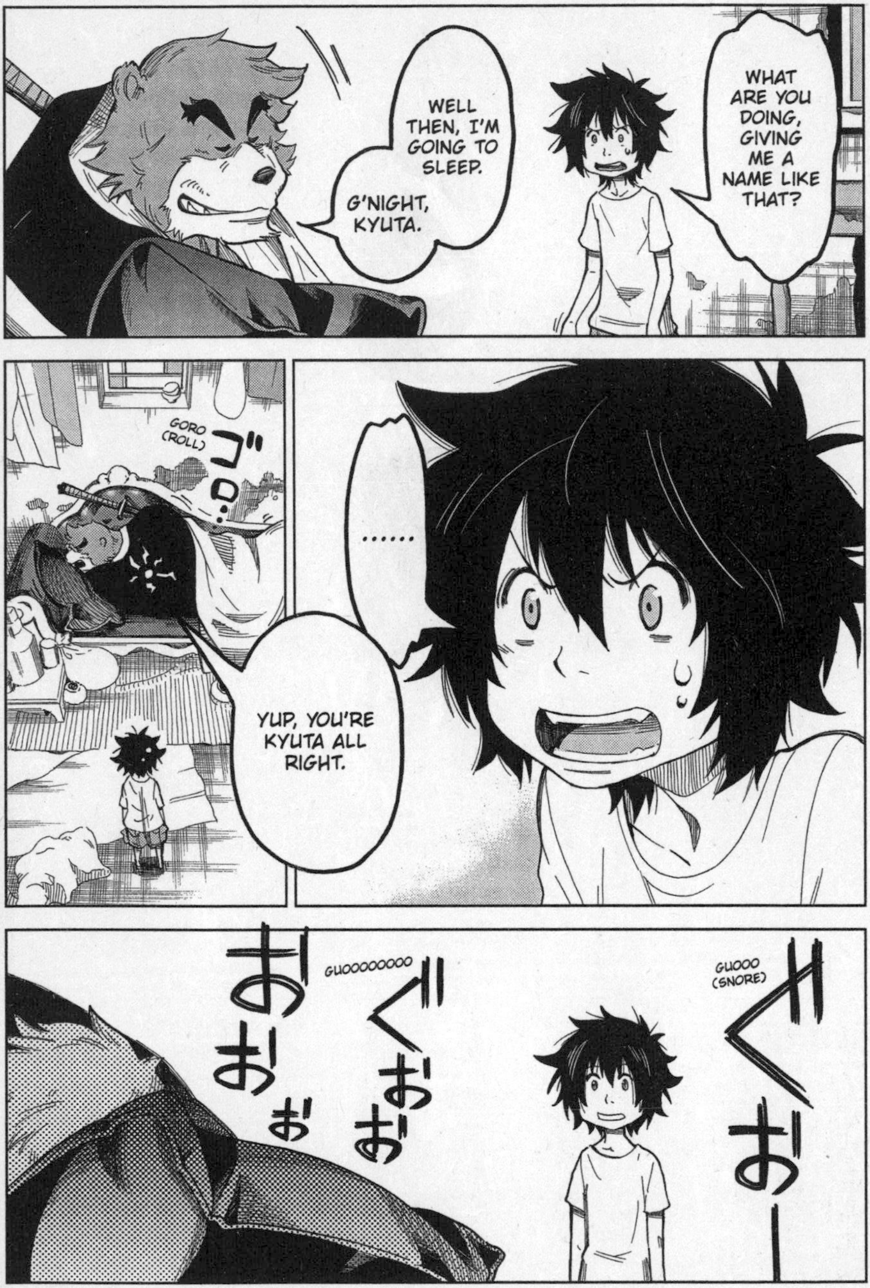
WHAT ARE YOU DOING, GIVING ME A NAME LIKE THAT?
WELL THEN, I'M GOING TO SLEEP.
G'NIGHT, KYUTA.
......
ゴロ…
GORO (ROLL)
YUP, YOU'RE KYUTA ALL RIGHT.
ぐおー
GUOOO (SNORE)
ぐおおぉ
おお
GUOOOOOOOO

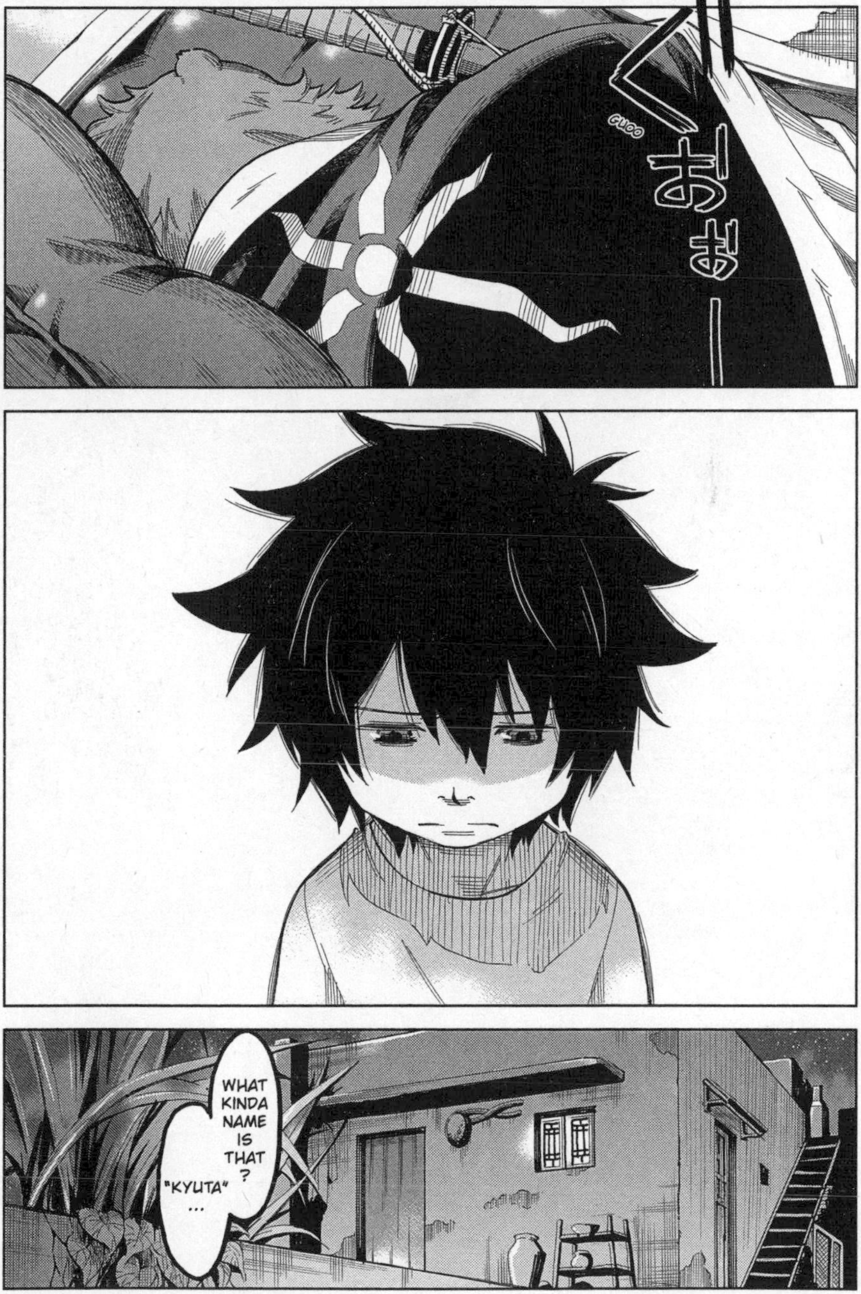
ぐおおー
GUOO
WHAT KINDA NAME IS THAT?
"KYUTA"...

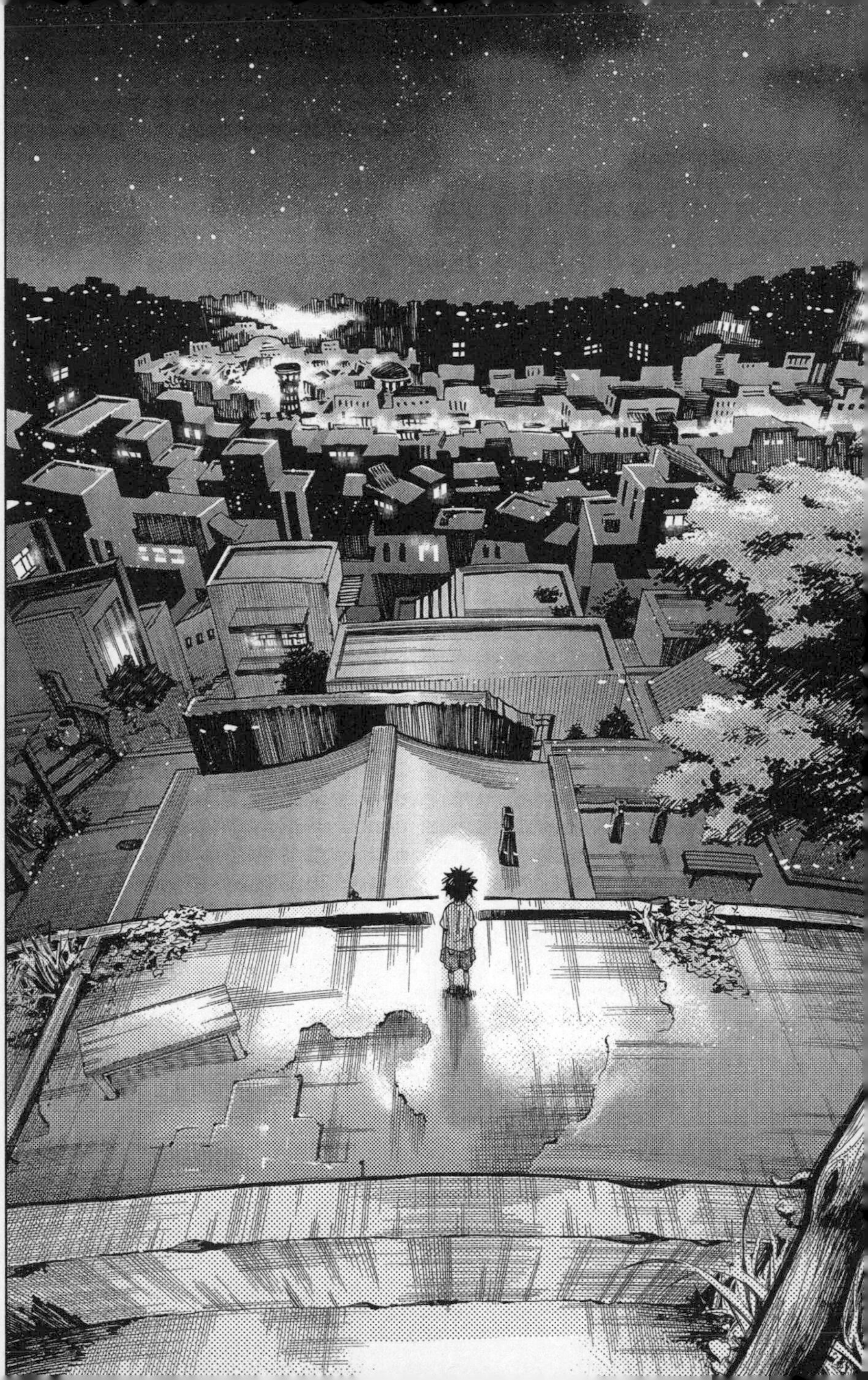

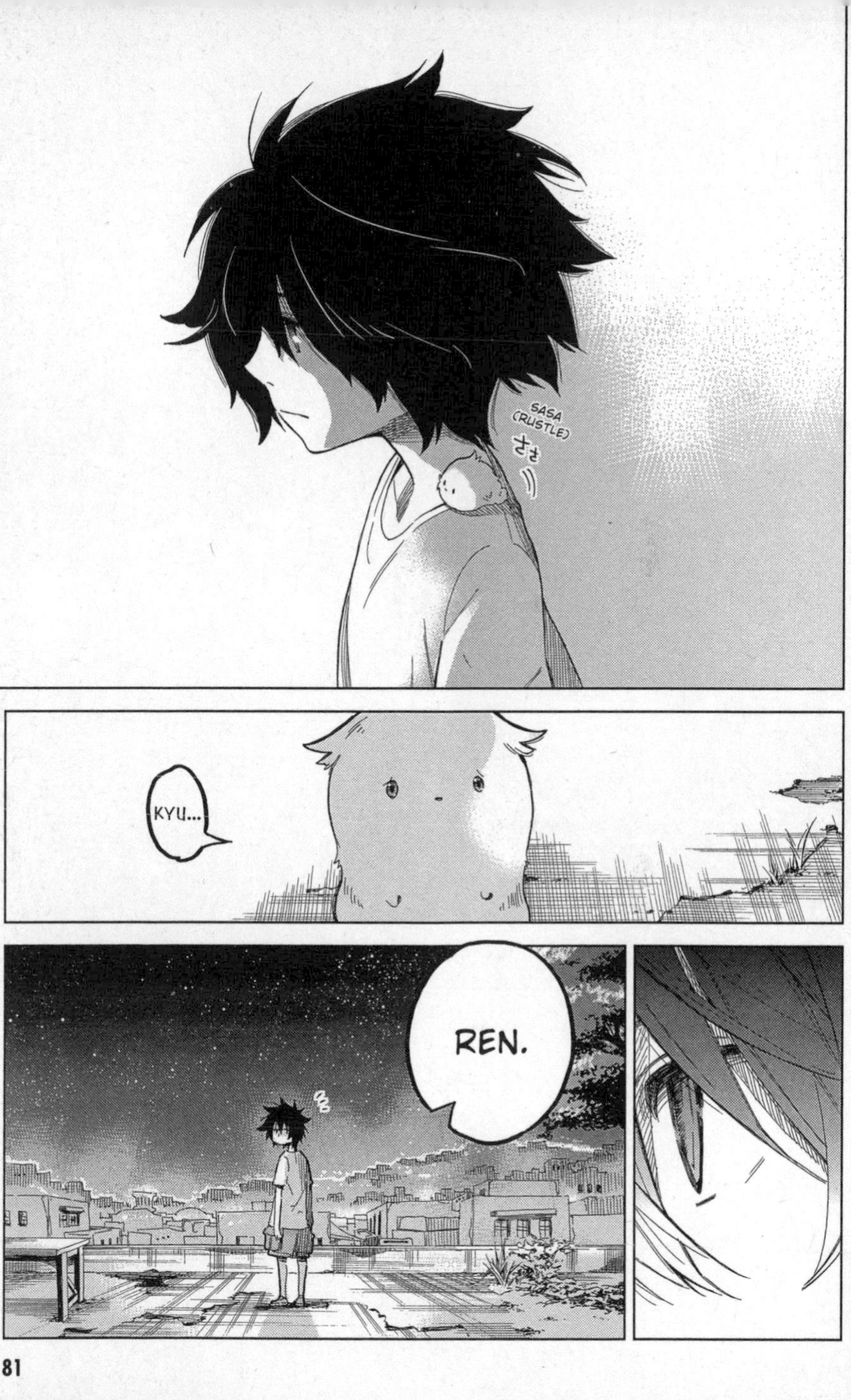
SASA (RUSTLE)
ささ
KYU...
REN.

I MADE YOUR FAVORITE, OMELET WITH HAM.

LET'S EAT IT TOGETHER.

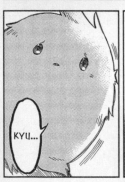

KYU...

FURA (DRIFT)

...OKAY.

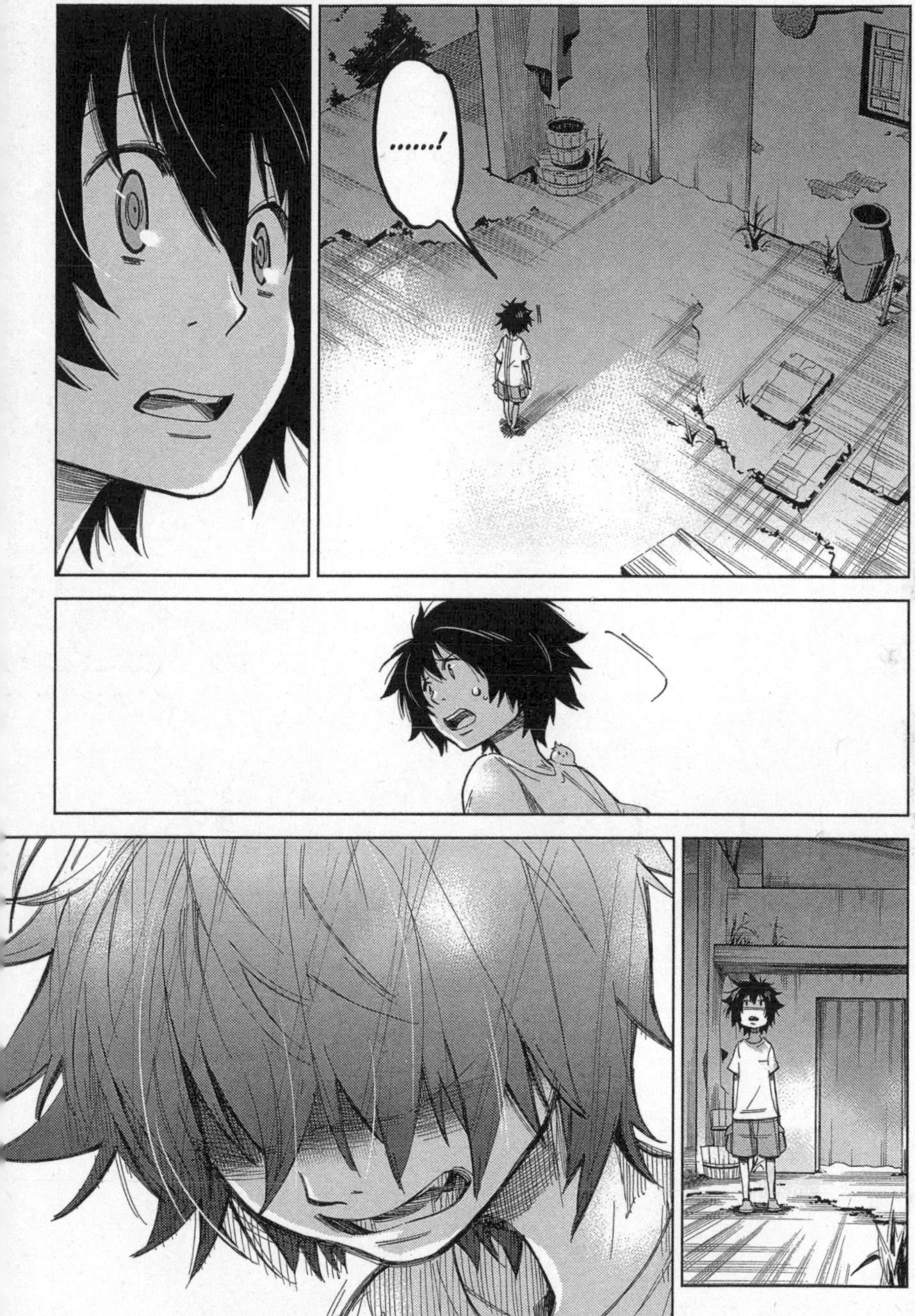

......!

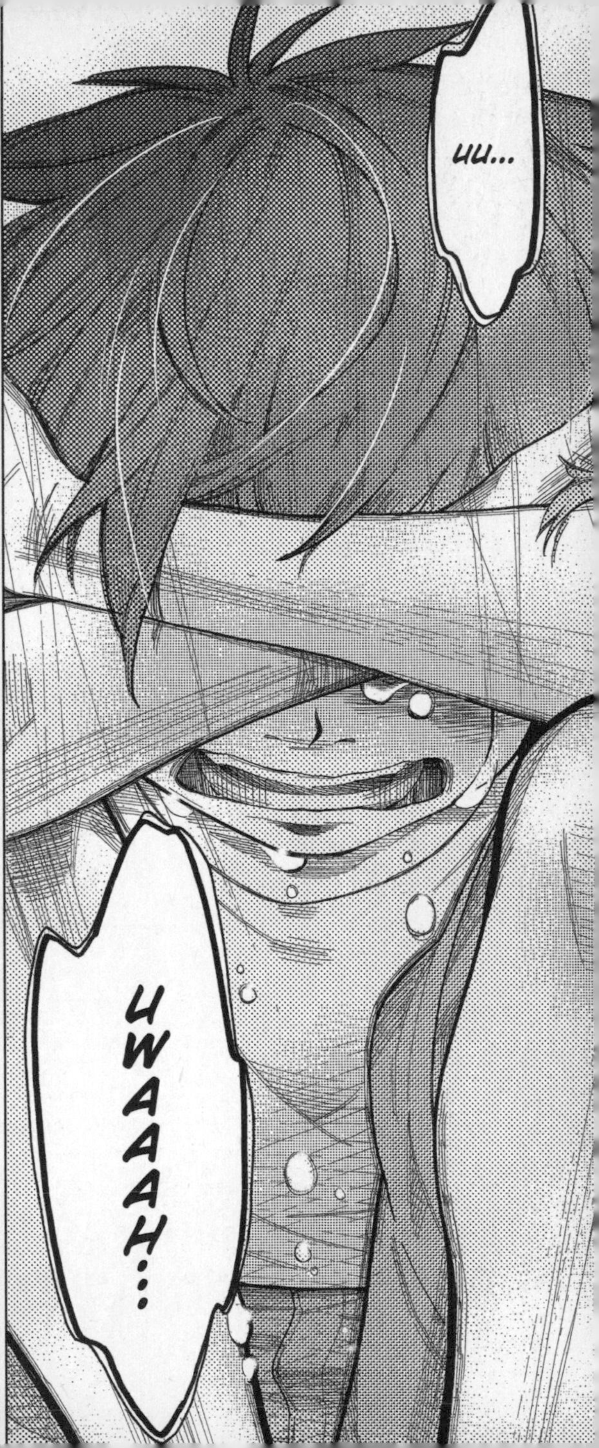
UU...
UWAAAAH...
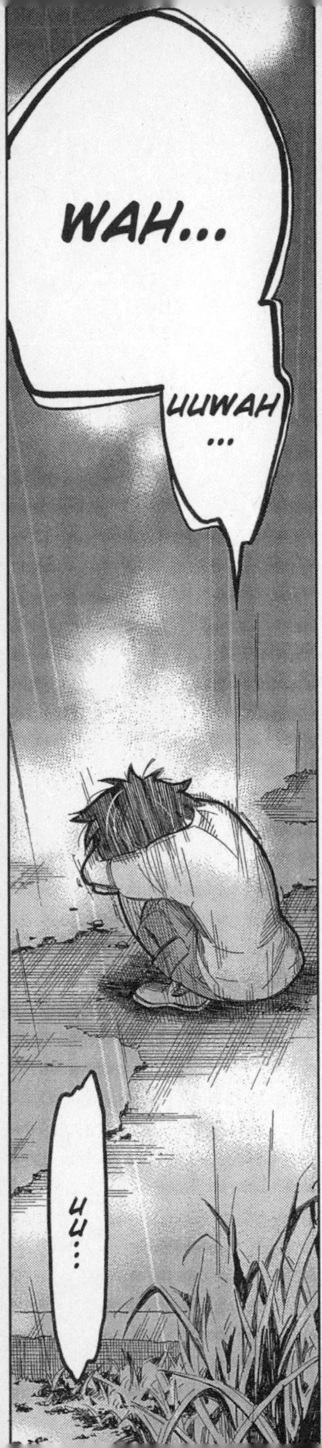
WAH...
UUWAH ...
UU...

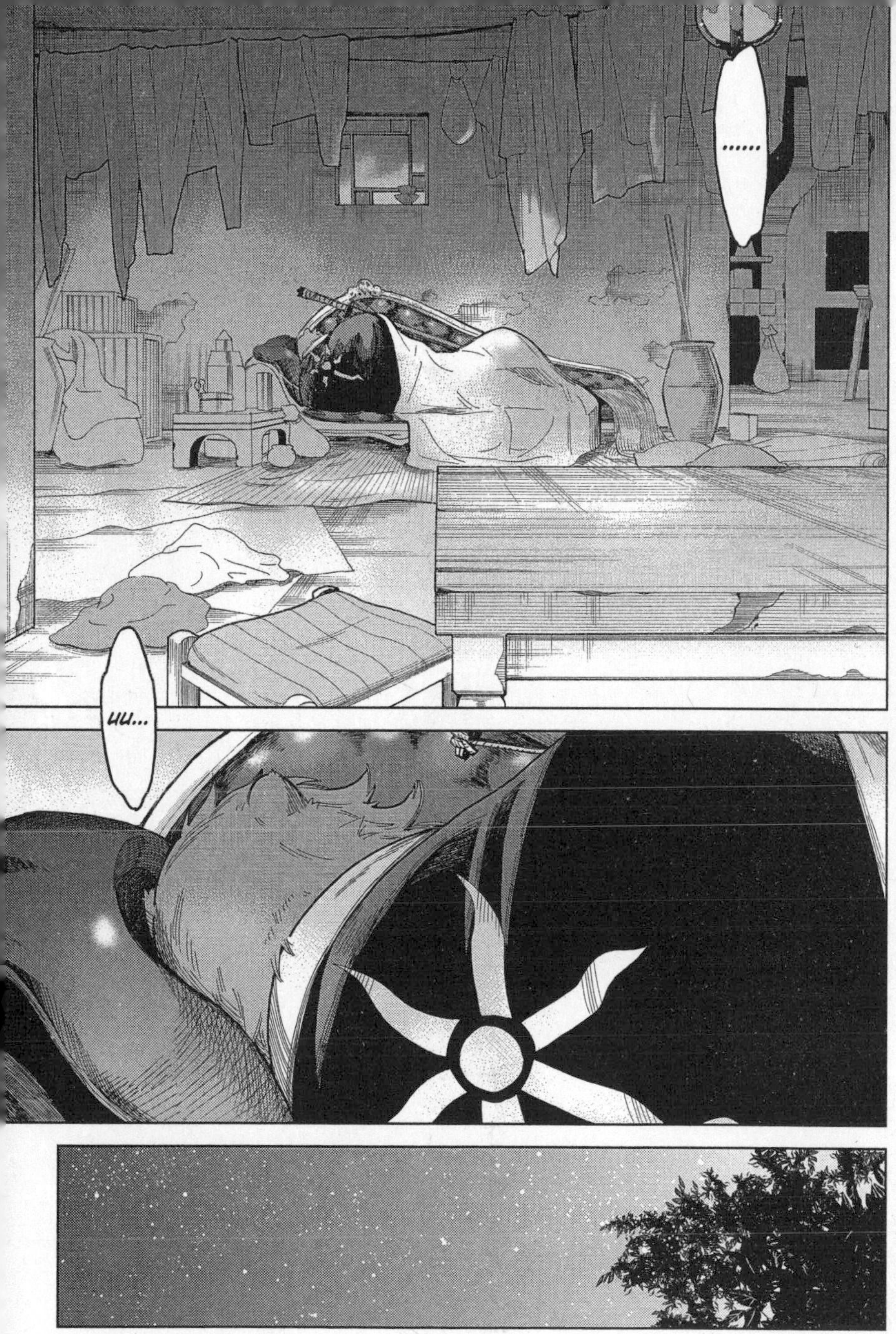
......
UU...

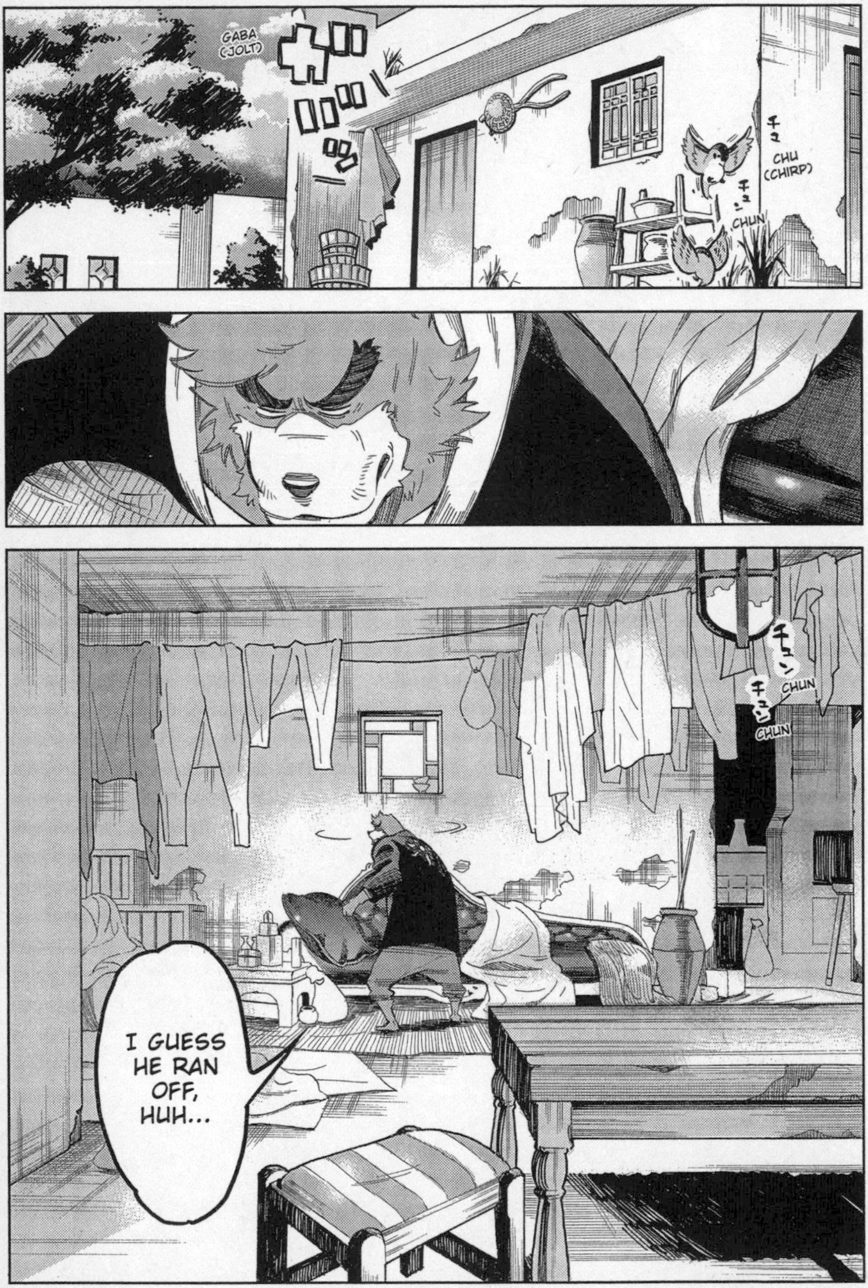
チュ
CHU (CHIRP)
チュン
CHUN
GABA (-JOLT)
チュン
CHUN
チュン
CHUN
I GUESS HE RAN OFF, HUH...

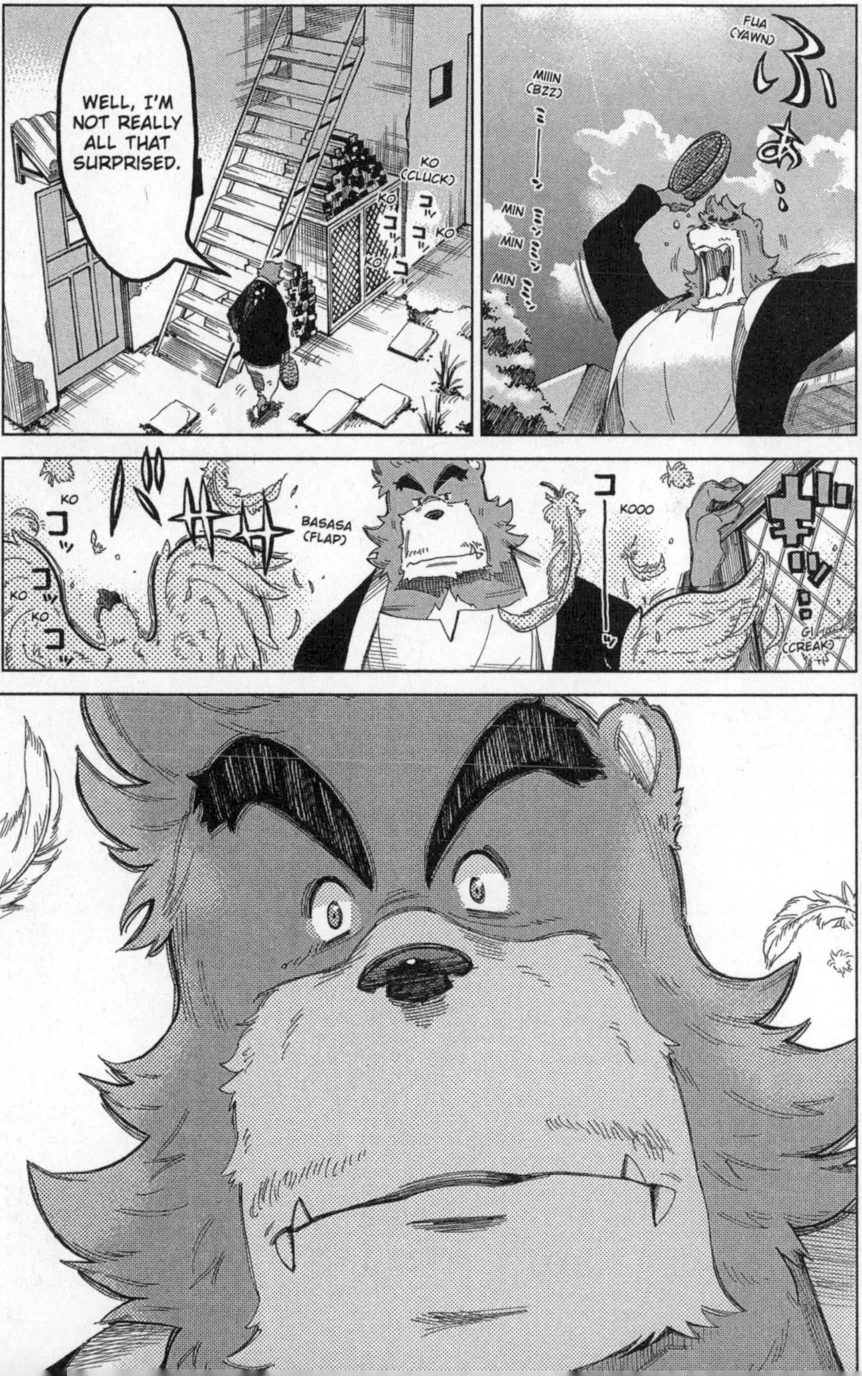
FUA (YAWN)
MIIIN (BZZ)
MIN MIN MIN
WELL, I'M NOT REALLY ALL THAT SURPRISED.
KO (CLUCK)
KO
KO
KO
GI (CREAK)
KOOO
BASASA (FLAP)
KO
KO
KO

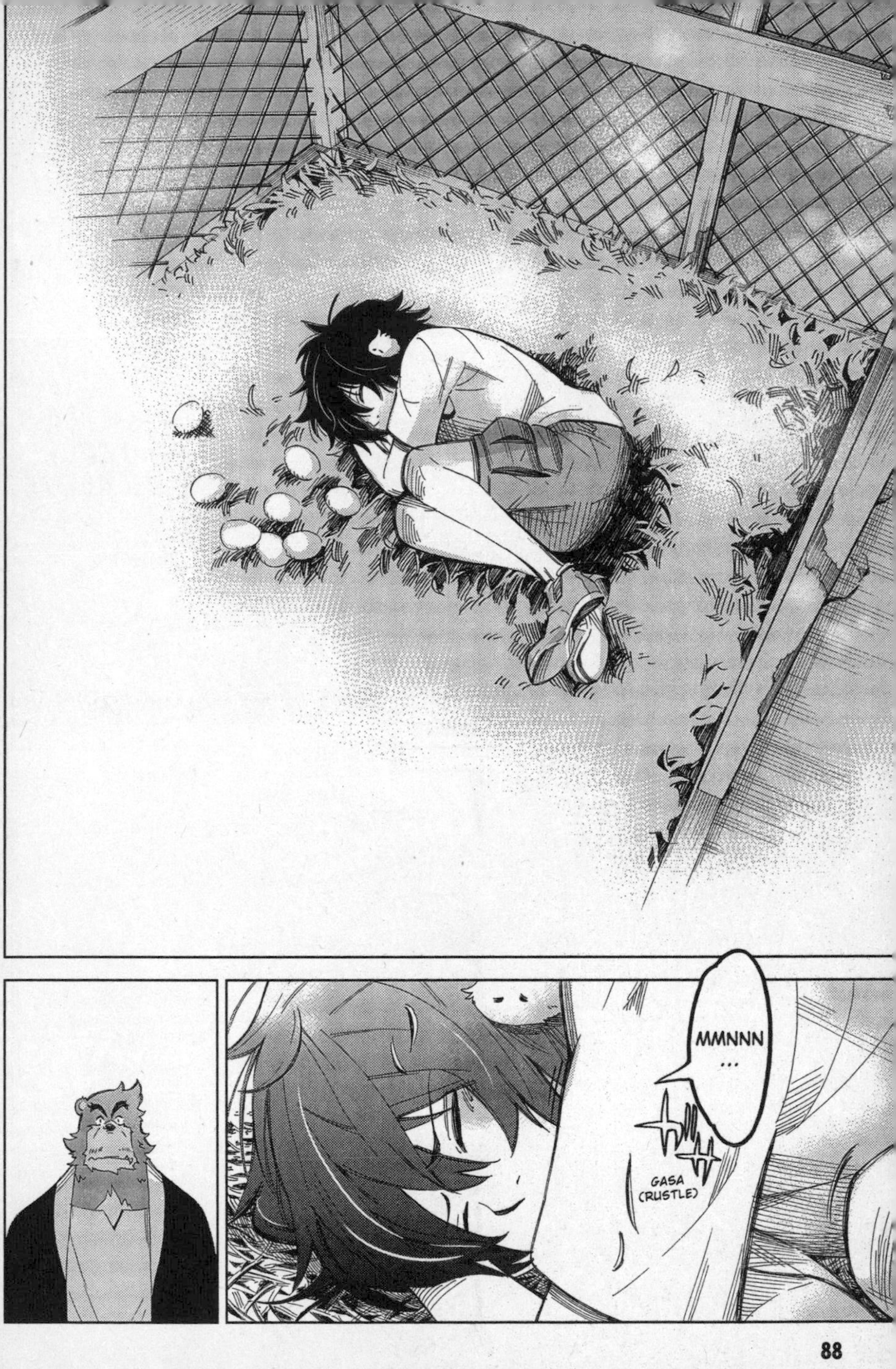
MMNNN
...
GASA
(RUSTLE)

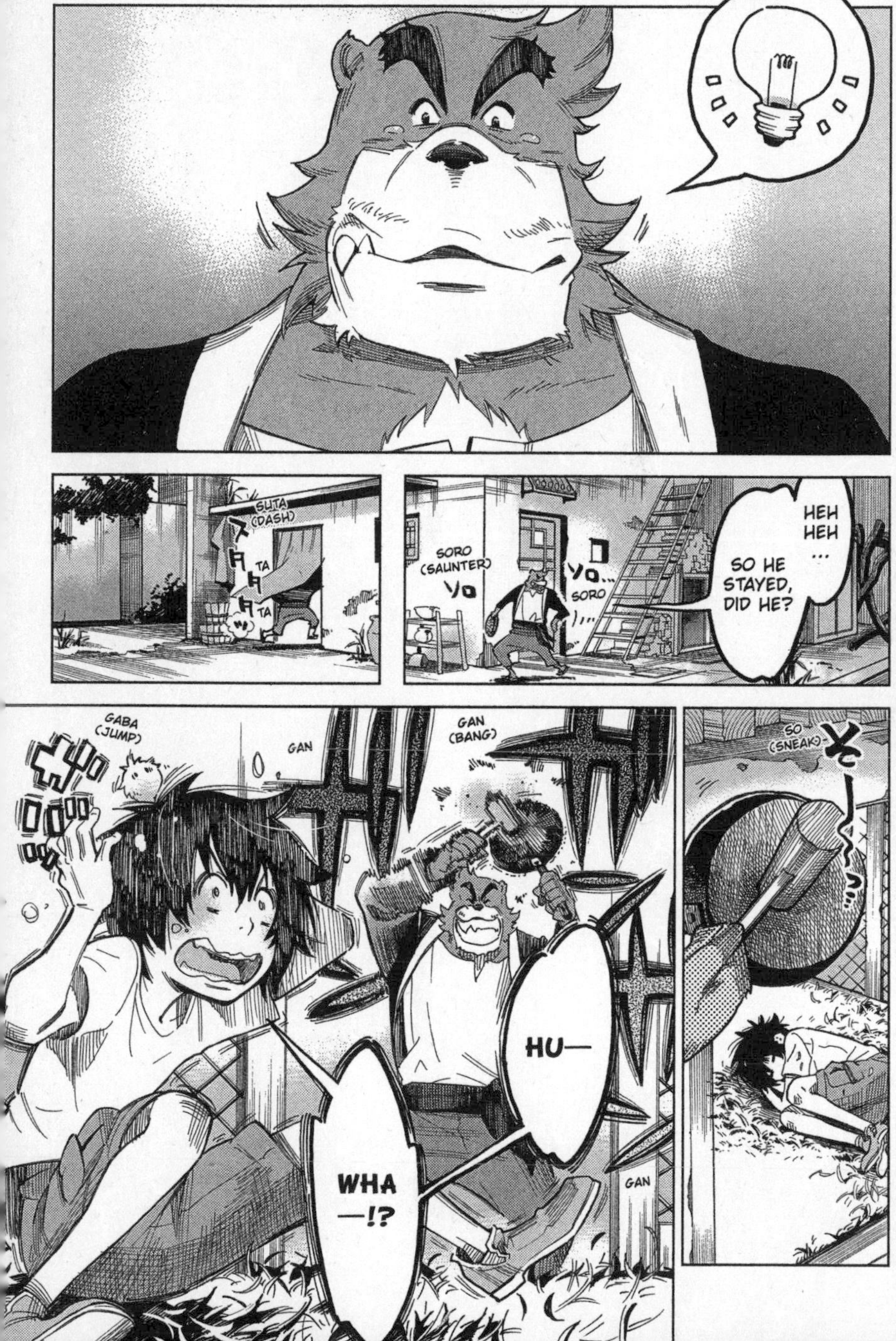
HEH HEH ...
SO HE STAYED, DID HE?
SORO (SAUNTER)
SORO
SUTA (DASH)
TA
TA
SO (SNEAK)
GAN (BANG)
GAN
GABA (JUMP)
HU—
WHA—!?
GAN

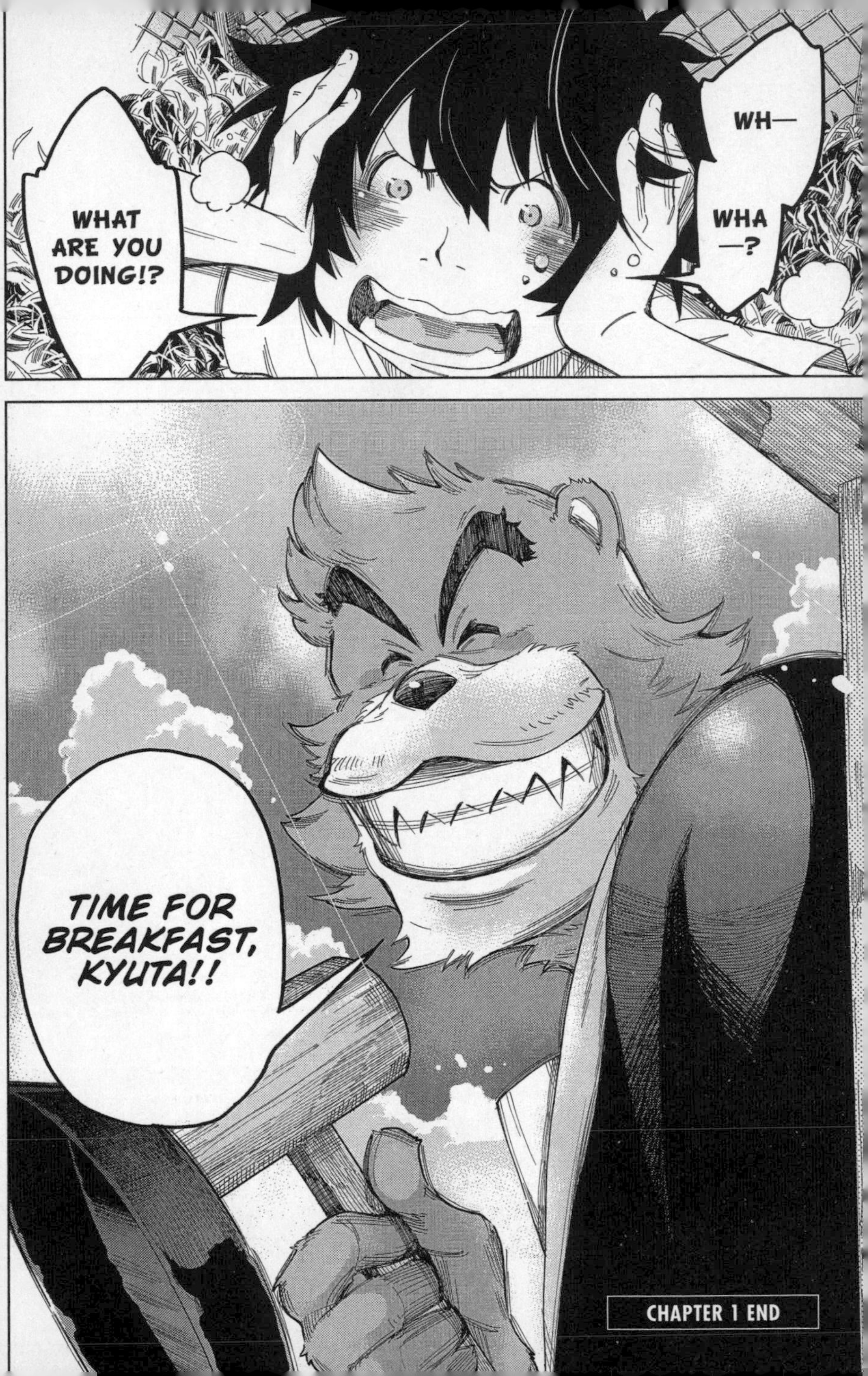
WH— WHA—?
WHAT ARE YOU DOING!?
TIME FOR BREAKFAST, KYUTA!!
CHAPTER 1 END

CHAPTER 2 "DISCIPLE!? WHO, ME!?"

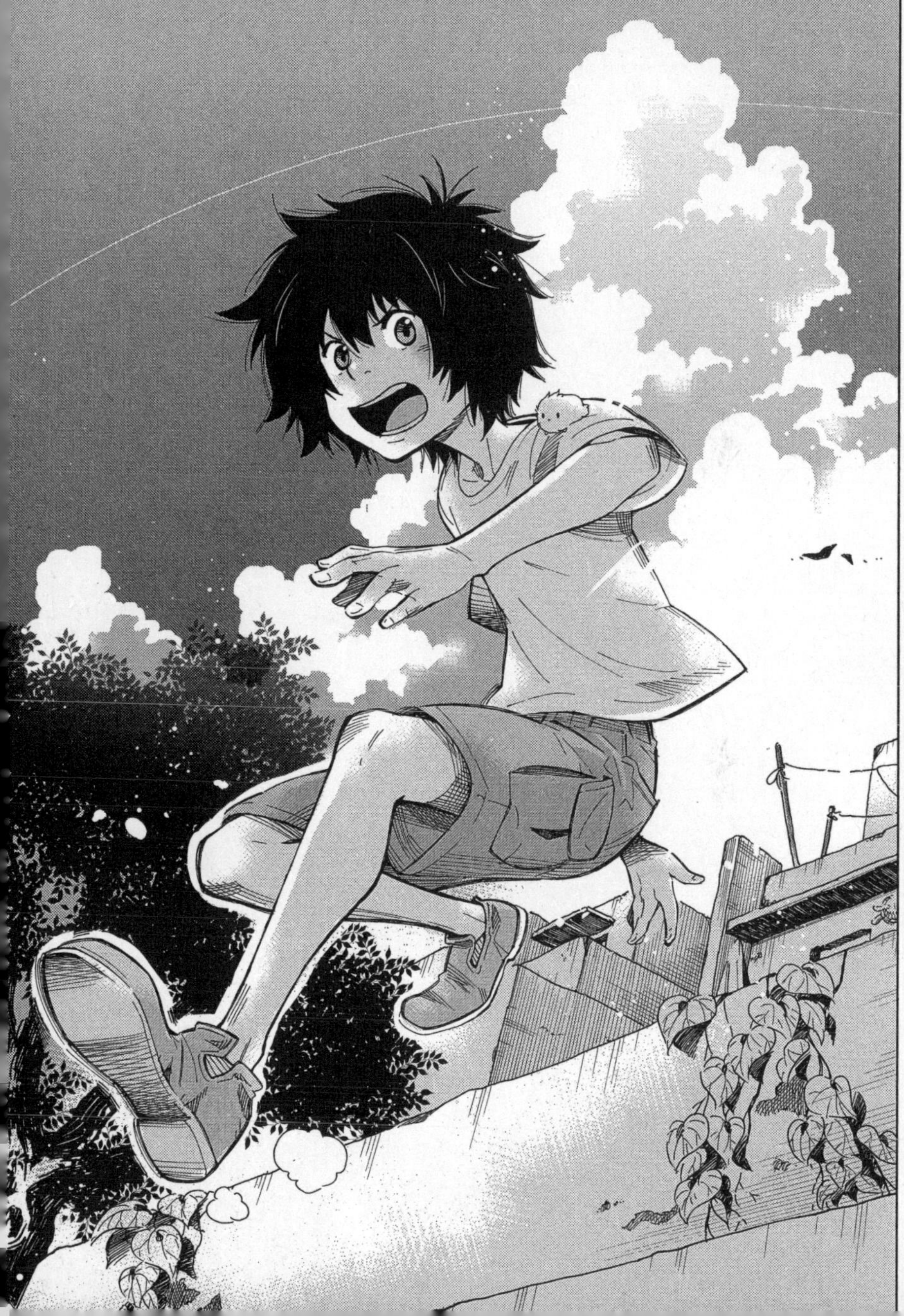

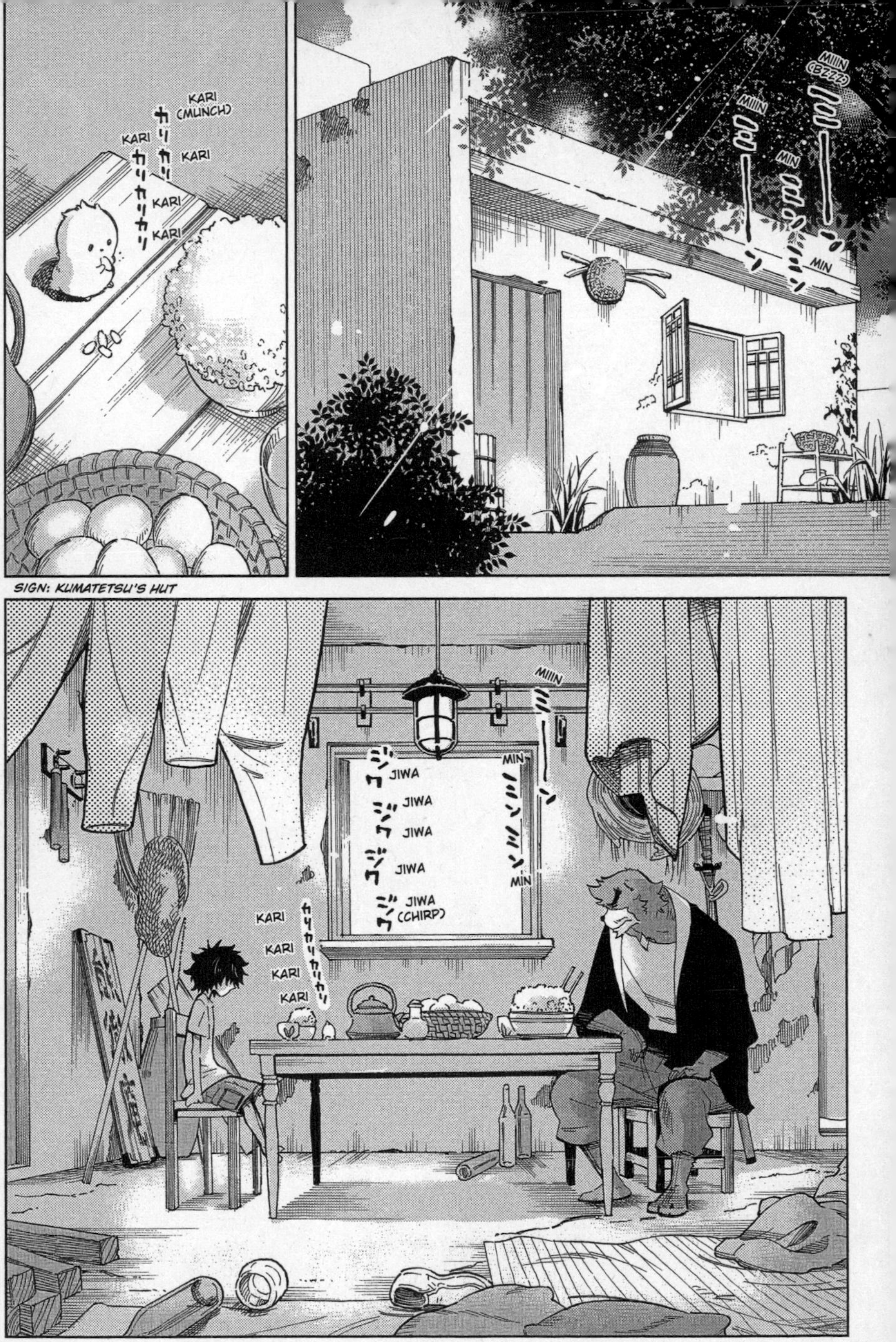
MIIN (BZZZ)
MIIN
MIN MIN
MIN
KARI (MUNCH)
KARI
KARI
KARI
KARI
SIGN: KUMATETSU'S HUT
MIIN
MIN
MIN
JIWA
JIWA
JIWA
JIWA
JIWA (CHIRP)
KARI
KARI
KARI
KARI

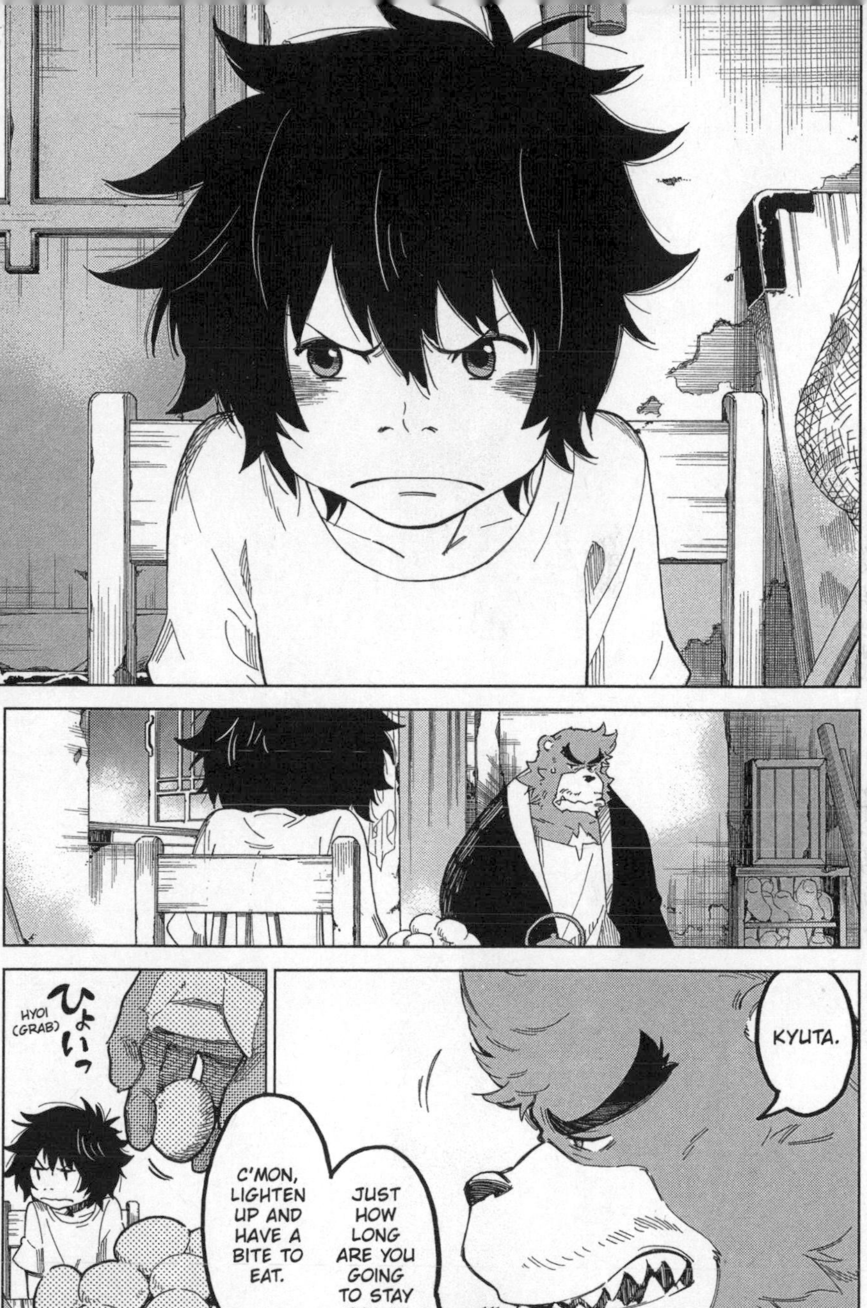
KYUTA.
JUST HOW LONG ARE YOU GOING TO STAY MAD AT ME?
C'MON, LIGHTEN UP AND HAVE A BITE TO EAT.
ひょいっ
HYOI (GRAB)

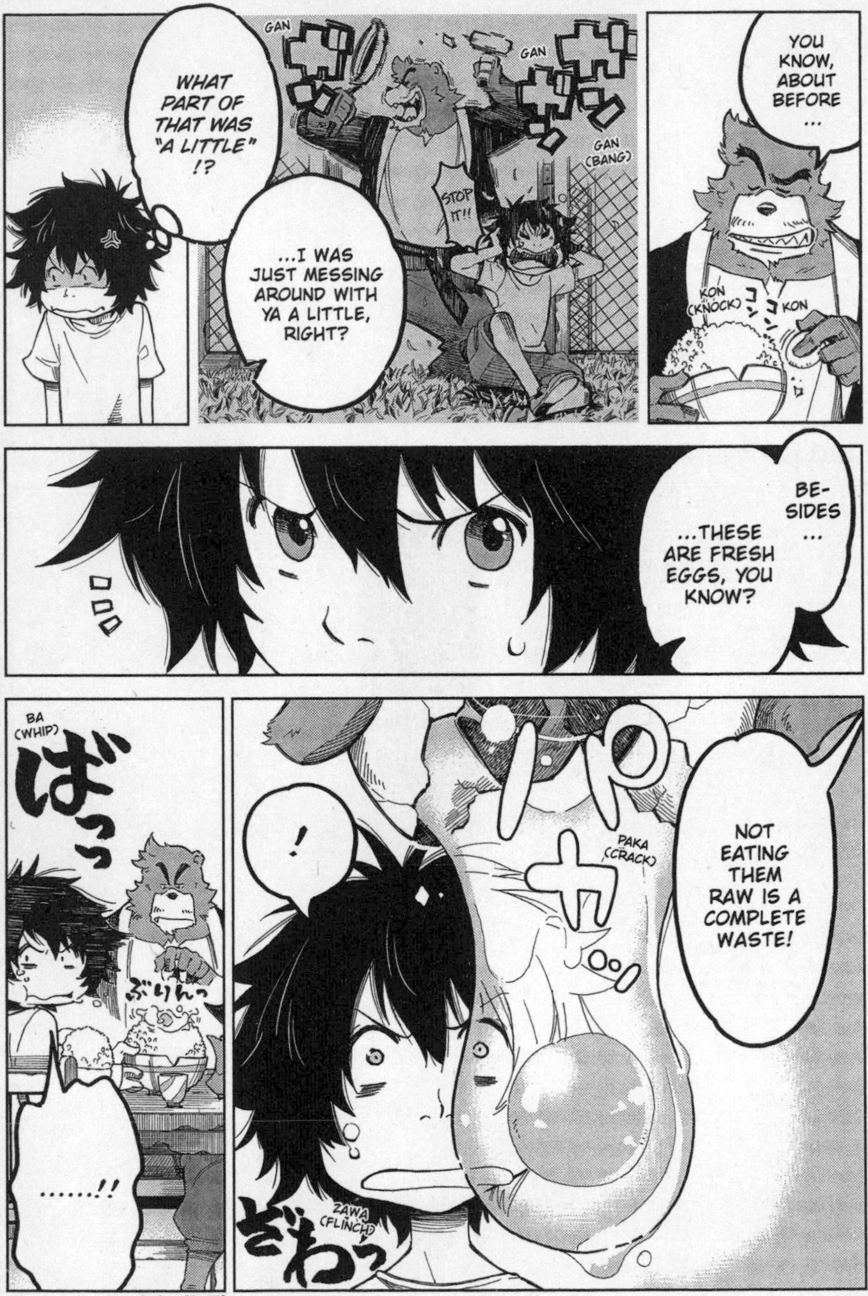
YOU KNOW, ABOUT BEFORE ...
KON (KNOCK) KON
GAN
GAN
GAN (BANG)
STOP IT!!
...I WAS JUST MESSING AROUND WITH YA A LITTLE, RIGHT?
WHAT PART OF THAT WAS "A LITTLE" !?
BE-SIDES ...
...THESE ARE FRESH EGGS, YOU KNOW?
NOT EATING THEM RAW IS A COMPLETE WASTE!
PAKA (CRACK)
!
ZAWA (FLINCH)
BA (WHIP)
......!!

SFX: BURIN (PLOP)

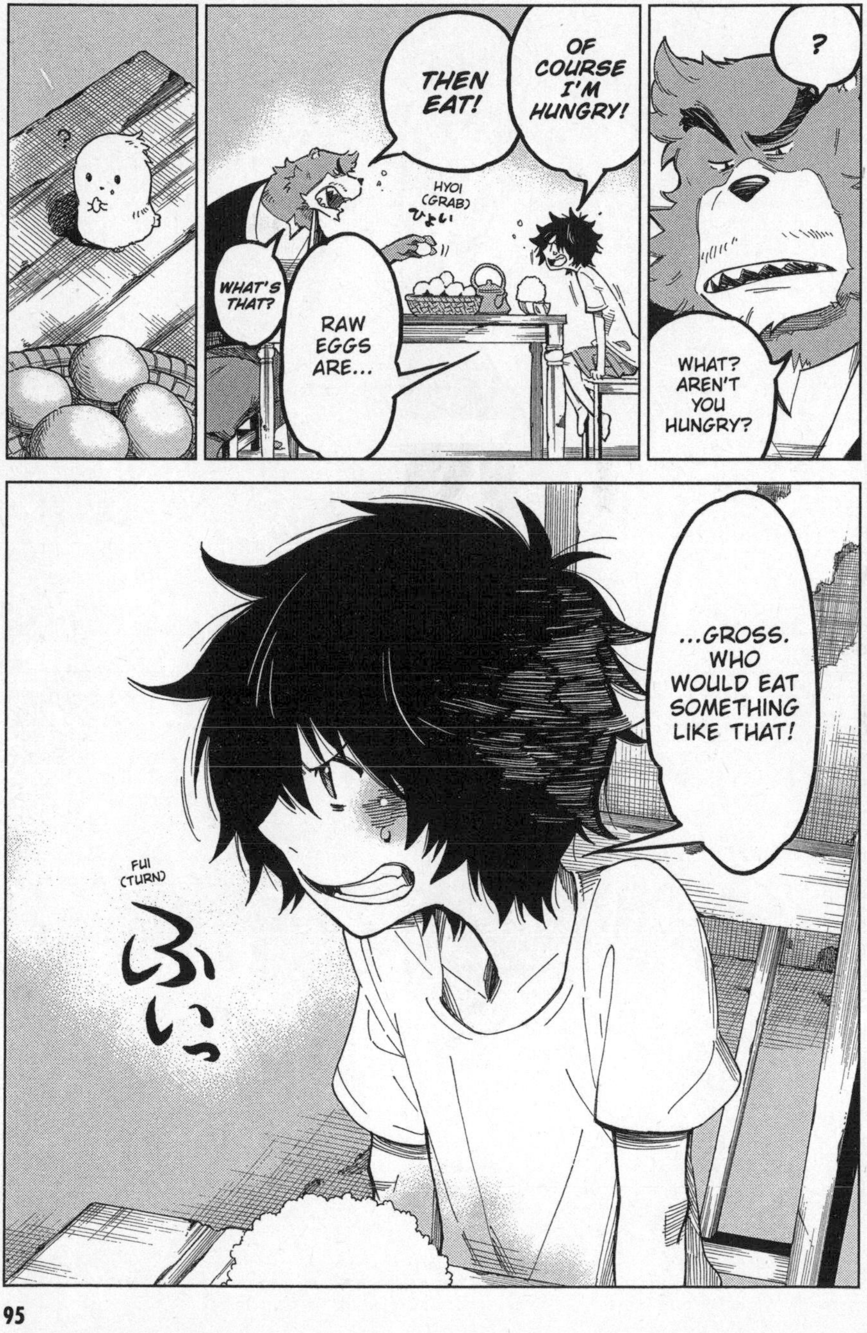
?
WHAT? AREN'T YOU HUNGRY?
OF COURSE I'M HUNGRY!
THEN EAT!
HYOI (GRAB) ひょい
RAW EGGS ARE...
WHAT'S THAT?
?
...GROSS. WHO WOULD EAT SOMETHING LIKE THAT!
FUI (TURN) ふいっ

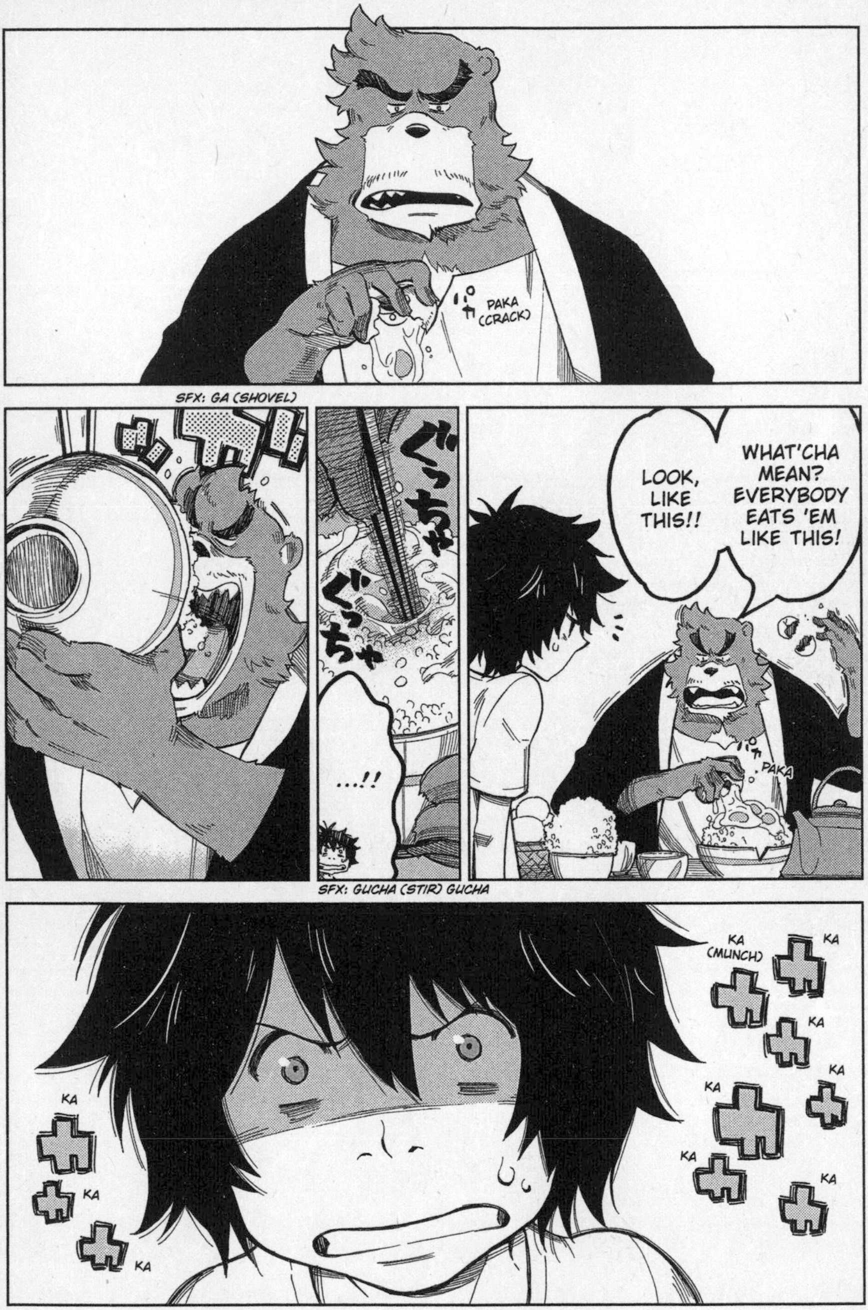
パカ
PAKA (CRACK)
WHAT'CHA MEAN? EVERYBODY EATS 'EM LIKE THIS!
LOOK, LIKE THIS!!
パカ
PAKA
ぐっちゃ
ぐっちゃ
...!!
SFX: GUCHA (STIR) GUCHA
SFX: GA (SHOVEL)
KA (MUNCH)
KA
KA
KA
KA
KA
KA
KA
KA
KA

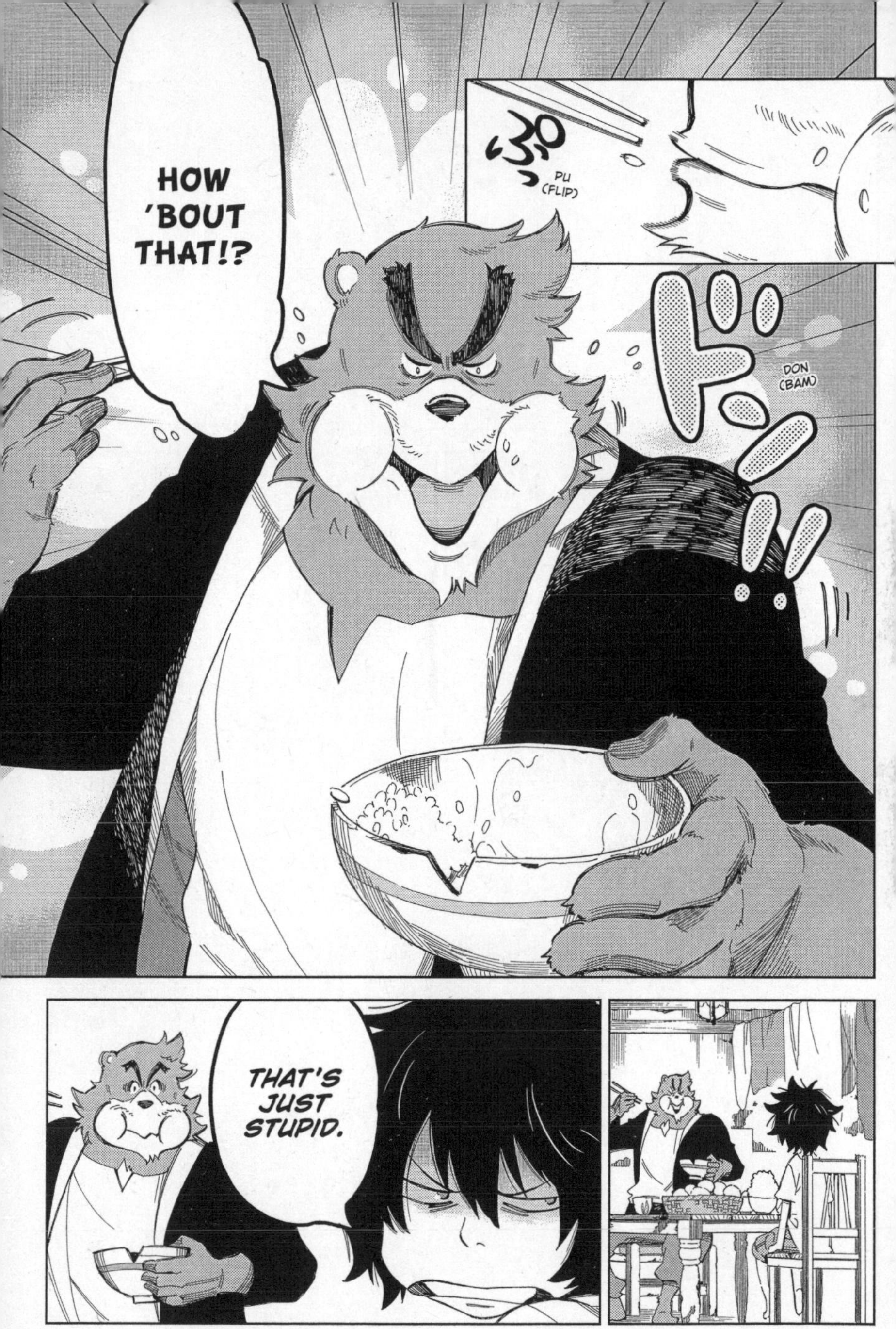
ぷっ
PU (FLIP)
HOW 'BOUT THAT!?
ドン!!
DON (BAM)
THAT'S JUST STUPID.

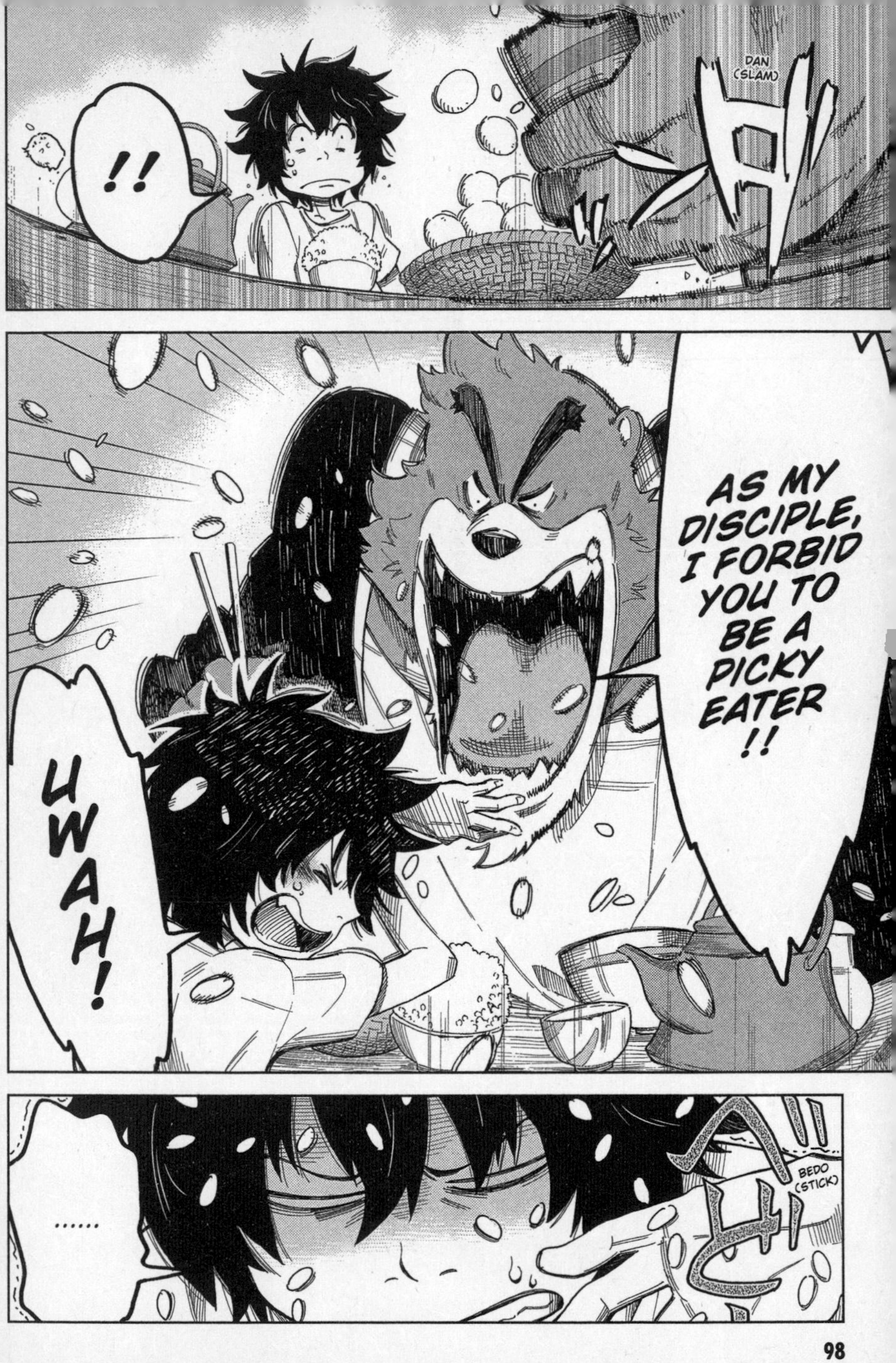
DAN (SLAM)
!!
AS MY DISCIPLE, I FORBID YOU TO BE A PICKY EATER!!
UWAH!
BEDO (STICK)
......

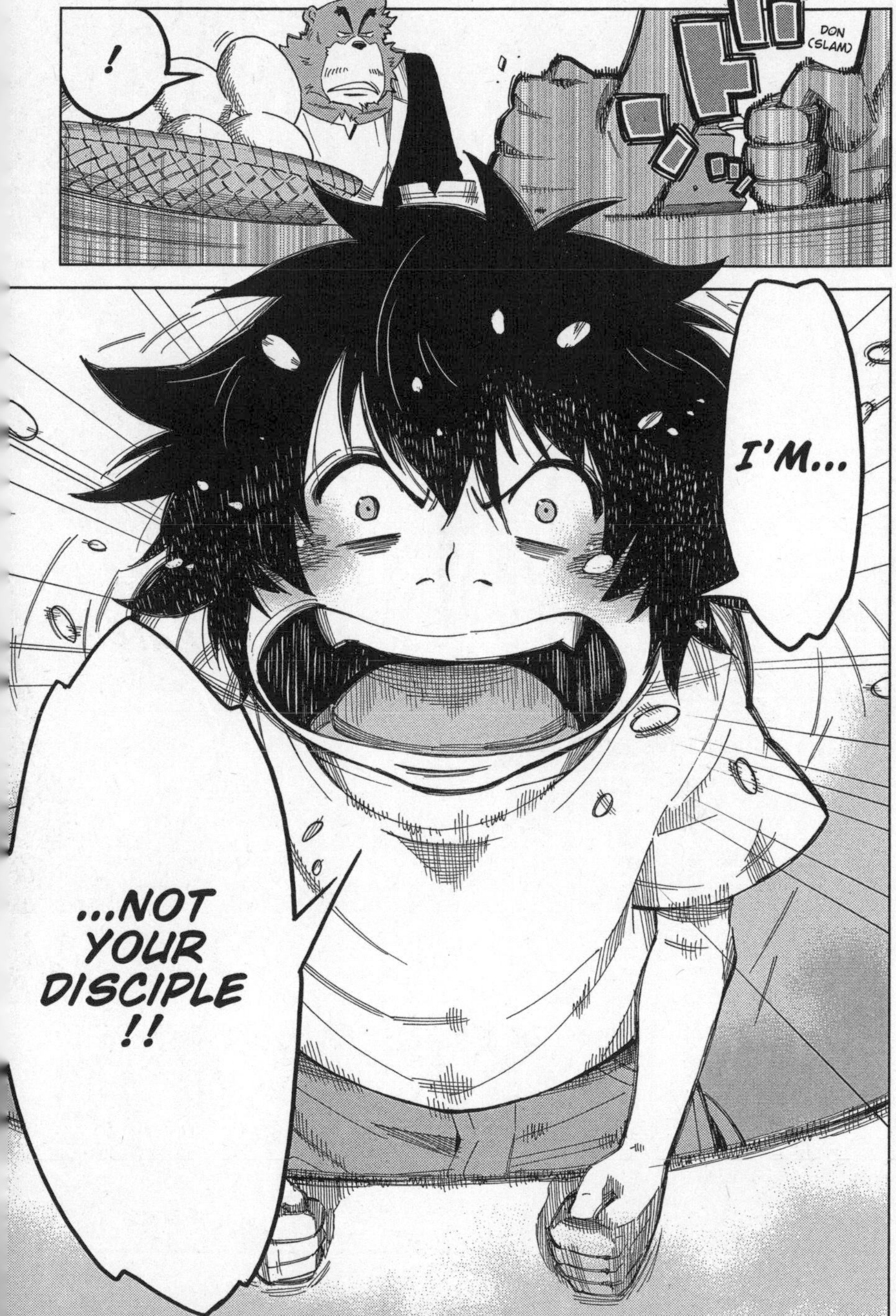
DON (SLAM)
!
I'M...
...NOT YOUR DISCIPLE !!

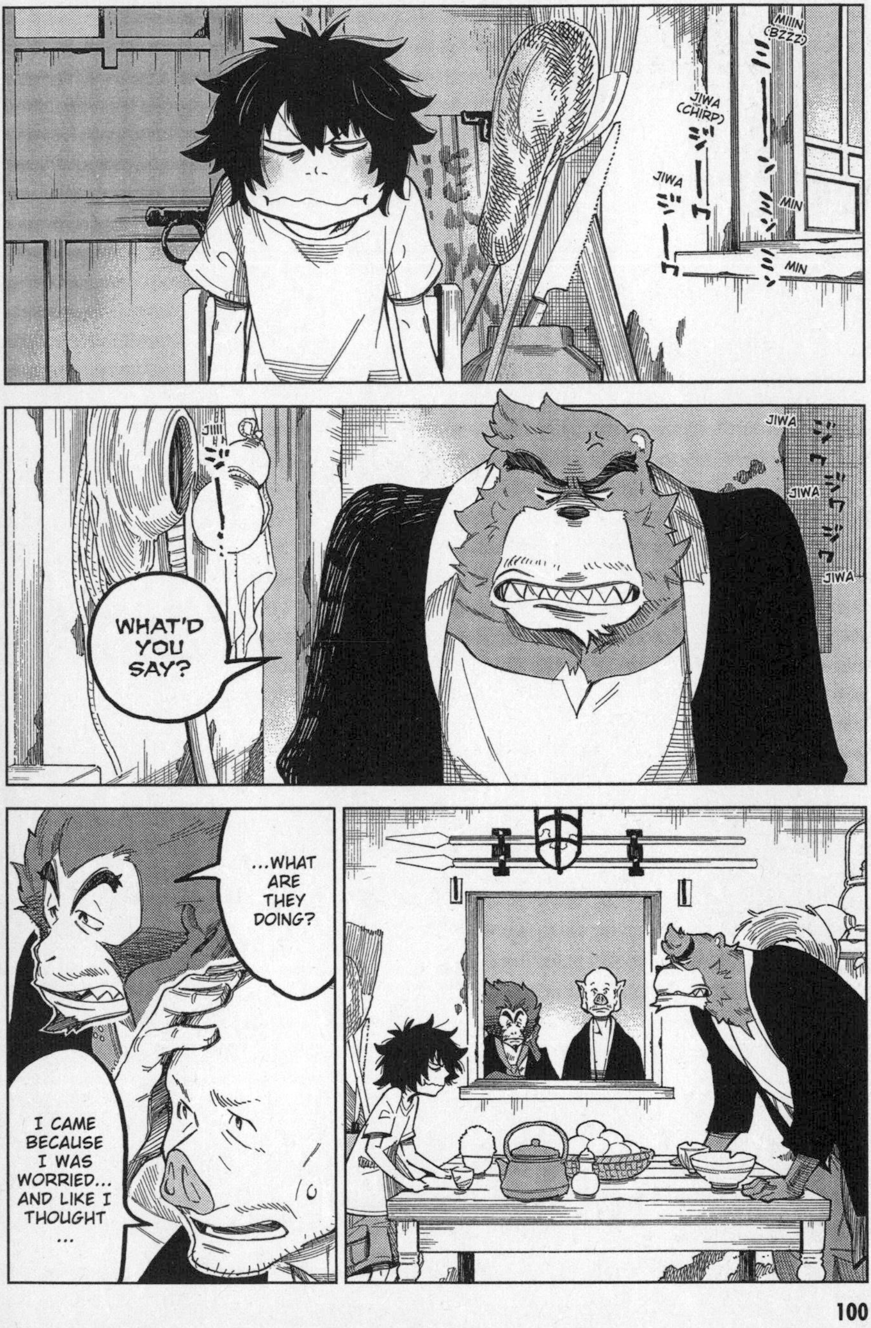
MIIN (BZZZ)
JIWA (CHIRP)
JIWA
MIN
MIN
JIWA
JIWA
JIWA
JIII
WHAT'D YOU SAY?
...WHAT ARE THEY DOING?
I CAME BECAUSE I WAS WORRIED... AND LIKE I THOUGHT ...

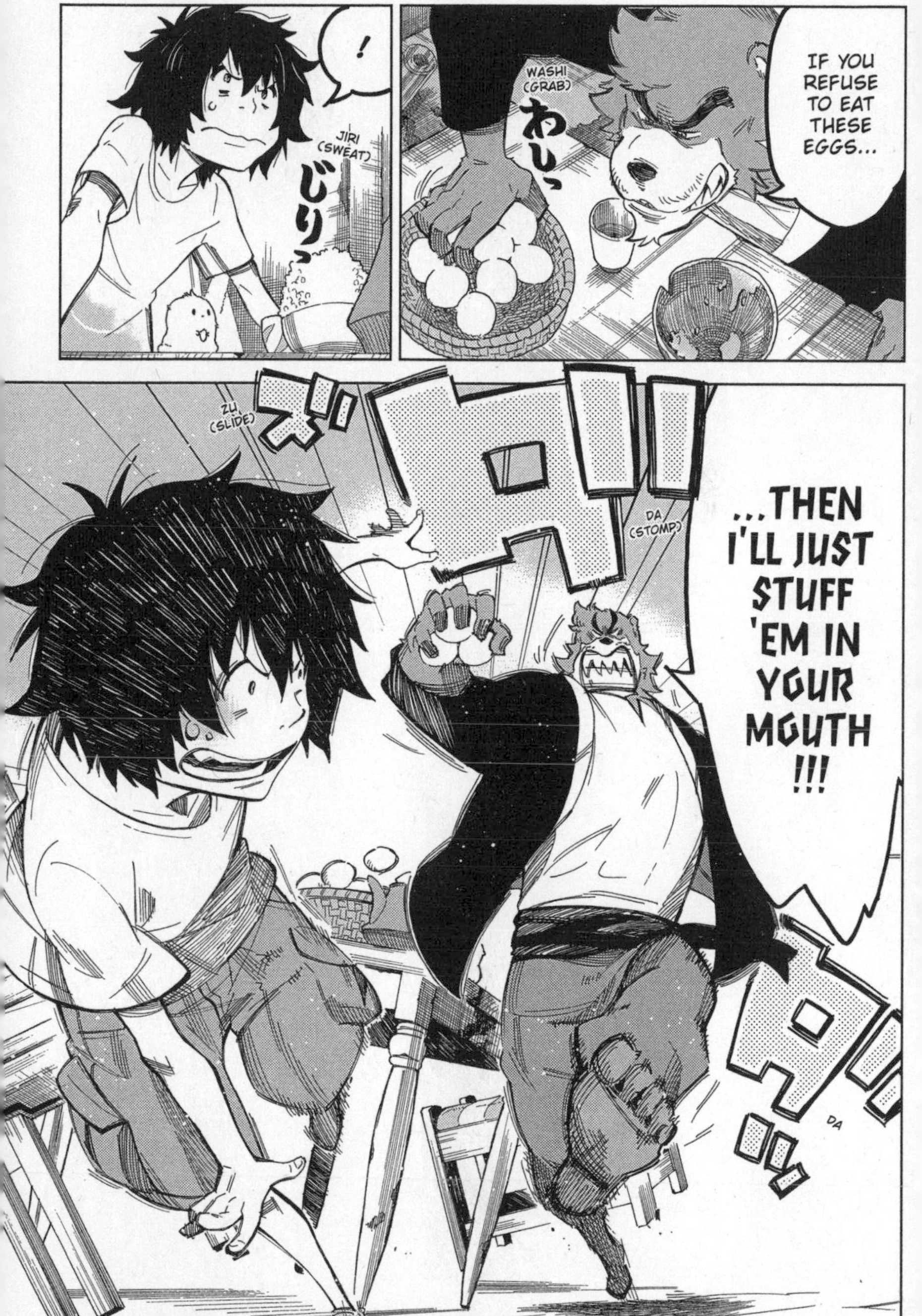
IF YOU REFUSE TO EAT THESE EGGS...
WASHI (GRAB)
わしっ
!
JIRI (SWEAT)
じりっ
ZU (SLIDE)
DA (STOMP)
...THEN I'LL JUST STUFF 'EM IN YOUR MOUTH!!!
DA

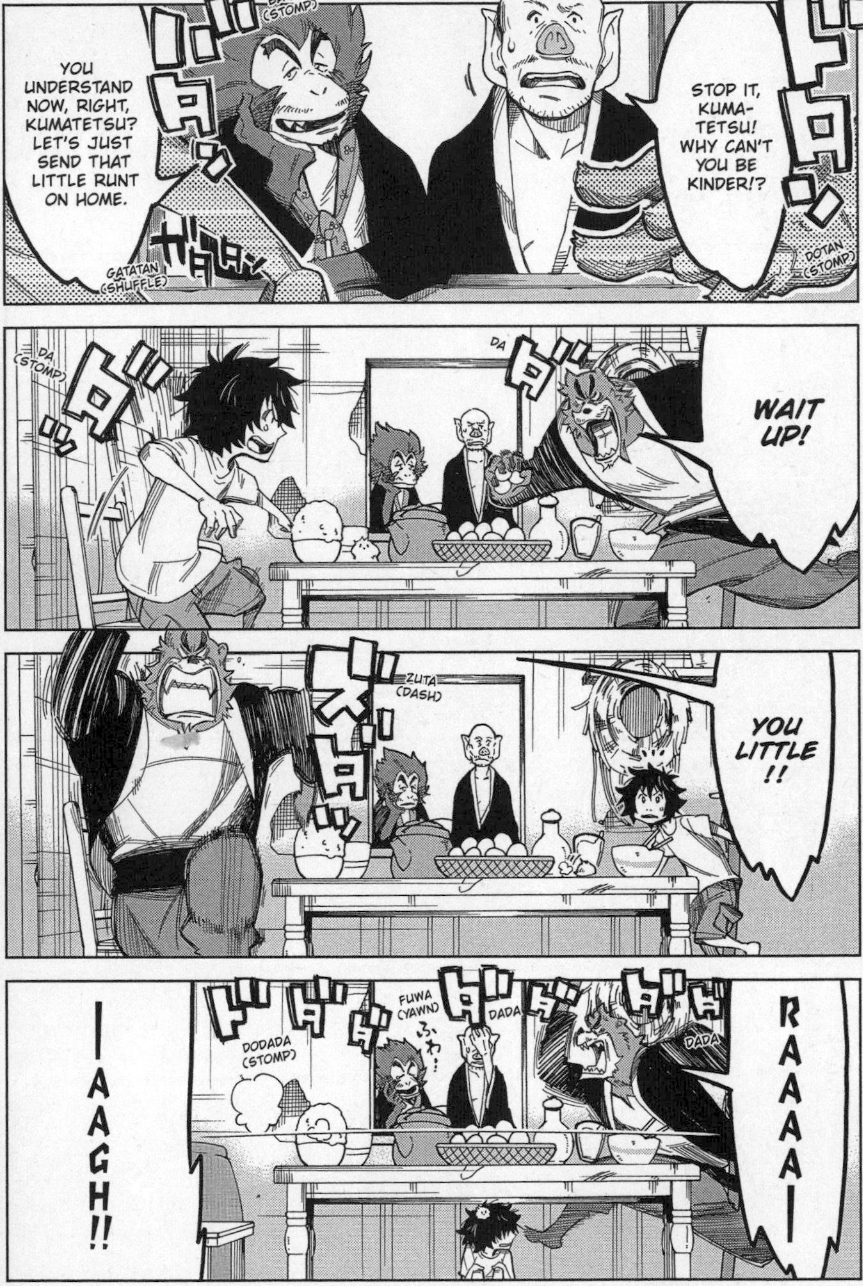

STOP IT, KUMA-TETSU! WHY CAN'T YOU BE KINDER!?
DOTAN (STOMP)
BATAN (STOMP)
YOU UNDERSTAND NOW, RIGHT, KUMATETSU? LET'S JUST SEND THAT LITTLE RUNT ON HOME.
GATATAN (SHUFFLE)
WAIT UP!
DA
DA (STOMP)
YOU LITTLE !!
ZUTA (DASH)
RAAAAI
DADA
DADA
FUWA (YAWN)
ふわ…
DODADA (STOMP)
IAAAGH!!

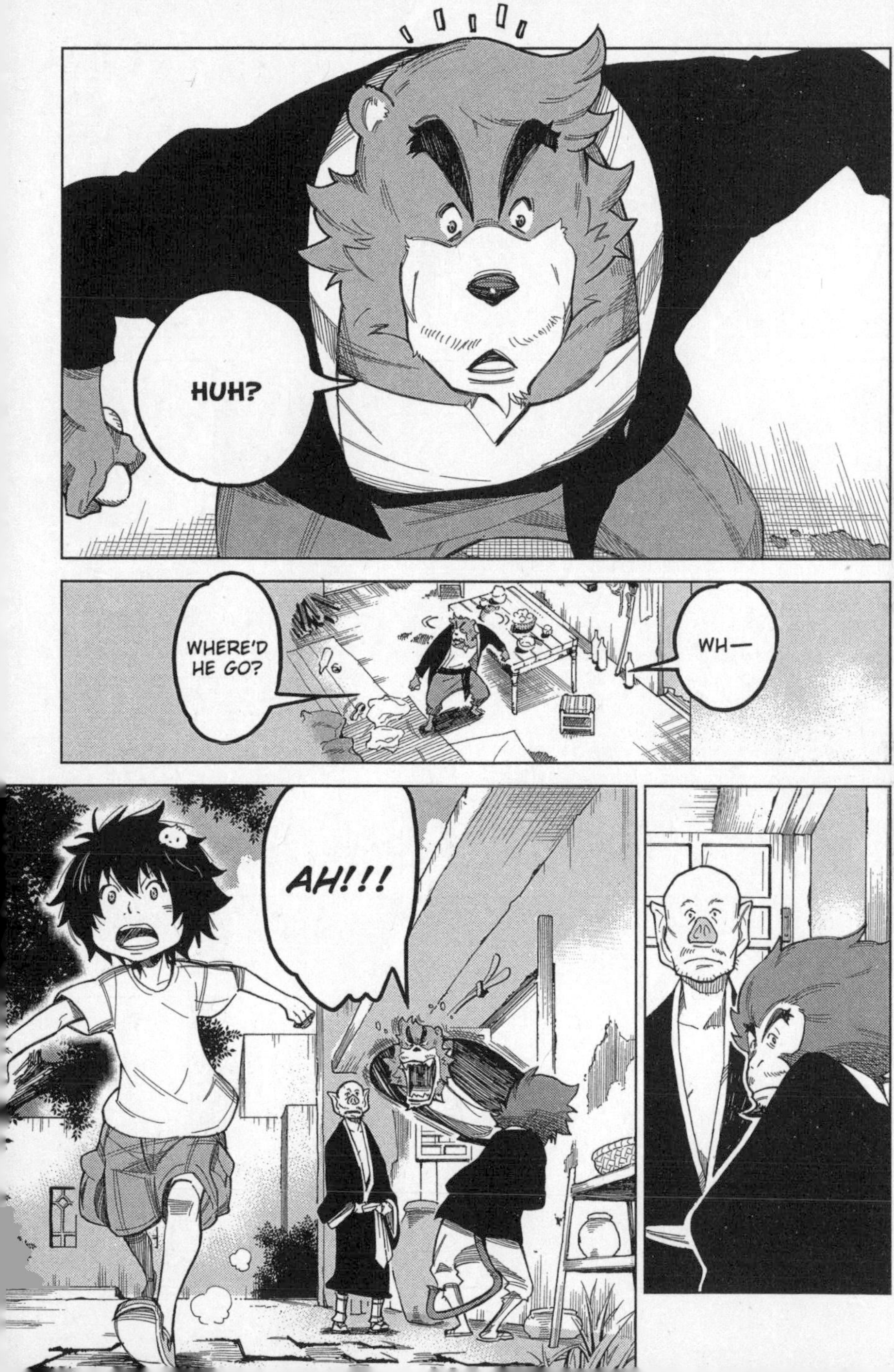
HUH?
WH—
WHERE'D HE GO?
AH!!!

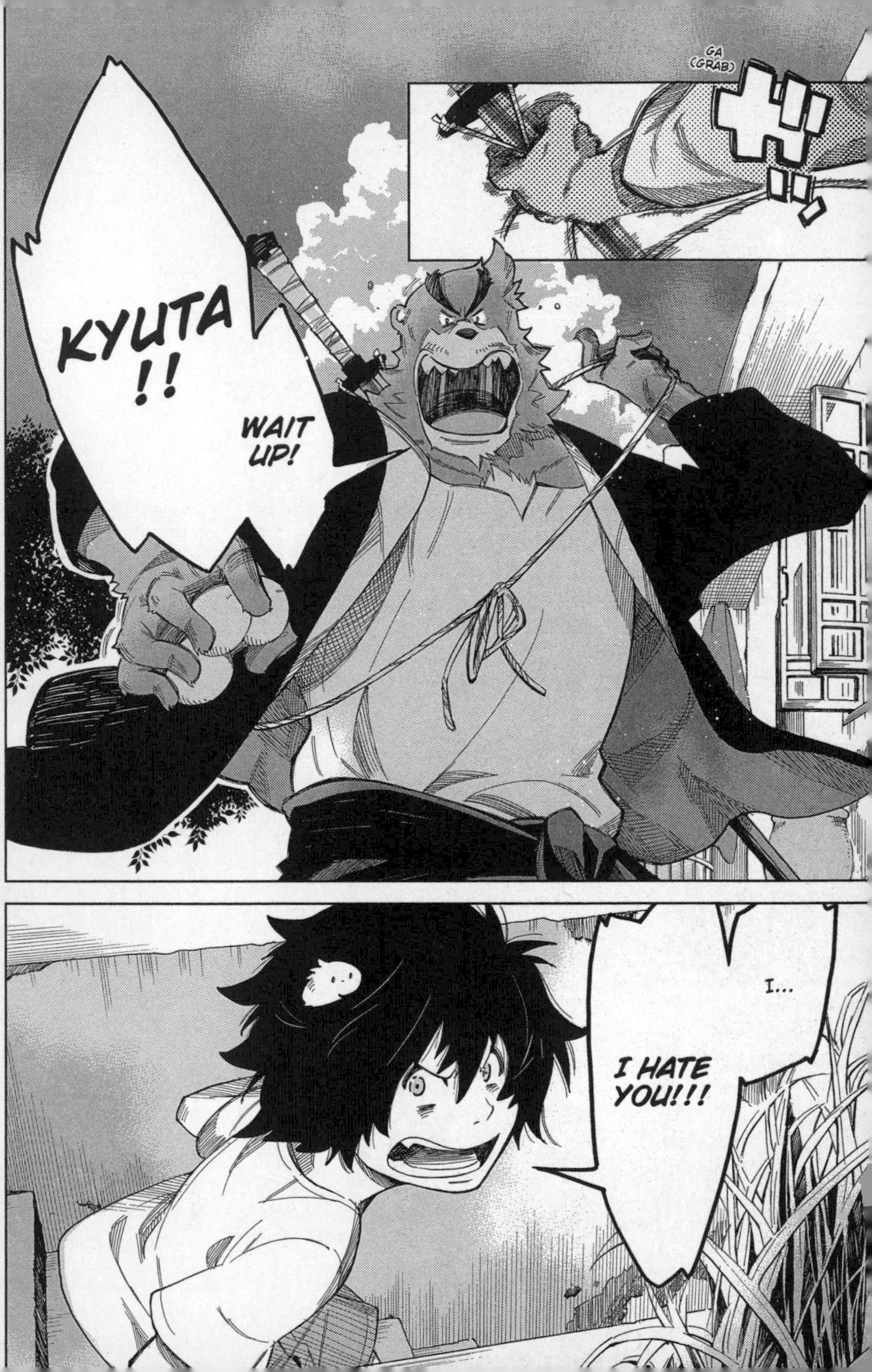
GA (GRAB)
KYUTA!!
WAIT UP!
I...
I HATE YOU!!!

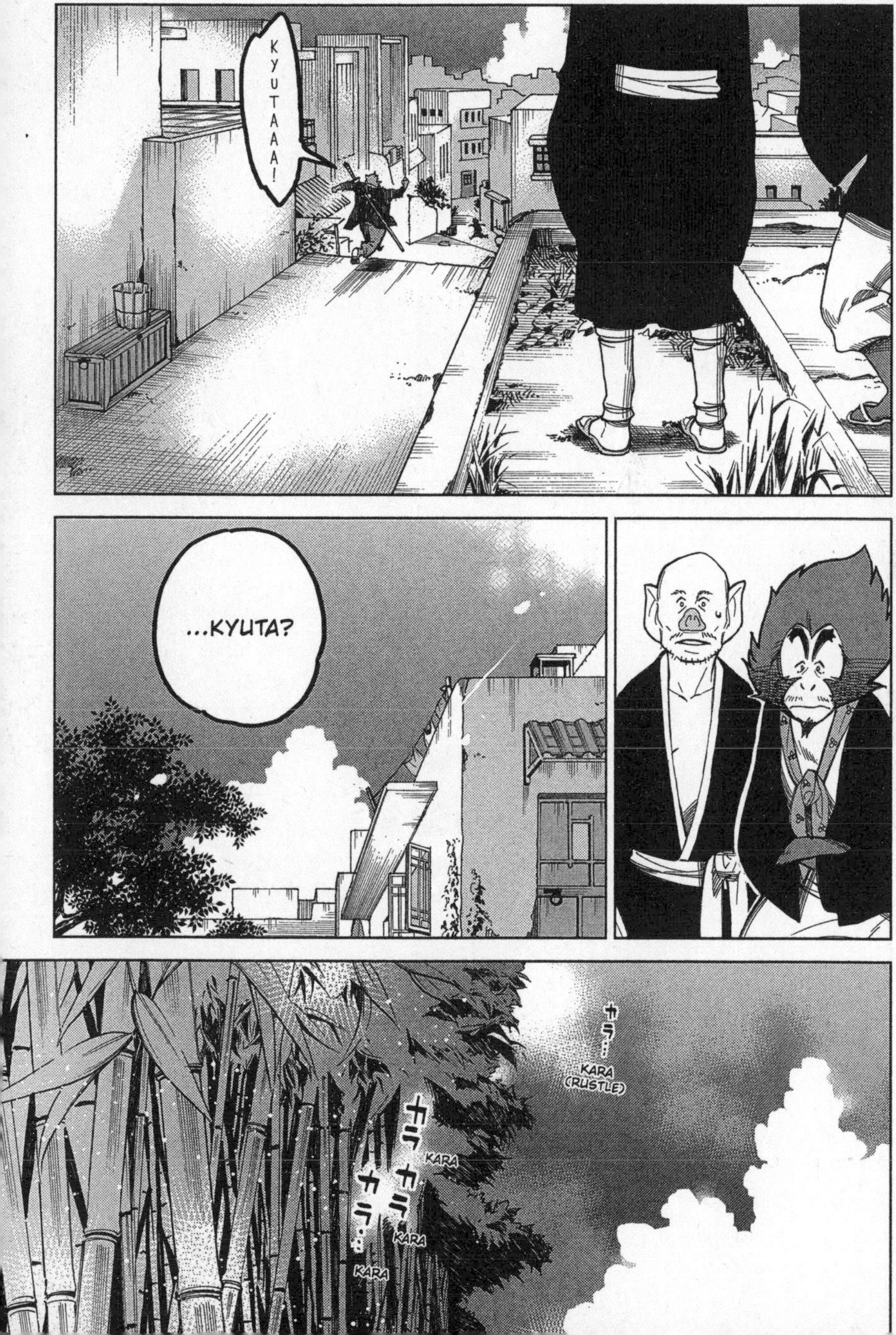
KYUTAAA!
...KYUTA?
カラ…
KARA (RUSTLE)
カラ
KARA
カラ
KARA
カラ…
KARA

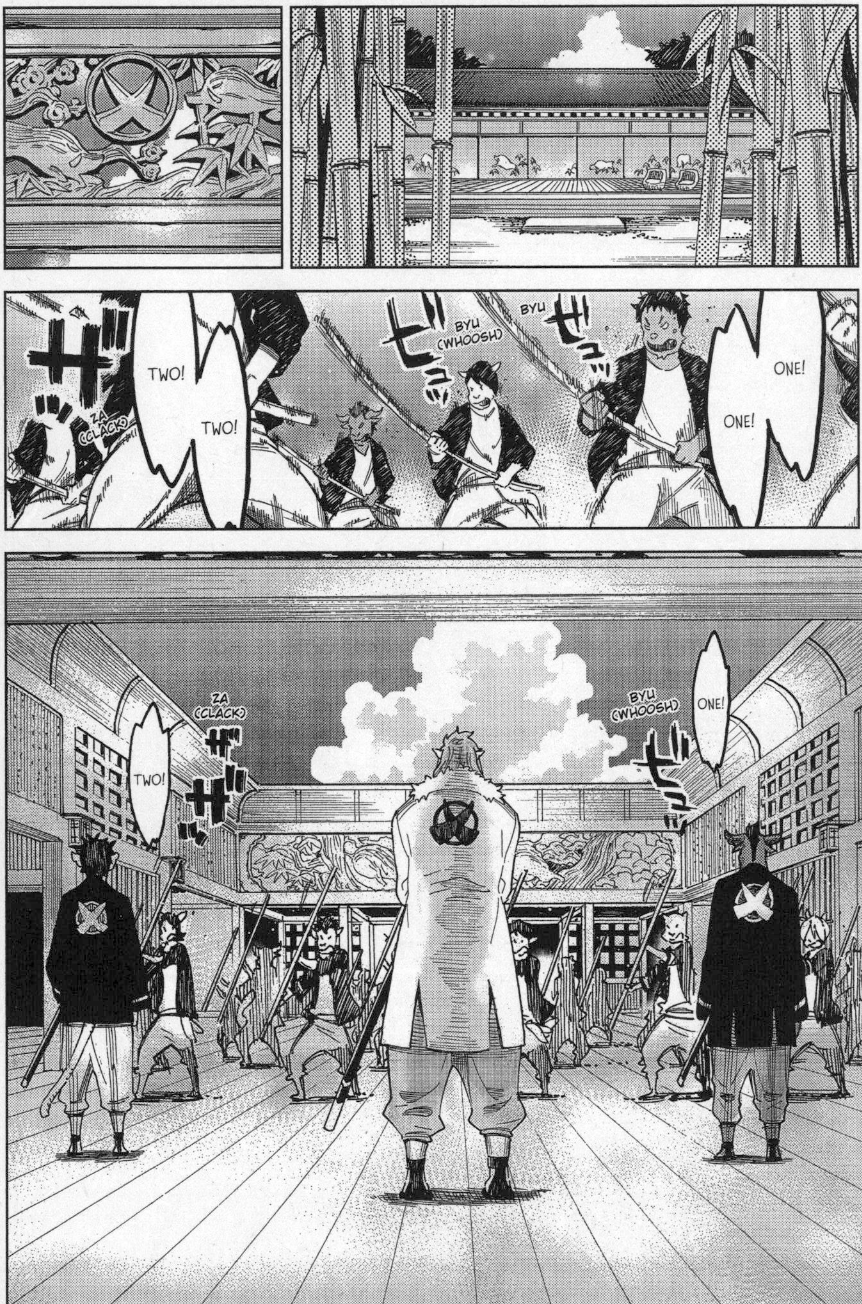

ONE!
ONE!
BYU
BYU (WHOOSH)
TWO!
TWO!
ZA (CLACK)
ONE!
BYU (WHOOSH)
ZA (CLACK)
TWO!

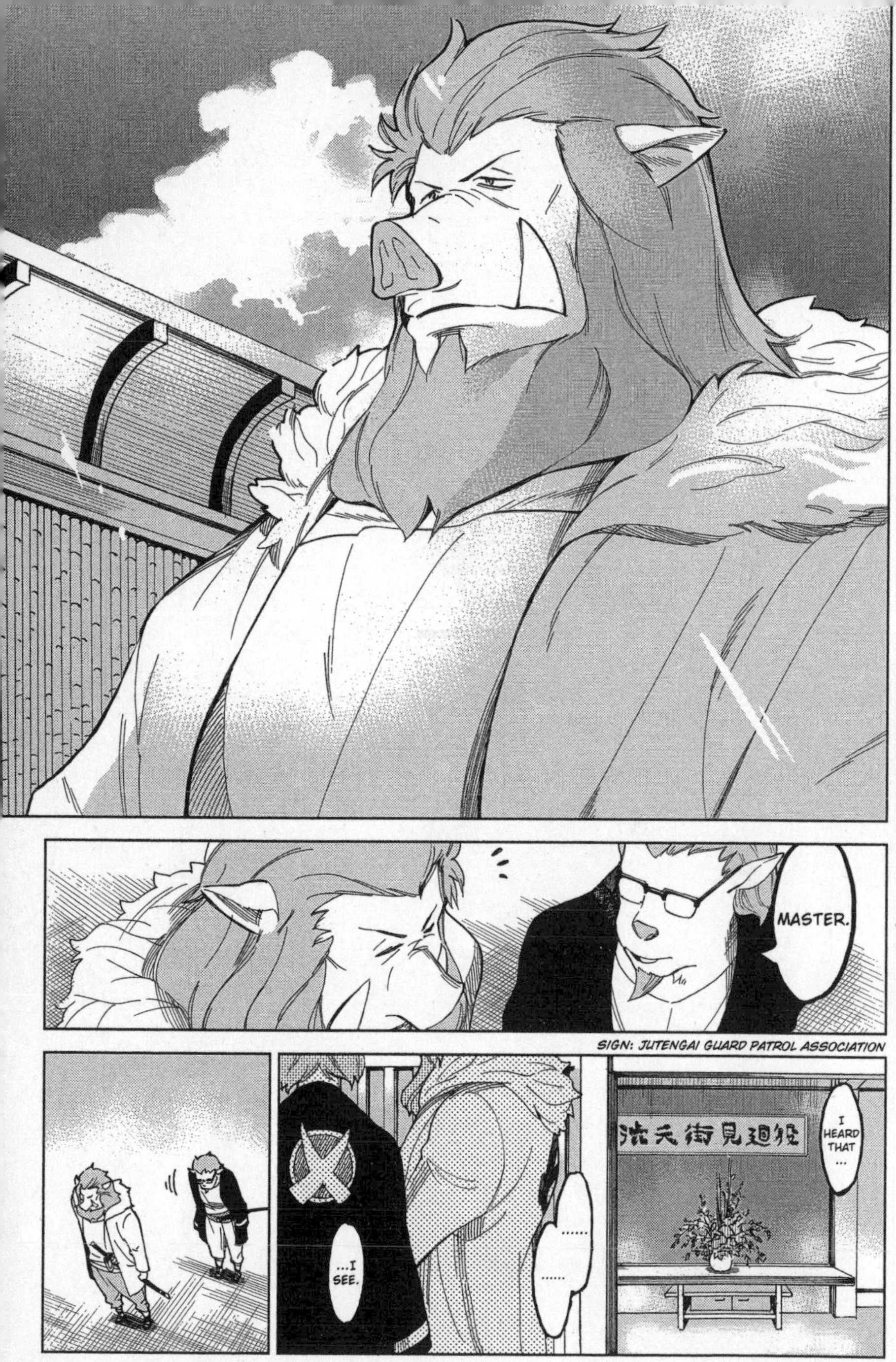
MASTER.
SIGN: JUTENGAI GUARD PATROL ASSOCIATION
I HEARD THAT ...
......
......
...I SEE.

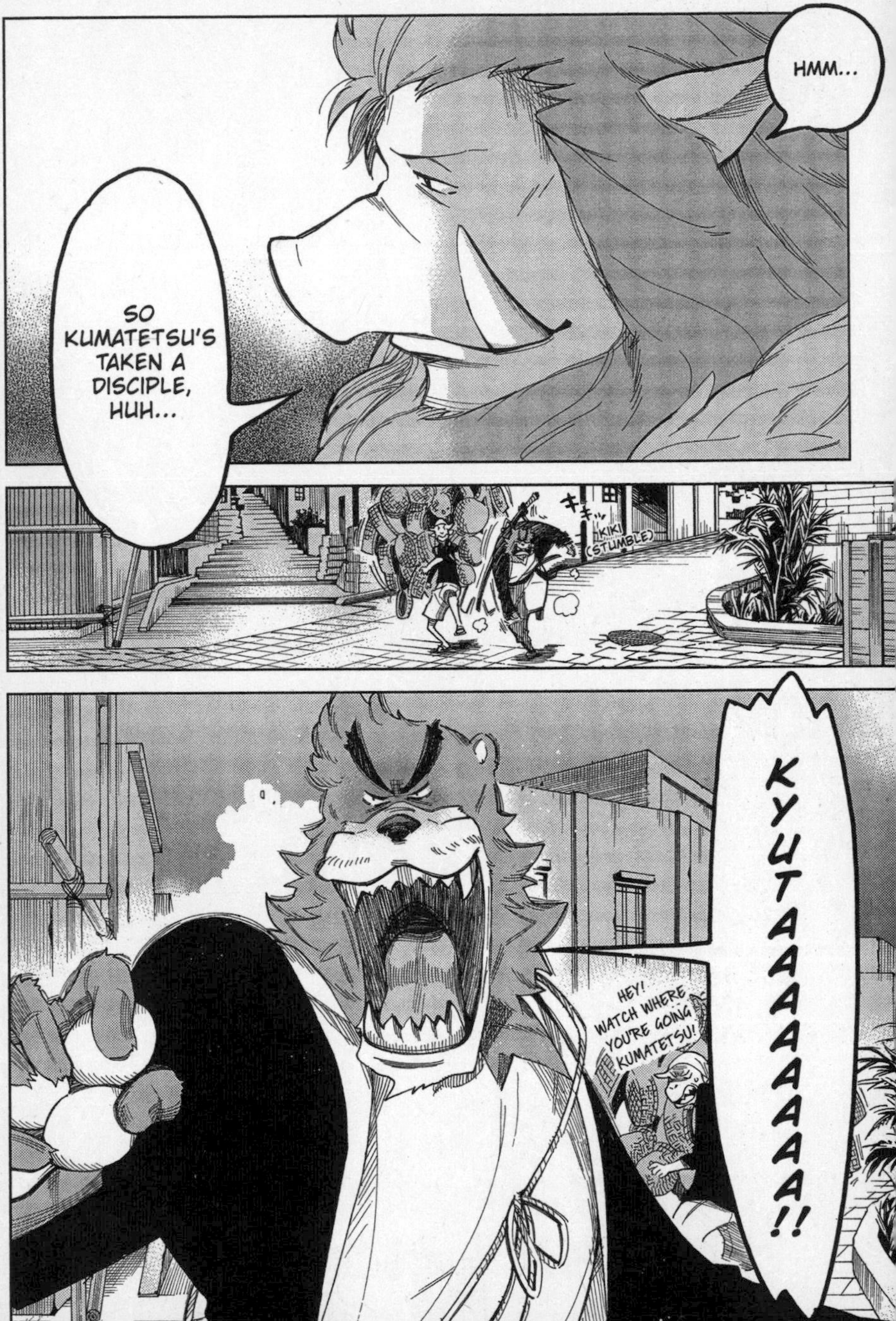
HMM...
SO KUMATETSU'S TAKEN A DISCIPLE, HUH...
キキッ
KIKI (STUMBLE)
KYUTAAAAAAAAA!!
HEY! WATCH WHERE YOU'RE GOING KUMATETSU!

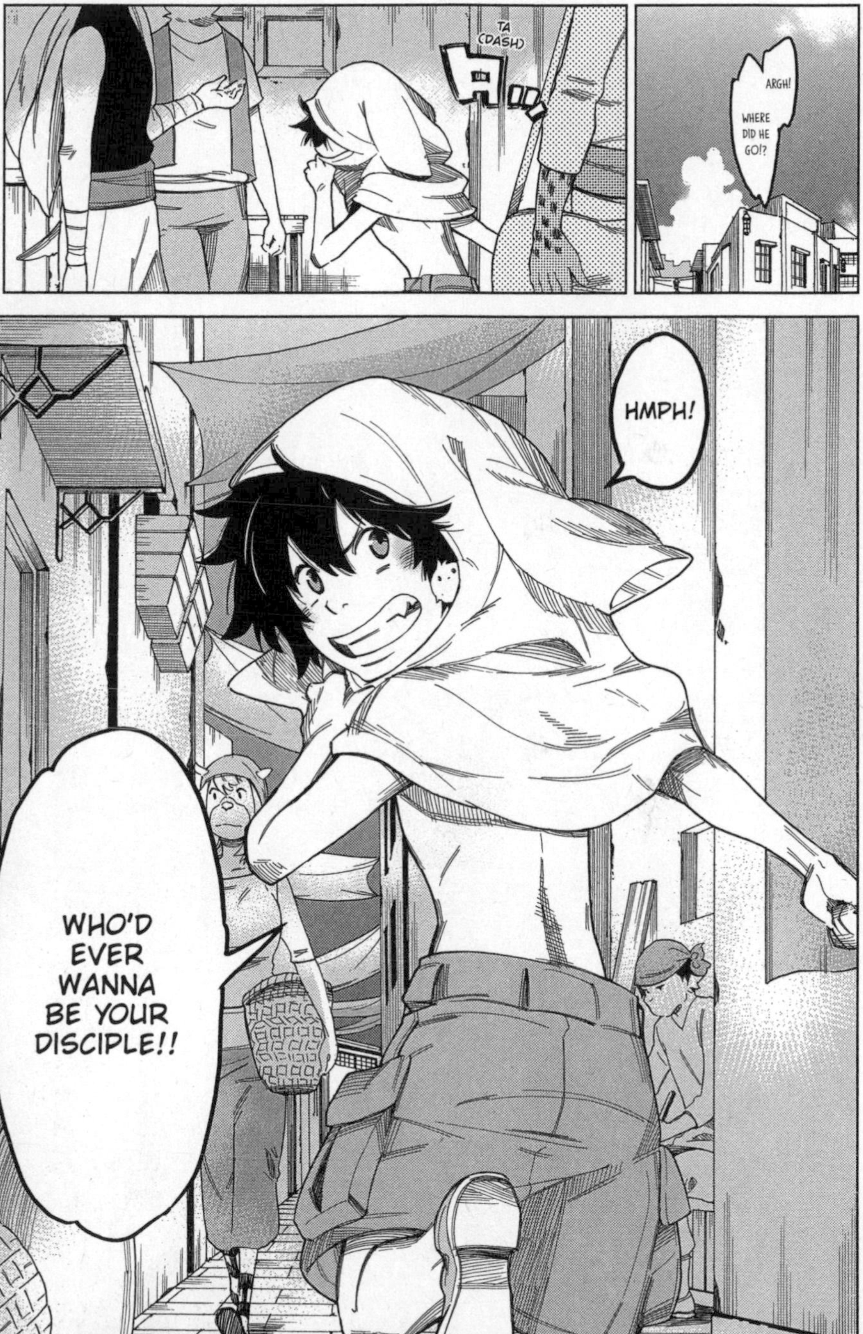
ARGH!
WHERE DID HE GO!?
TA (DASH)
HMPH!
WHO'D EVER WANNA BE YOUR DISCIPLE!!

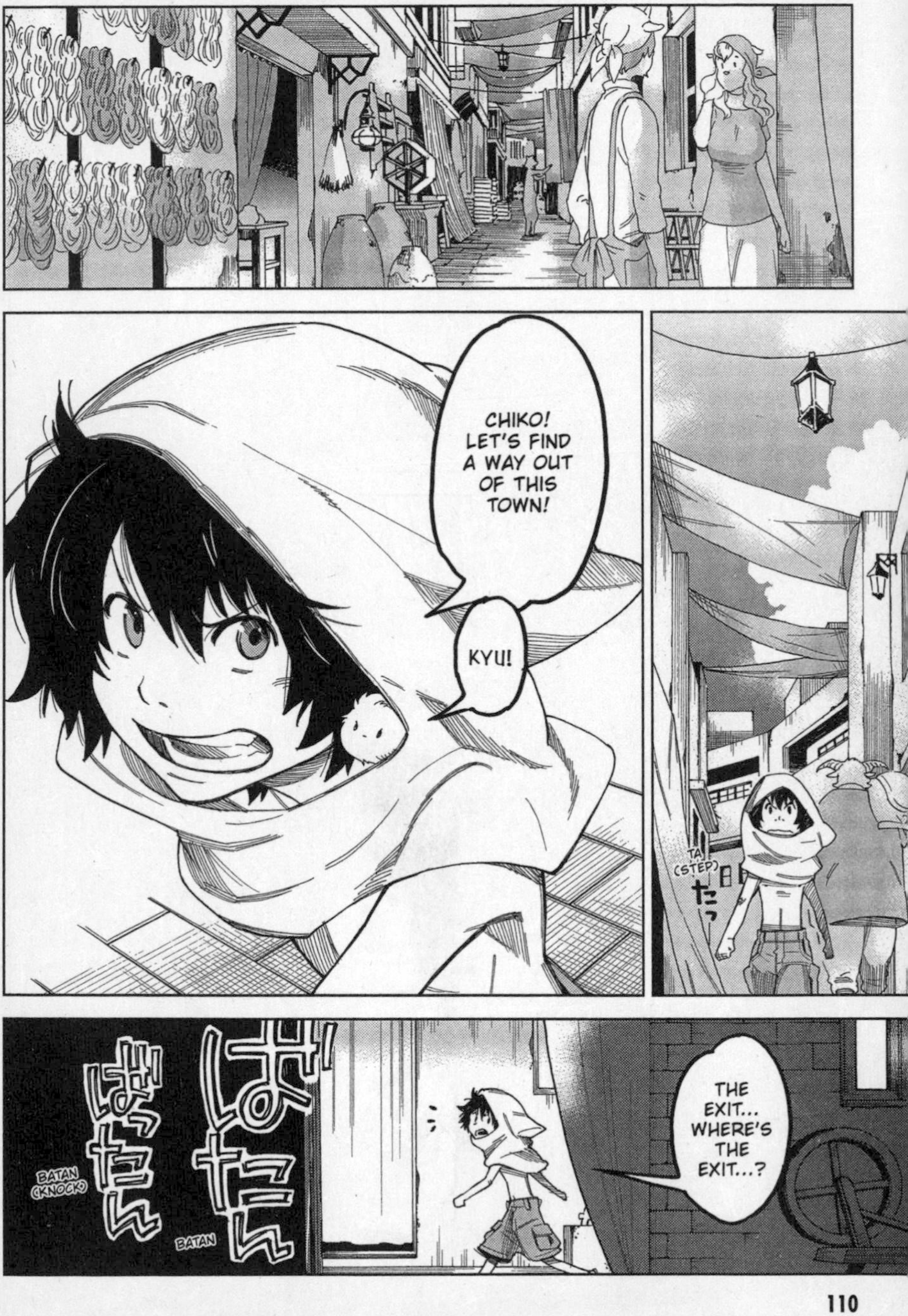
TA (STEP)
たっ
CHIKO! LET'S FIND A WAY OUT OF THIS TOWN!
KYU!
THE EXIT... WHERE'S THE EXIT...?
ばったん
BATAN
ばったん
BATAN (KNOCK)

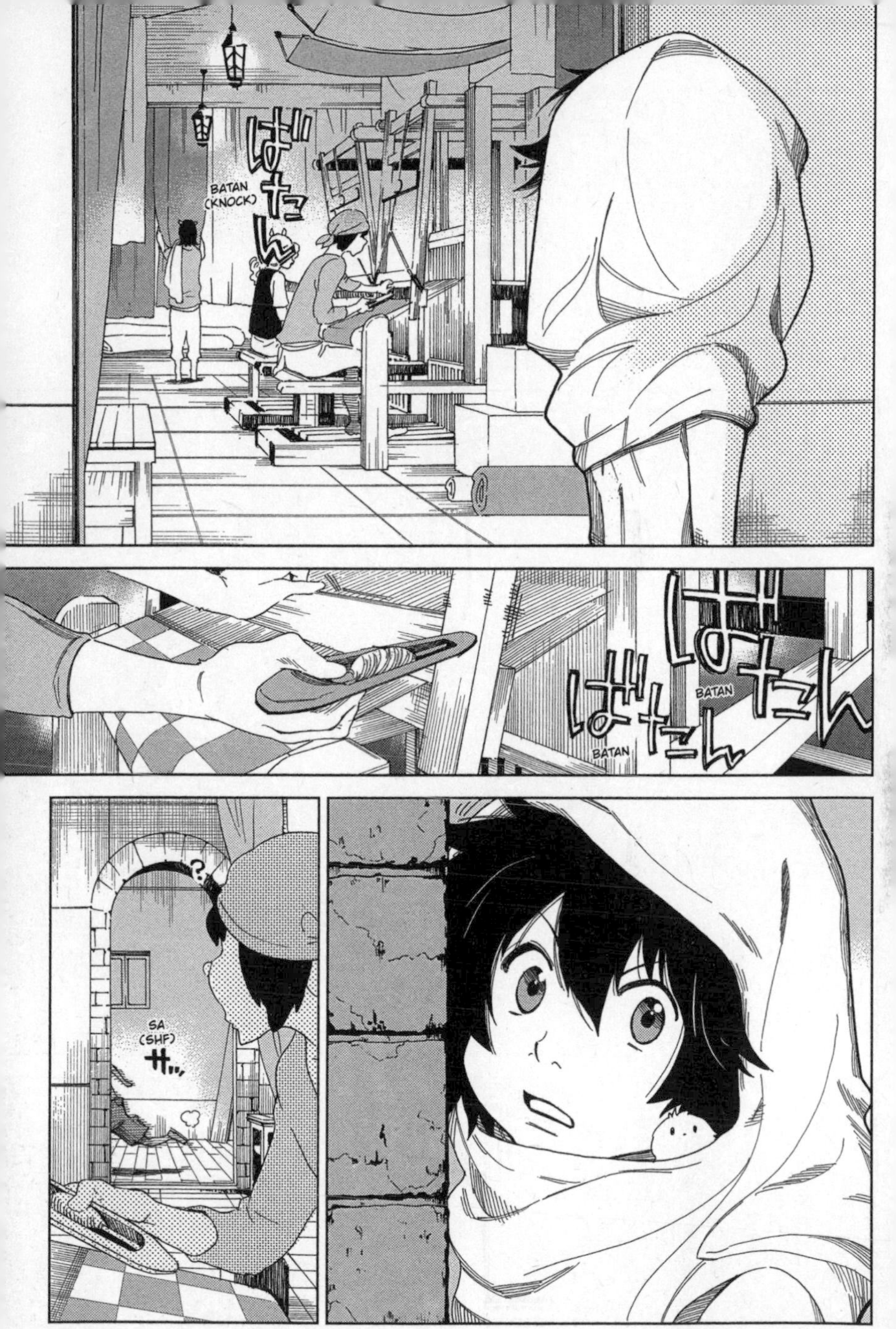
ばたん
BATAN (KNOCK)
ばたん
BATAN
ばたん
BATAN
?
SA (SHF)
サッ

KAN
(CLANG)

KAN

KAN

KAN

KAN

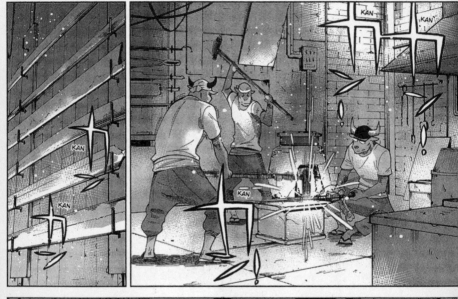

SURA
(SLIDE)

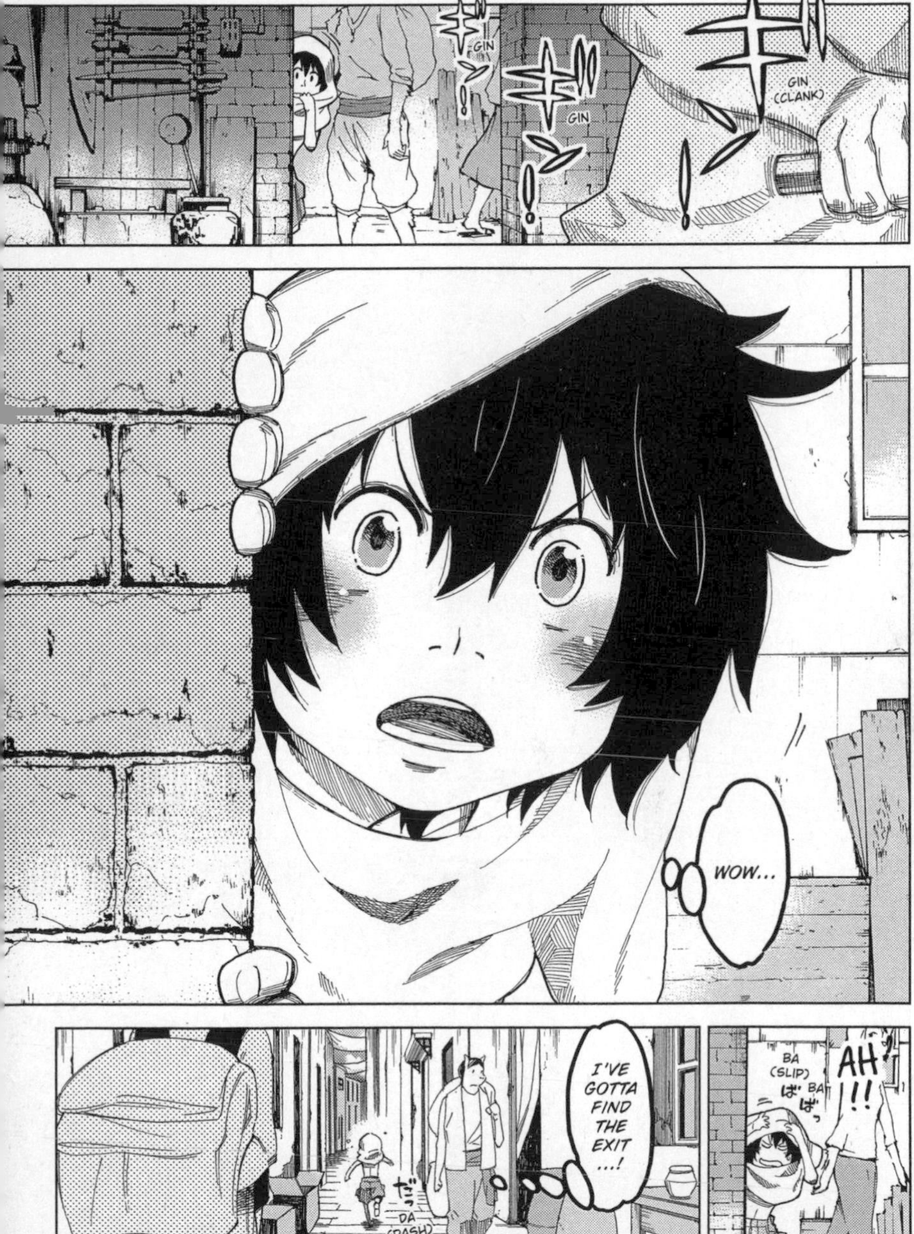
ギン!
GIN (CLANK)
ギン!
GIN
ギン!
GIN
WOW...
ばっ
BA (SLIP)
ばっ
BA
AH!!
I'VE GOTTA FIND THE EXIT...!
だっ
DA (DASH)

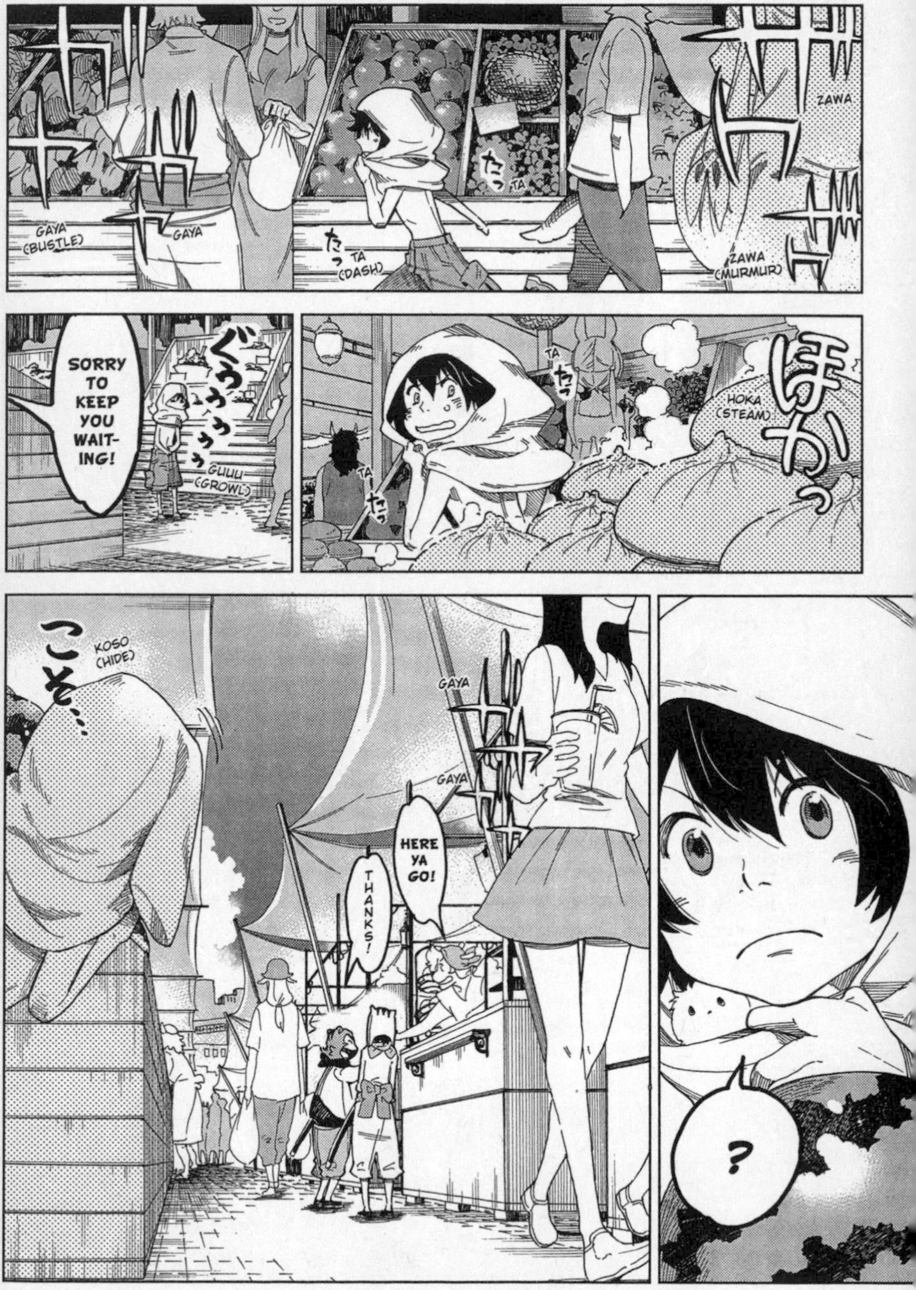
ZAWA
たっ
TA
ZAWA (MURMUR)
たっ
TA (DASH)
GAYA
GAYA (BUSTLE)
ほわっ
HOKA (STEAM)
たっ
TA
たっ
TA
ぐうううう
GUUU (GROWL)
SORRY TO KEEP YOU WAITING!
?
GAYA
GAYA
HERE YA GO!
THANKS!
こそ…
KOSO (HIDE)

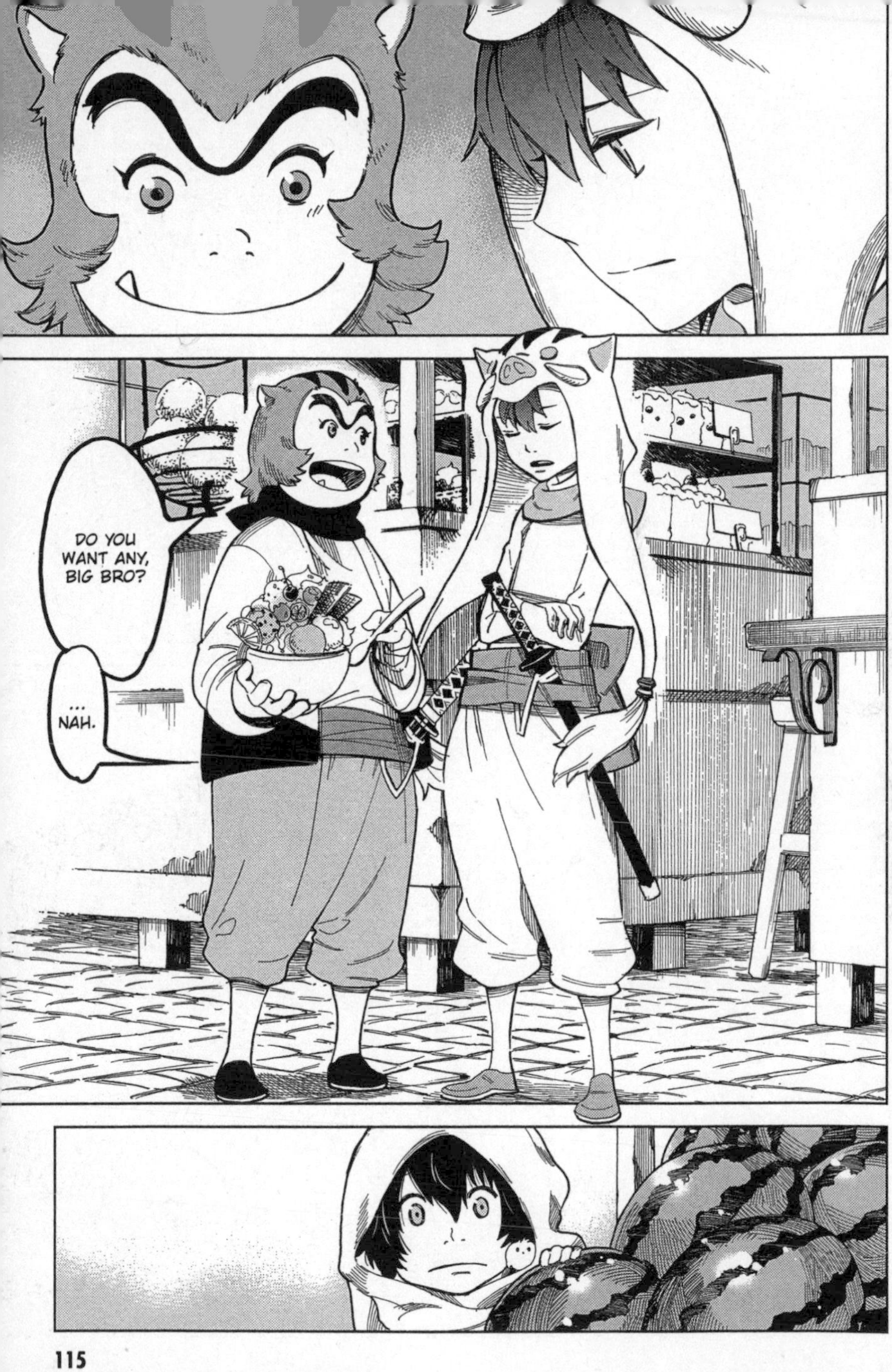
DO YOU WANT ANY, BIG BRO?
... NAH.

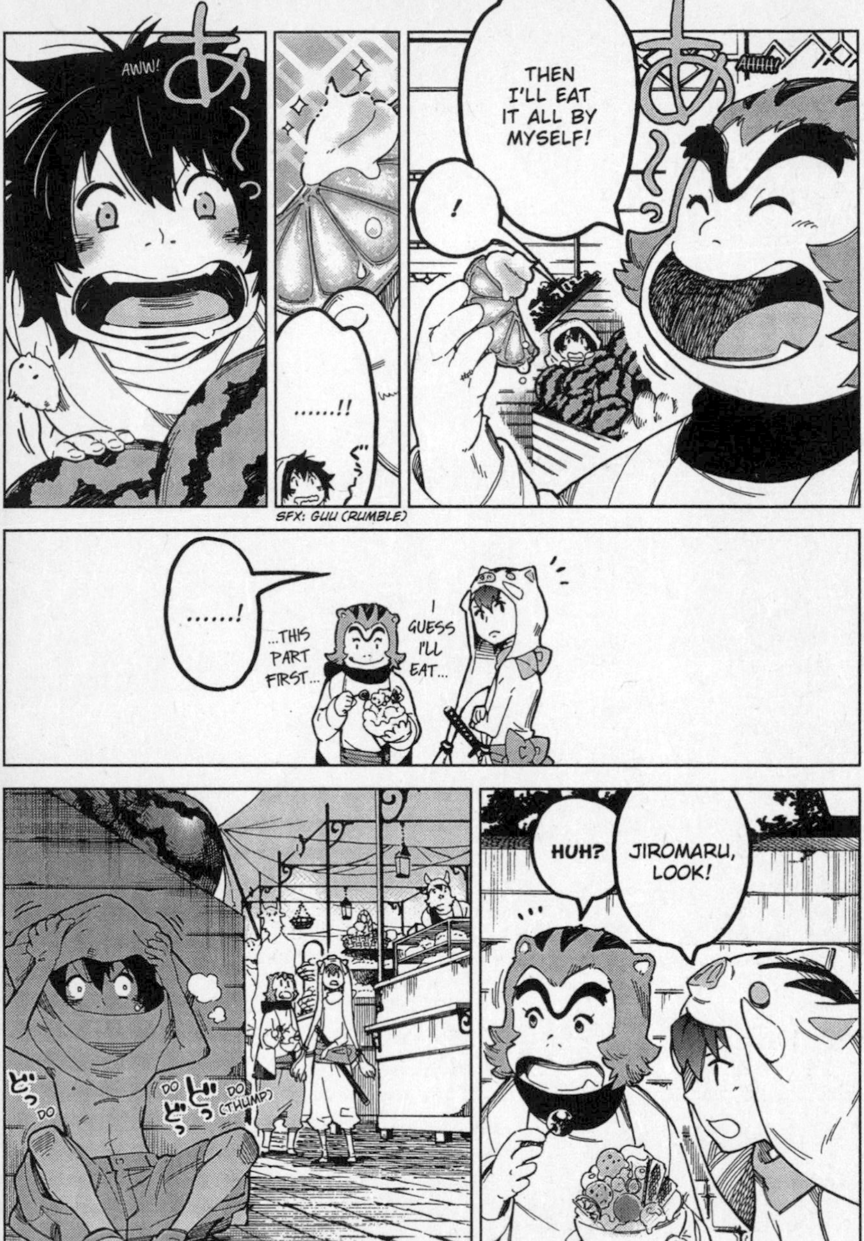
AHHH!
THEN I'LL EAT IT ALL BY MYSELF!
!
......!!
AWW!
SFX: GUU (RUMBLE)
I GUESS I'LL EAT...
...THIS PART FIRST...
......!
JIROMARU, LOOK!
HUH?
DO DO DO (THUMP)

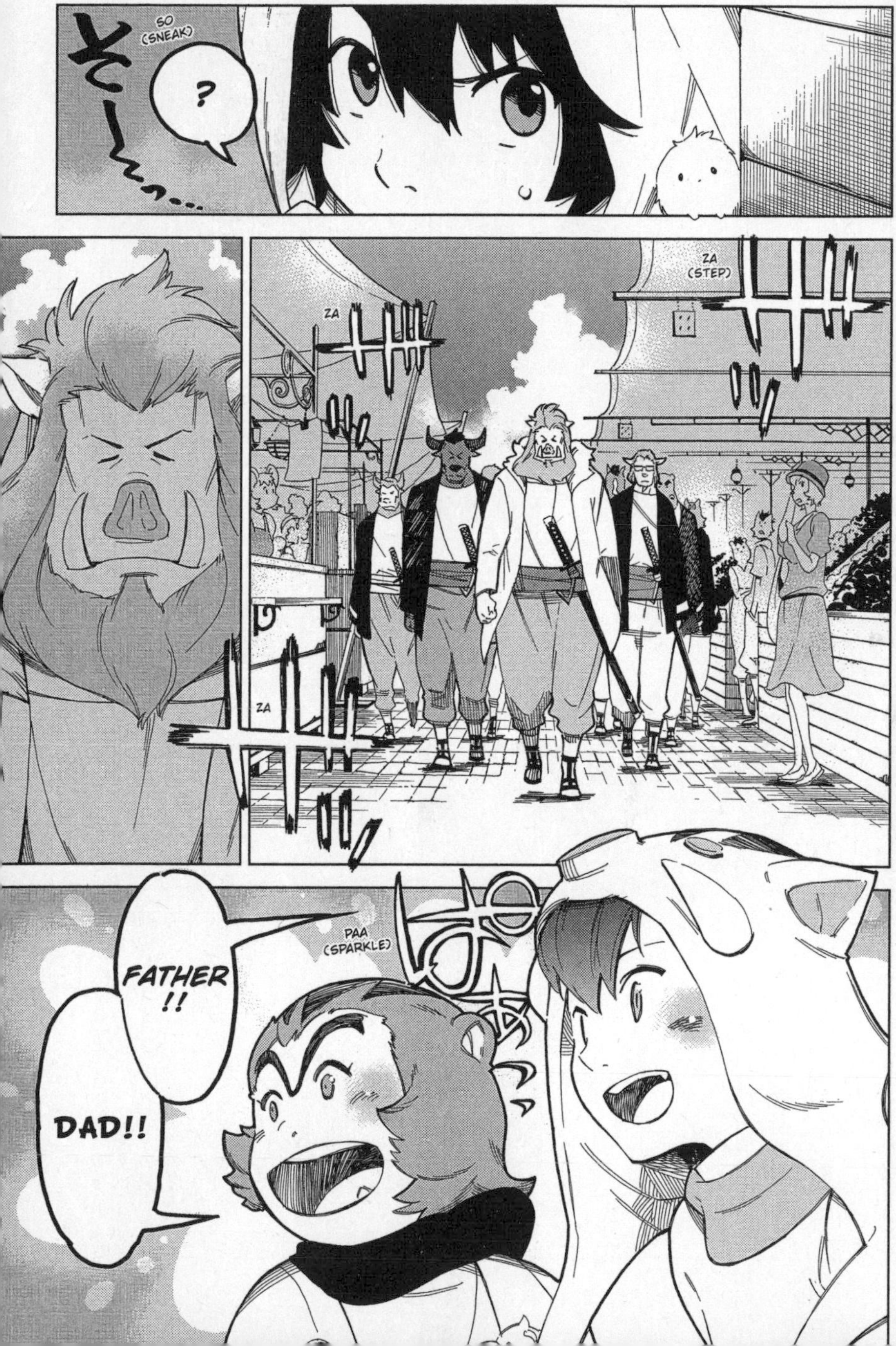
SO (SNEAK)
?
ZA (STEP)
ZA
ZA
PAA (SPARKLE)
FATHER!!
DAD!!

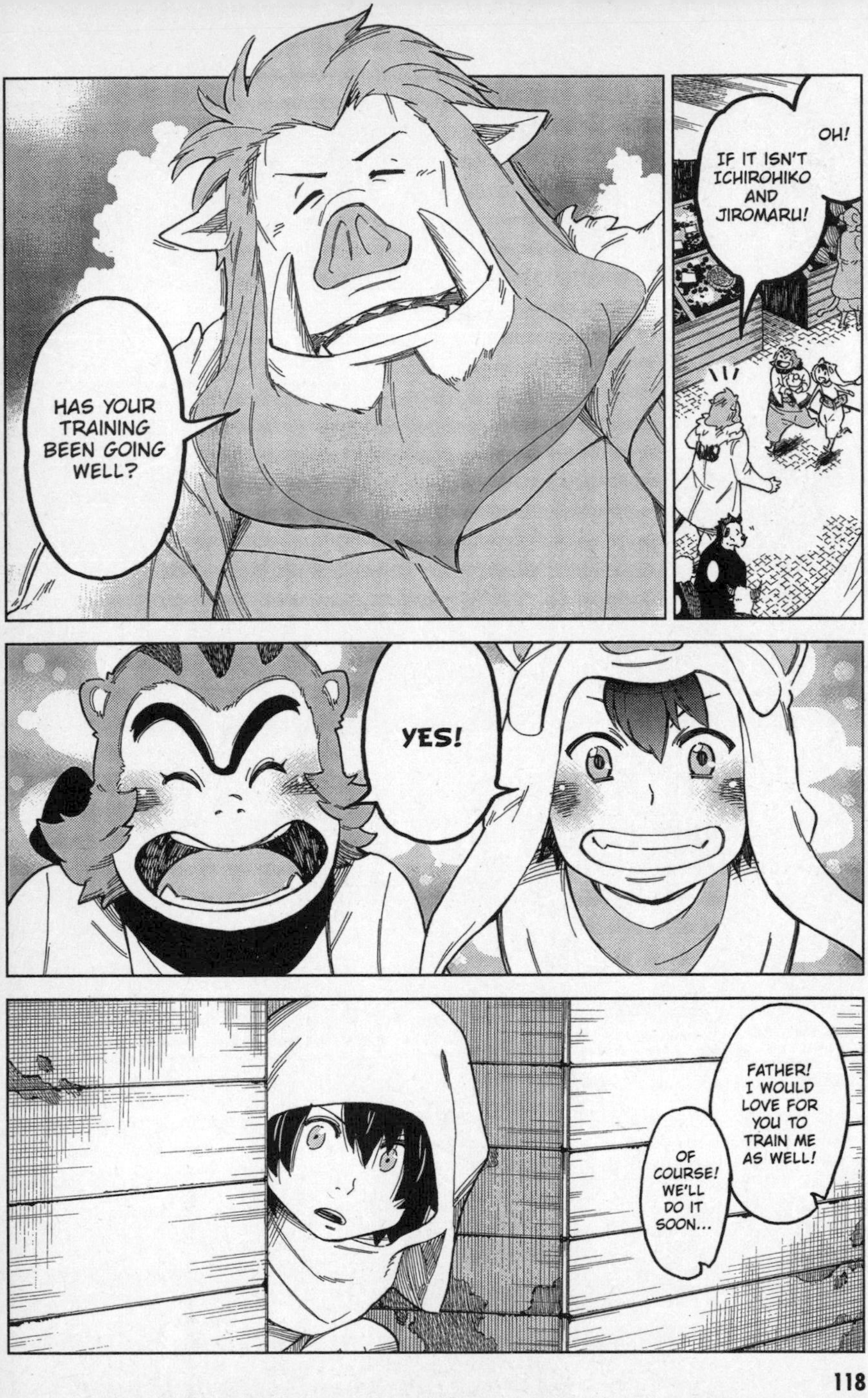
OH!
IF IT ISN'T ICHIROHIKO AND JIROMARU!
HAS YOUR TRAINING BEEN GOING WELL?
YES!
FATHER! I WOULD LOVE FOR YOU TO TRAIN ME AS WELL!
OF COURSE! WE'LL DO IT SOON...

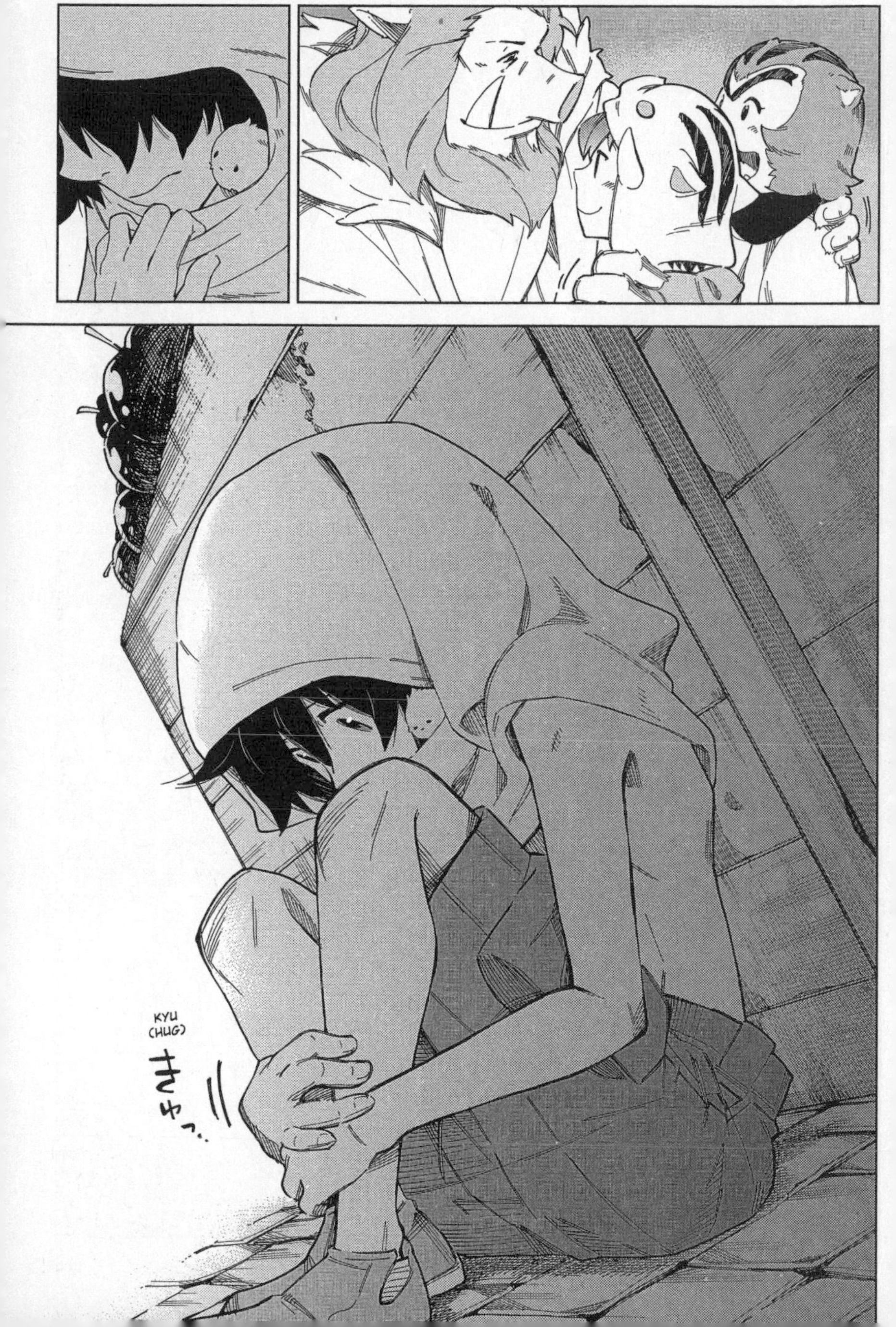
KYU
(HUG)
きゅっ…

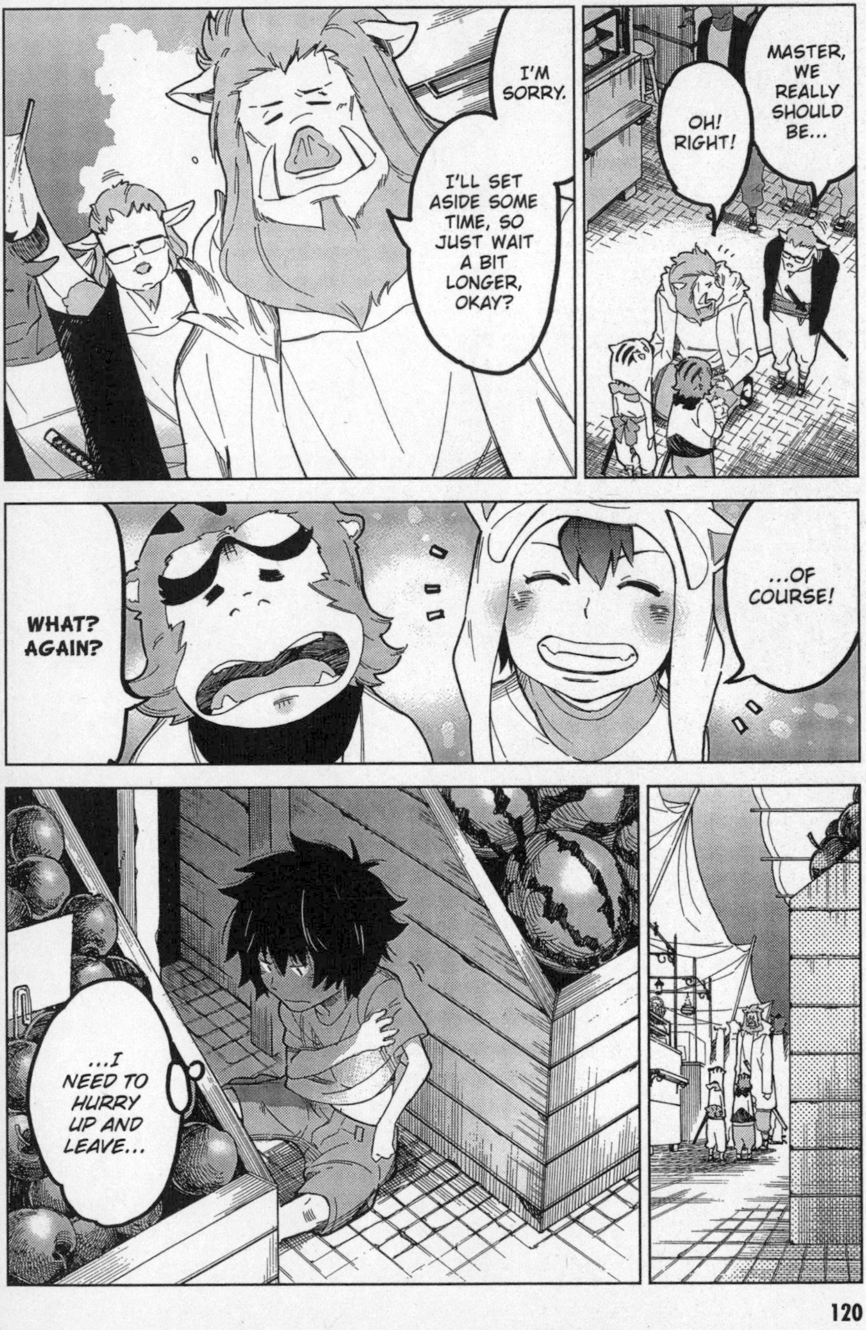
MASTER, WE REALLY SHOULD BE...
OH! RIGHT!
I'M SORRY.
I'LL SET ASIDE SOME TIME, SO JUST WAIT A BIT LONGER, OKAY?
...OF COURSE!
WHAT? AGAIN?
...I NEED TO HURRY UP AND LEAVE...

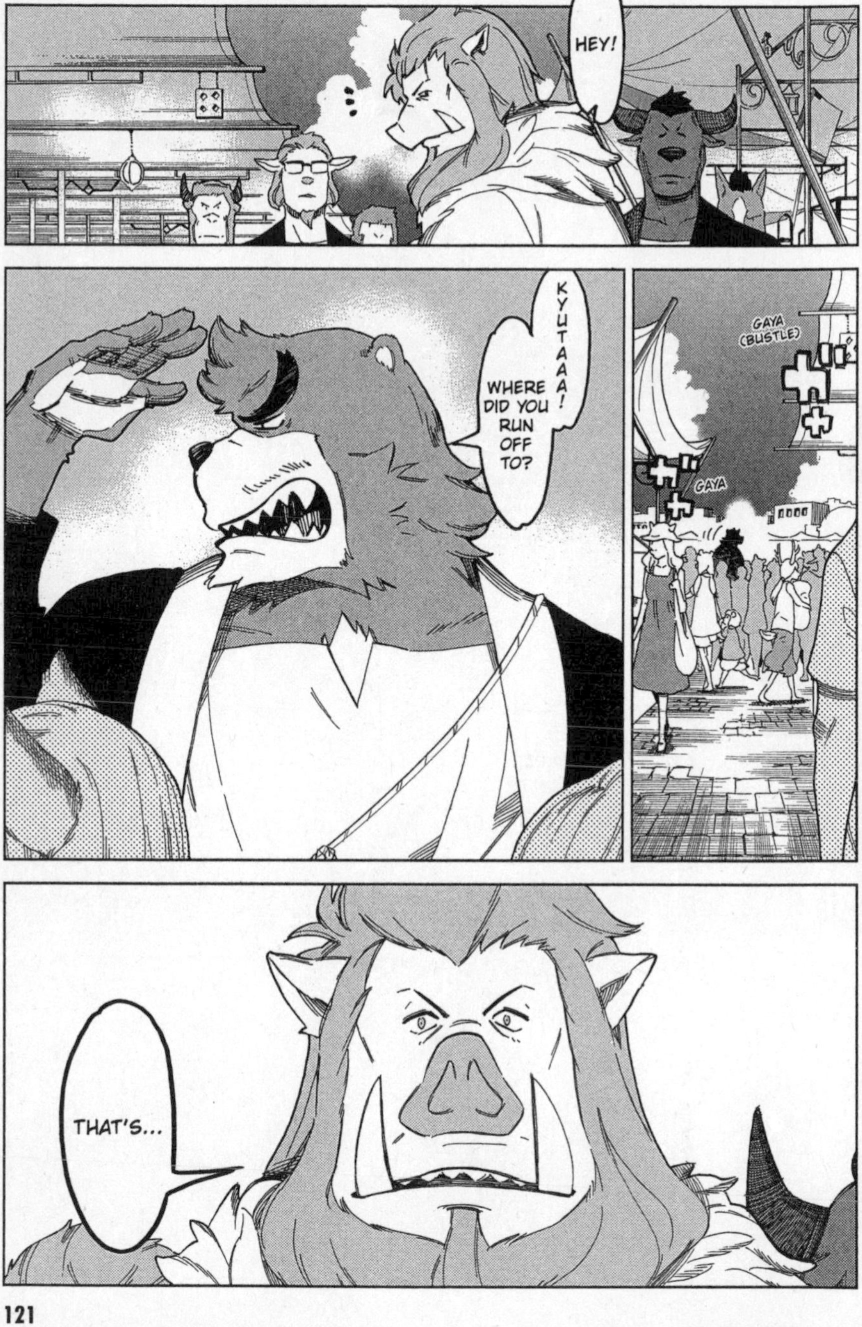
HEY!
GAYA (BUSTLE)
GAYA
KYUTAAAA! WHERE DID YOU RUN OFF TO?
THAT'S...

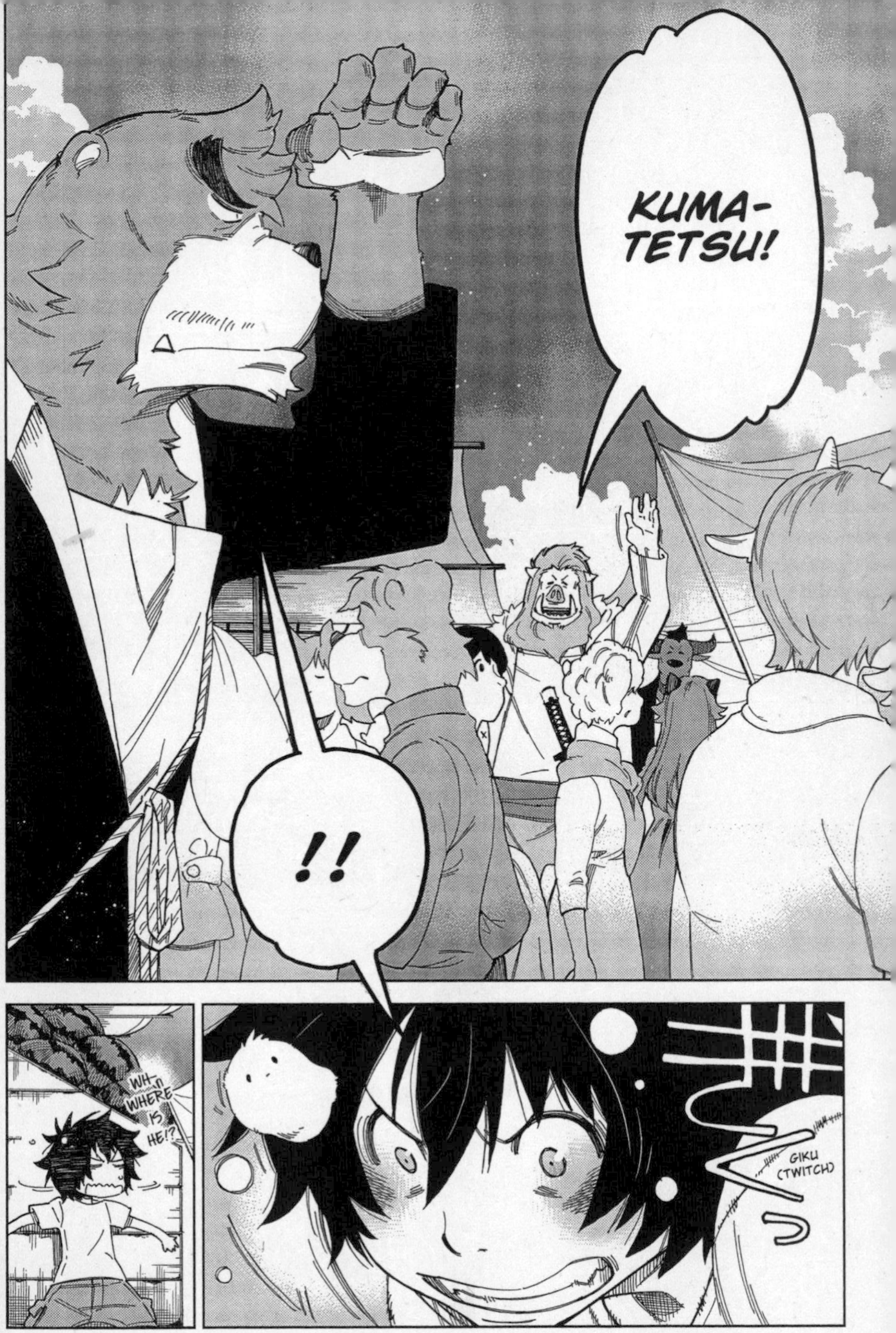
KUMA-TETSU!
!!
GIKU (TWITCH)
WH- WHERE IS HE!?

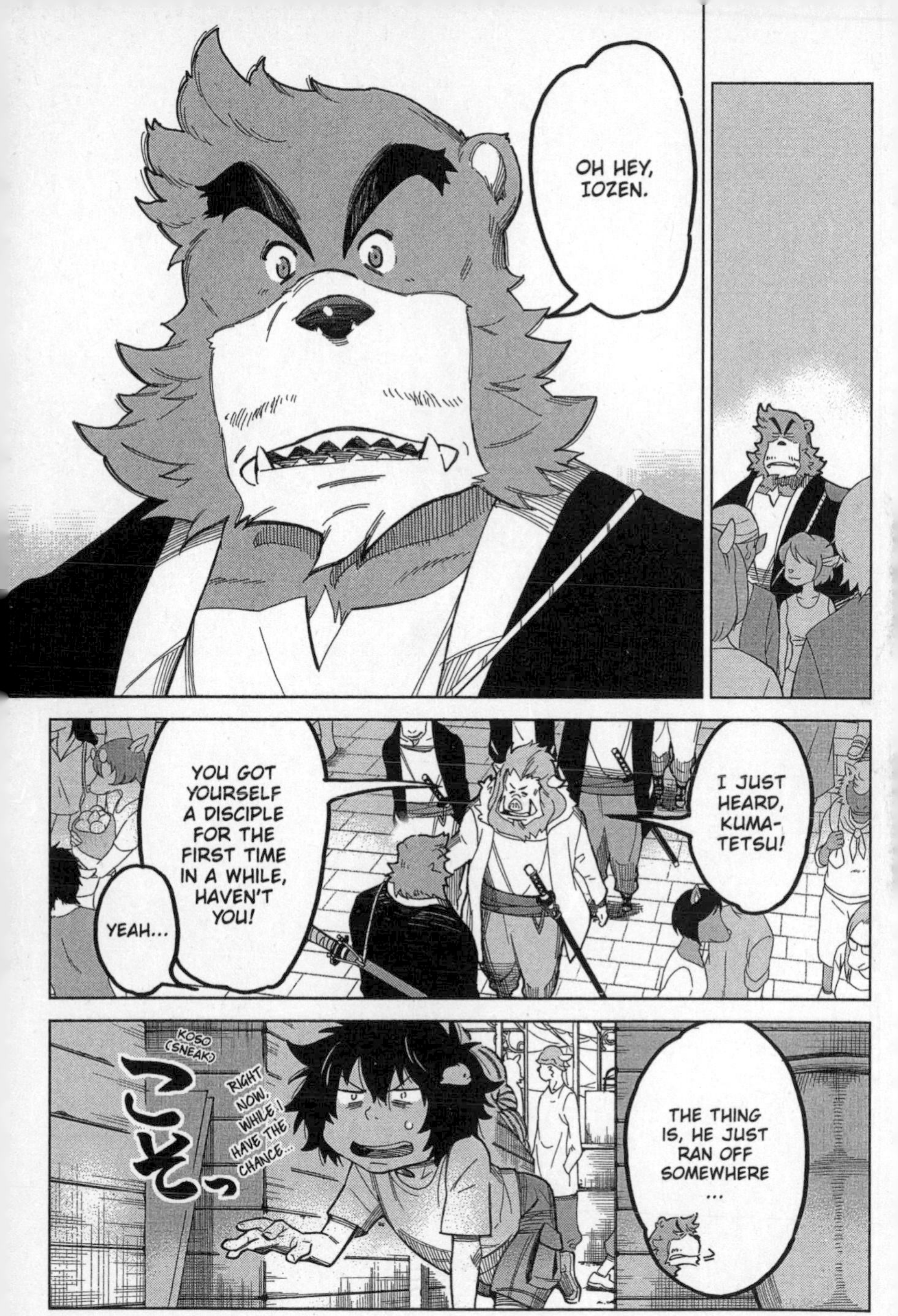
OH HEY, IOZEN.
I JUST HEARD, KUMA-TETSU!
YOU GOT YOURSELF A DISCIPLE FOR THE FIRST TIME IN A WHILE, HAVEN'T YOU!
YEAH...
THE THING IS, HE JUST RAN OFF SOMEWHERE ...
KOSO (SNEAK)
こそっ
RIGHT NOW, WHILE I HAVE THE CHANCE...

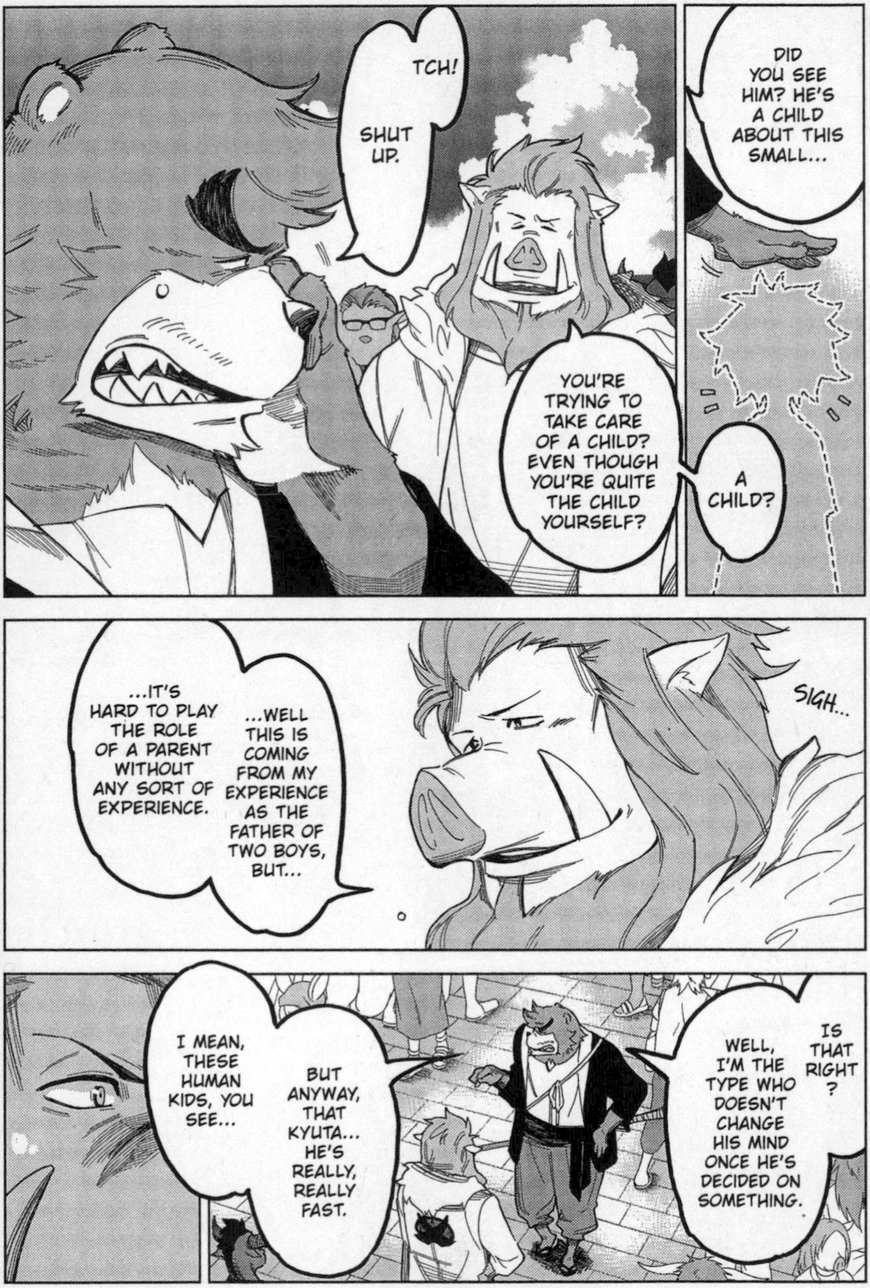
DID YOU SEE HIM? HE'S A CHILD ABOUT THIS SMALL...
A CHILD?
YOU'RE TRYING TO TAKE CARE OF A CHILD? EVEN THOUGH YOU'RE QUITE THE CHILD YOURSELF?
TCH!
SHUT UP.
SIGH...
...WELL THIS IS COMING FROM MY EXPERIENCE AS THE FATHER OF TWO BOYS, BUT...
...IT'S HARD TO PLAY THE ROLE OF A PARENT WITHOUT ANY SORT OF EXPERIENCE.
IS THAT RIGHT?
WELL, I'M THE TYPE WHO DOESN'T CHANGE HIS MIND ONCE HE'S DECIDED ON SOMETHING.
BUT ANYWAY, THAT KYUTA... HE'S REALLY, REALLY FAST.
I MEAN, THESE HUMAN KIDS, YOU SEE...

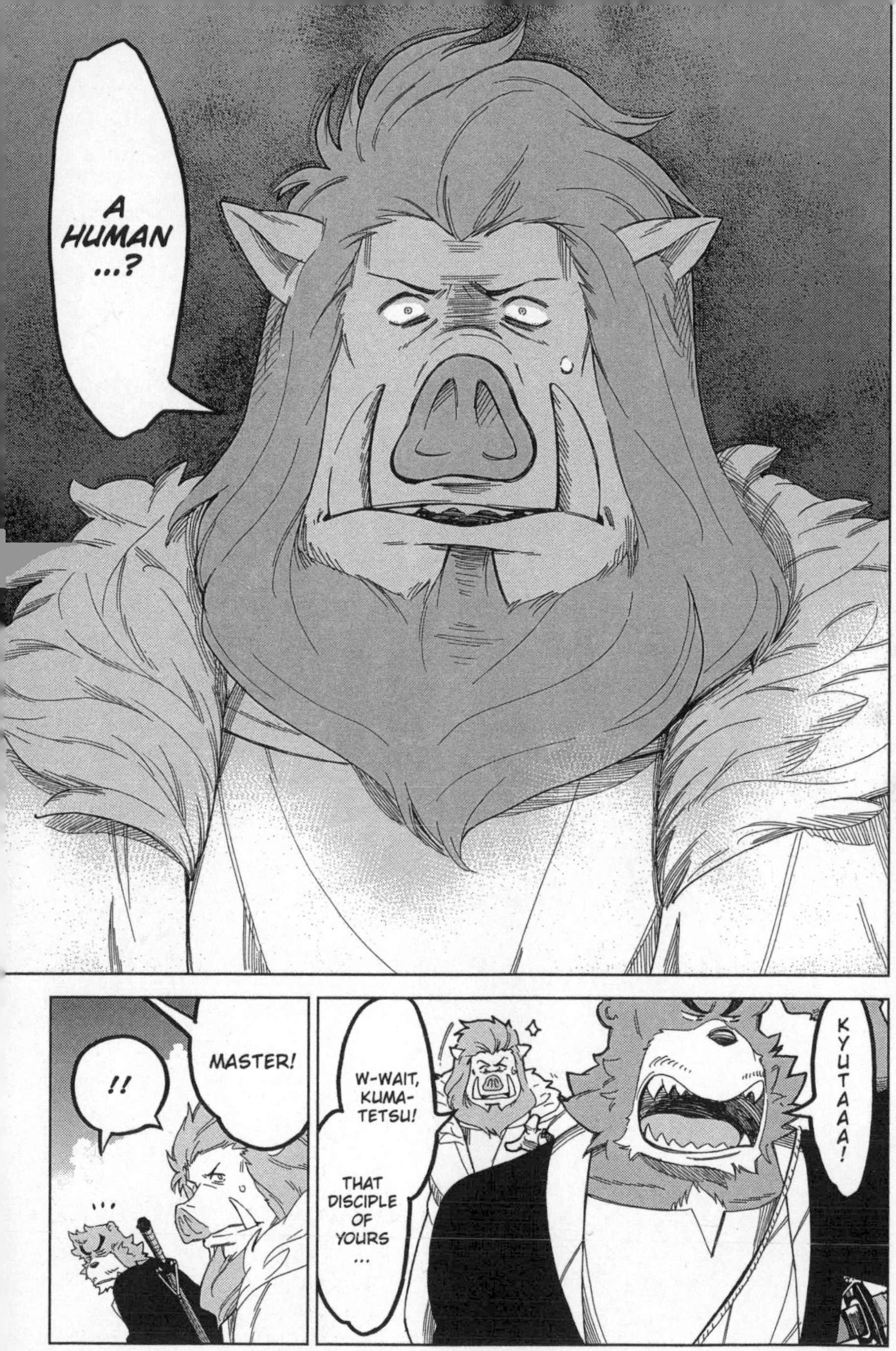
A HUMAN ...?
KYUTAAA!
W-WAIT, KUMA-TETSU!
THAT DISCIPLE OF YOURS ...
MASTER!
!!
...

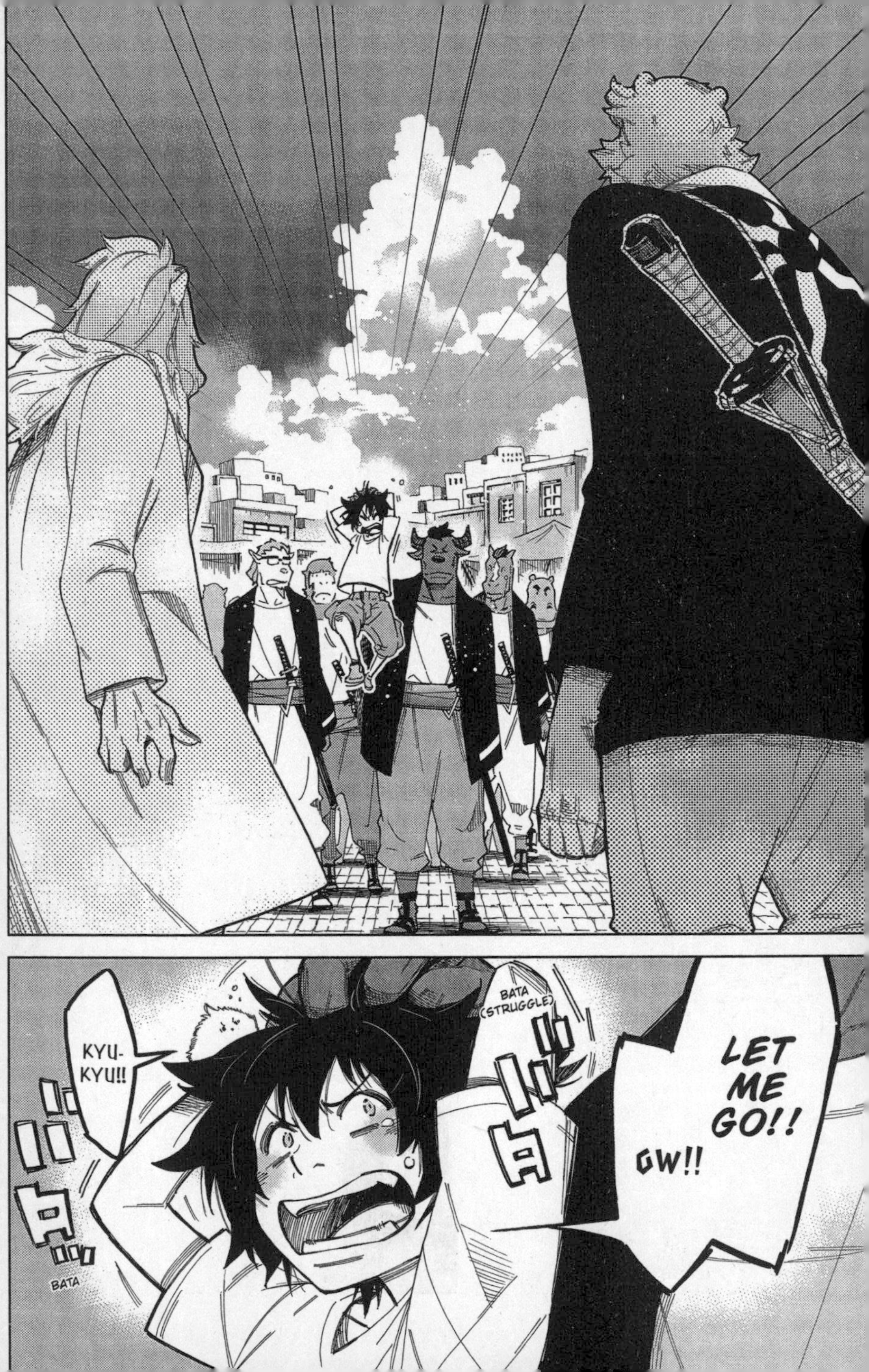
BATA (STRUGGLE)
LET ME GO!!
OW!!
KYU-KYU!!
BATA

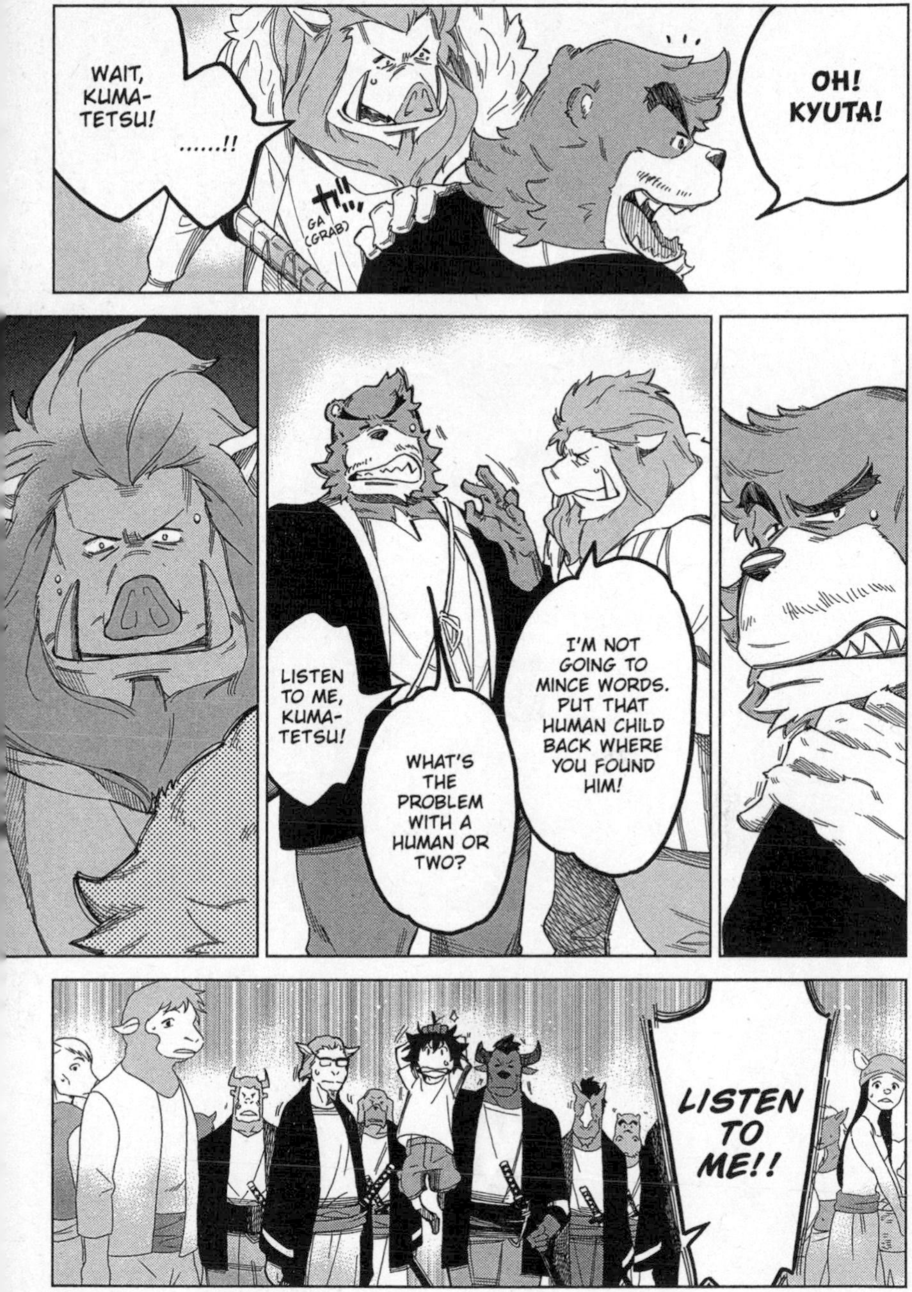
OH! KYUTA!
WAIT, KUMA-TETSU!
......!!
GA (GRAB)
I'M NOT GOING TO MINCE WORDS. PUT THAT HUMAN CHILD BACK WHERE YOU FOUND HIM!
LISTEN TO ME, KUMA-TETSU!
WHAT'S THE PROBLEM WITH A HUMAN OR TWO?
LISTEN TO ME!!

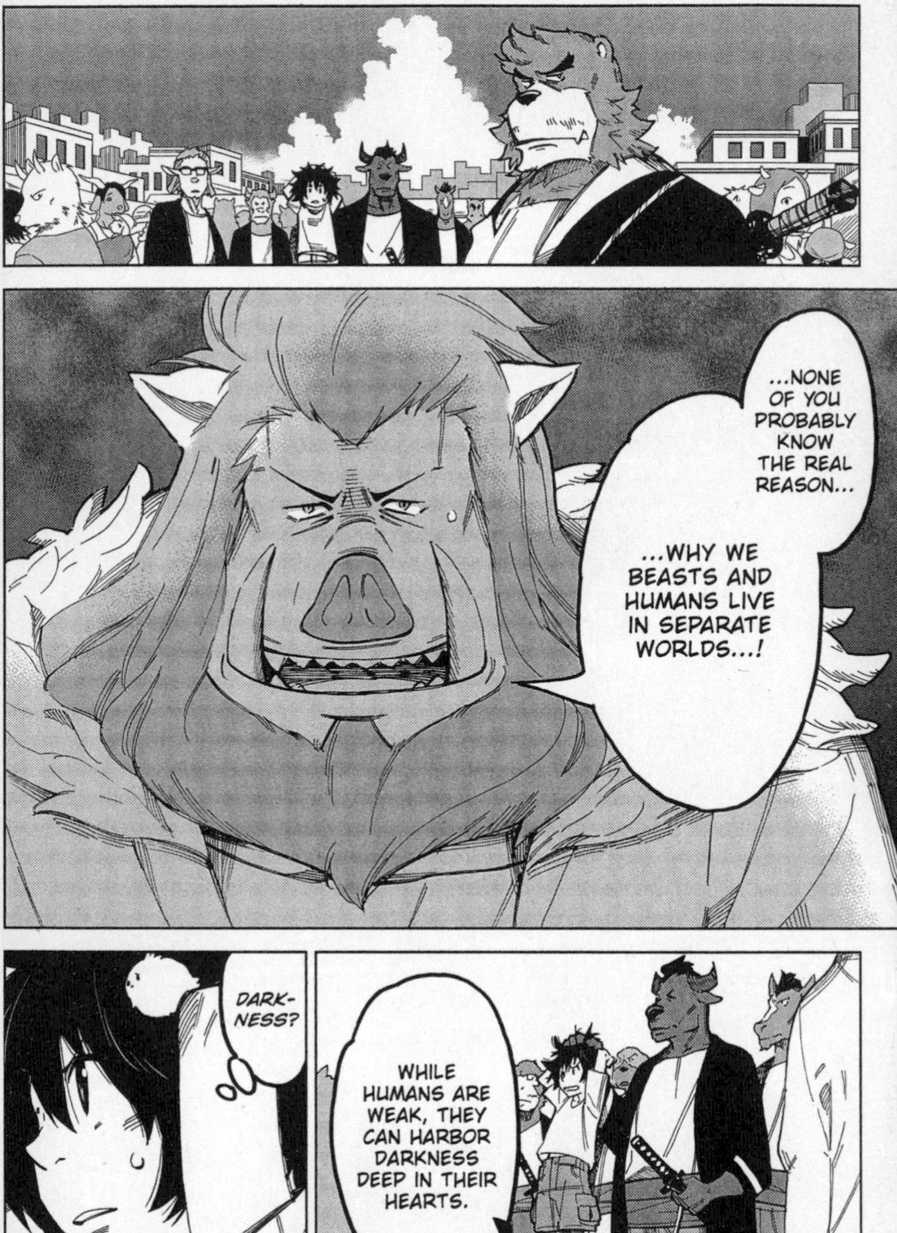
...NONE OF YOU PROBABLY KNOW THE REAL REASON...
...WHY WE BEASTS AND HUMANS LIVE IN SEPARATE WORLDS...!
WHILE HUMANS ARE WEAK, THEY CAN HARBOR DARKNESS DEEP IN THEIR HEARTS.
DARK-NESS?

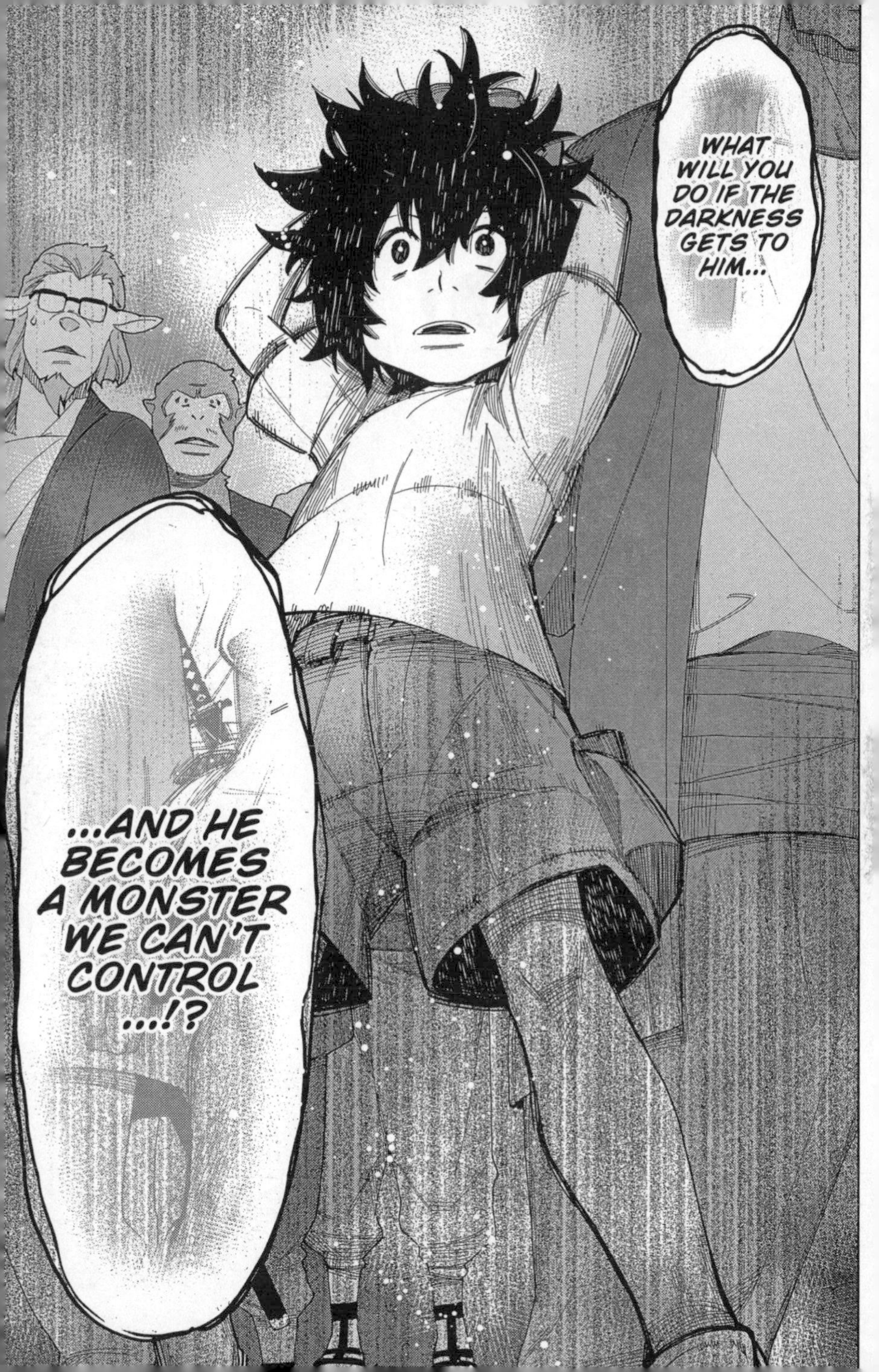
WHAT WILL YOU DO IF THE DARKNESS GETS TO HIM...
...AND HE BECOMES A MONSTER WE CAN'T CONTROL ...!?

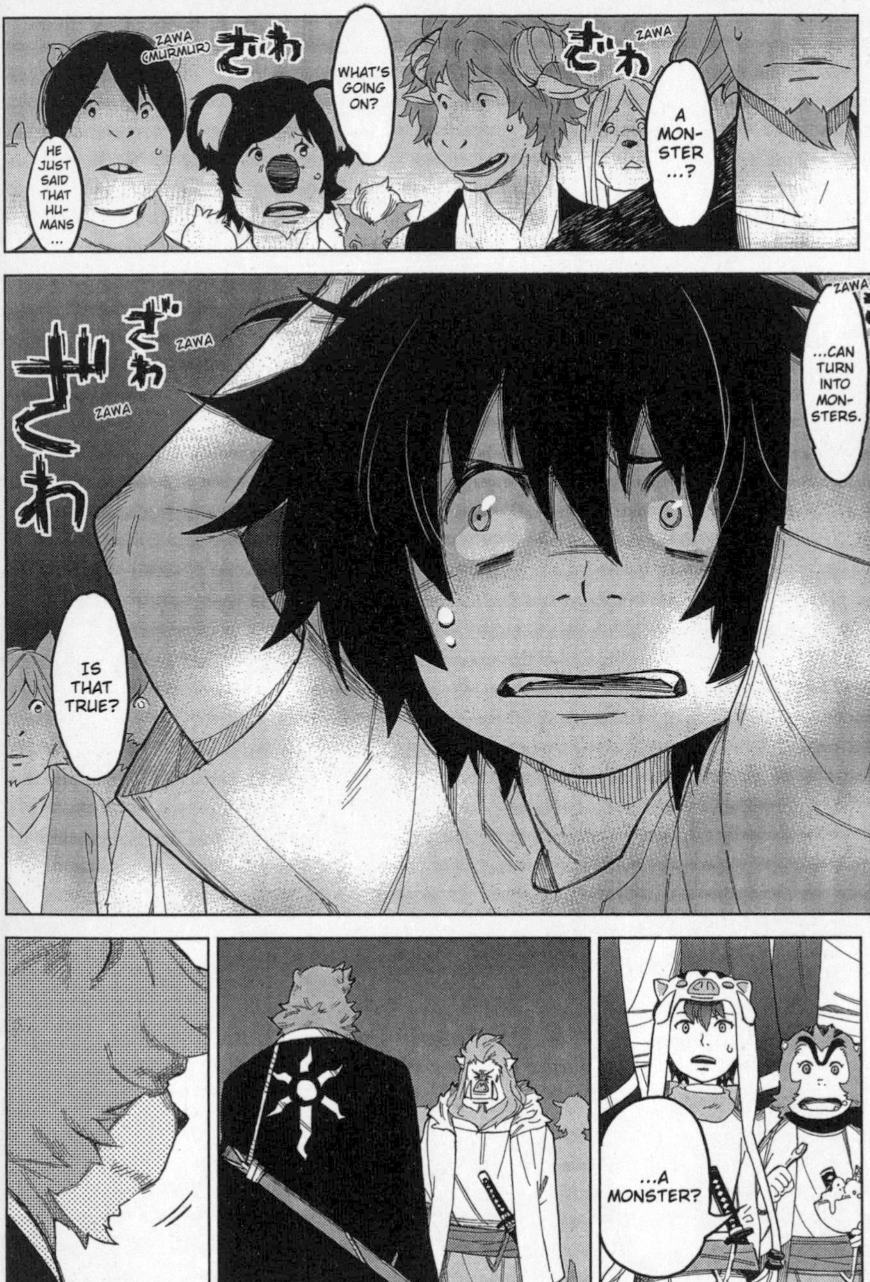
ZAWA
ざわ
A MONSTER...?
WHAT'S GOING ON?
ZAWA (MURMUR)
ざわ
HE JUST SAID THAT HUMANS...
ZAWA
ざわ
...CAN TURN INTO MONSTERS.
ZAWA
ざわ
ZAWA
ざわ
IS THAT TRUE?
...A MONSTER?

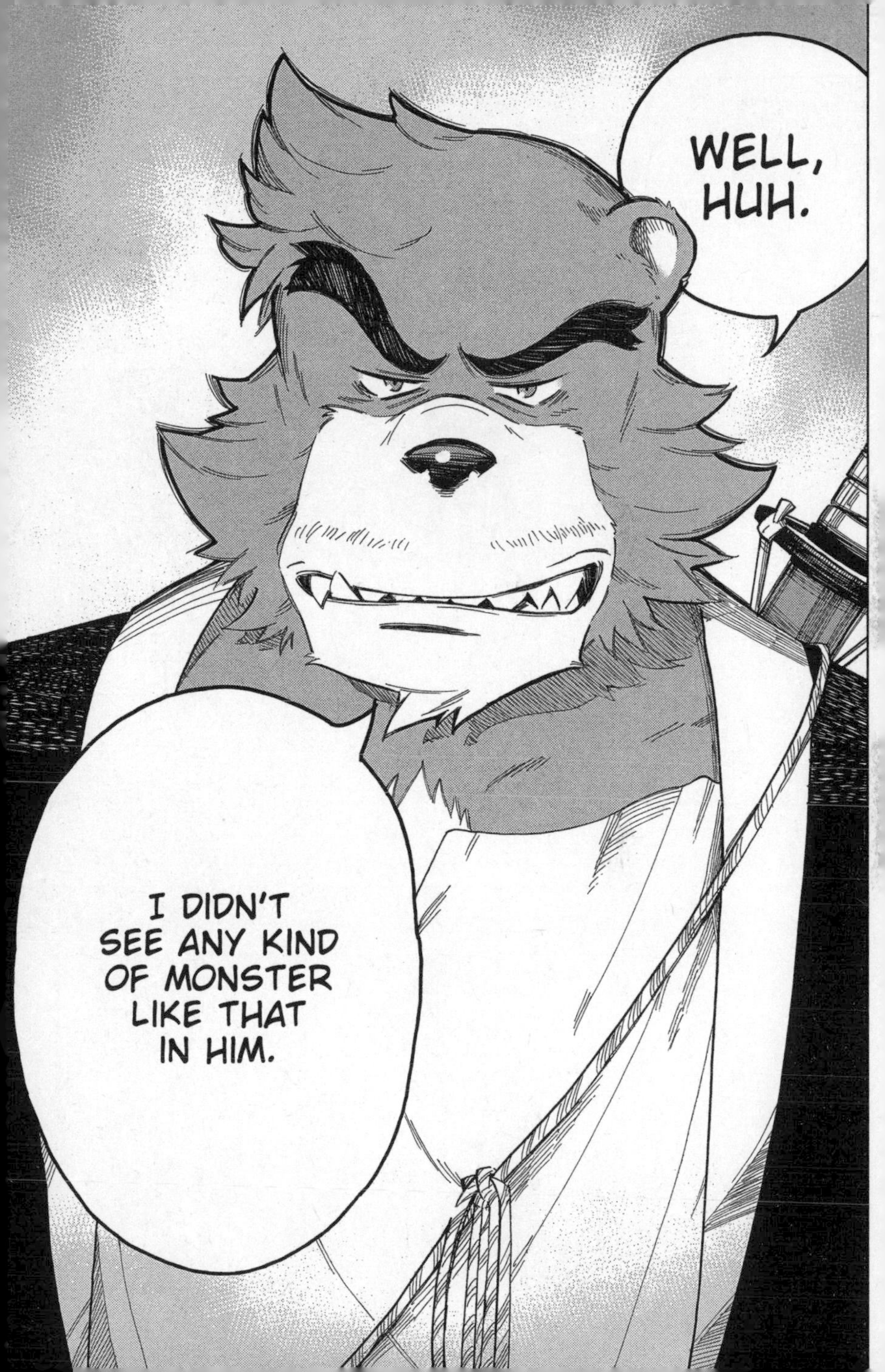
WELL, HUH.
I DIDN'T SEE ANY KIND OF MONSTER LIKE THAT IN HIM.

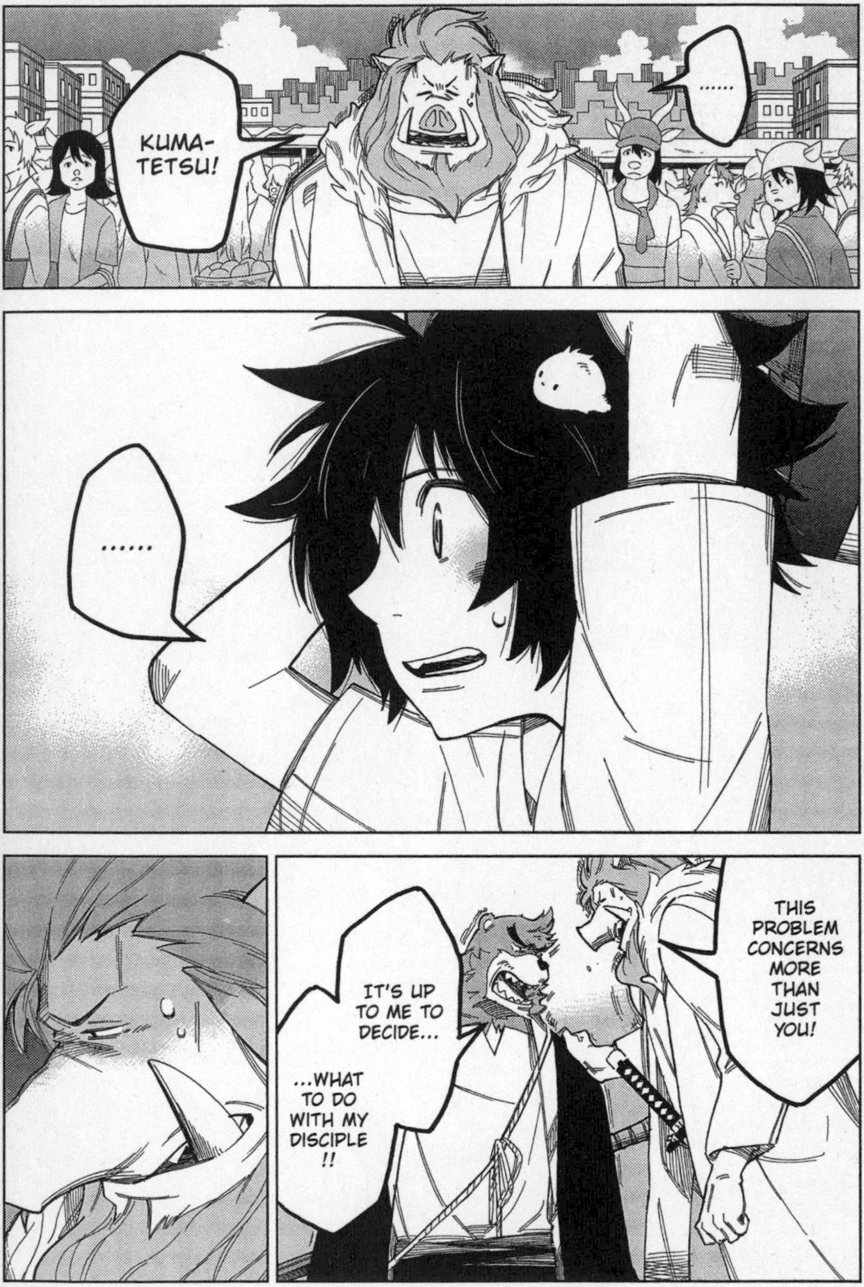
......
KUMA-TETSU!
......
THIS PROBLEM CONCERNS MORE THAN JUST YOU!
IT'S UP TO ME TO DECIDE...
...WHAT TO DO WITH MY DISCIPLE !!

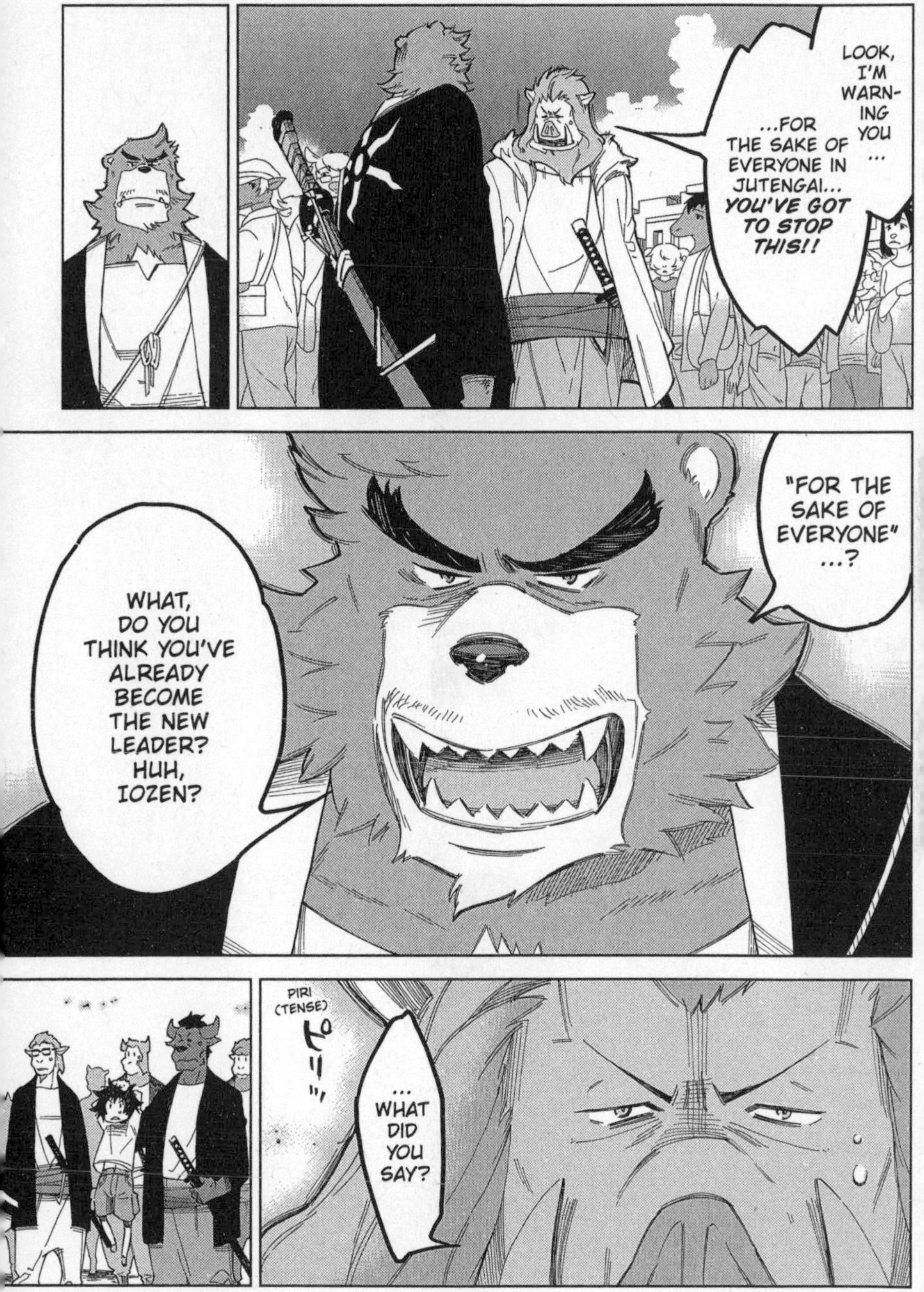
LOOK, I'M WARNING YOU ...
...FOR THE SAKE OF EVERYONE IN JUTENGAI... *YOU'VE GOT TO STOP THIS!!*
...
"FOR THE SAKE OF EVERYONE" ...?
WHAT, DO YOU THINK YOU'VE ALREADY BECOME THE NEW LEADER? HUH, IOZEN?
PIRI (TENSE)
... WHAT DID YOU SAY?

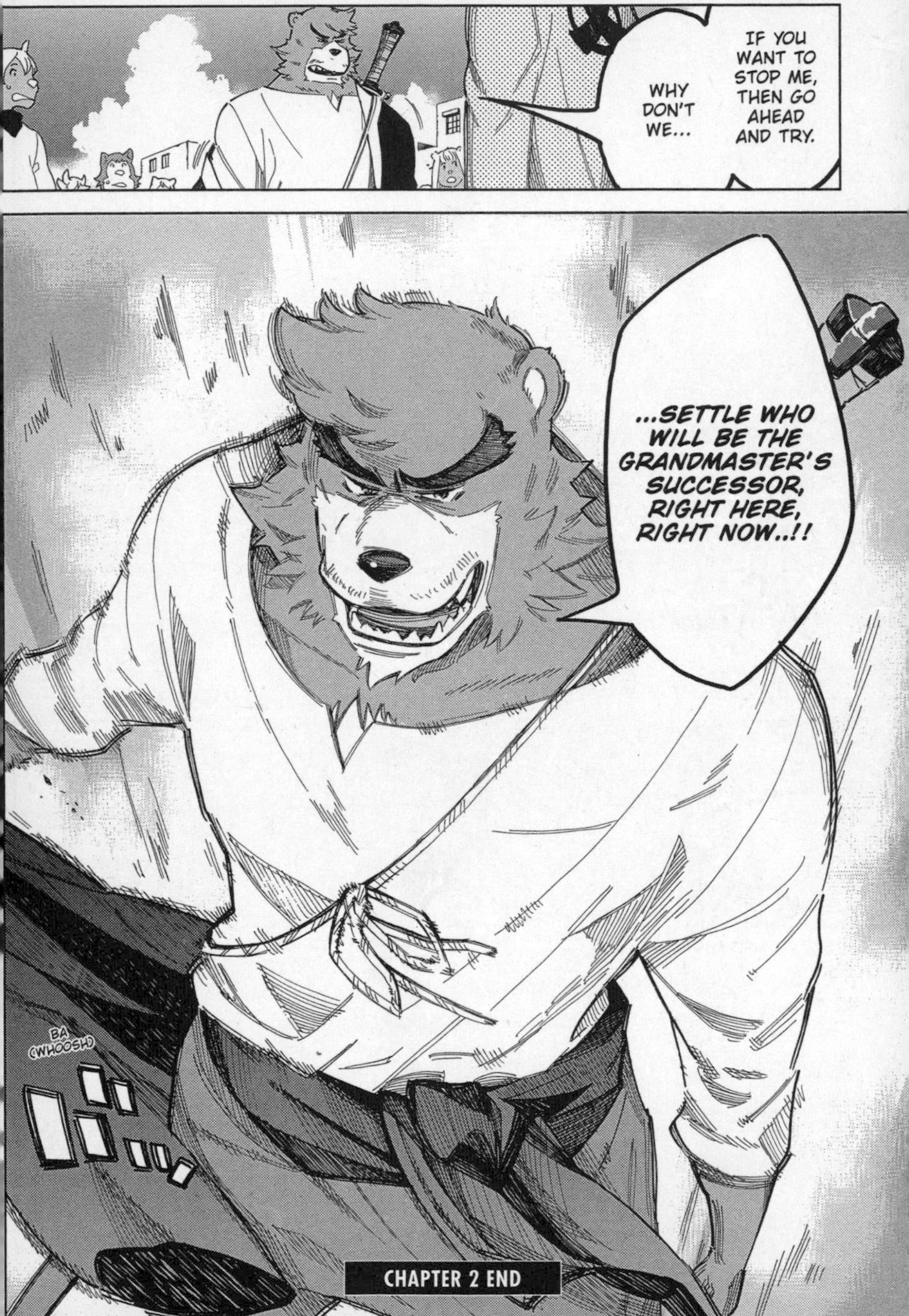
IF YOU WANT TO STOP ME, THEN GO AHEAD AND TRY.
WHY DON'T WE...
...SETTLE WHO WILL BE THE GRANDMASTER'S SUCCESSOR, RIGHT HERE, RIGHT NOW..!!
BA (WHOOSH)
CHAPTER 2 END

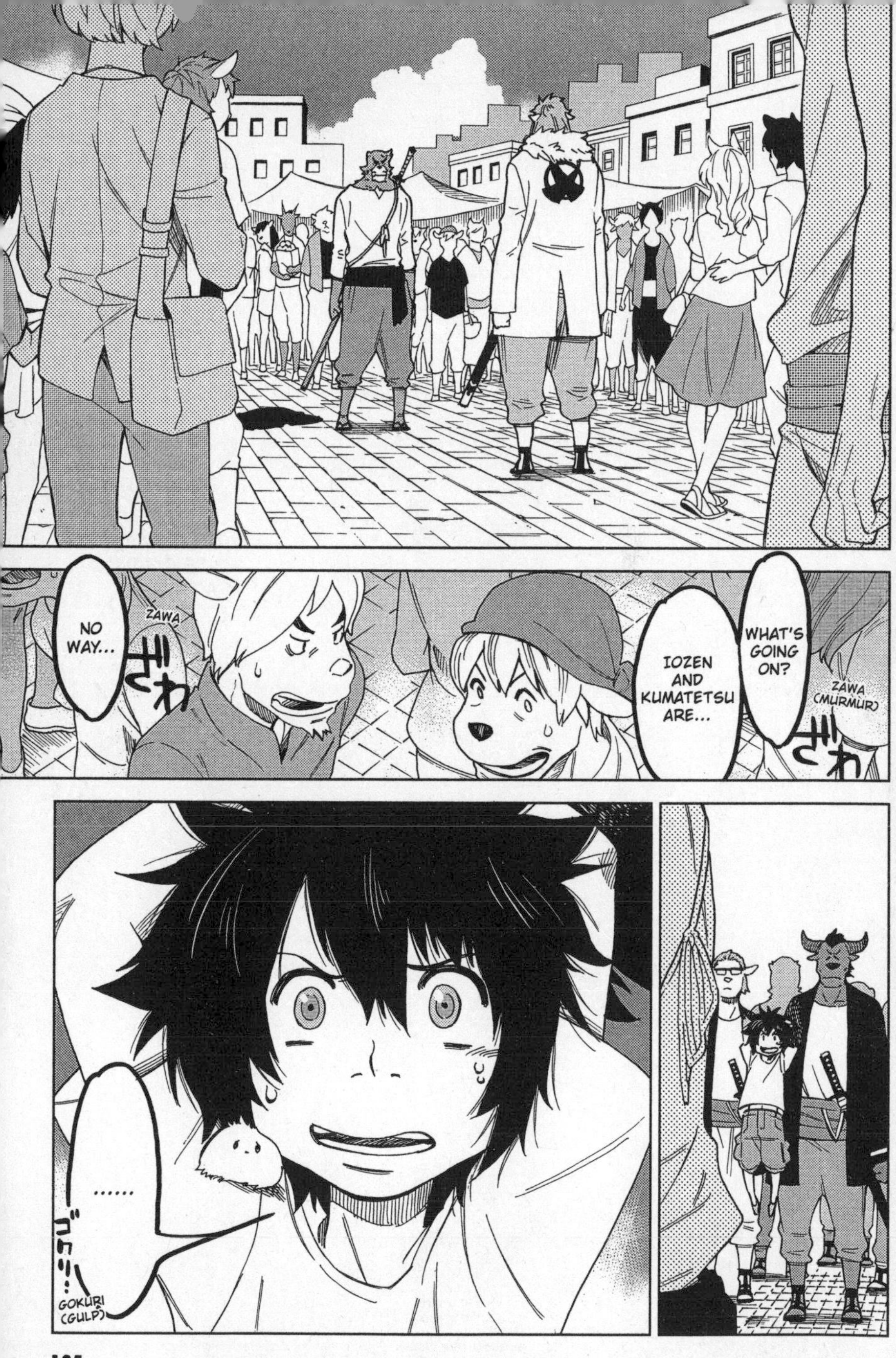

ZAWA (MURMUR)
ざわ
WHAT'S GOING ON?
IOZEN AND KUMATETSU ARE...
ZAWA
ざわ
NO WAY...
......
ゴクリ..
GOKURI (GULP)

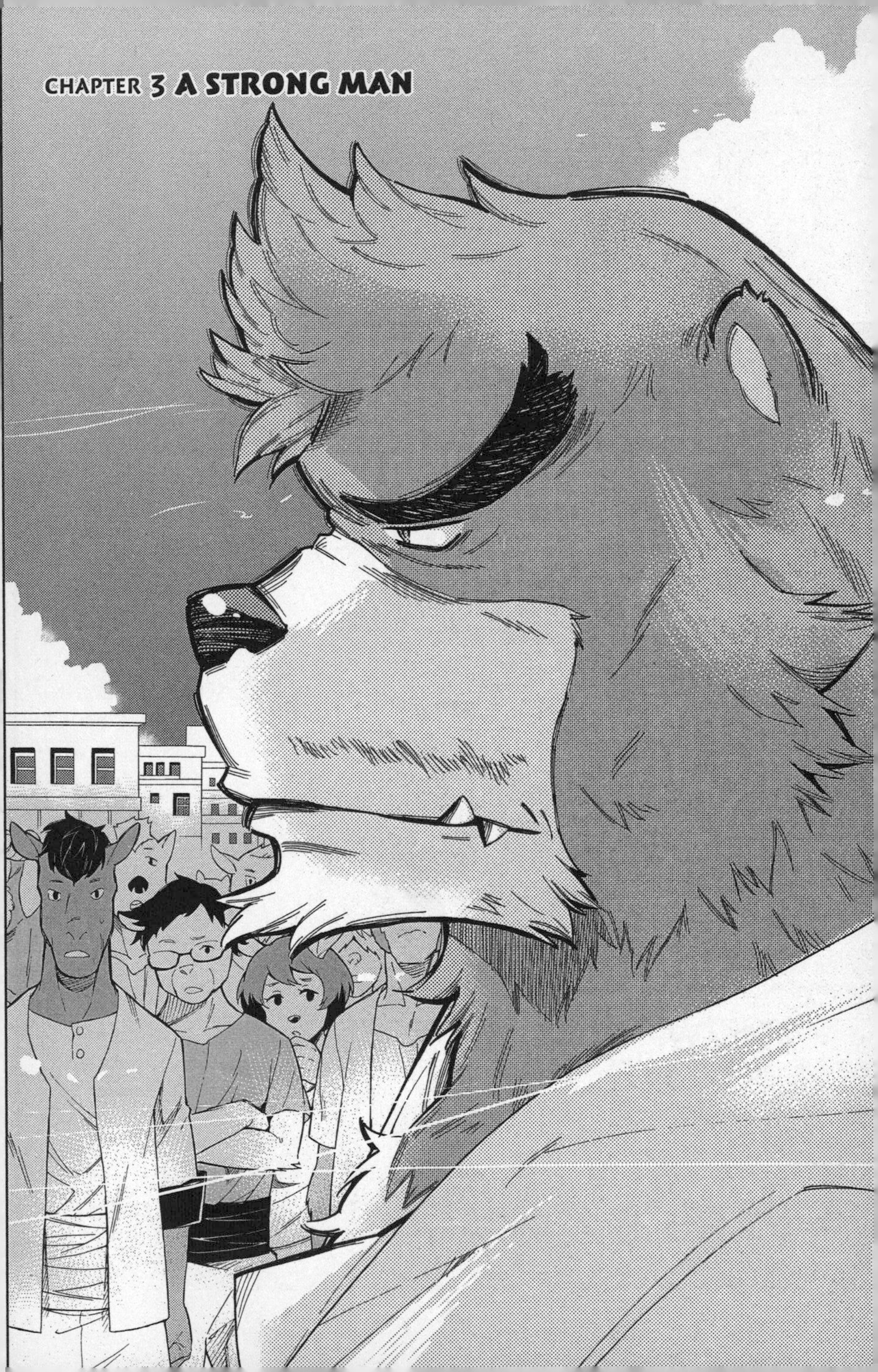
CHAPTER 3 A STRONG MAN

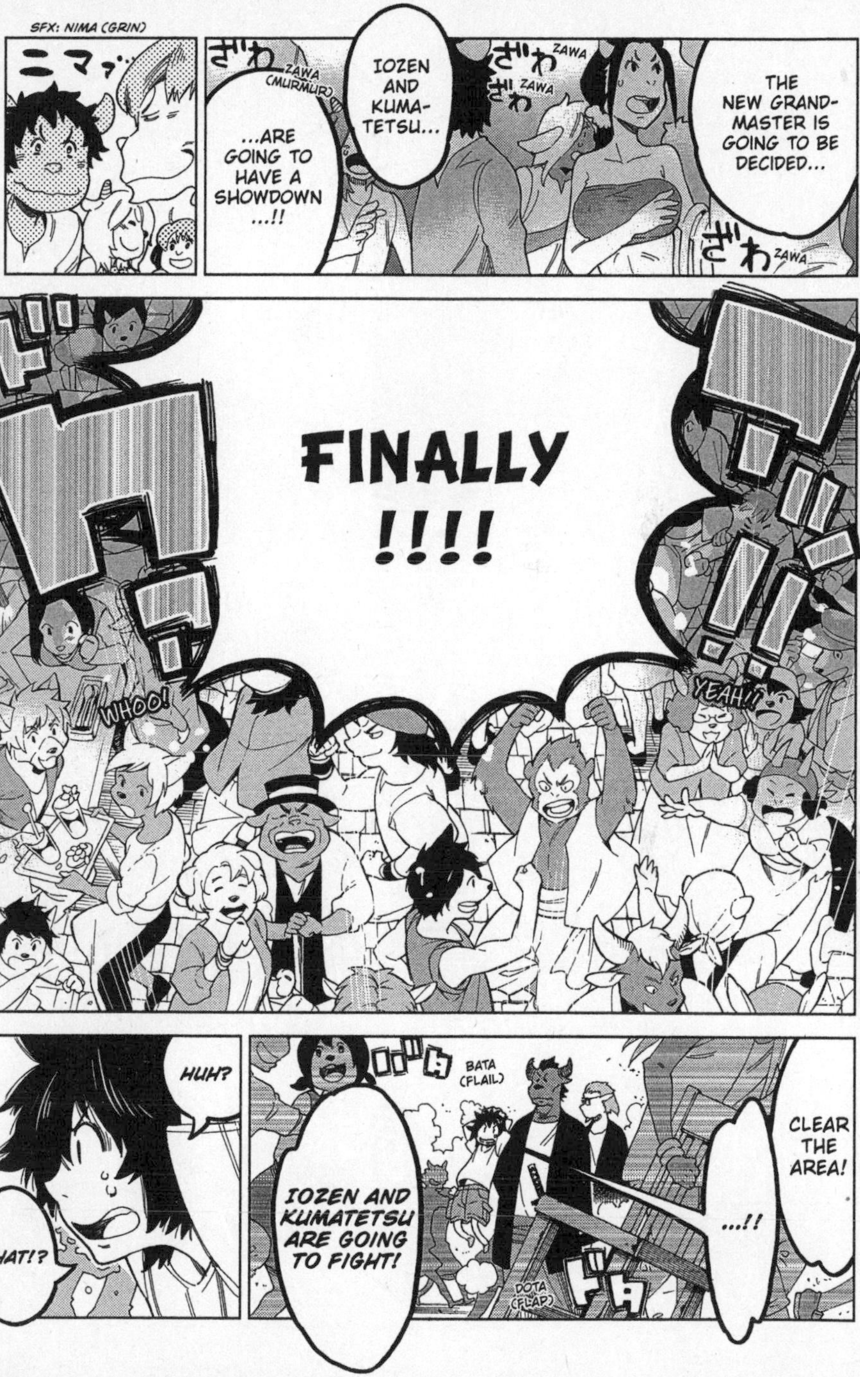
ざわ ZAWA
THE NEW GRAND-MASTER IS GOING TO BE DECIDED...
ざわ ZAWA
ざわ ZAWA
IOZEN AND KUMA-TETSU...
ざわ ZAWA (MURMUR)
...ARE GOING TO HAVE A SHOWDOWN ...!!
SFX: NIMA (GRIN)
ニマッ
FINALLY !!!!
YEAH!!
WHOO!
CLEAR THE AREA!
...!!
BATA (FLAIL)
IOZEN AND KUMATETSU ARE GOING TO FIGHT!
DOTA (FLAP)
HUH?
WHAT!?

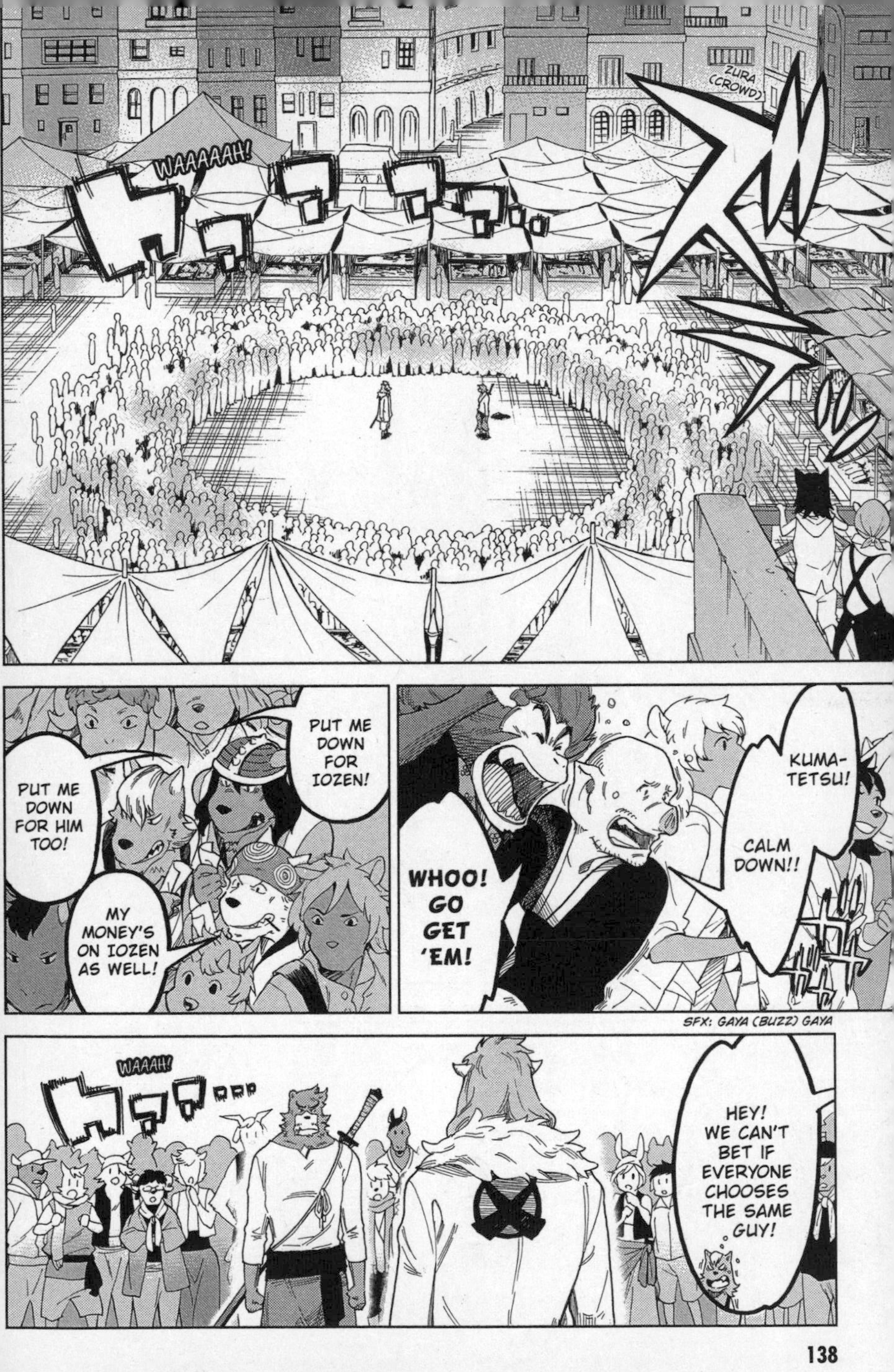
ZURA (CROWD)
WAAAAAH!
KUMA-TETSU!
CALM DOWN!!
WHOO! GO GET 'EM!
SFX: GAYA (BUZZ) GAYA
PUT ME DOWN FOR IOZEN!
PUT ME DOWN FOR HIM TOO!
MY MONEY'S ON IOZEN AS WELL!
HEY! WE CAN'T BET IF EVERYONE CHOOSES THE SAME GUY!
WAAAH!

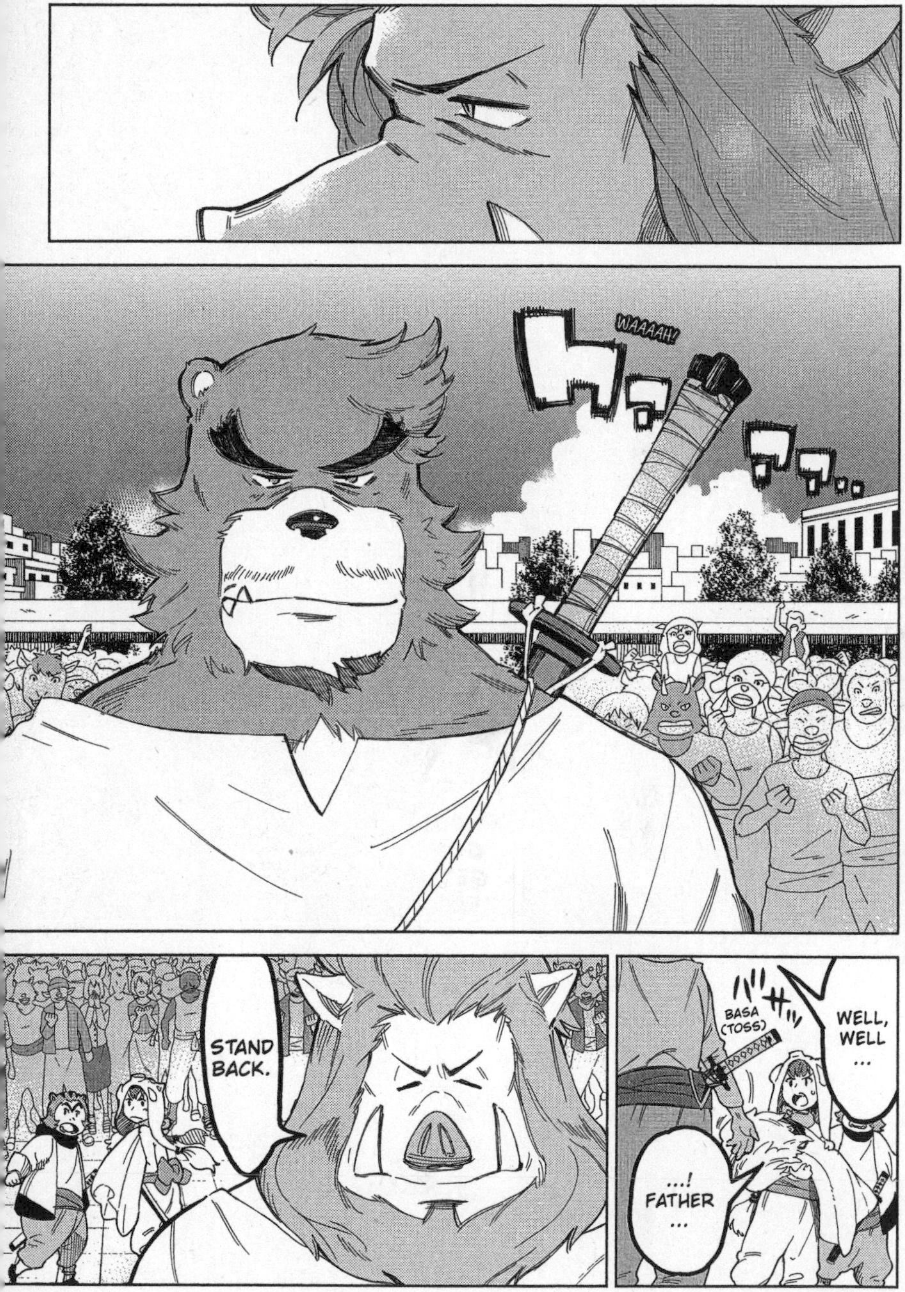
WAAAAH!
WELL, WELL ...
BASA (TOSS)
...! FATHER ...
STAND BACK.

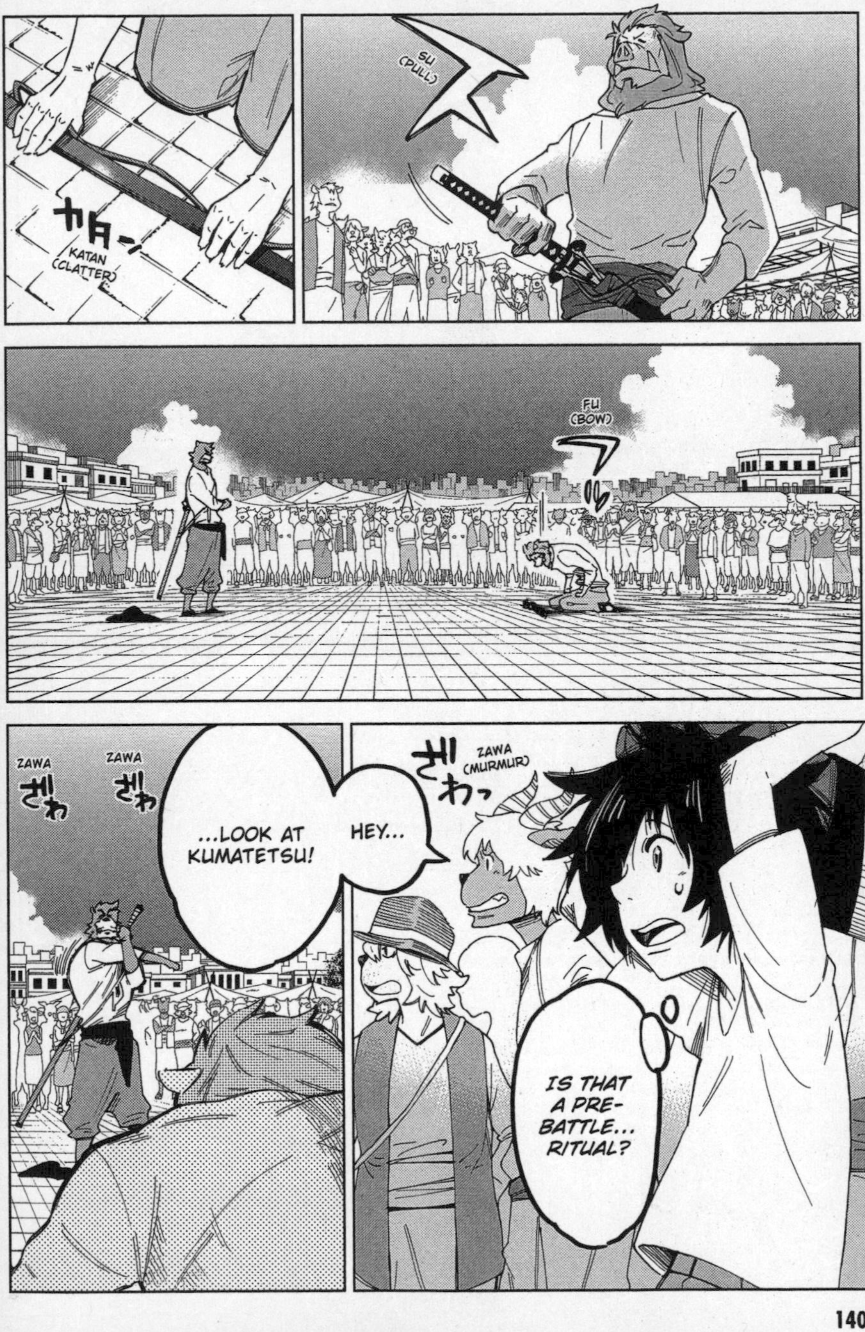
SU (PULL)
カタン
KATAN (CLATTER)
FU (BOW)
ざわっ
ZAWA (MURMUR)
HEY...
...LOOK AT KUMATETSU!
IS THAT A PRE-BATTLE... RITUAL?
ざわ
ZAWA
ざわ
ZAWA

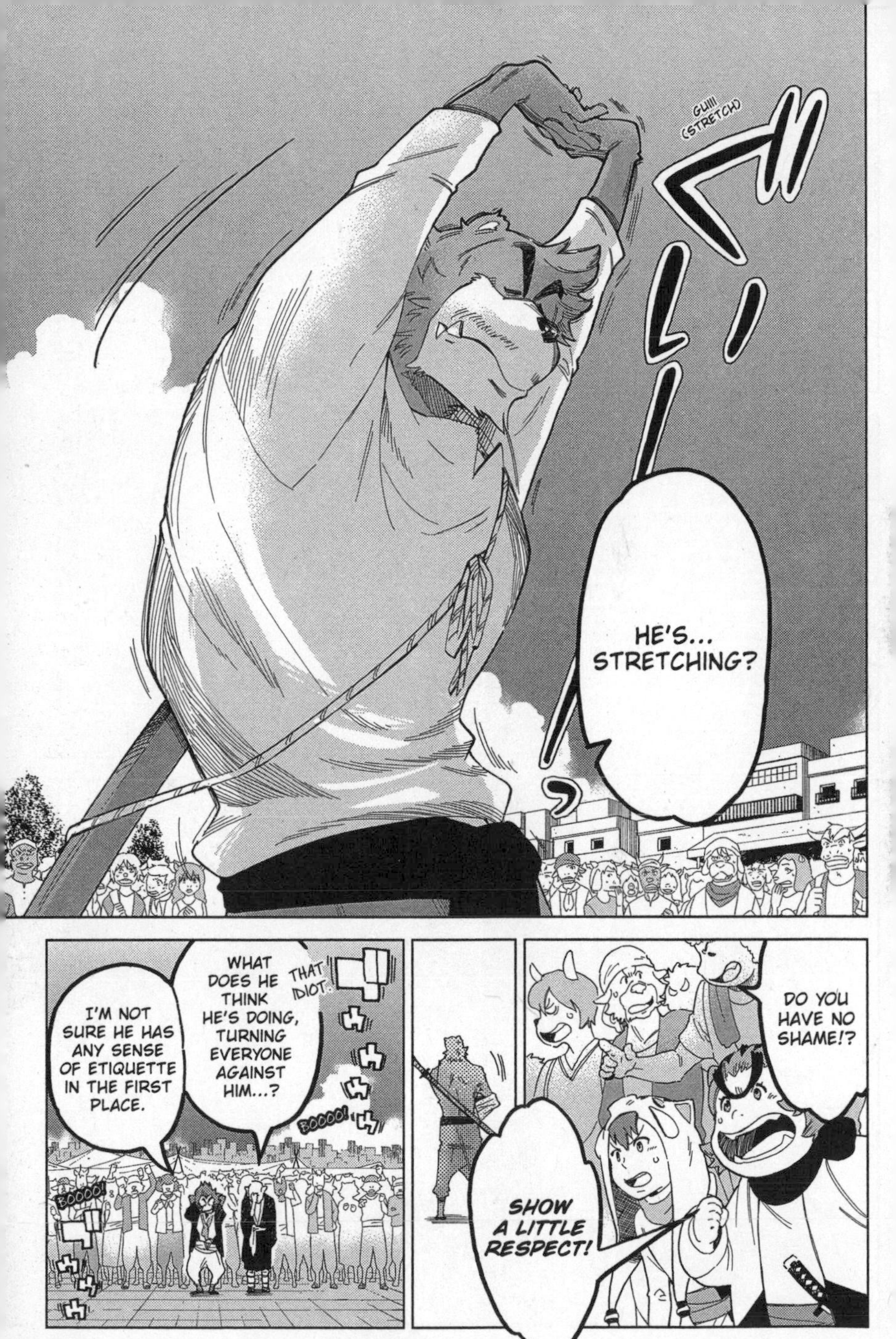
GUIII (STRETCH)
HE'S... STRETCHING?
DO YOU HAVE NO SHAME!?
SHOW A LITTLE RESPECT!
THAT IDIOT.
WHAT DOES HE THINK HE'S DOING, TURNING EVERYONE AGAINST HIM...?
I'M NOT SURE HE HAS ANY SENSE OF ETIQUETTE IN THE FIRST PLACE.
BOOOO!
BOOOO!

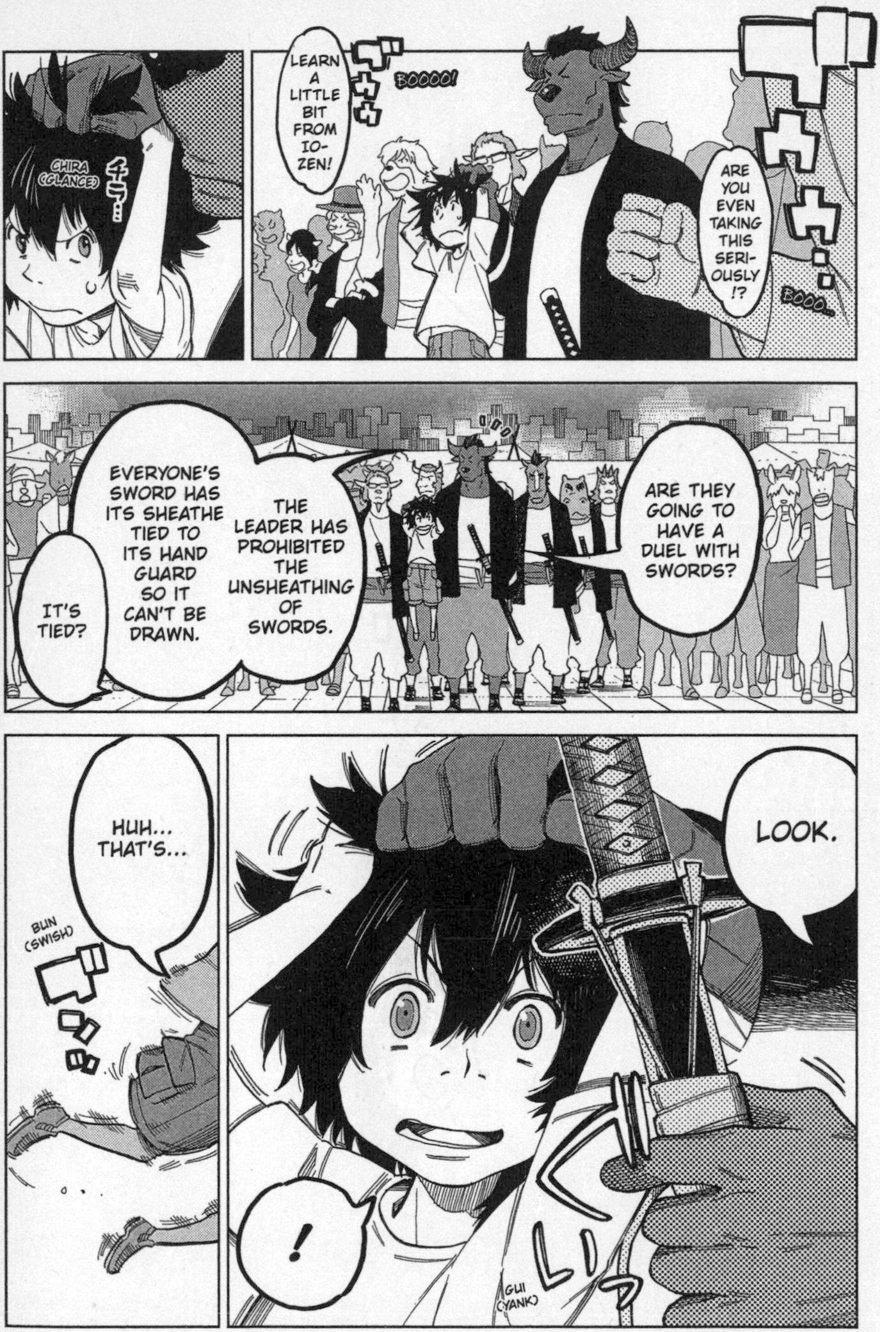
ARE YOU EVEN TAKING THIS SERIOUSLY!?
BOOO...
BOOOO!
LEARN A LITTLE BIT FROM IO-ZEN!
CHIRA (GLANCE)
ARE THEY GOING TO HAVE A DUEL WITH SWORDS?
THE LEADER HAS PROHIBITED THE UNSHEATHING OF SWORDS.
EVERYONE'S SWORD HAS ITS SHEATHE TIED TO ITS HAND GUARD SO IT CAN'T BE DRAWN.
IT'S TIED?
LOOK.
!
GUI (YANK)
HUH... THAT'S...
BUN (SWISH)

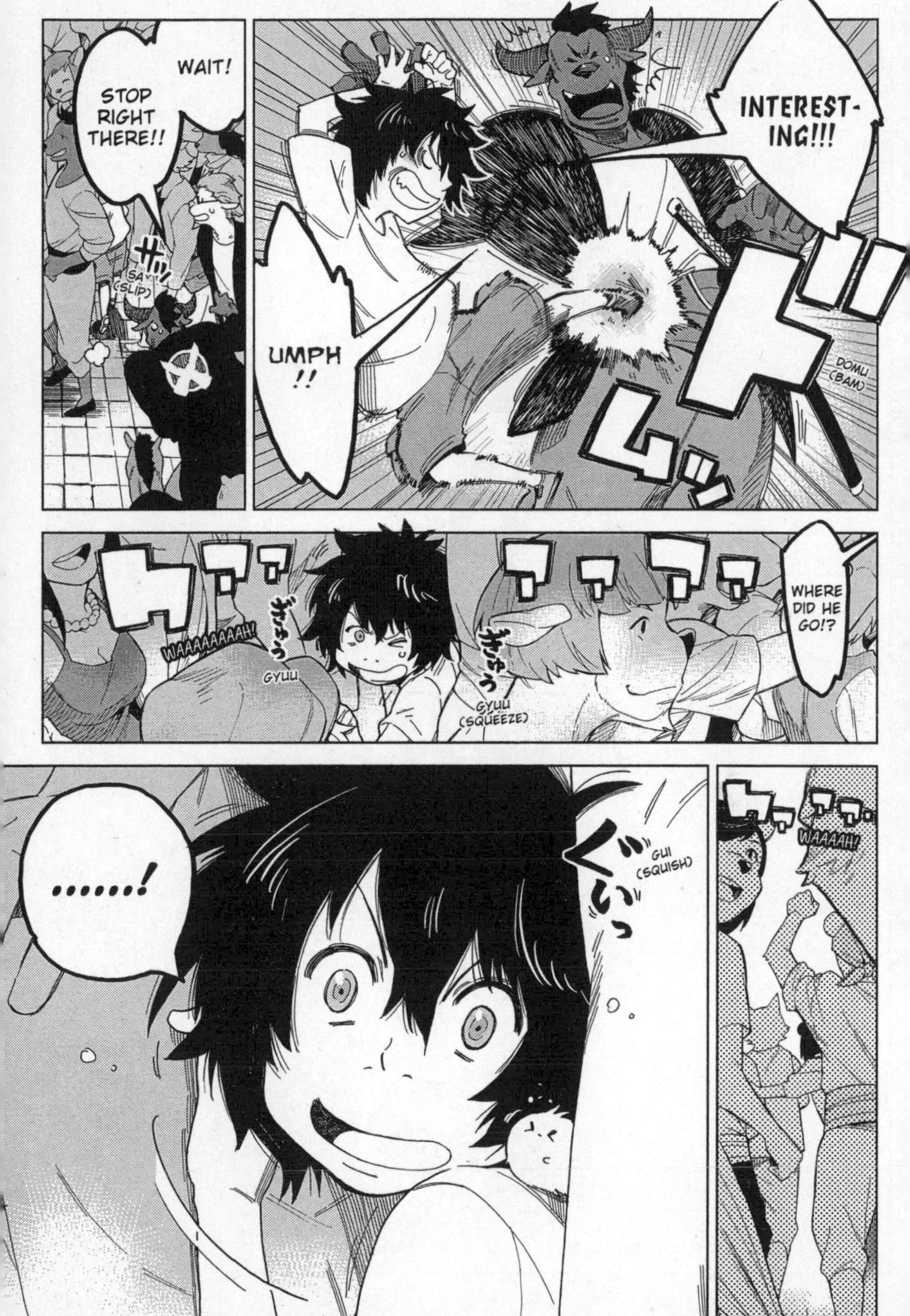
INTEREST-ING!!!
UMPH!!
DOMU (BAM)
WAIT! STOP RIGHT THERE!!
SA (SLIP)
WHERE DID HE GO!?
ぎゅう
GYUU (SQUEEZE)
ぎゅう
GYUU
WAAAAAAAAH!
WAAAAH!
GUI (SQUISH)
......!

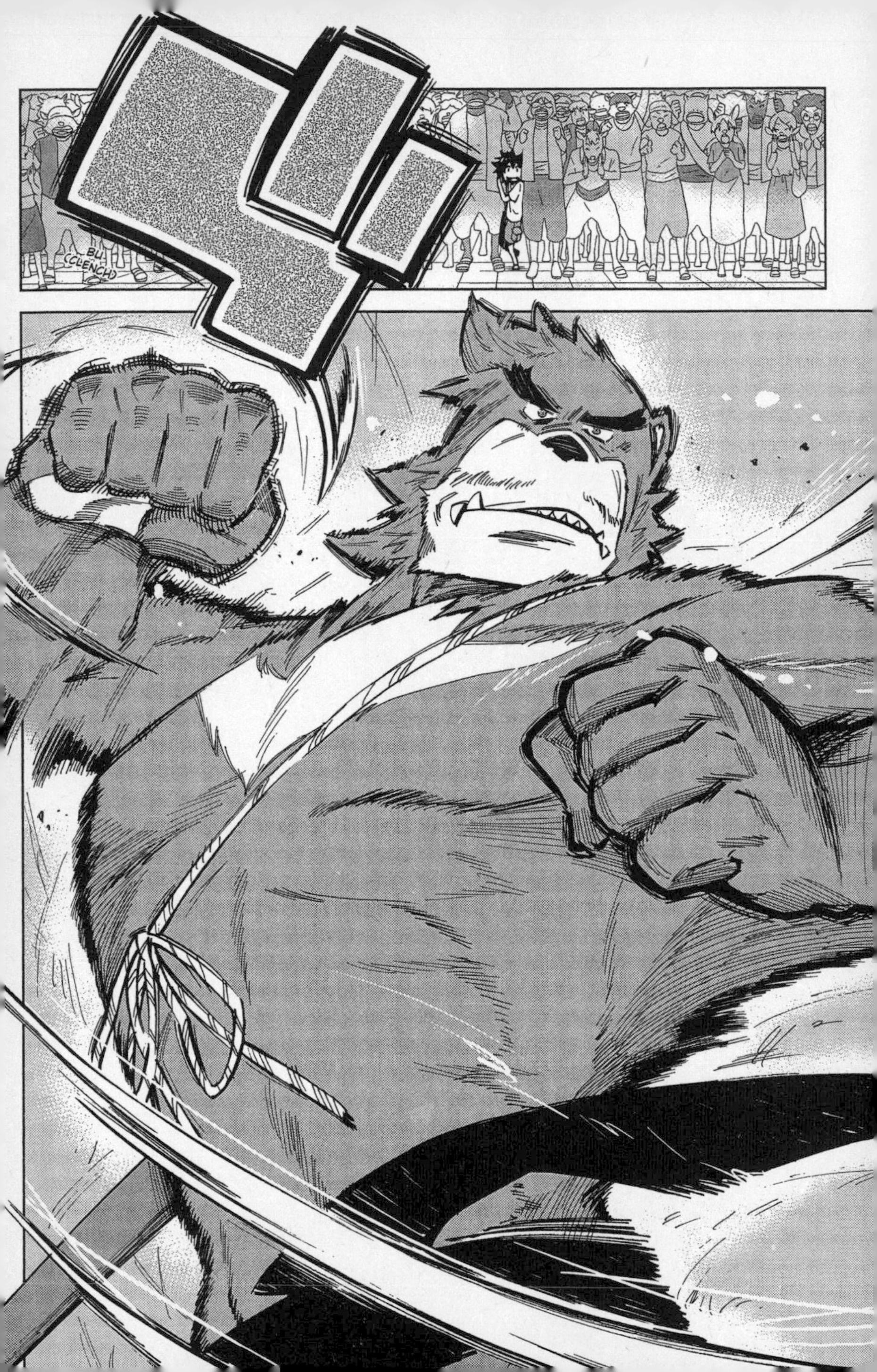
BU (CLENCH)

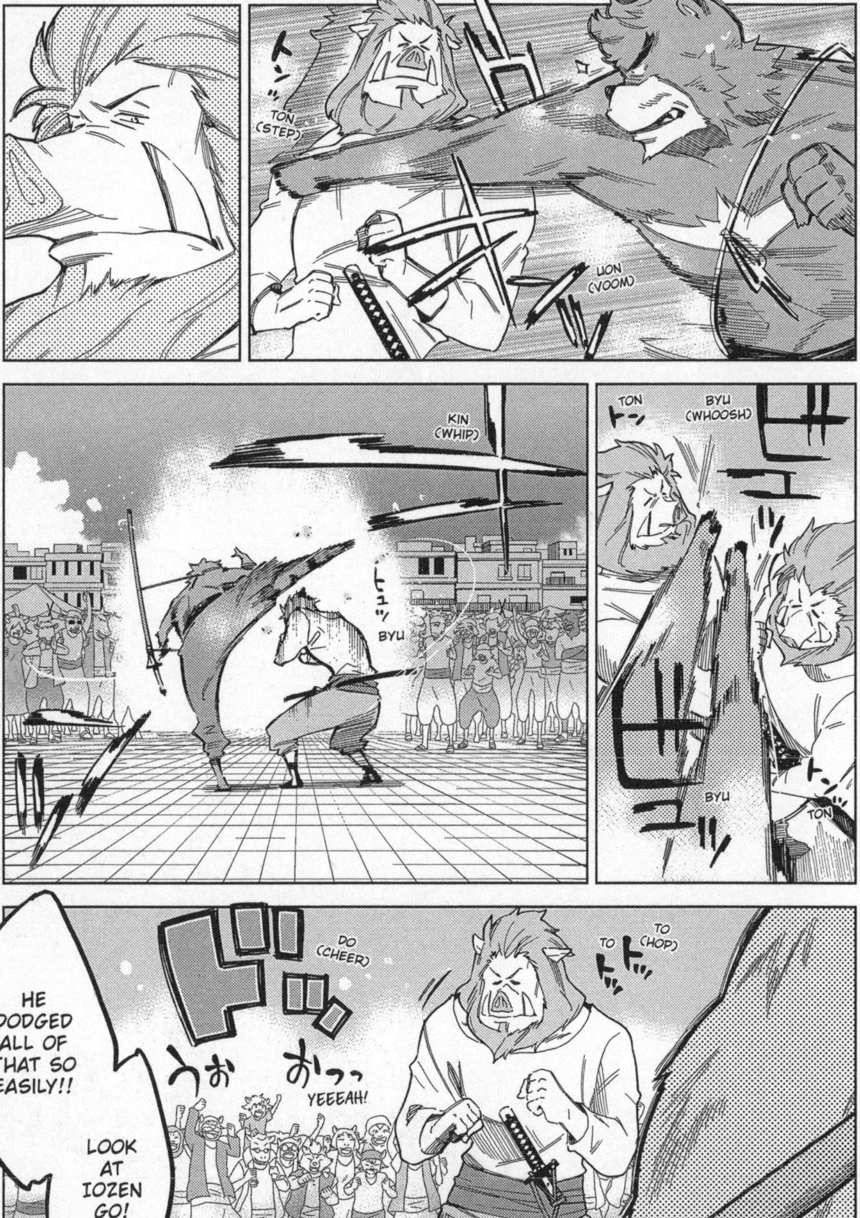
TON (STEP)
UON (VOOM)
TON
BYU (WHOOSH)
BYU
TON
KIN (WHIP)
BYU
TO TO (HOP)
DO (CHEER)
うお おっっ
YEEEAH!
HE DODGED ALL OF THAT SO EASILY!! LOOK AT IOZEN GO!

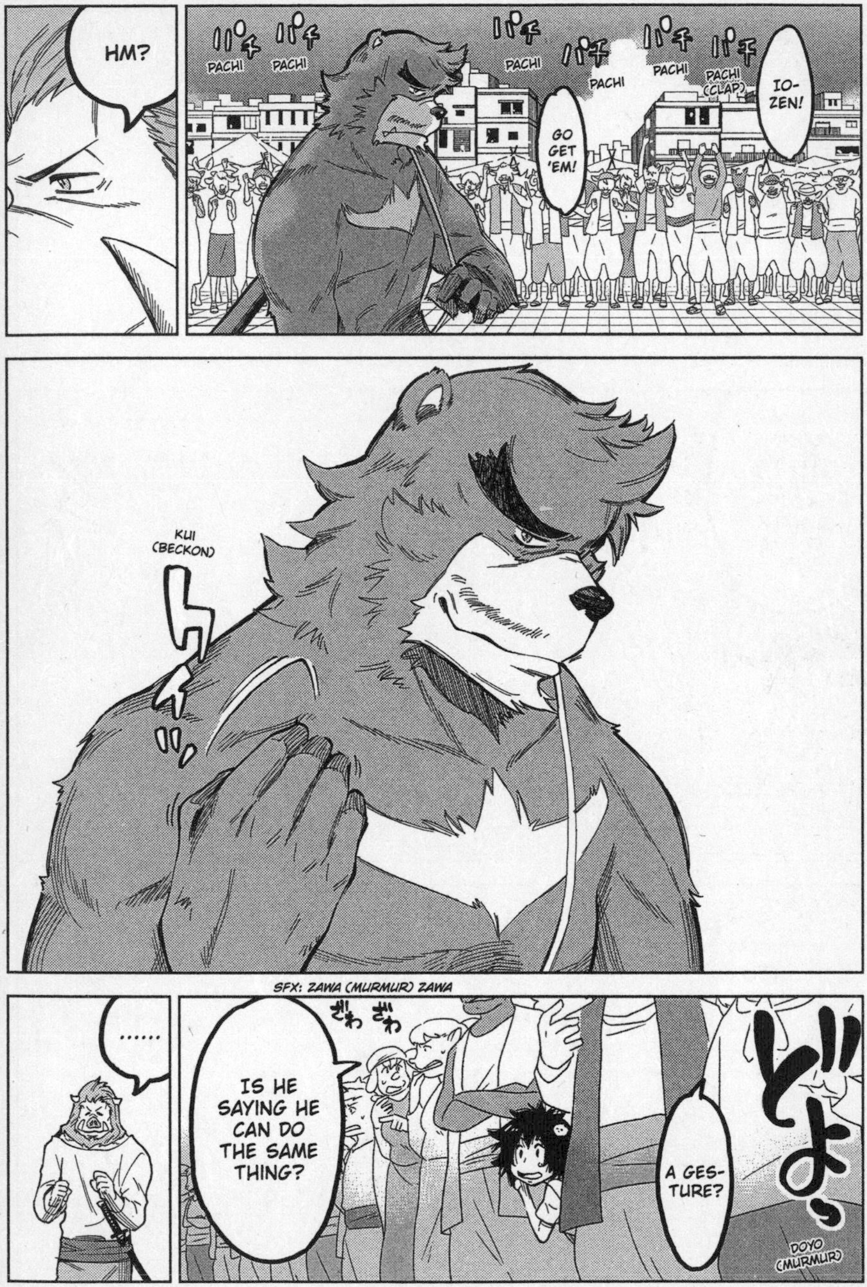
PACHI (CLAP)
PACHI
PACHI
PACHI
PACHI
PACHI
IO-ZEN!
GO GET 'EM!
HM?
KUI (BECKON)
SFX: ZAWA (MURMUR) ZAWA
DOYO (MURMUR)
A GES-TURE?
IS HE SAYING HE CAN DO THE SAME THING?
......

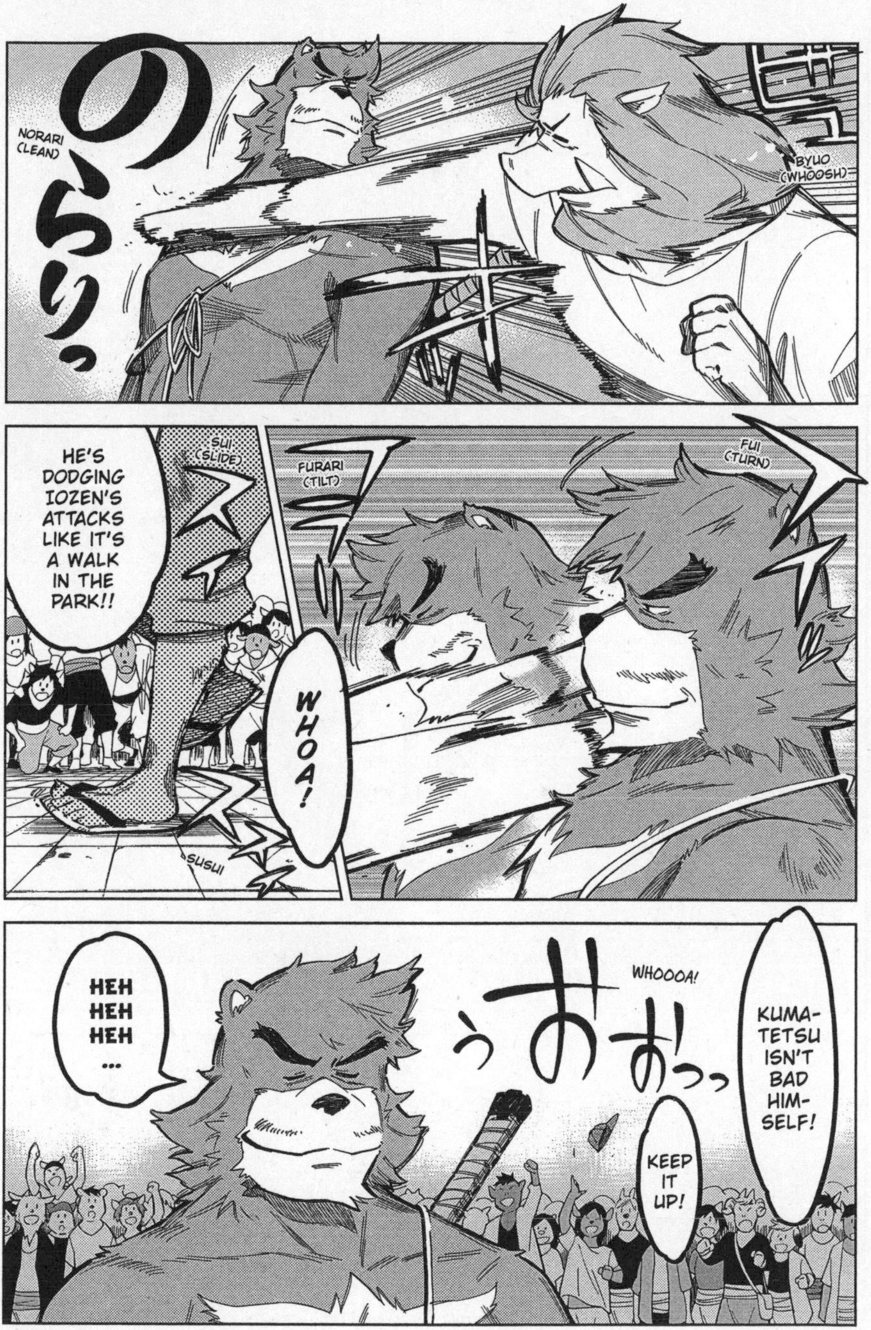
BYUO (WHOOSH)
のらりっ
NORARI (LEAN)
FUI (TURN)
FURARI (TILT)
SUI (SLIDE)
HE'S DODGING IOZEN'S ATTACKS LIKE IT'S A WALK IN THE PARK!!
WHOA!
SUSUI
KUMA-TETSU ISN'T BAD HIM-SELF!
うおおっっ
WHOOOA!
KEEP IT UP!
HEH HEH HEH ...

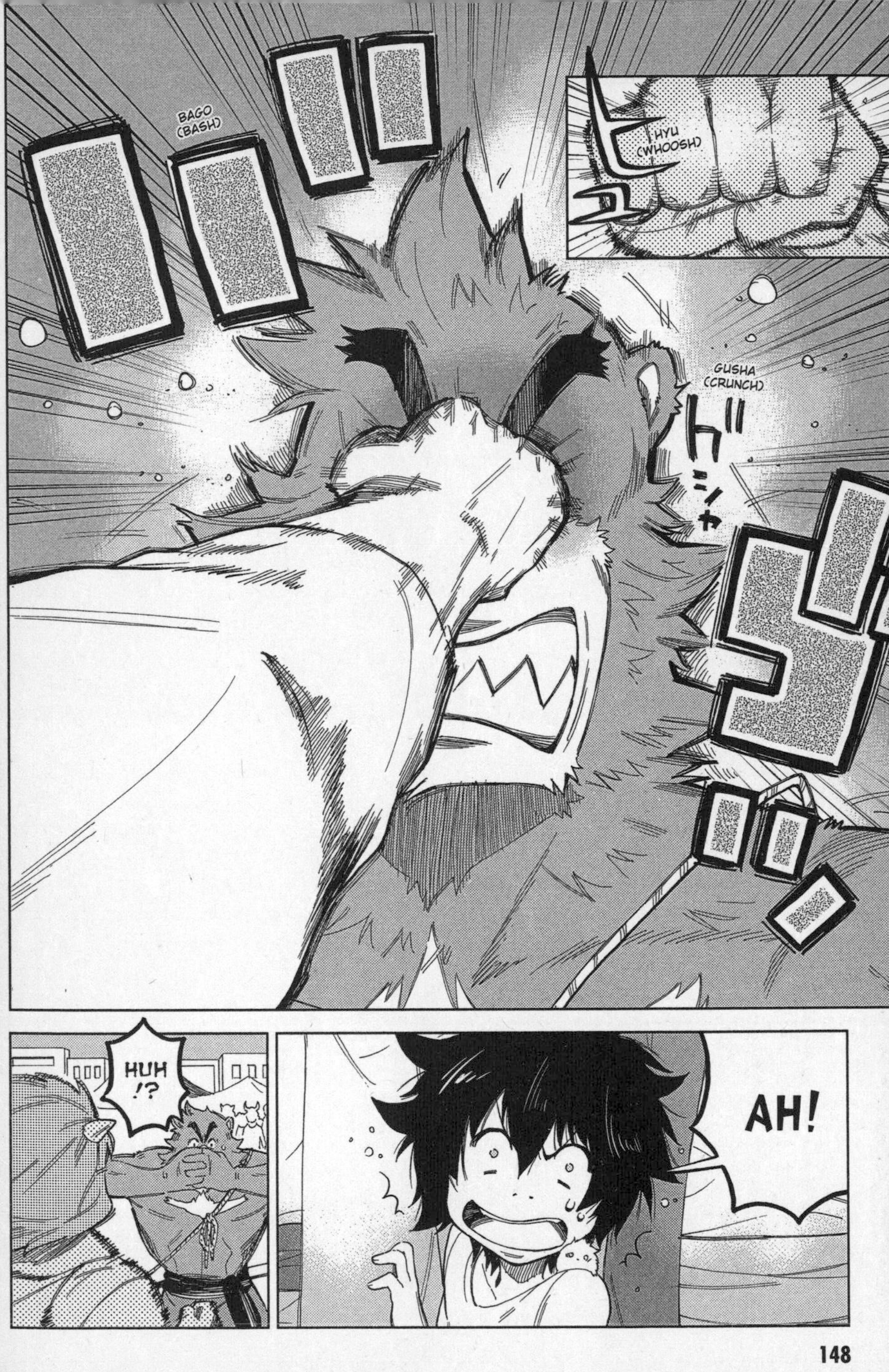
HYU (WHOOSH)
BAGO (BASH)
GUSHA (CRUNCH)
AH!
HUH!?

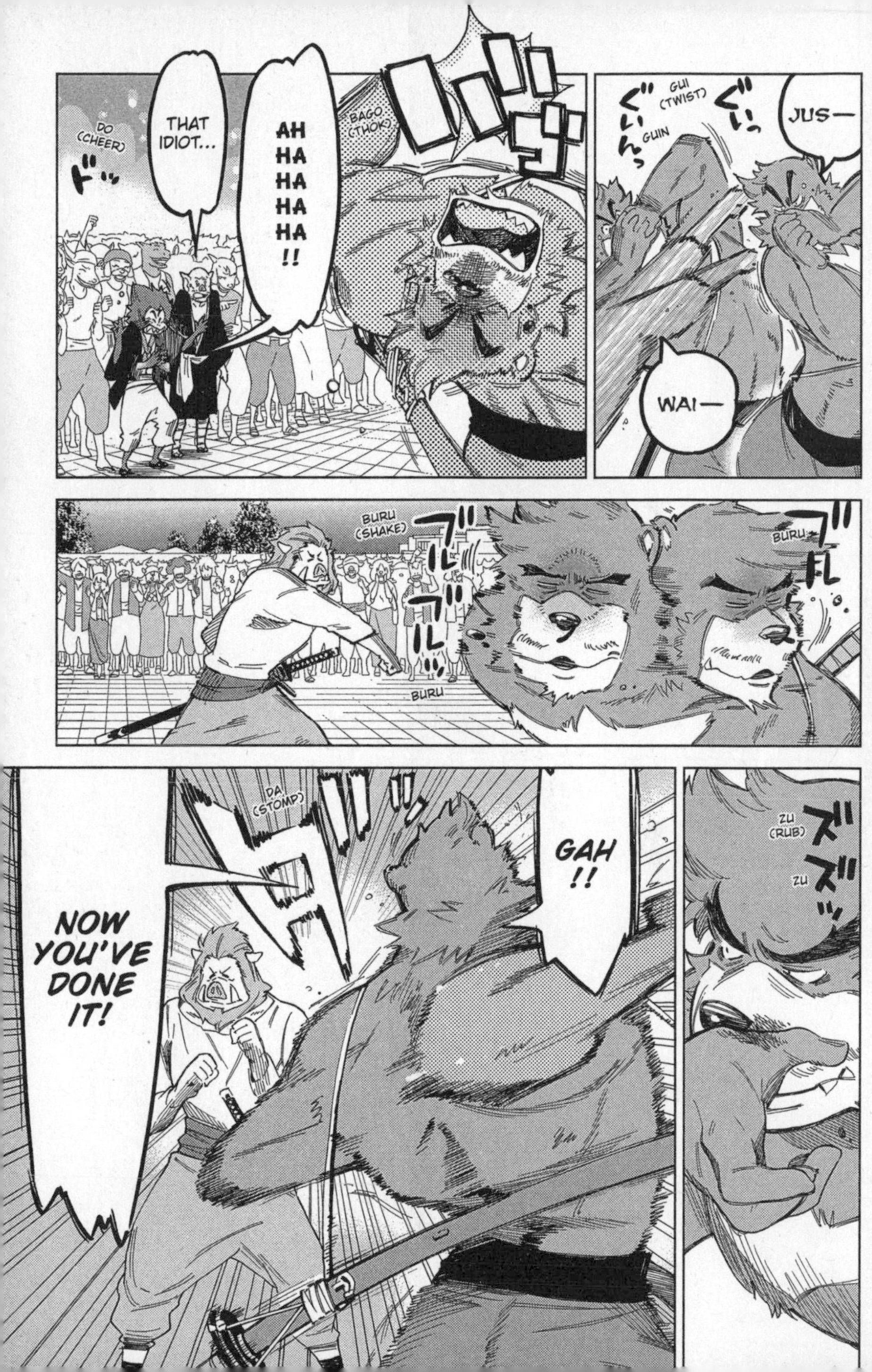
JUS—
GUI (TWIST)
GUIN
WAI—
BAGO (THOK)
AH HA HA HA HA!!
THAT IDIOT...
DO (CHEER)
BURU
BURU (SHAKE)
BURU
ZU (RUB)
ZU
GAH!!
DA (STOMP)
NOW YOU'VE DONE IT!

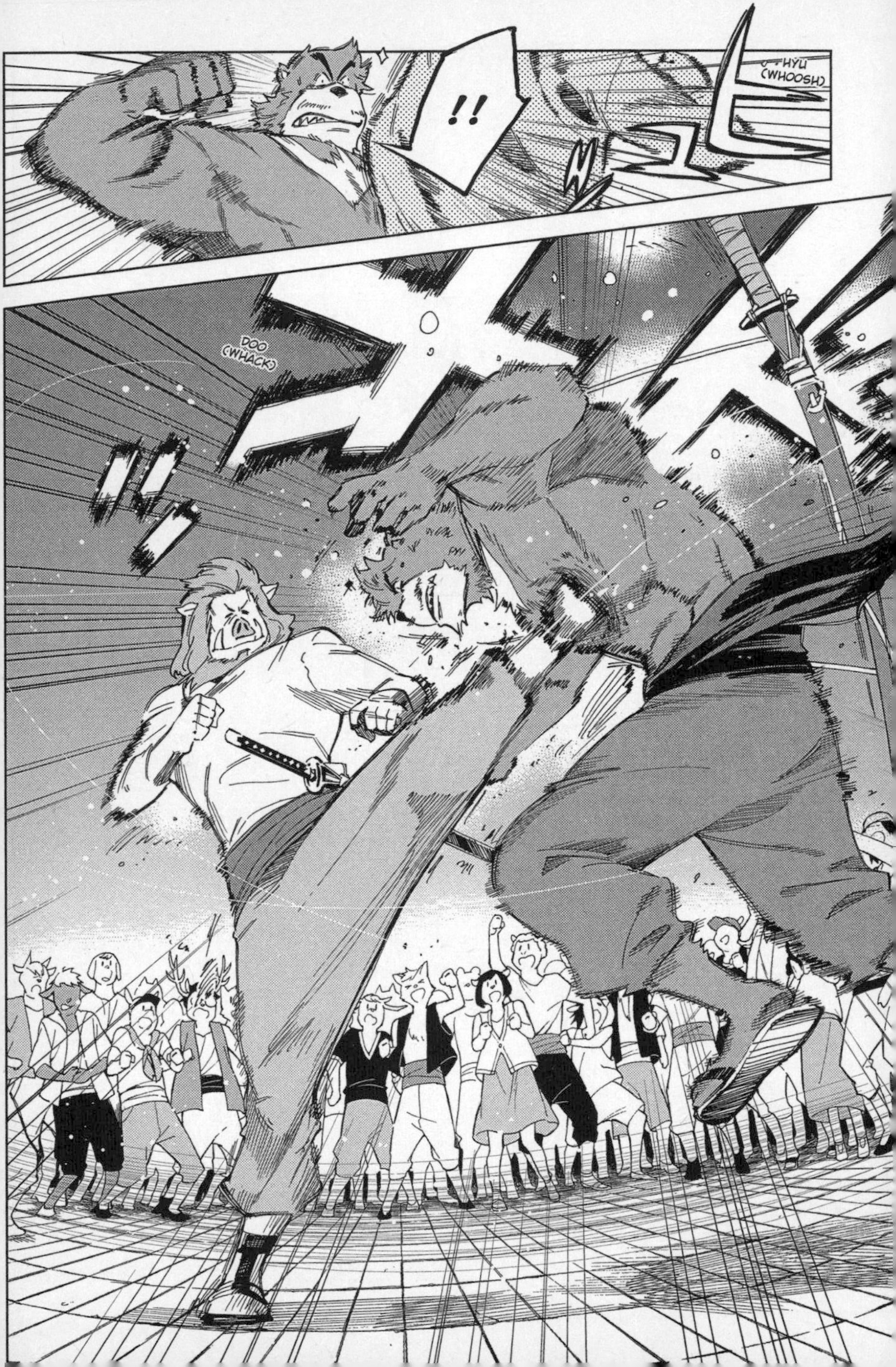
HYU (WHOOSH)
!!
DOO (WHACK)

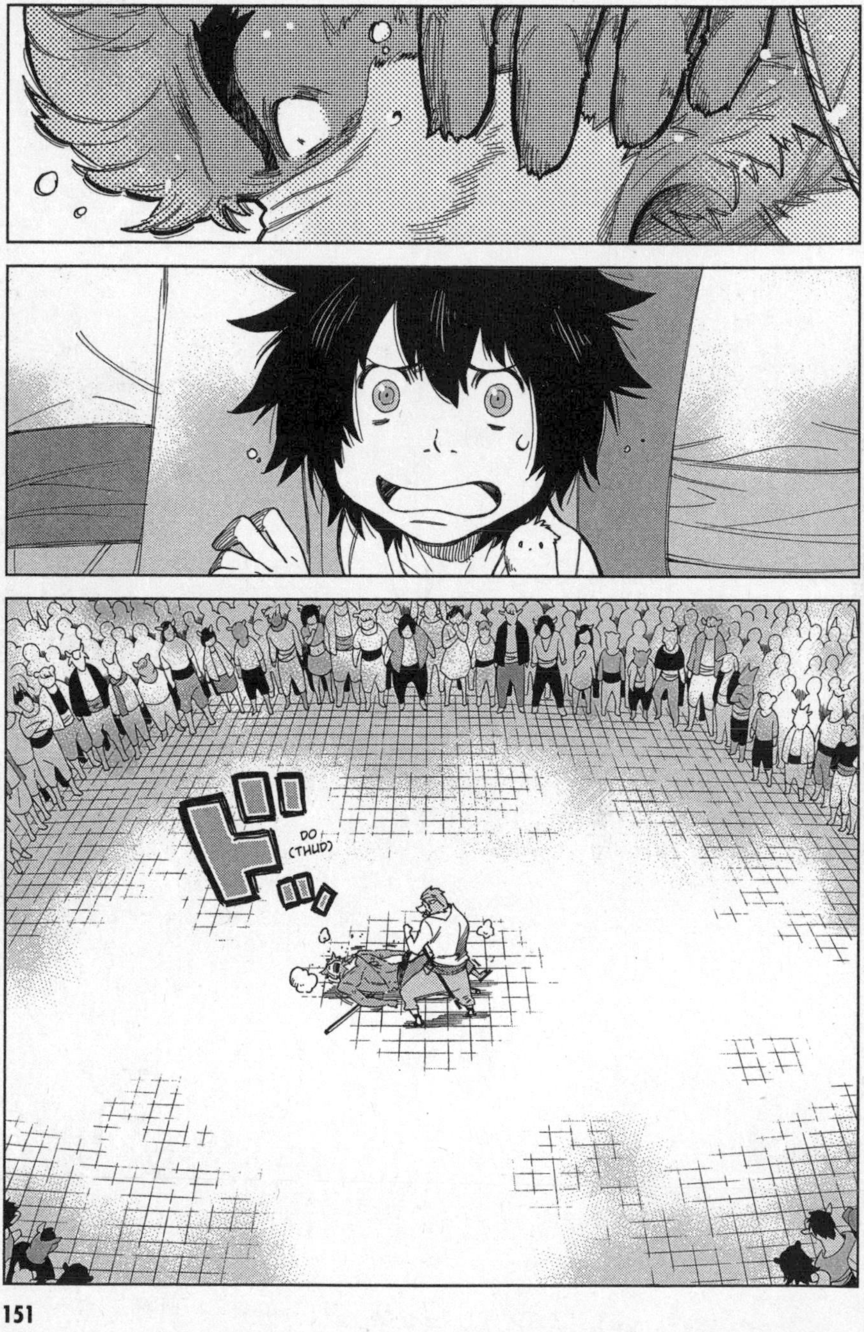
DO
(THUD)

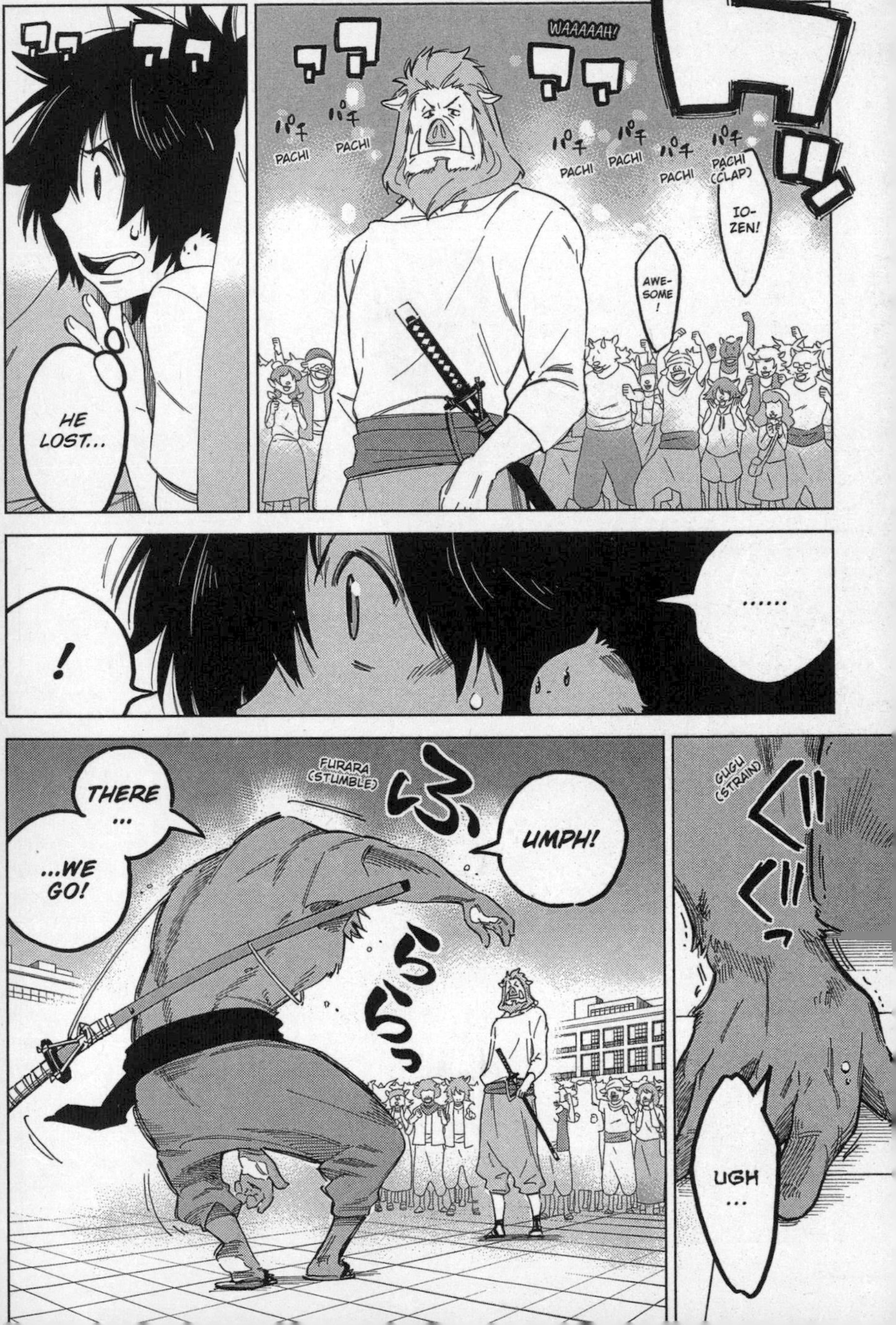
WAAAAAH!
PACHI (CLAP)
PACHI
PACHI
PACHI
PACHI
PACHI
IO-ZEN!
AWE-SOME!
HE LOST...
......
!
GUGU (STRAIN)
UGH ...
FURARA (STUMBLE)
UMPH!
THERE ...
...WE GO!

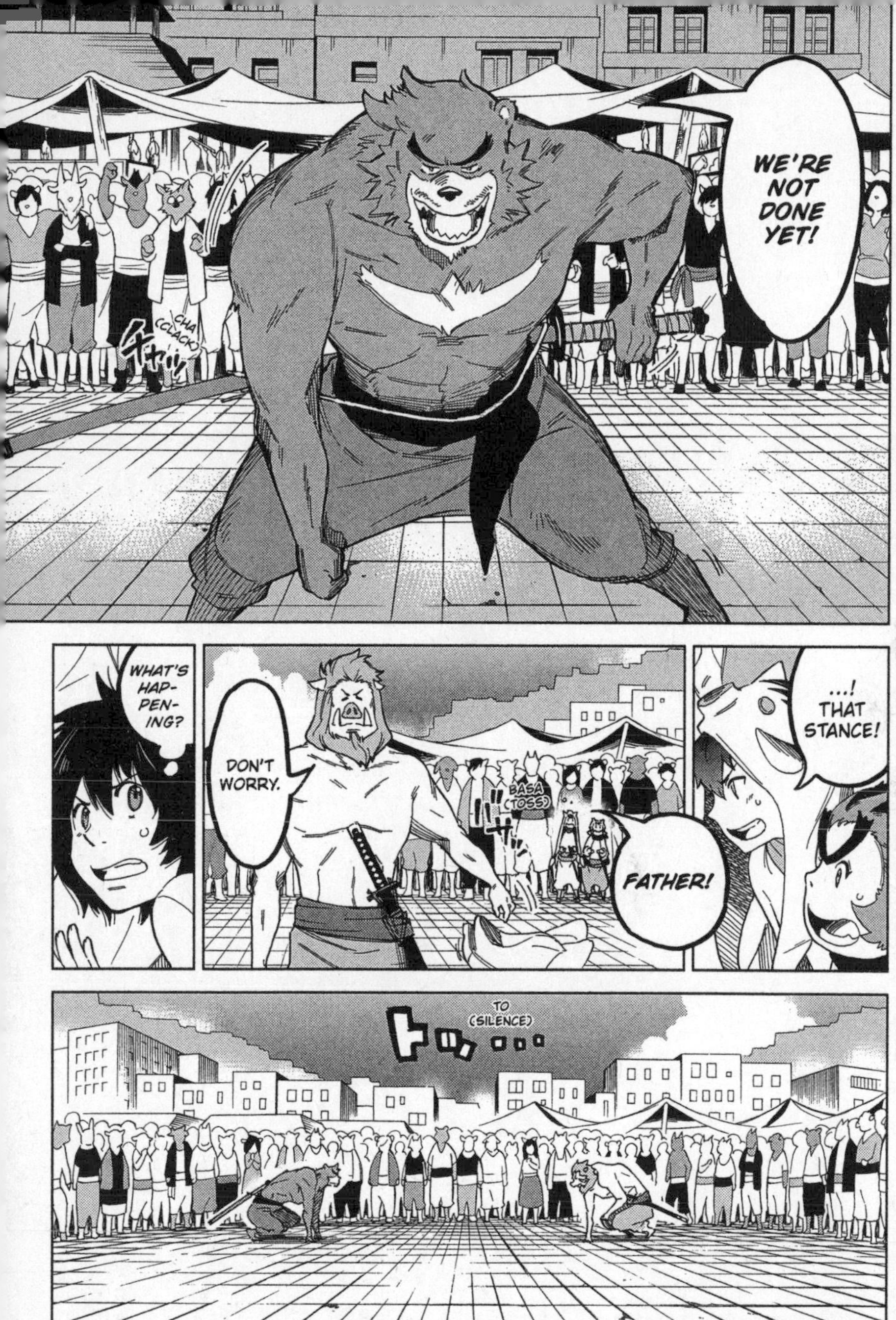
WE'RE NOT DONE YET!
CHA (CLACK)
...! THAT STANCE!
FATHER!
DON'T WORRY.
BASA (TOSS)
WHAT'S HAP-PEN-ING?
TO (SILENCE)

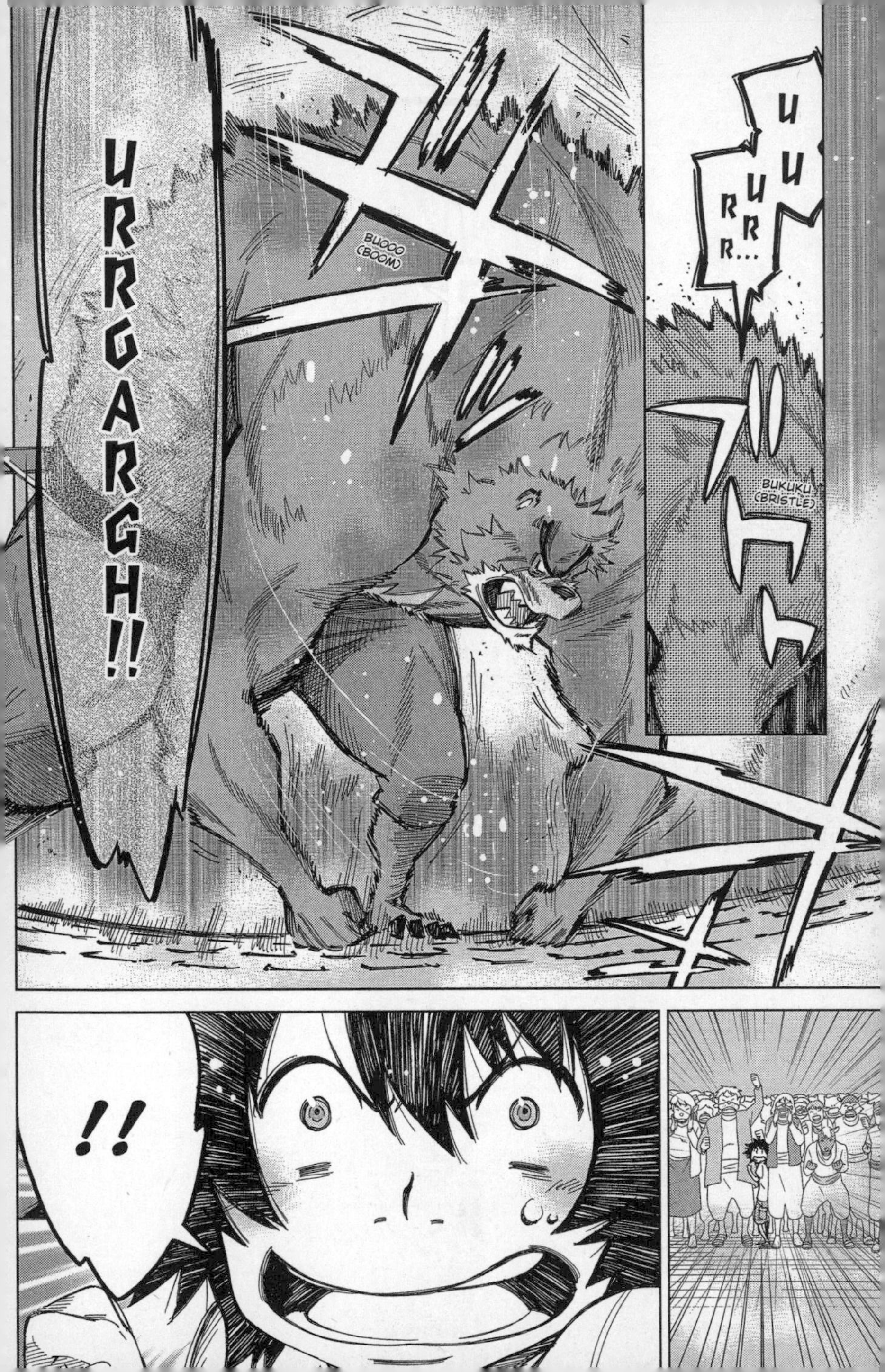
UUURRR...
BUKUKU (BRISTLE)
BUOOO (BOOM)
URRGARGH!!
!!

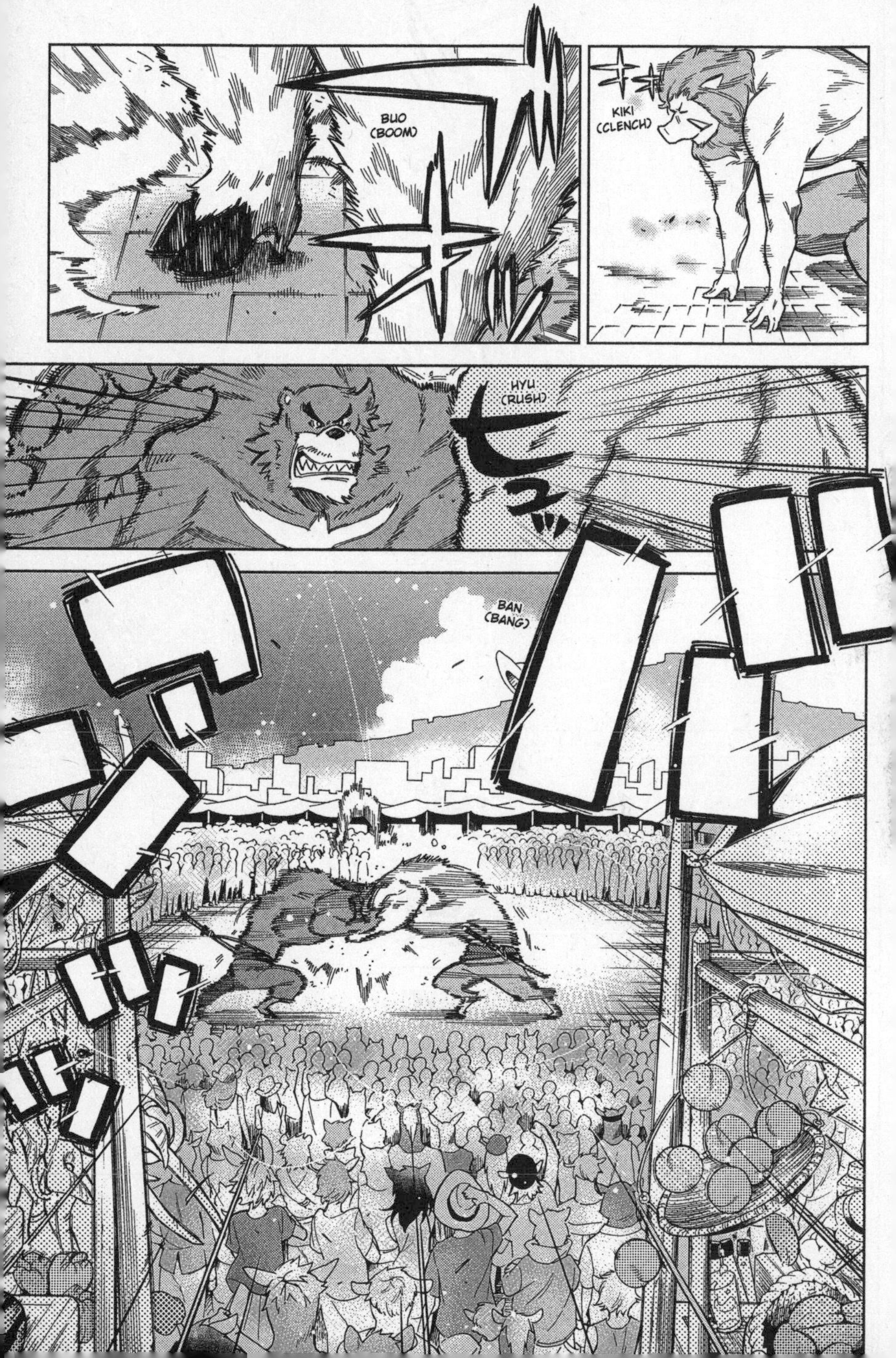
KIKI (CLENCH)
BUO (BOOM)
HYU (RUSH)
BAN (BANG)

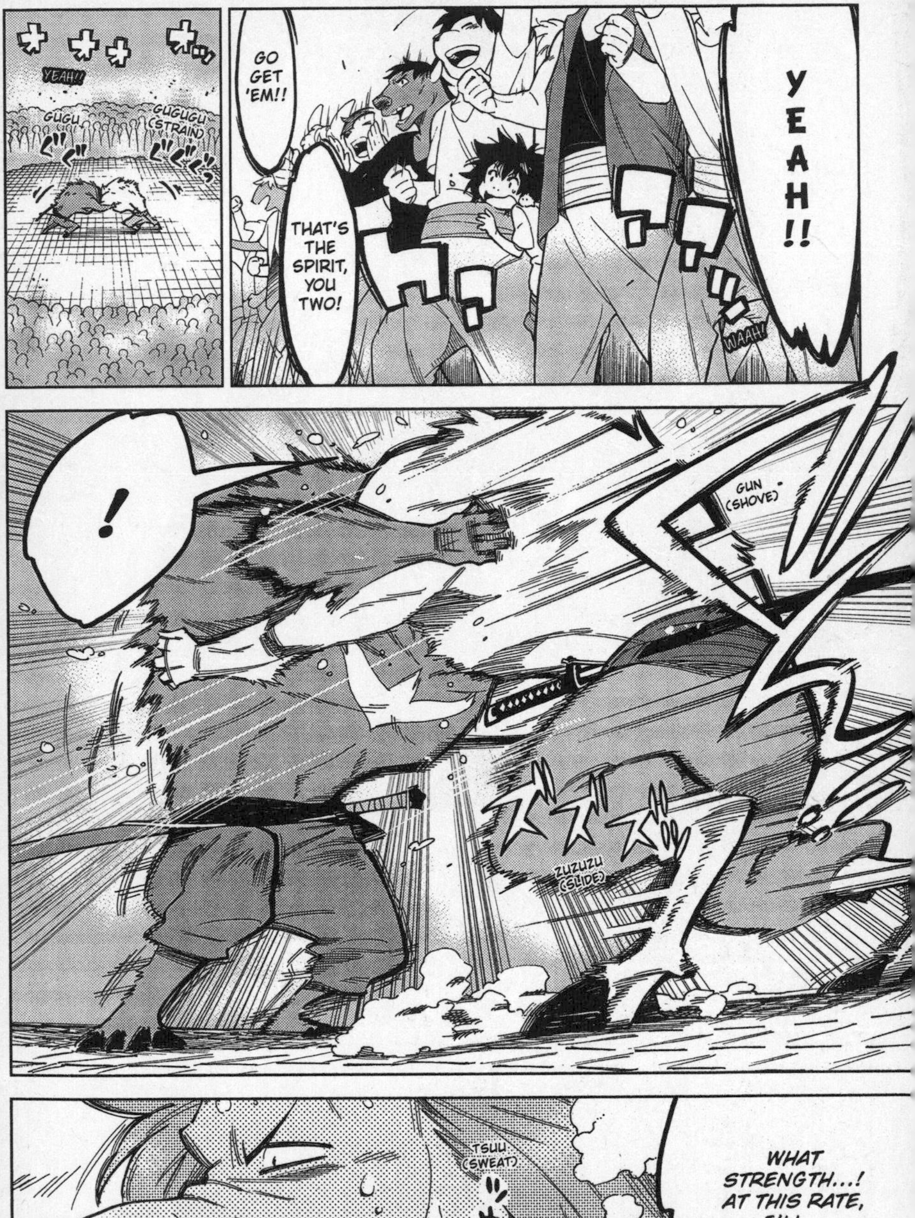
YEAH!!
WAAH!
GO GET 'EM!!
THAT'S THE SPIRIT, YOU TWO!
YEAH!!
GUGUGU (STRAIN)
GUGU
GUN (SHOVE)
ZUZUZU (SLIDE)
!
WHAT STRENGTH...! AT THIS RATE, I'LL...
TSUU (SWEAT)

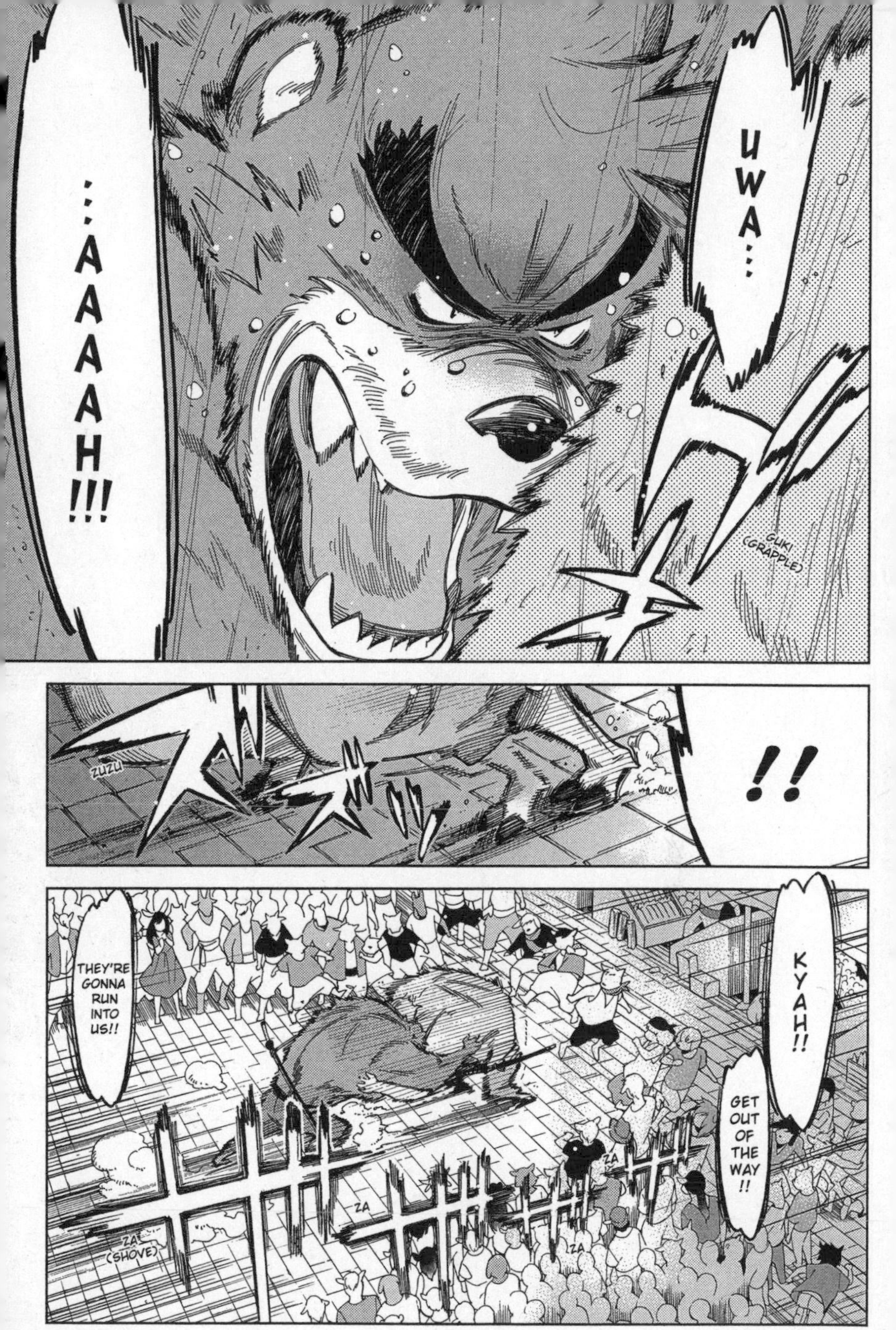
UWA...
...AAAAAH!!!
GUKI (GRAPPLE)
!!
ZUZU
KYAH!!
GET OUT OF THE WAY!!
THEY'RE GONNA RUN INTO US!!
ZA
ZA
ZA
ZA (SHOVE)

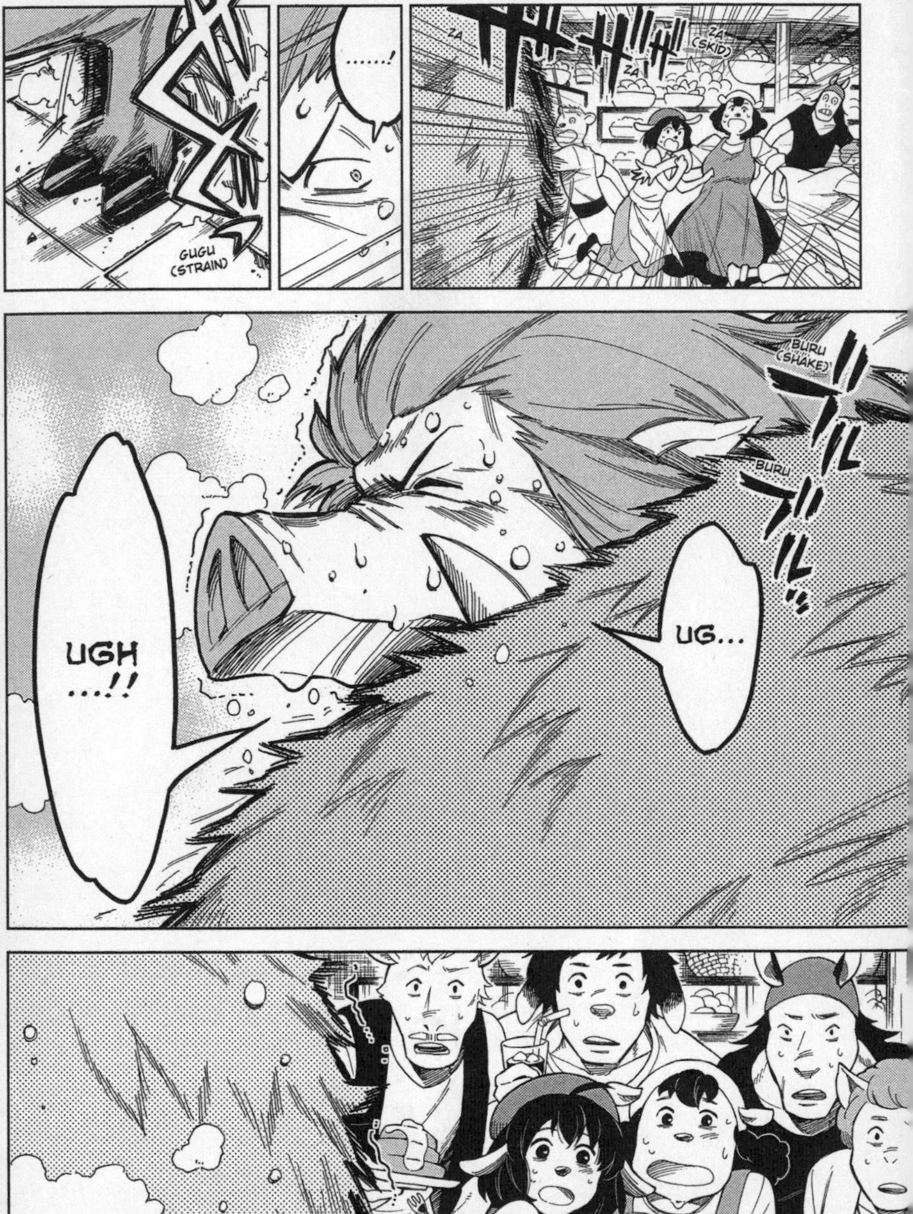
ZA
ZA (SKID)
ZA
......!
GUGU (STRAIN)
BURU (SHAKE)
BURU
UG...
UGH ...!!

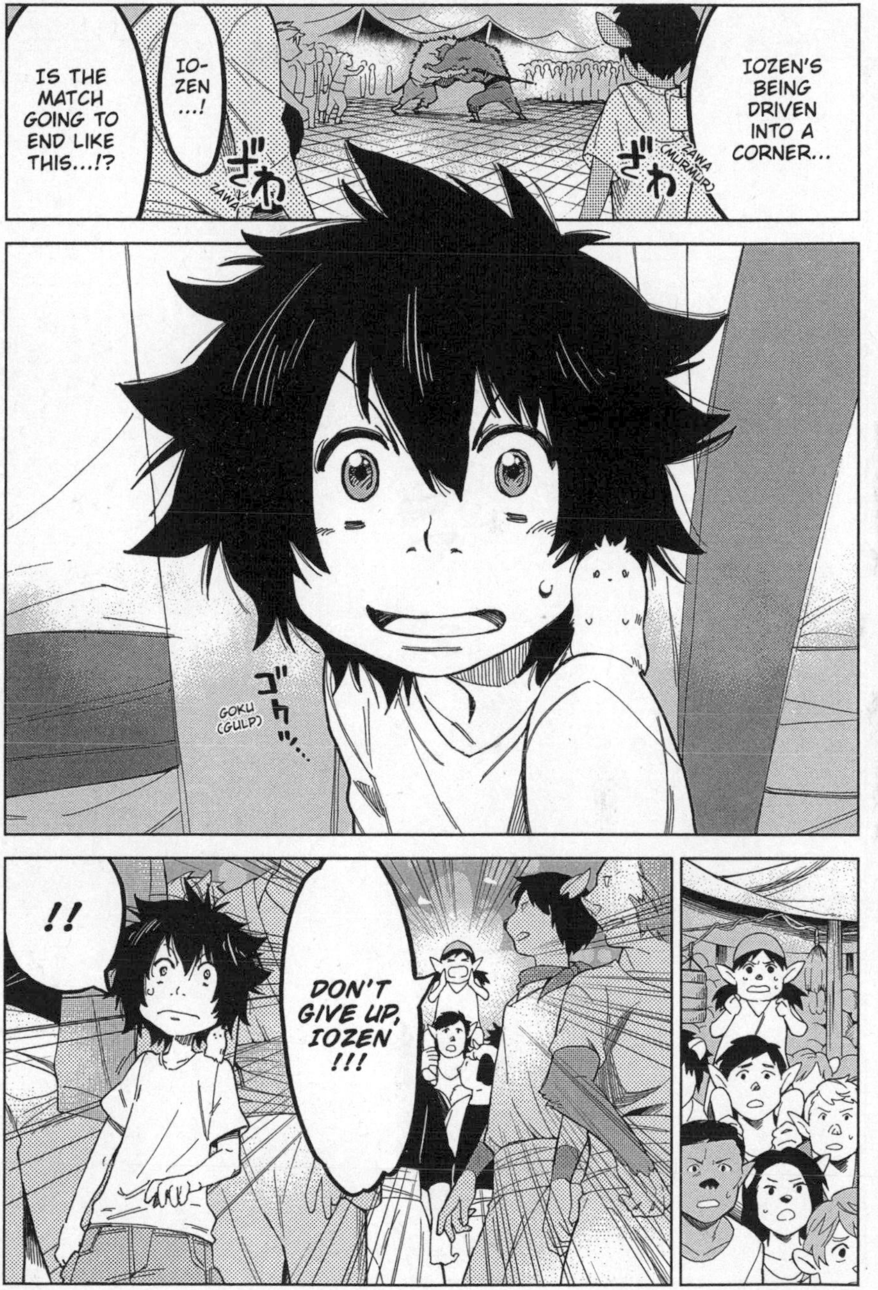
IOZEN'S BEING DRIVEN INTO A CORNER...
ざわ
ZAWA (MURMUR)
ざわ
ZAWA
IO-ZEN ...!
IS THE MATCH GOING TO END LIKE THIS...!?
ゴクッ...
GOKU (GULP)
DON'T GIVE UP, IOZEN !!!
!!

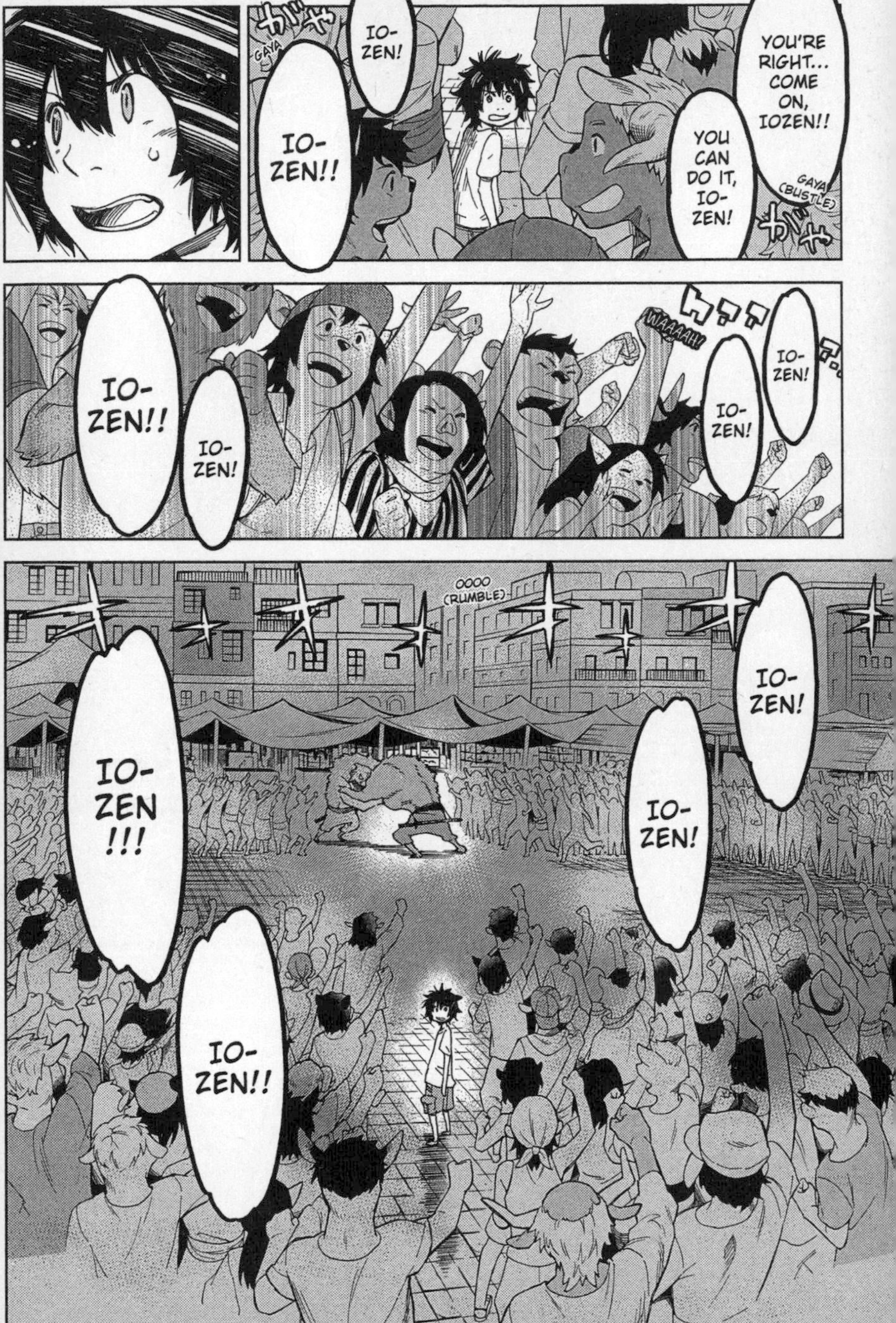
YOU'RE RIGHT... COME ON, IOZEN!!
GAYA (BUSTLE)
YOU CAN DO IT, IO-ZEN!
IO-ZEN!
IO-ZEN!!
GAYA
WAAAAH!!
IO-ZEN!
IO-ZEN!
IO-ZEN!
IO-ZEN!!
IO-ZEN!
OOOO (RUMBLE)
IO-ZEN!
IO-ZEN!!!
IO-ZEN!!

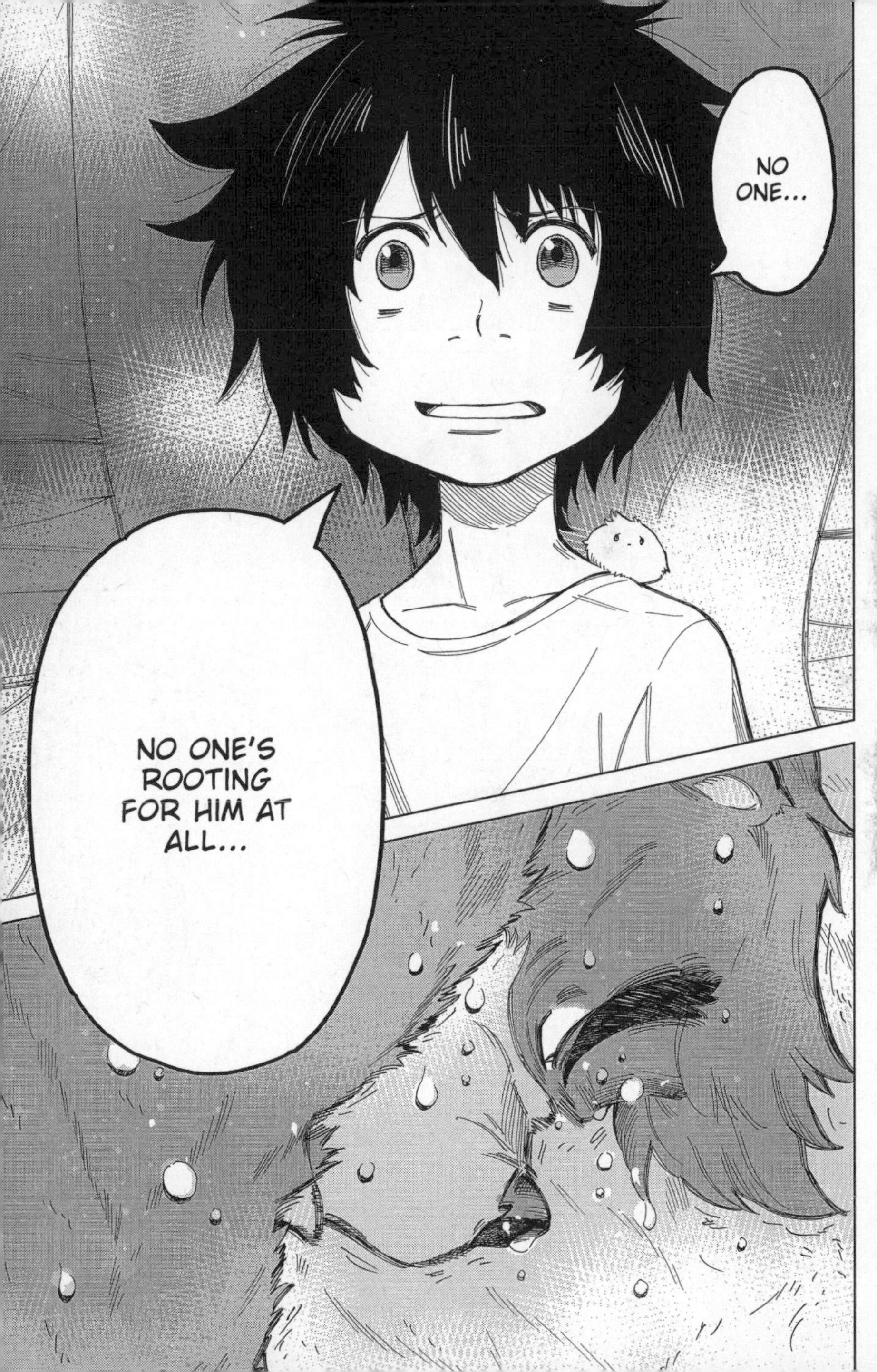
NO ONE...
NO ONE'S ROOTING FOR HIM AT ALL...

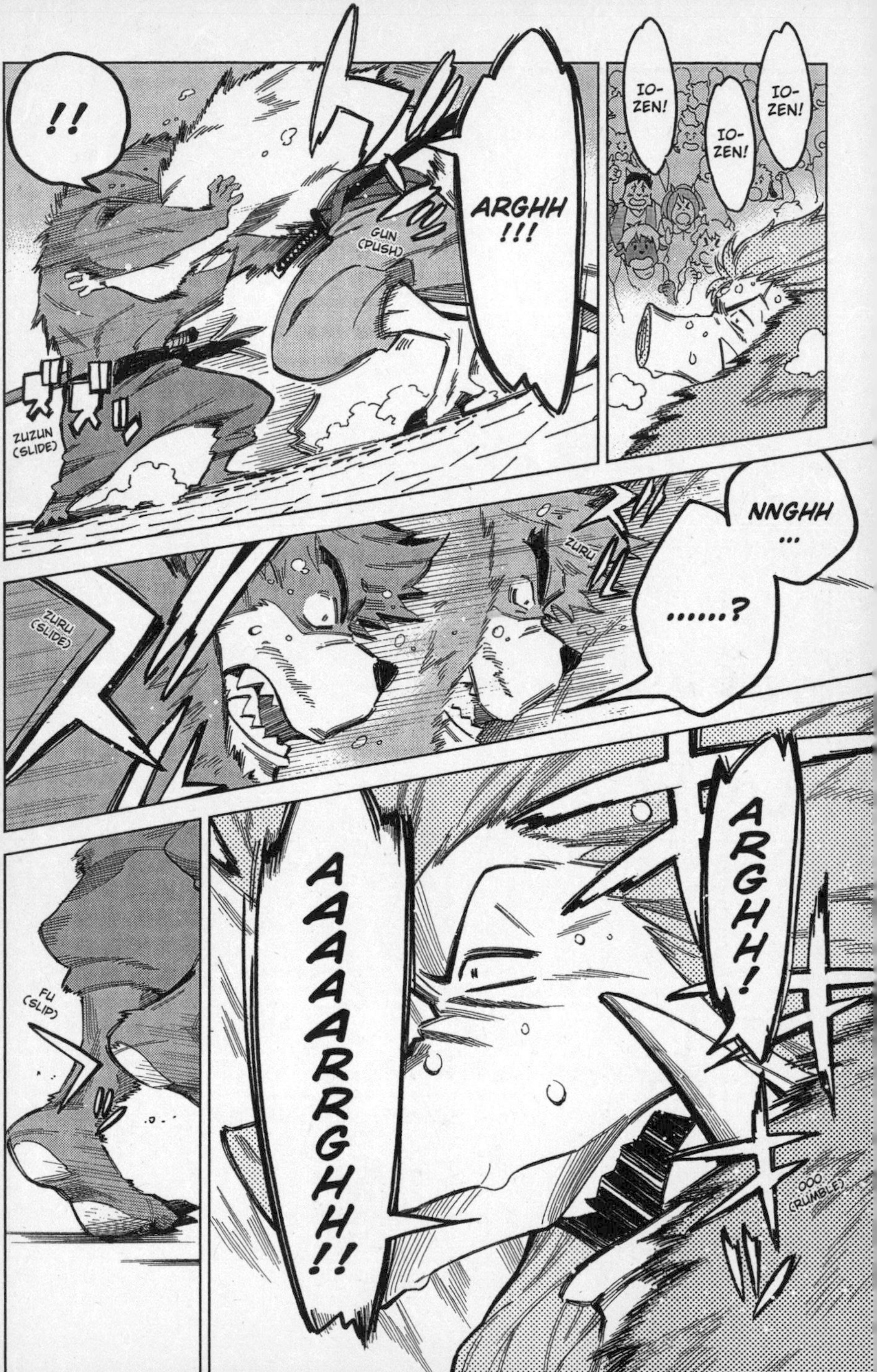
IO-ZEN!
IO-ZEN!
IO-ZEN!
ARGHH!!!
GUN (PUSH)
!!
ZUZUN (SLIDE)
NNGHH...
......?
ZURU
ZURU (SLIDE)
ARGHH!
AAAAARRGHH!!
OOO (RUMBLE)
FU (SLIP)

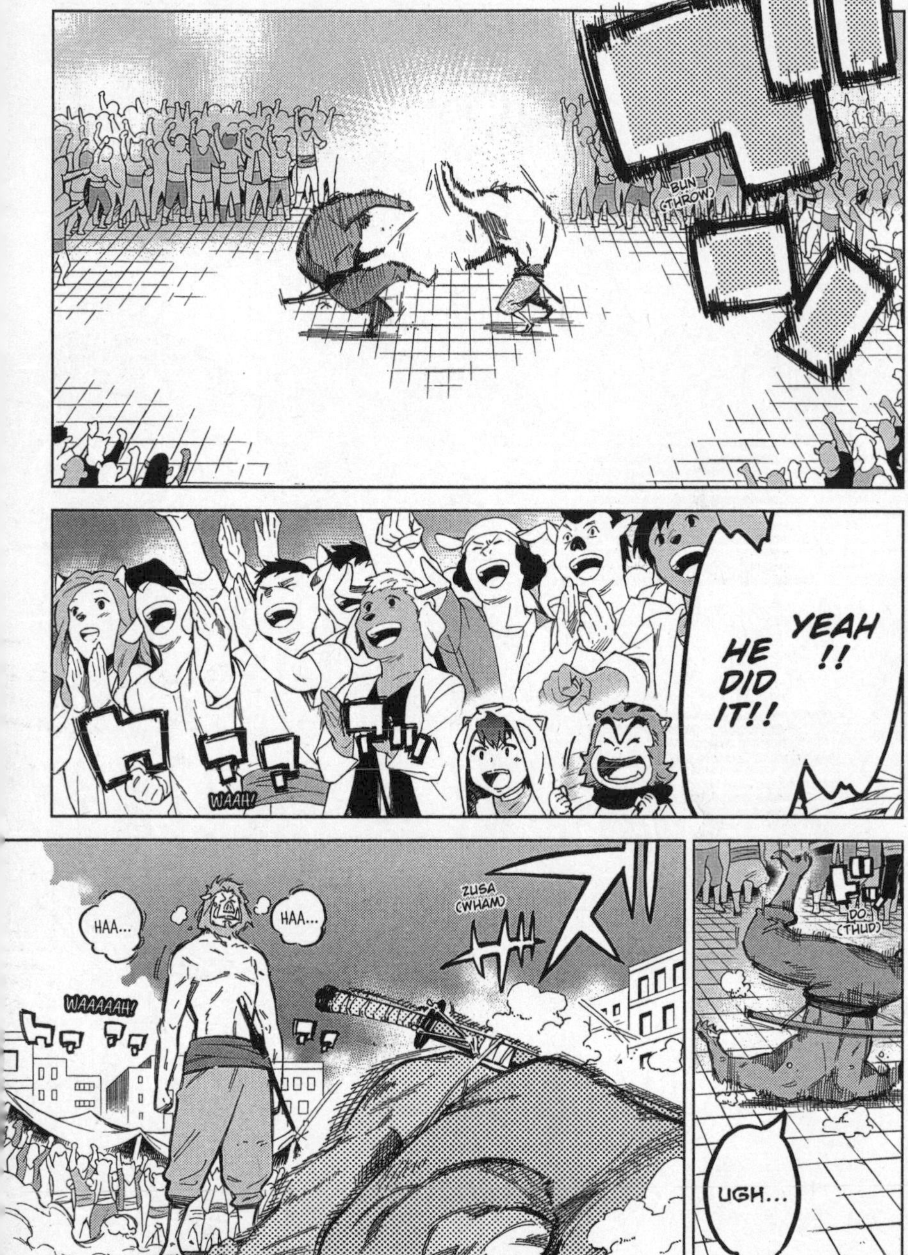
BUN (THROW)
YEAH!!
HE DID IT!!
WAAH!
DO (THUD)
UGH...
ZUSA (WHAM)
HAA...
HAA...
WAAAAAH!

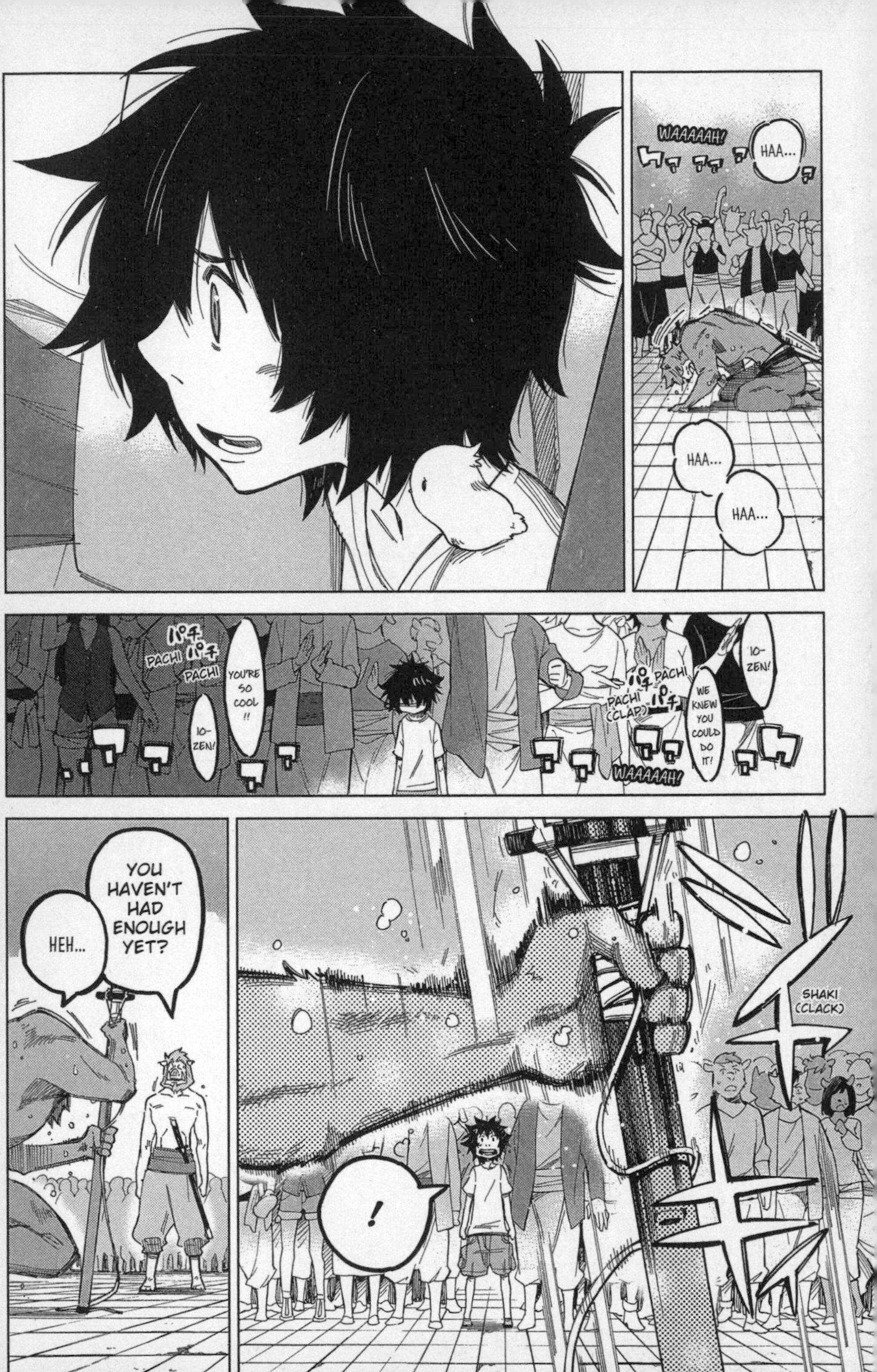
WAAAAAH!
HAA...
HAA...
HAA...
IO-ZEN!
WE KNEW YOU COULD DO IT!
パチ PACHI PACHI パチ (CLAP)
WAAAAAH!
YOU'RE SO COOL!!
パチ PACHI パチ PACHI
IO-ZEN!
SHAKI (CLACK)
!
YOU HAVEN'T HAD ENOUGH YET?
HEH...

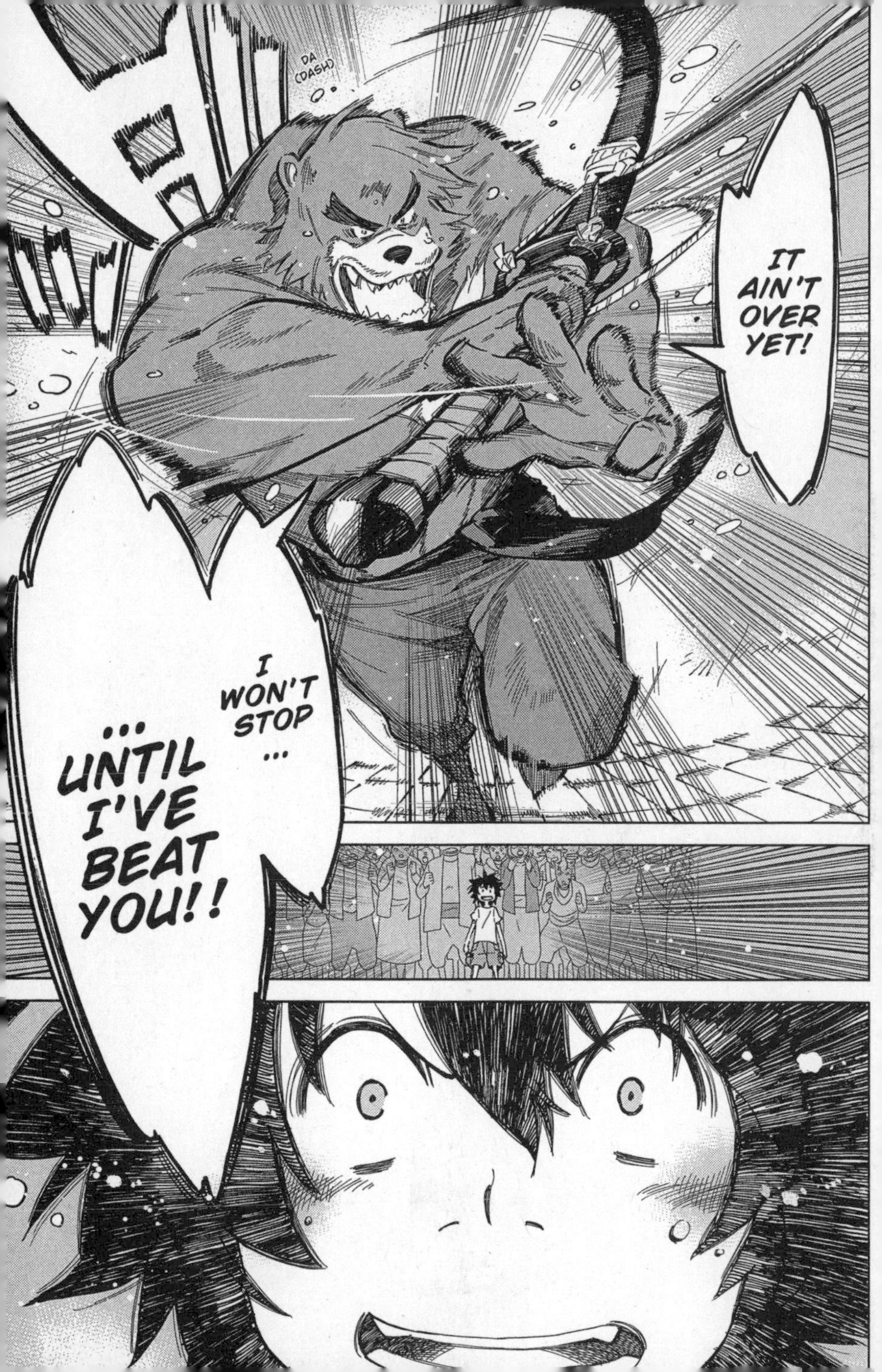
IT AIN'T OVER YET!
DA (DASH)
I WON'T STOP ...
... UNTIL I'VE BEAT YOU!!

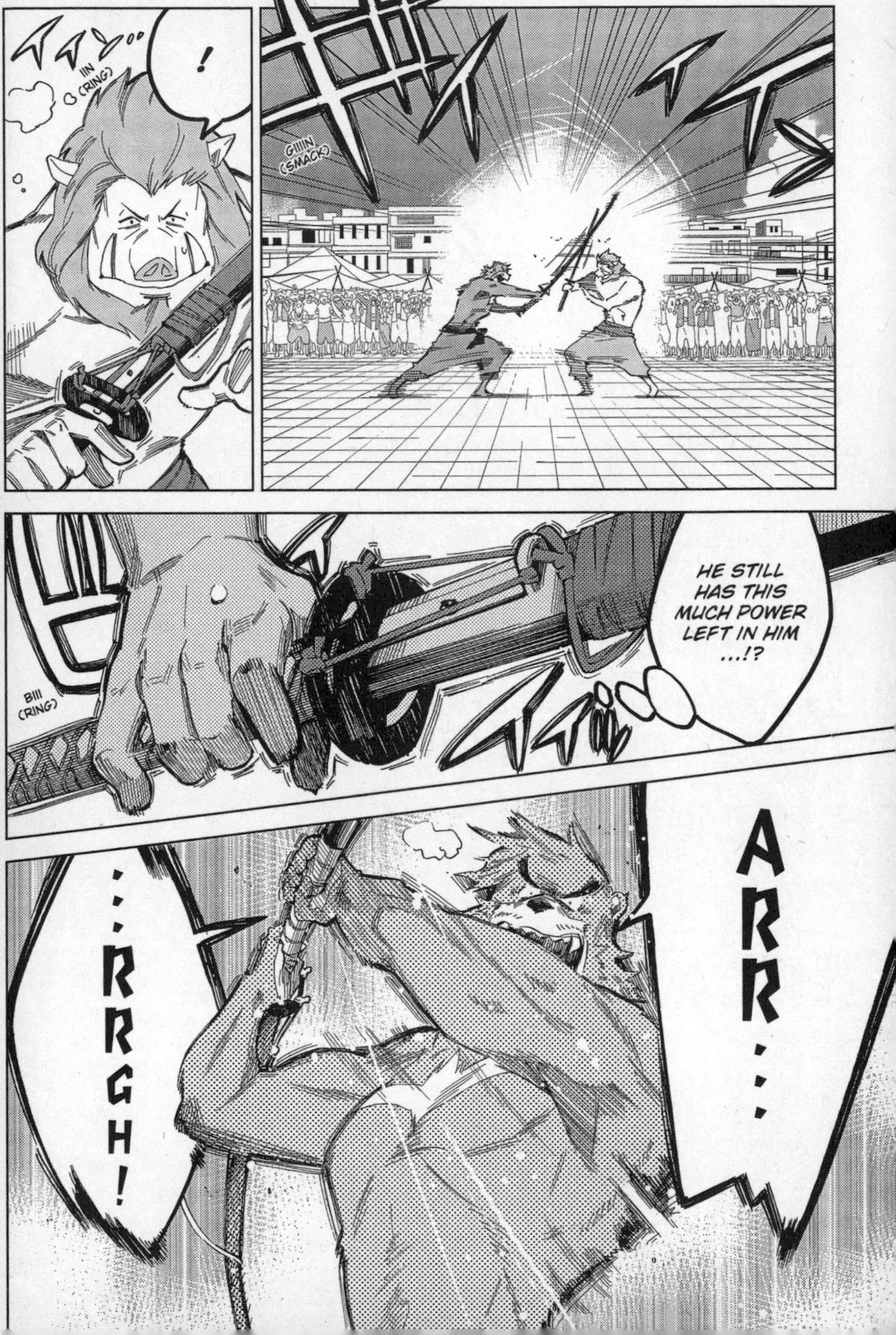
GIIIN (SMACK)
IIN (RING)
!
HE STILL HAS THIS MUCH POWER LEFT IN HIM ...!?
BIII (RING)
ARR...
...RRRGH!

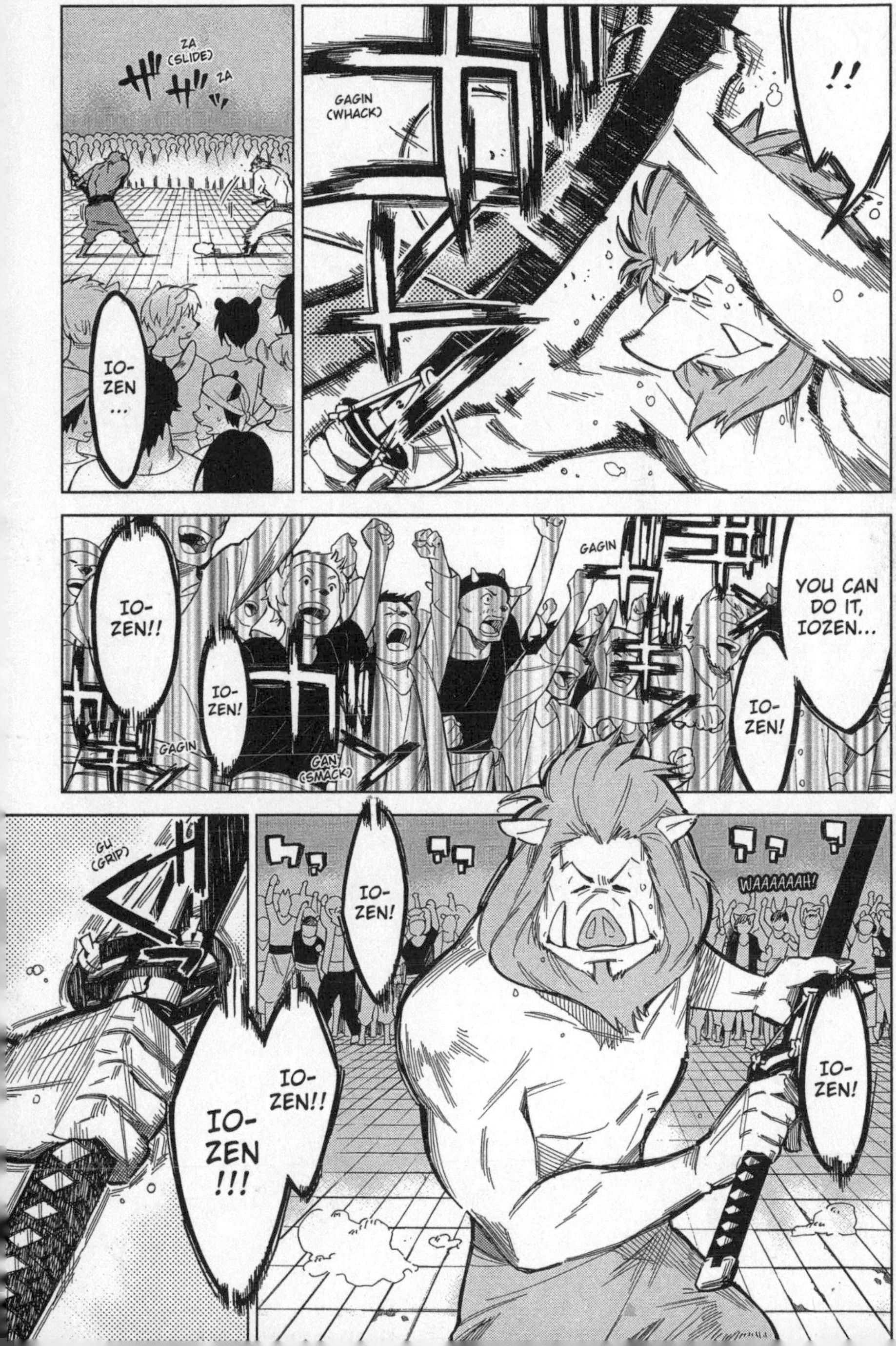
!!
GAGIN (WHACK)
ZA (SLIDE)
ZA
IO-ZEN...
YOU CAN DO IT, IOZEN...
IO-ZEN!
GAGIN
GAN (SMACK)
IO-ZEN!!
IO-ZEN!
GAGIN
WAAAAAAH!
IO-ZEN!
IO-ZEN!
IO-ZEN!!
IO-ZEN!!!
GU (GRIP)

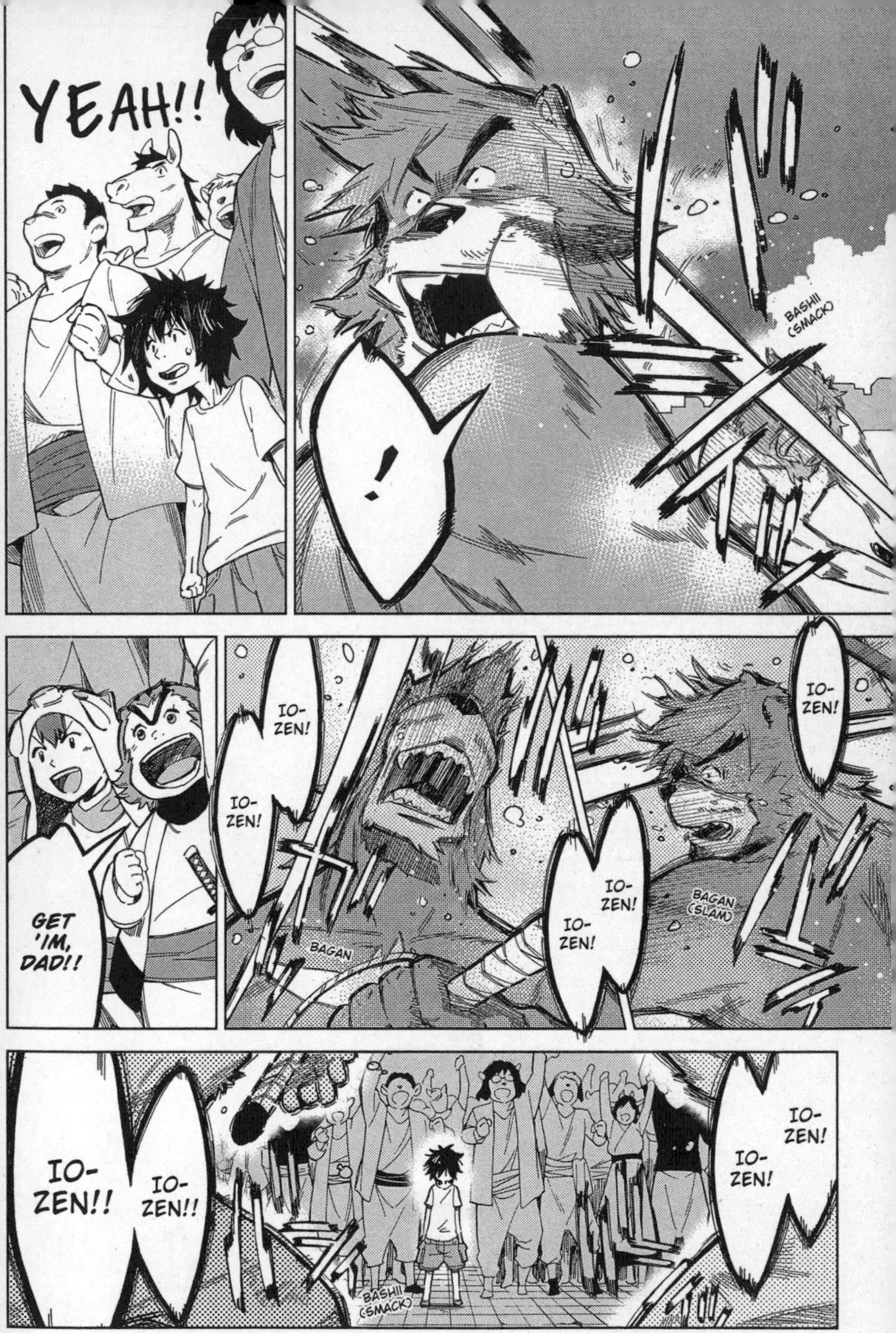
!
BASHI (SMACK)
YEAH!!
IO-ZEN!
IO-ZEN!
IO-ZEN!
BAGAN (SLAM)
IO-ZEN!
IO-ZEN!
BAGAN
GET 'IM, DAD!!
IO-ZEN!
IO-ZEN!
BASHI (SMACK)
IO-ZEN!!
IO-ZEN!!

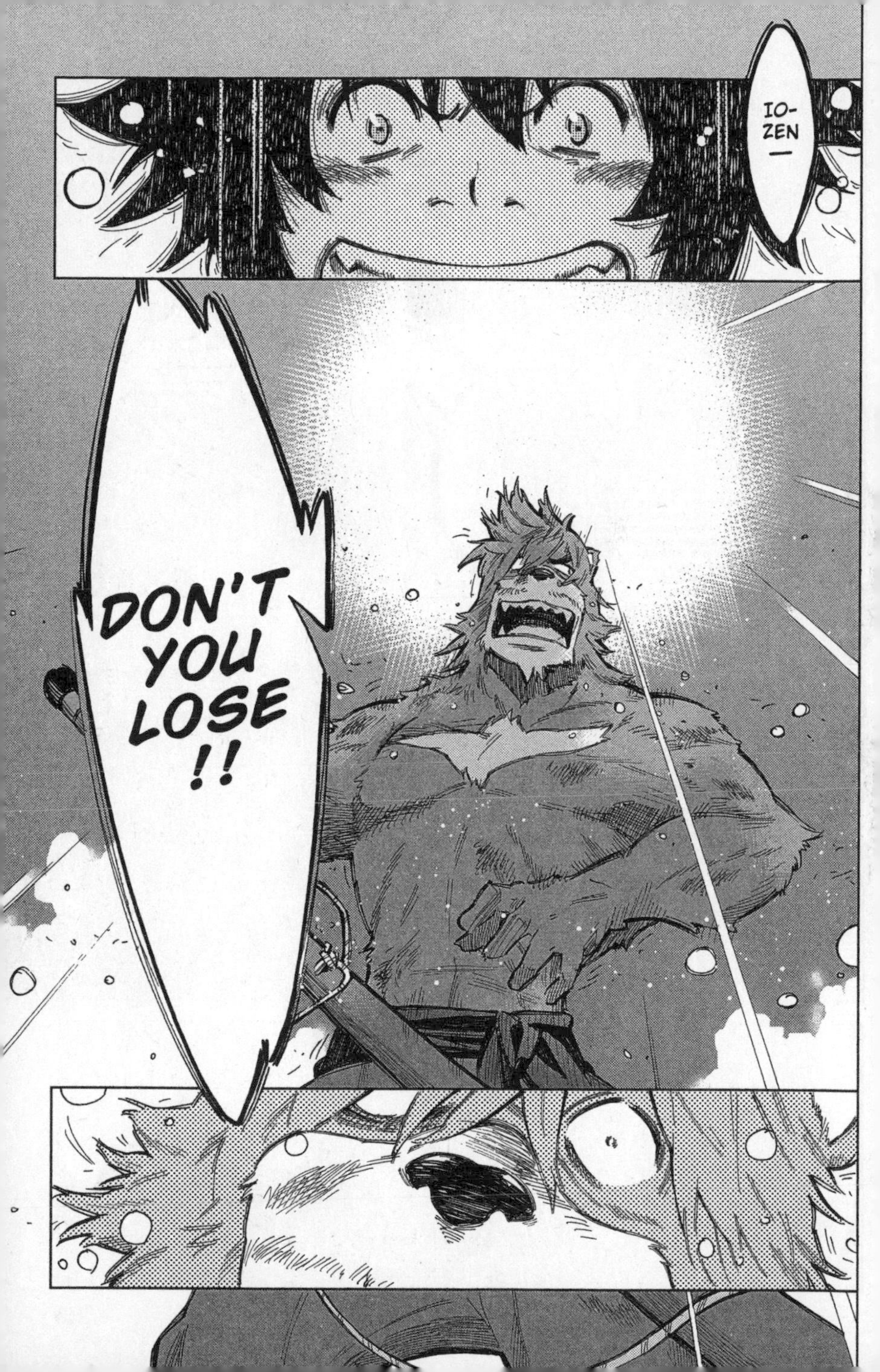

IO-ZEN—
DON'T YOU LOSE!!

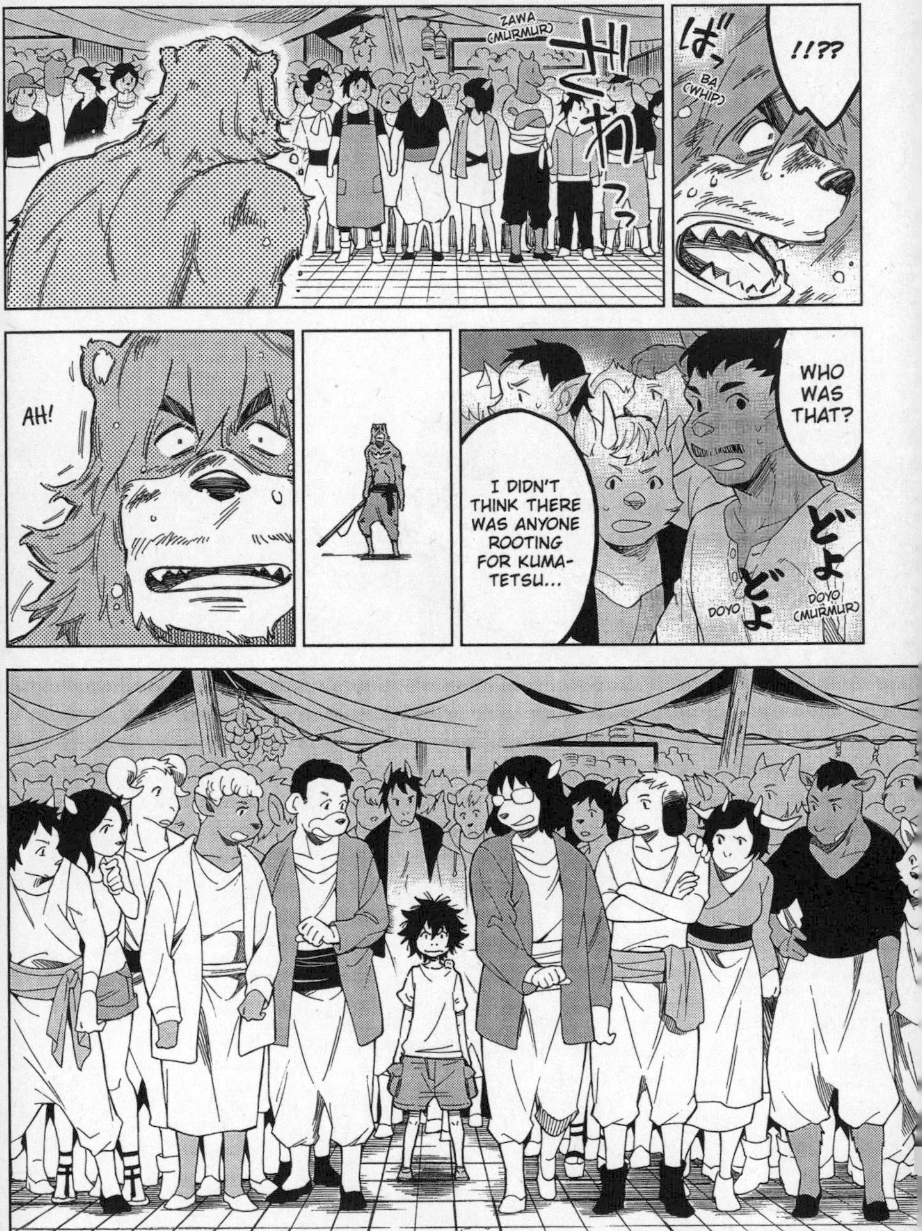
!!??
ばっ
BA (WHIP)
ざわっ
ZAWA (MURMUR)
WHO WAS THAT?
I DIDN'T THINK THERE WAS ANYONE ROOTING FOR KUMA-TETSU...
どよ
DOYO (MURMUR)
どよ
DOYO
AH!

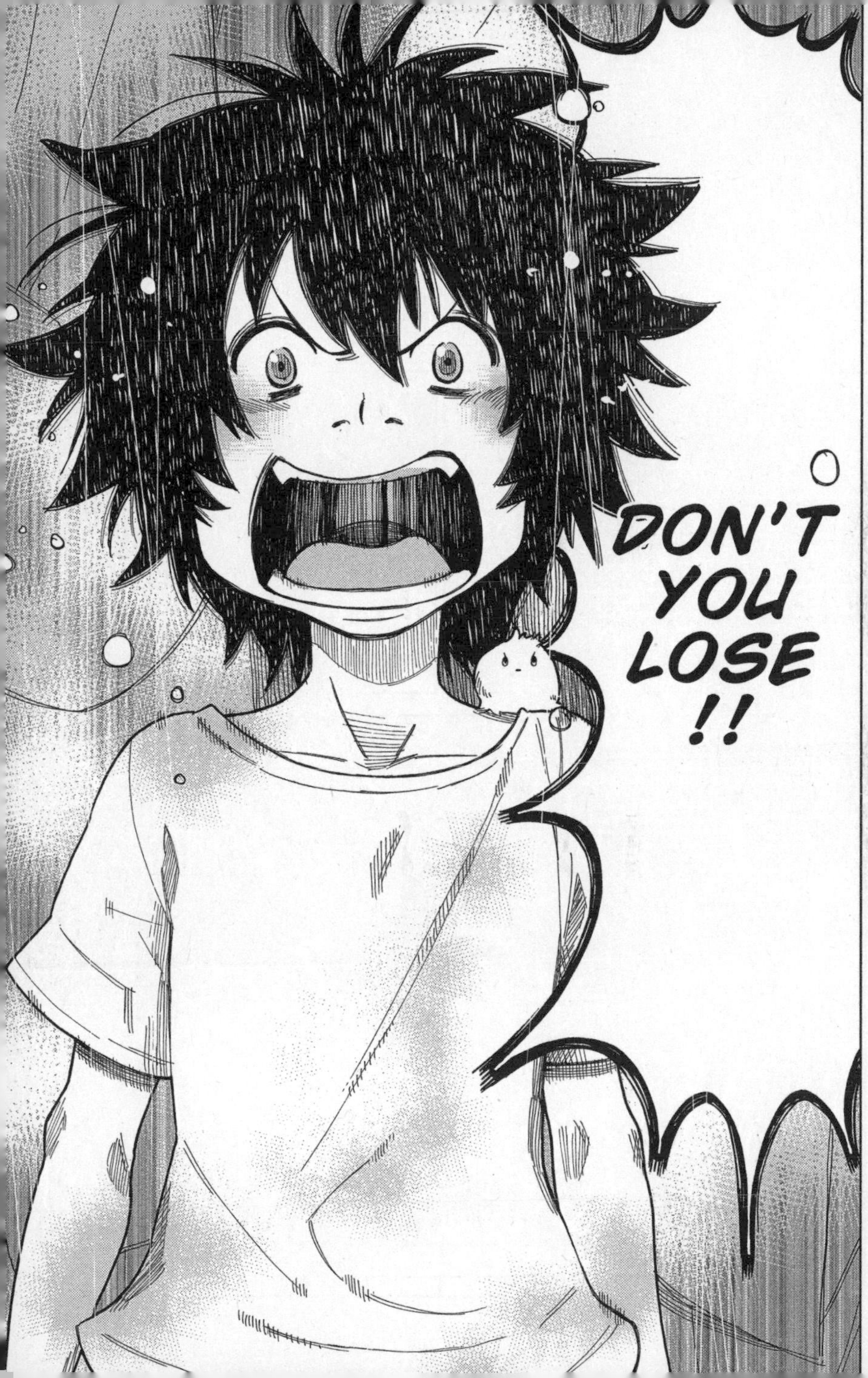
DON'T YOU LOSE !!

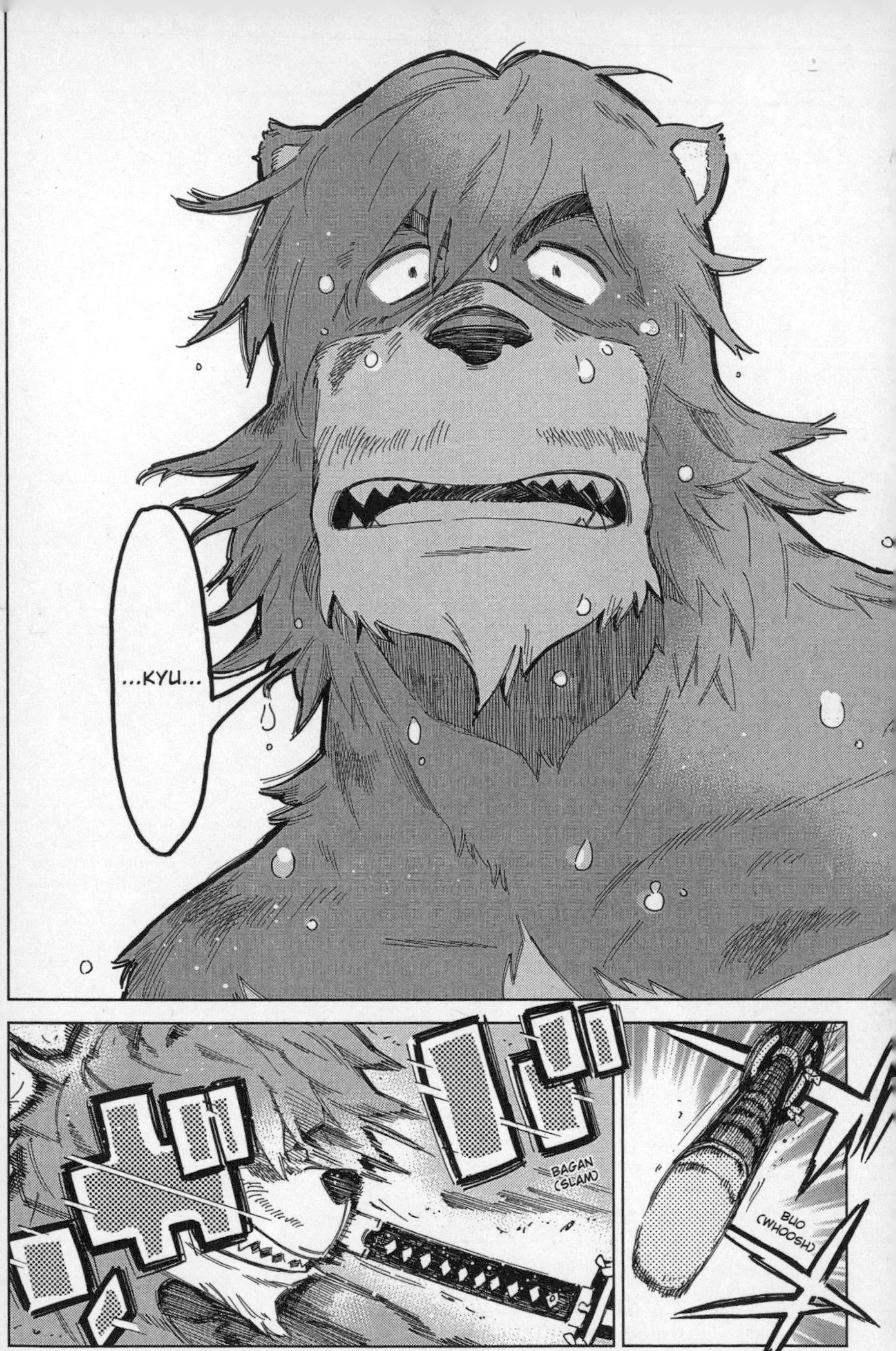
...KYU...
BUO (WHOOSH)
BAGAN (SLAM)

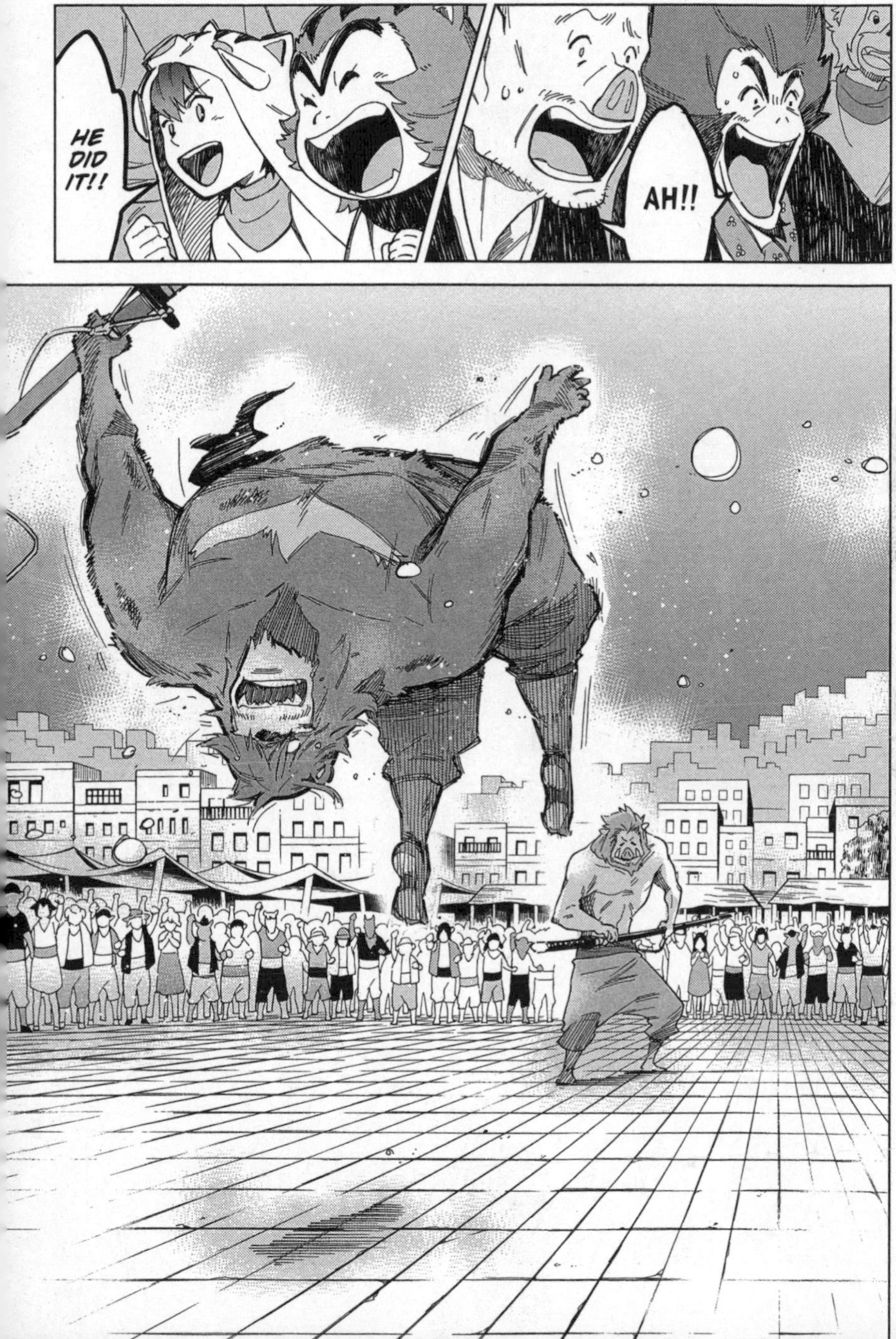
AH!!
HE DID IT!!

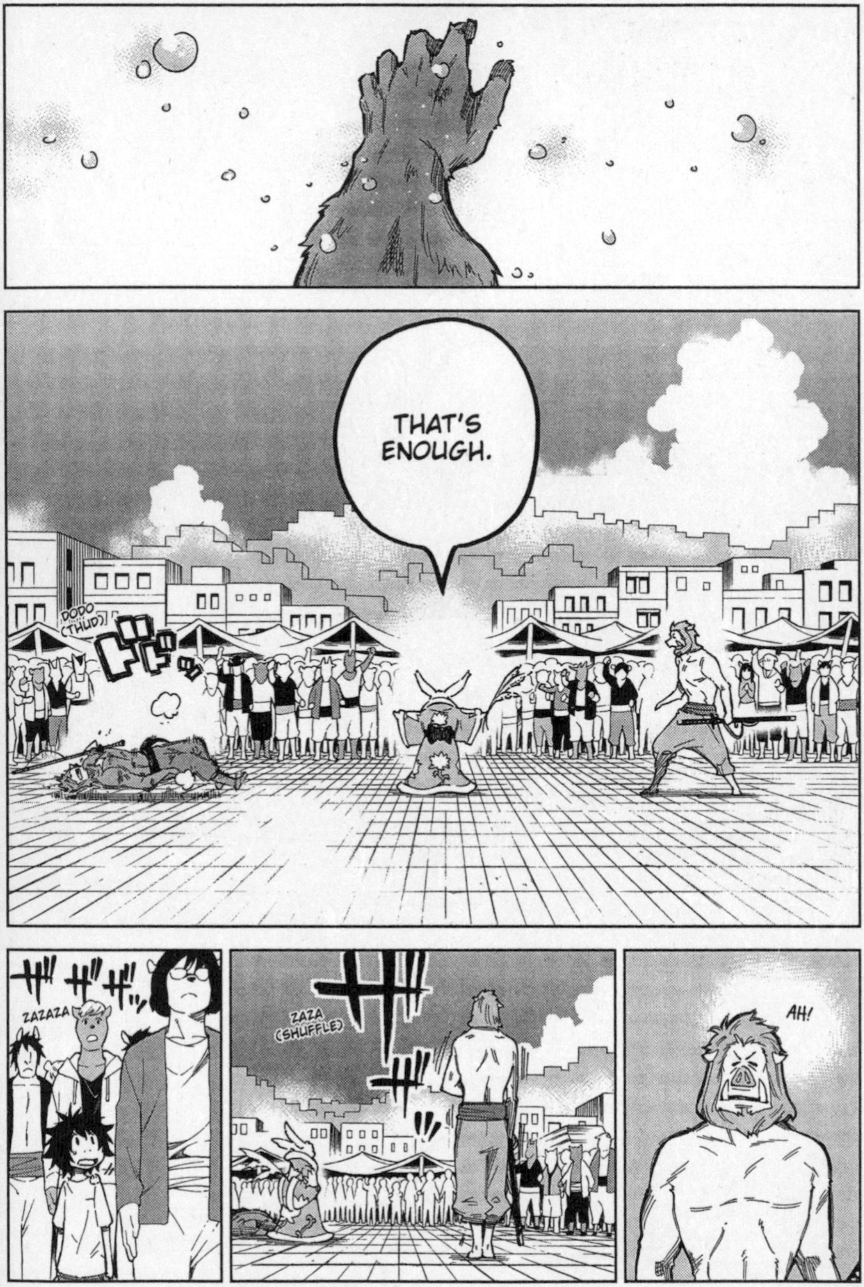
THAT'S ENOUGH.
DODO (THUD)
AH!
ZAZA (SHUFFLE)
ZAZAZA

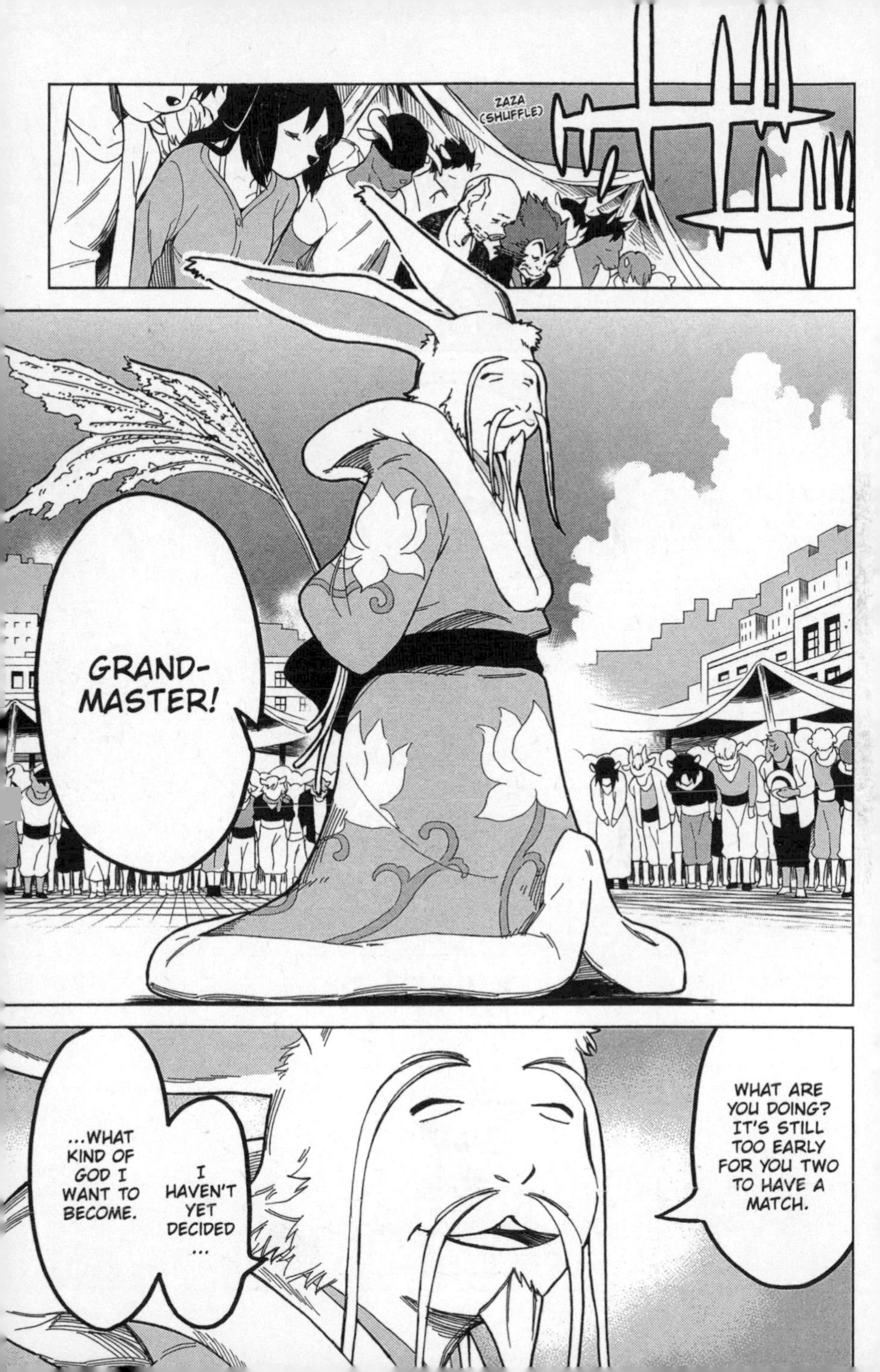
ZAZA (SHUFFLE)
GRAND-MASTER!
WHAT ARE YOU DOING? IT'S STILL TOO EARLY FOR YOU TWO TO HAVE A MATCH.
I HAVEN'T YET DECIDED ...
...WHAT KIND OF GOD I WANT TO BECOME.

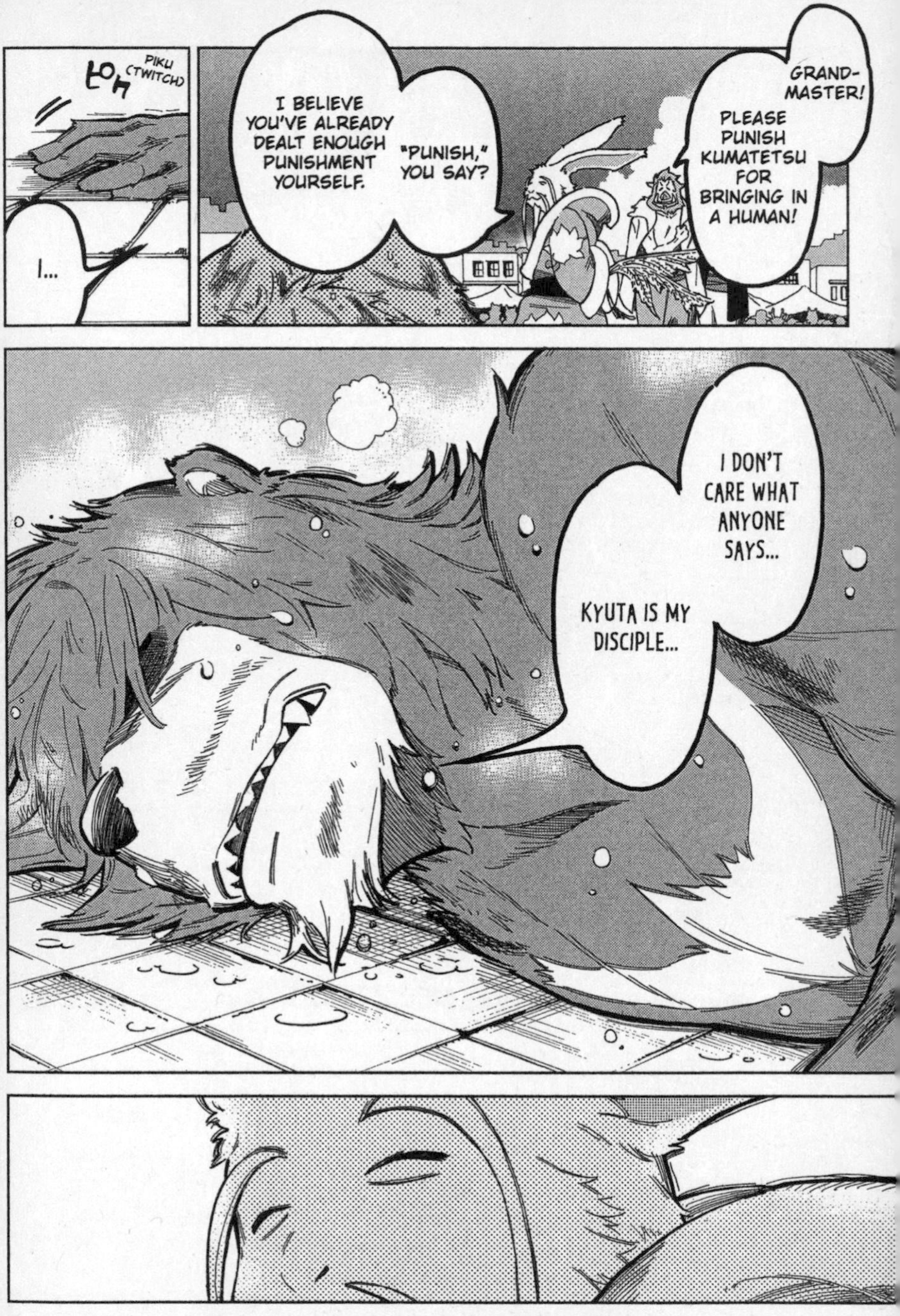
GRAND-MASTER!
PLEASE PUNISH KUMATETSU FOR BRINGING IN A HUMAN!
"PUNISH," YOU SAY?
I BELIEVE YOU'VE ALREADY DEALT ENOUGH PUNISHMENT YOURSELF.
ピク PIKU (TWITCH)
I...
I DON'T CARE WHAT ANYONE SAYS...
KYUTA IS MY DISCIPLE...

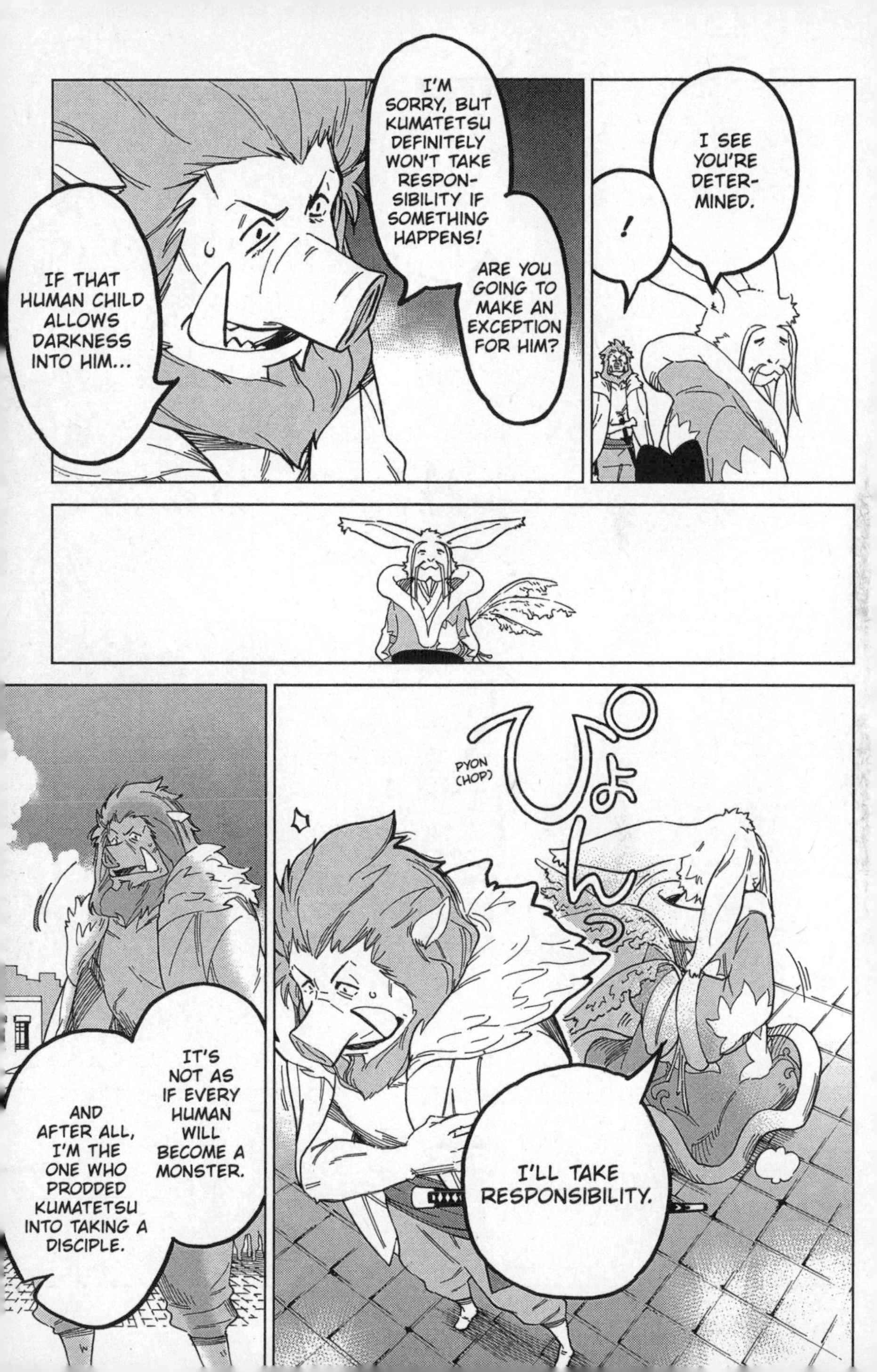
I SEE YOU'RE DETERMINED.
!
I'M SORRY, BUT KUMATETSU DEFINITELY WON'T TAKE RESPON-SIBILITY IF SOMETHING HAPPENS!
ARE YOU GOING TO MAKE AN EXCEPTION FOR HIM?
IF THAT HUMAN CHILD ALLOWS DARKNESS INTO HIM...
ぴょんっ
PYON (HOP)
I'LL TAKE RESPONSIBILITY.
IT'S NOT AS IF EVERY HUMAN WILL BECOME A MONSTER.
AND AFTER ALL, I'M THE ONE WHO PRODDED KUMATETSU INTO TAKING A DISCIPLE.

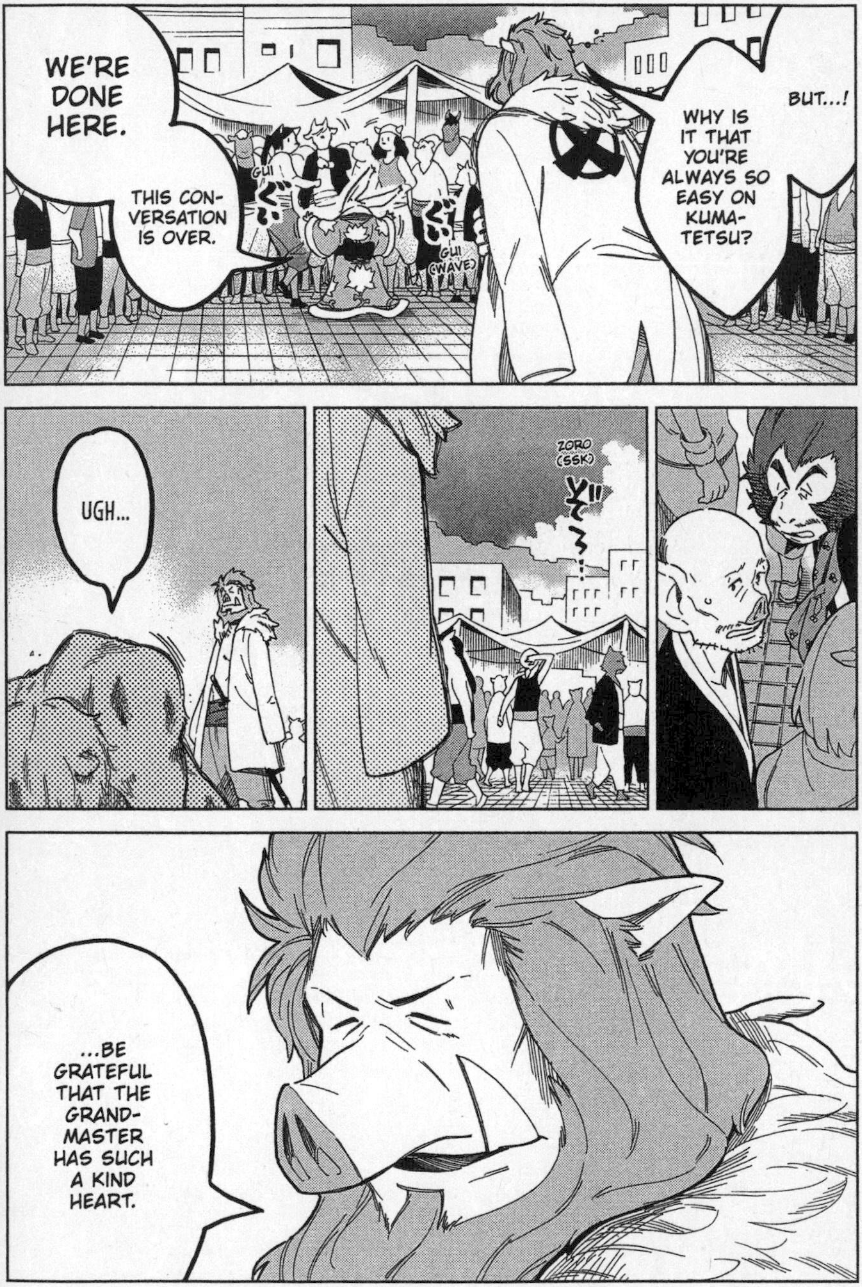
BUT...!
WHY IS IT THAT YOU'RE ALWAYS SO EASY ON KUMA-TETSU?
WE'RE DONE HERE.
GUI
THIS CON-VERSATION IS OVER.
GUI (WAVE)
ZORO (SSK)
UGH...
...BE GRATEFUL THAT THE GRAND-MASTER HAS SUCH A KIND HEART.

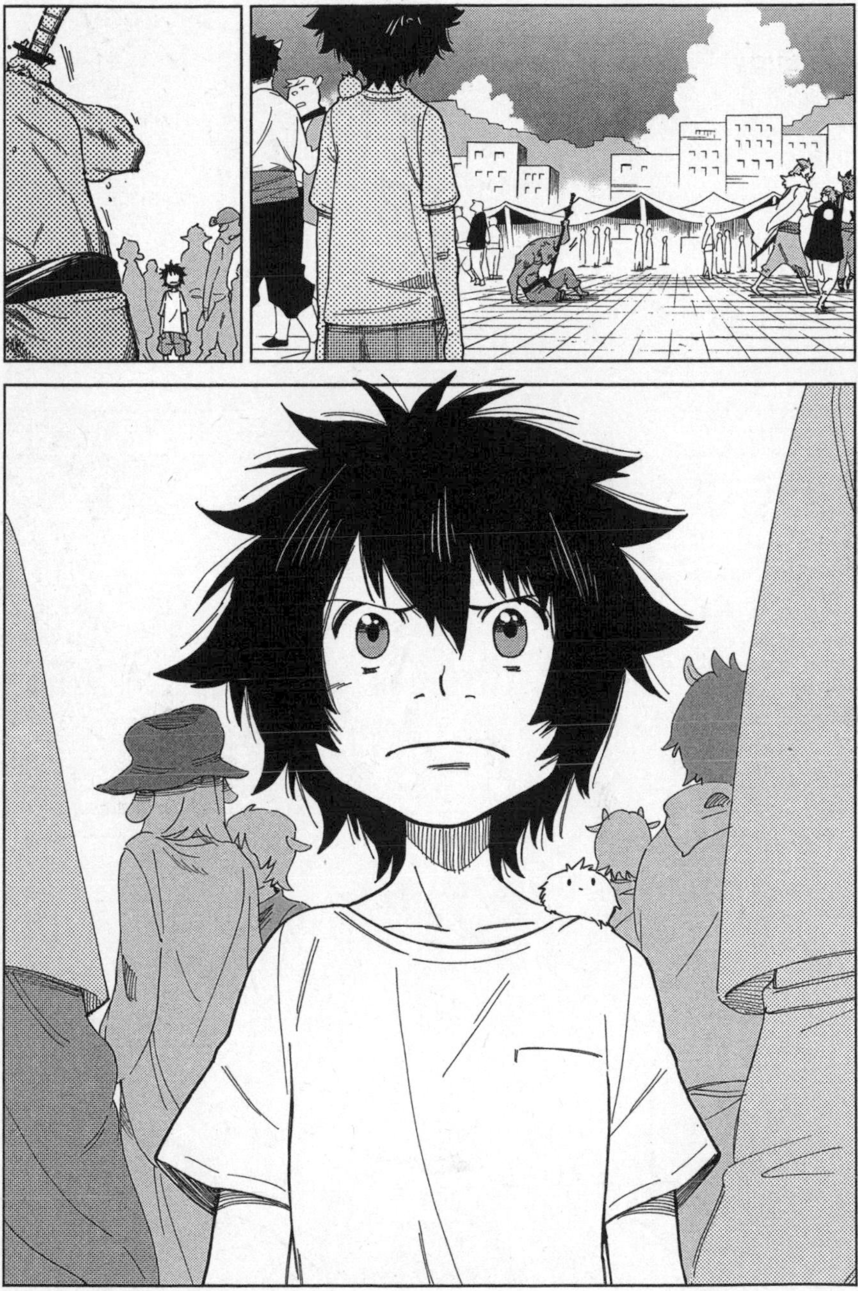

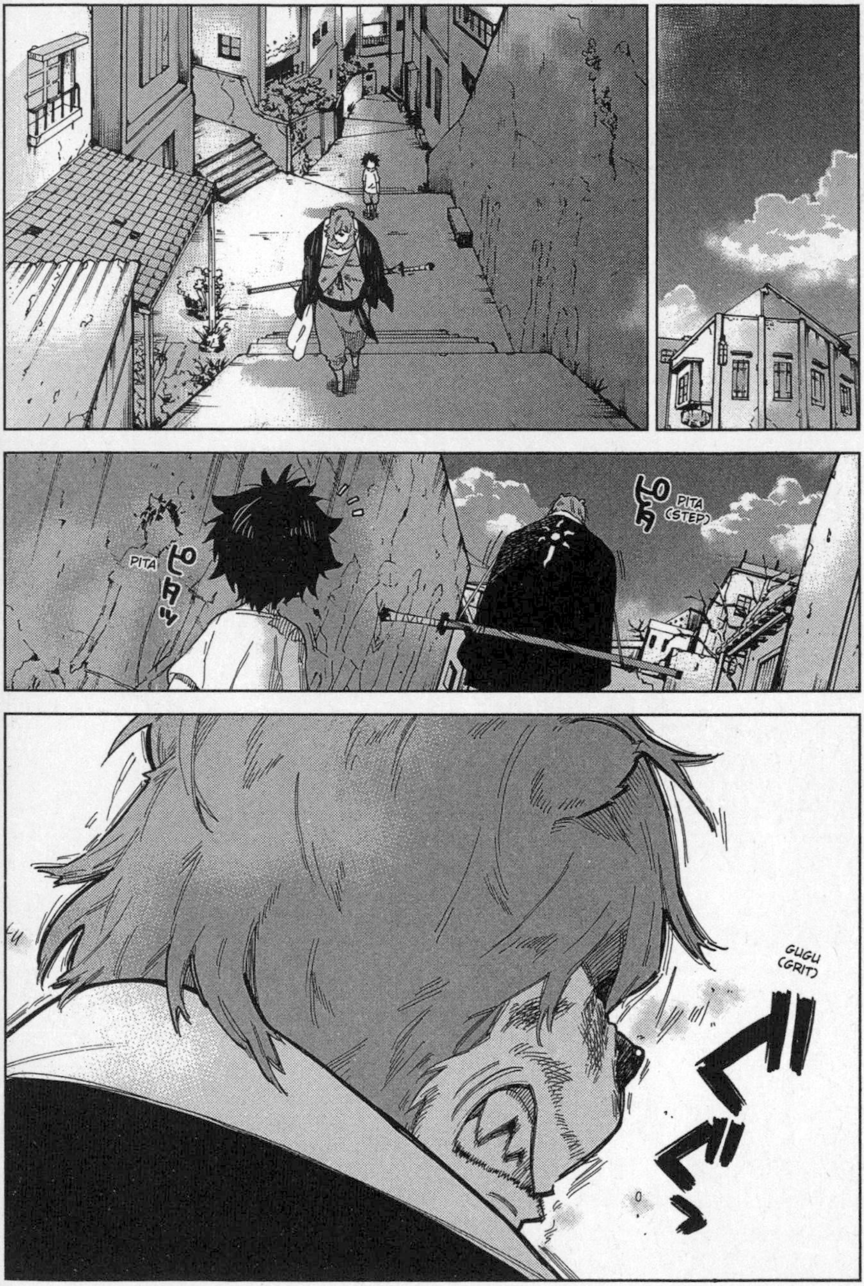
PITA (STEP)
PITA
GUGU (GRIT)

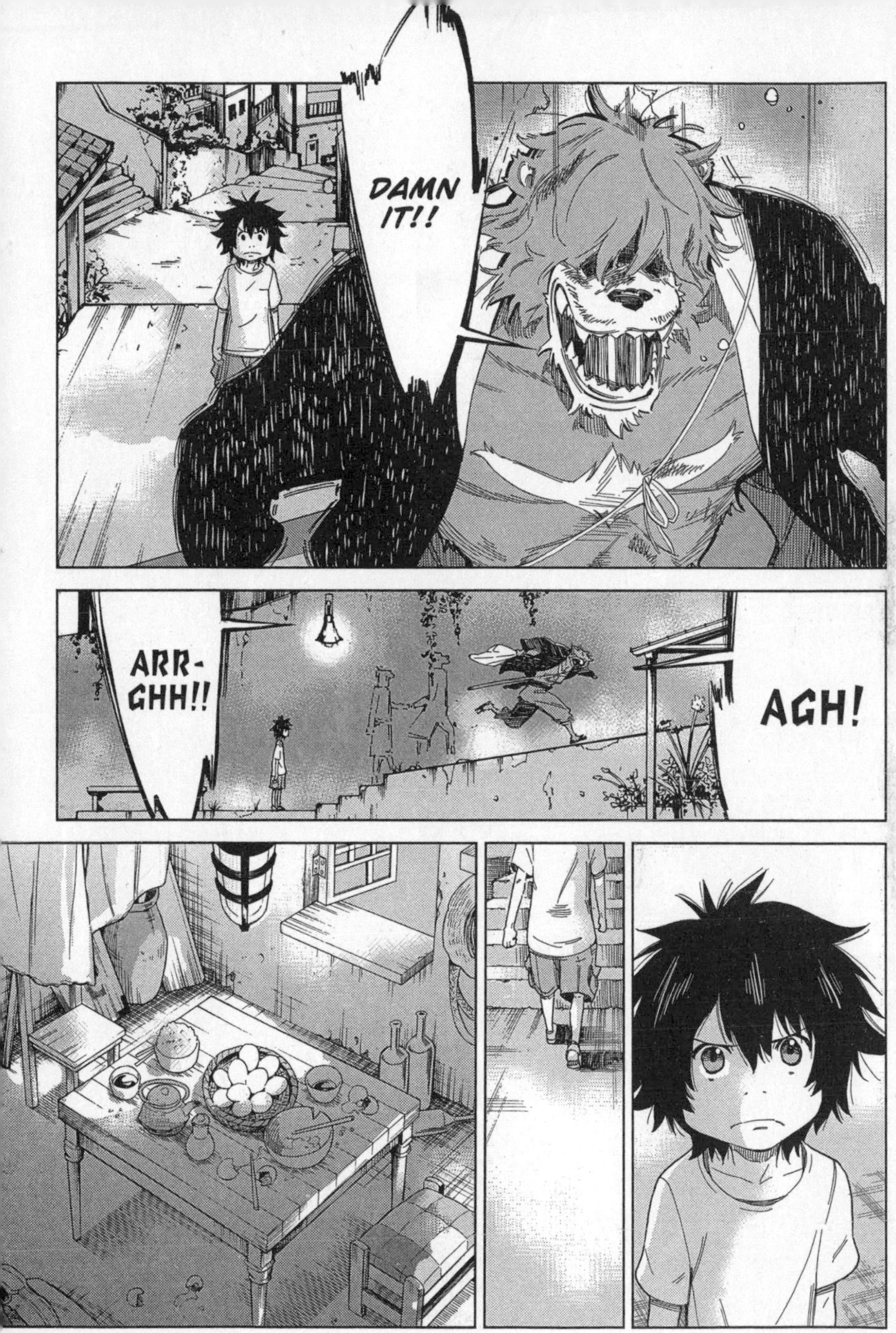
DAMN IT!!
AGH!
ARR-GHH!!

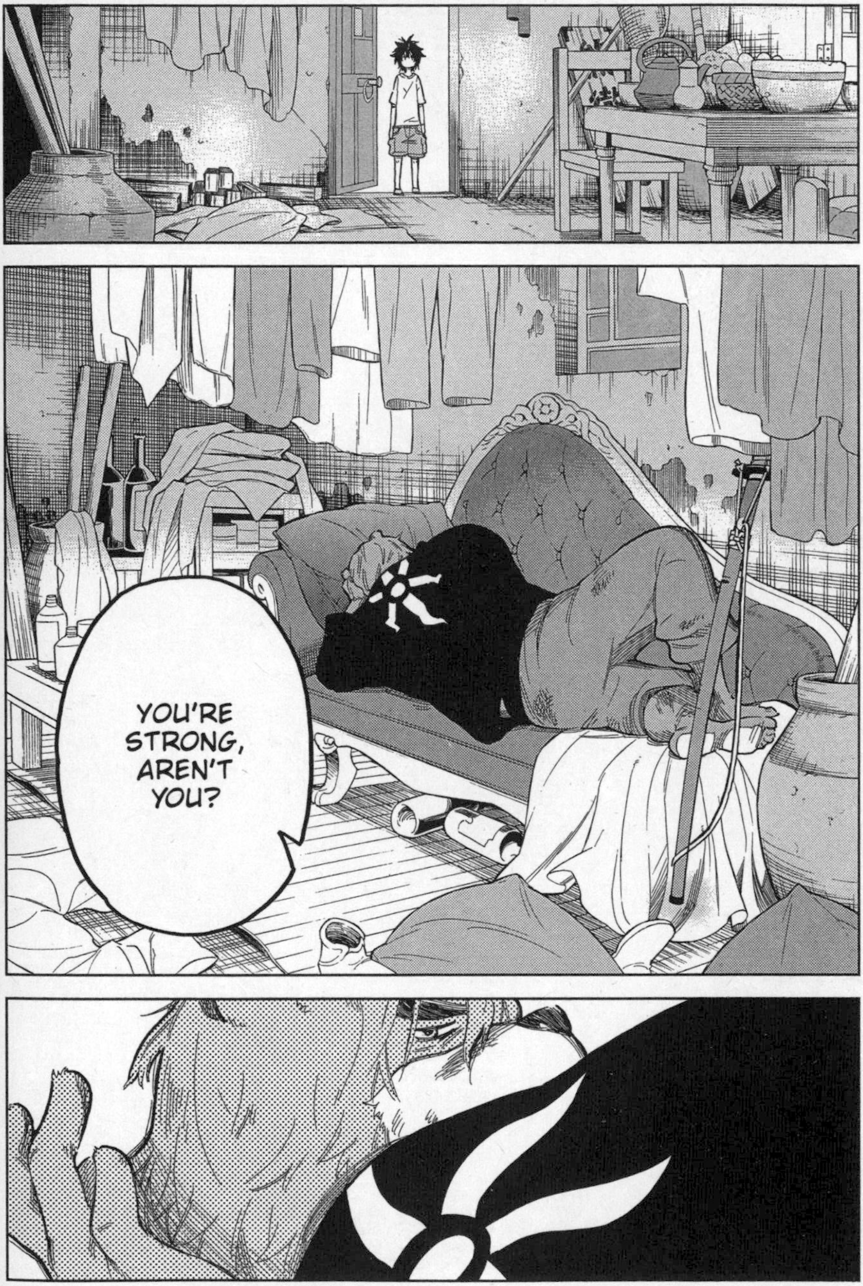
YOU'RE STRONG, AREN'T YOU?

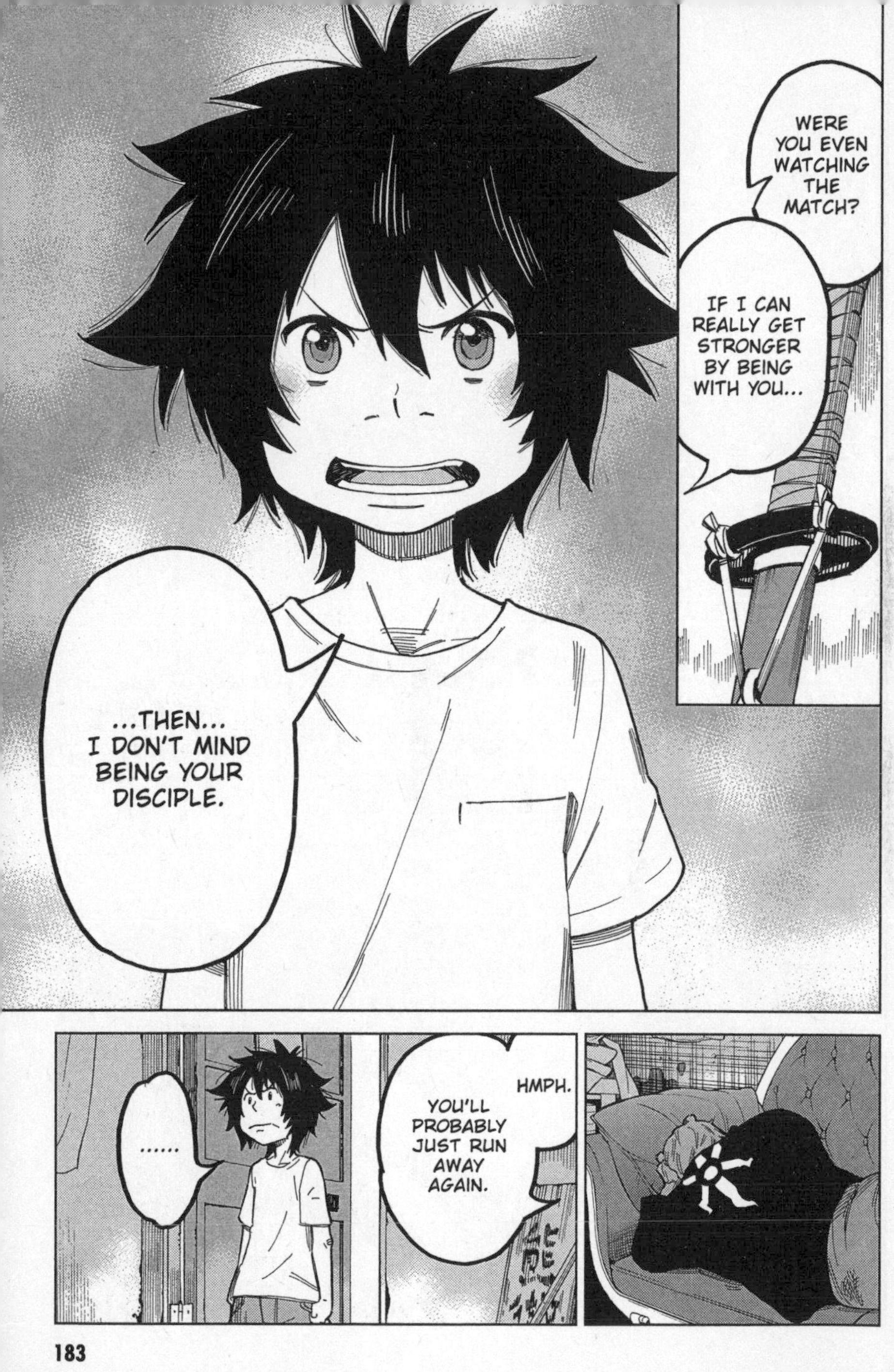
WERE YOU EVEN WATCHING THE MATCH?
IF I CAN REALLY GET STRONGER BY BEING WITH YOU...
...THEN... I DON'T MIND BEING YOUR DISCIPLE.
HMPH.
YOU'LL PROBABLY JUST RUN AWAY AGAIN.
......

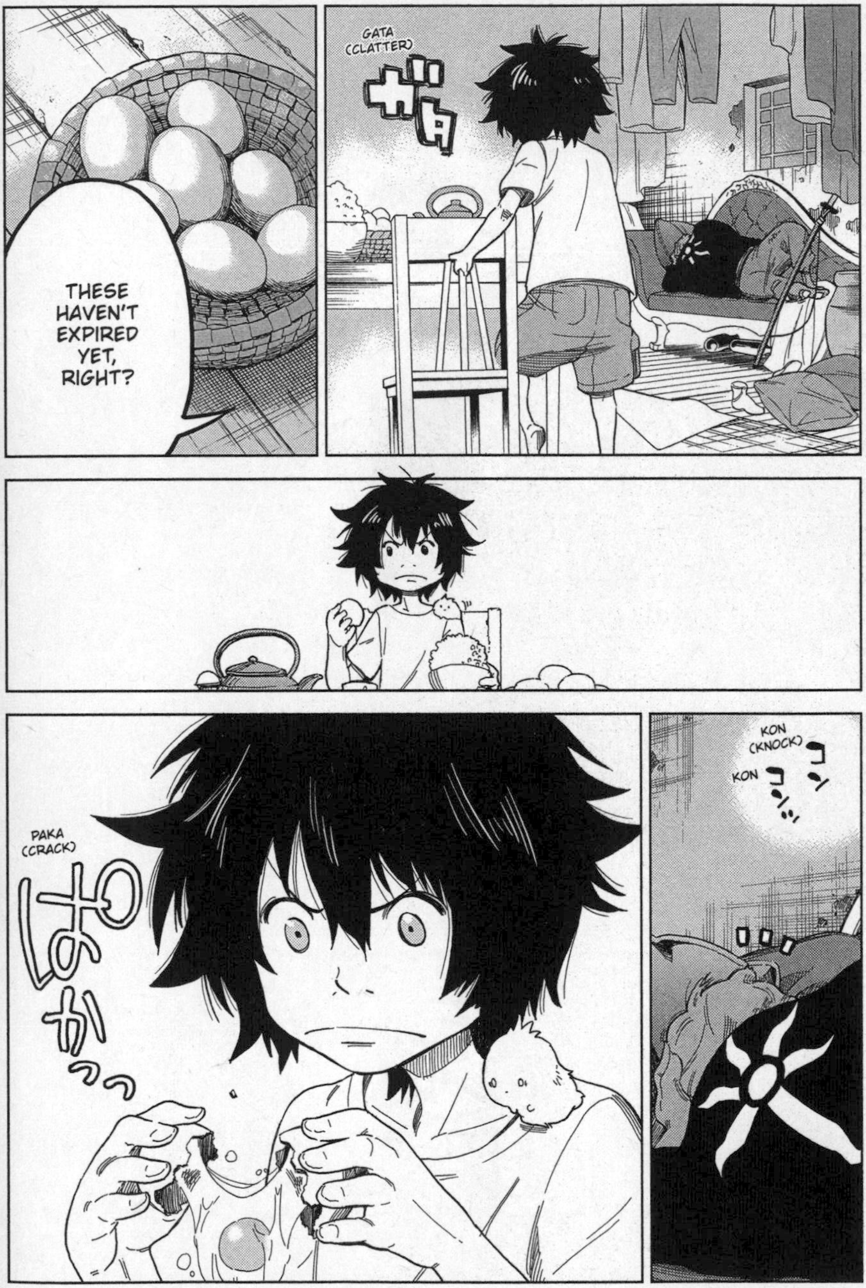
GATA (CLATTER)
ガタ
THESE HAVEN'T EXPIRED YET, RIGHT?
KON (KNOCK)
コン
KON
コンッ
PAKA (CRACK)
ぱかっ

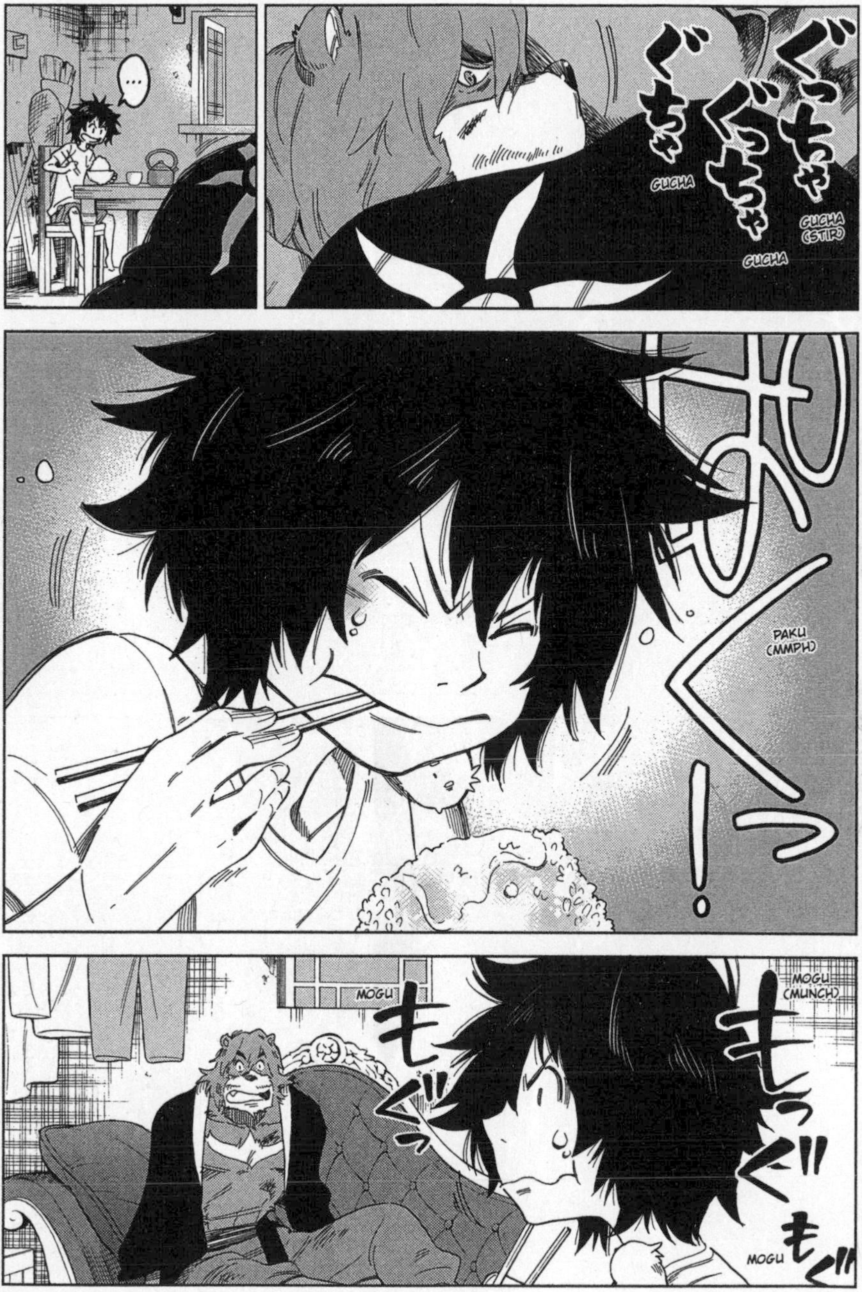
ぐっちゃ
ぐっちゃ
ぐちゃ
GUCHA
GUCHA (STIR)
GUCHA
...
PAKU (MMPH)
MOGU (MUNCH)
MOGU
MOGU

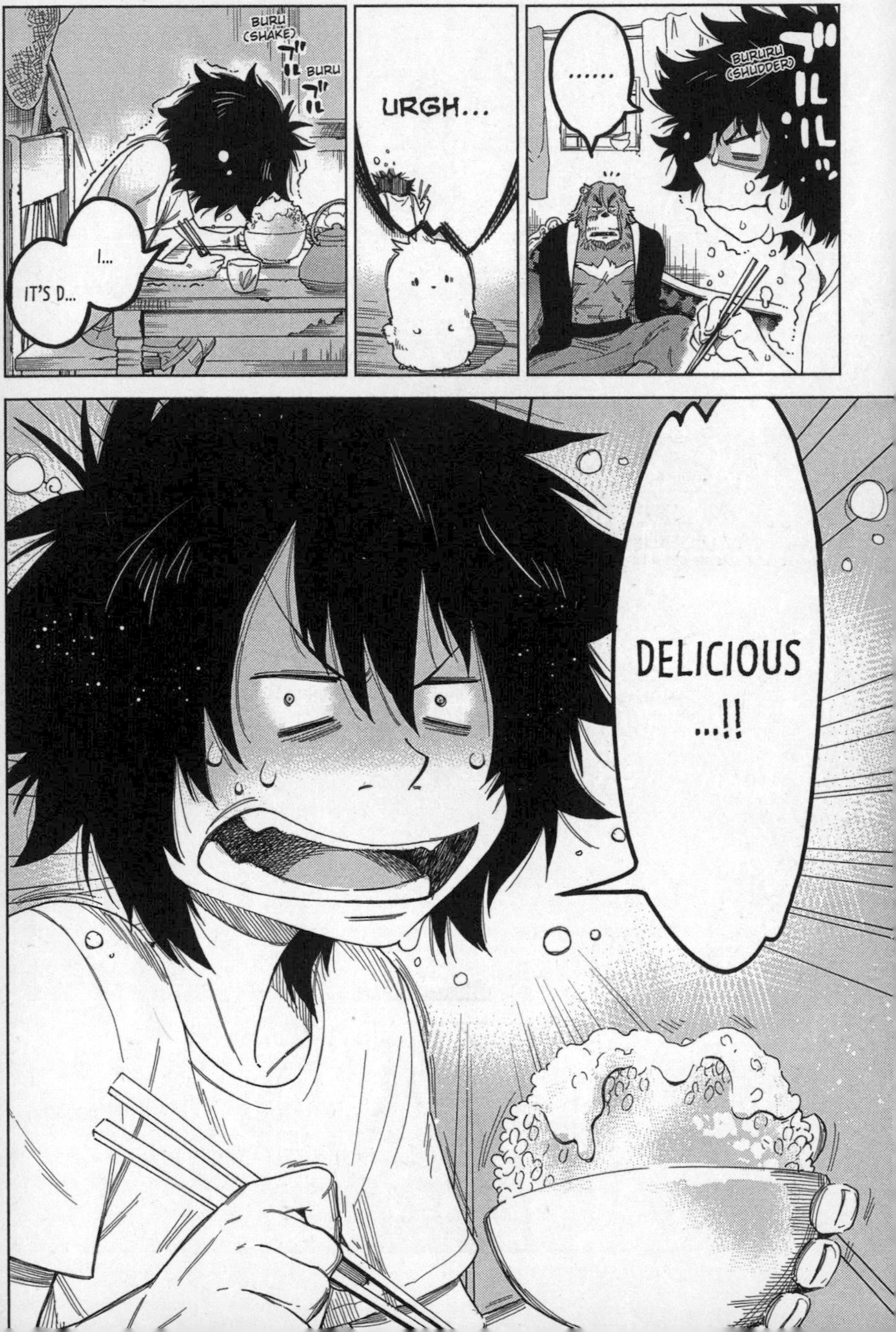
BURURU (SHUDDER)
......
URGH...
BURU (SHAKE)
BURU
I...
IT'S D...
DELICIOUS ...!!

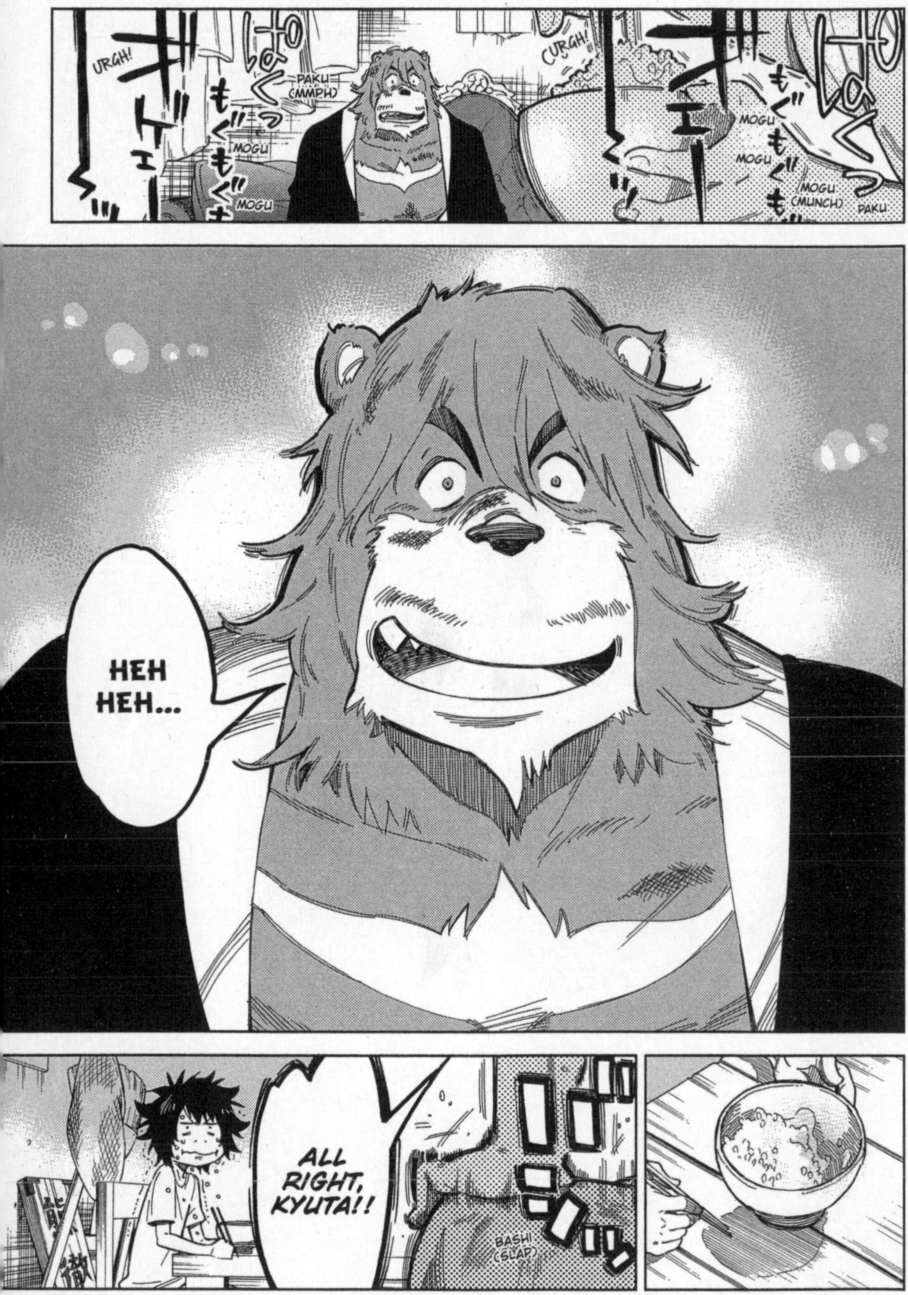
PAKU
MOGU (MUNCH)
MOGU
MOGU
CURGH!
PAKU (MMPH)
MOGU
MOGU
URGH!
HEH HEH...
BASHI (SLAP)
ALL RIGHT, KYUTA!!

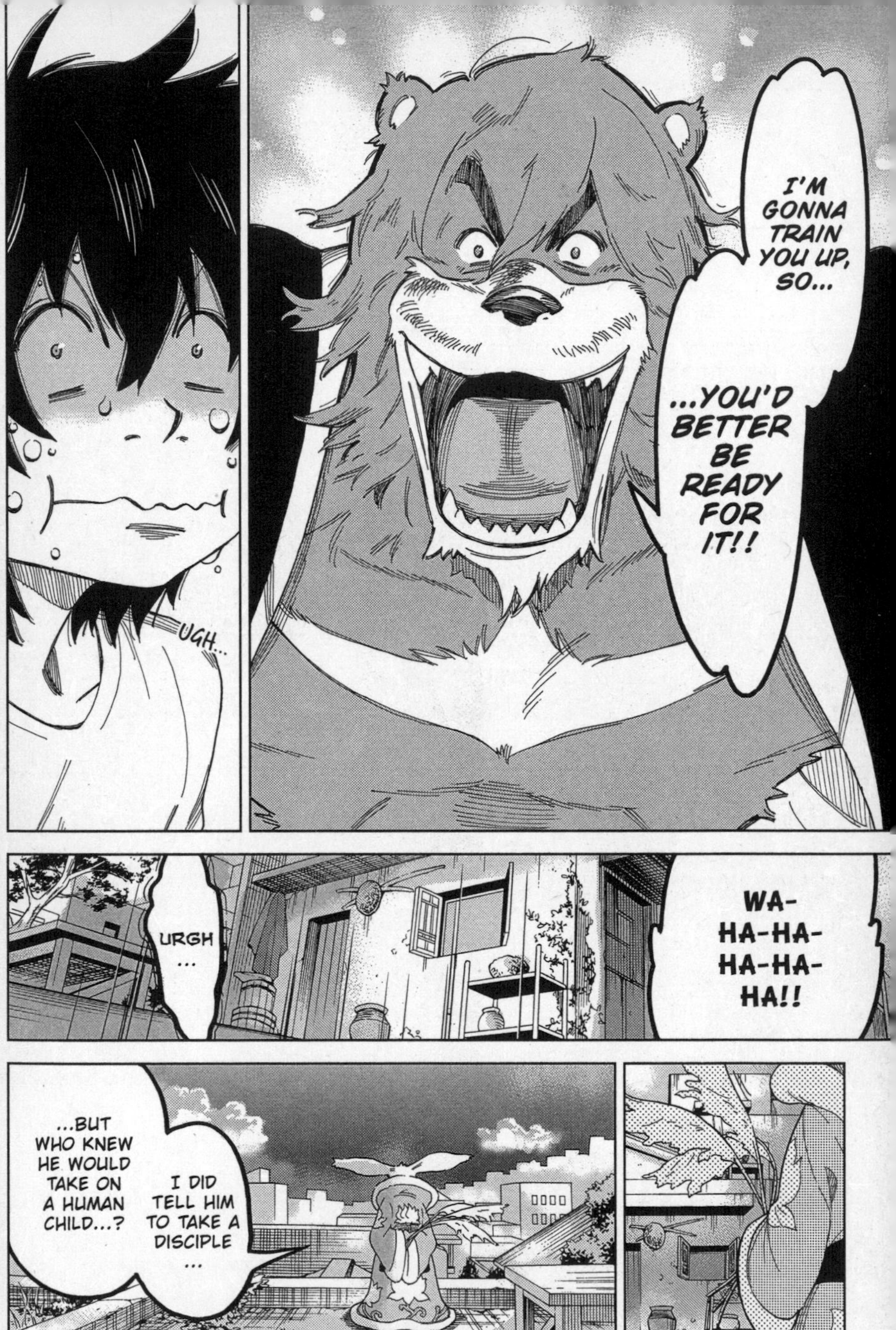
I'M GONNA TRAIN YOU UP, SO...
...YOU'D BETTER BE READY FOR IT!!
UGH...
WA-HA-HA-HA-HA-HA!!
URGH ...
I DID TELL HIM TO TAKE A DISCIPLE ...
...BUT WHO KNEW HE WOULD TAKE ON A HUMAN CHILD...?

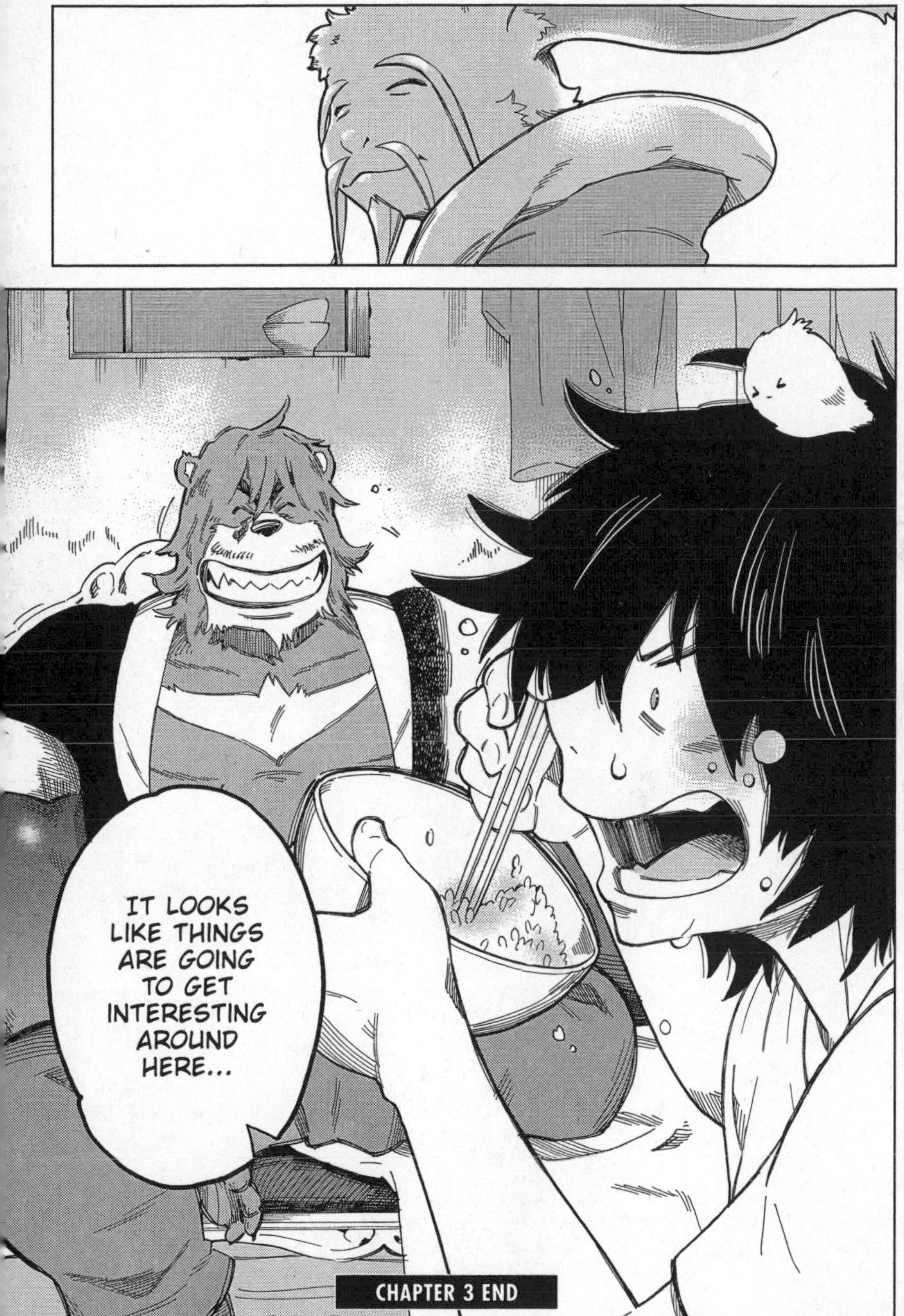
IT LOOKS LIKE THINGS ARE GOING TO GET INTERESTING AROUND HERE...
CHAPTER 3 END

THANK YOU FOR READING THE FIRST VOLUME OF *THE BOY AND THE BEAST*!

Hello, I am the artist of this comic, Renji Asai.
By the time this volume is on sale, I think many people will be waiting to see the public showing of the film, *The Boy and the Beast*. Actually, I will be one of those people! When I wrote this afterword, I still had not seen Kyuta or any of the others actually move on screen. However, while I was making this comic based off of the storyboards and other materials I had received, I really felt the sense that everyone in Jutengai was alive, from the characters' expressions to the little things like the glass bottles rolling around in Kumatetsu's room. I had real fun drawing all of them!

I hope that before you see the film—and even afterward—you would keep this book and its story's wonderful worldview in your hearts. Well then, I'll see you in volume 2!

Renji Asai

SPECIAL THANKS TO
Yuho Ueji-sensei, Akira Kasugai-sensei, Akira Katou-san, Miki Kamiya-san
Takuma Ishii-san, Sunabe-san, Oohashi, NAOKI

To Yuu-sensei, who sent me a congratulatory piece,
and my editor Ittoku Kimura-san — Thank you very much!

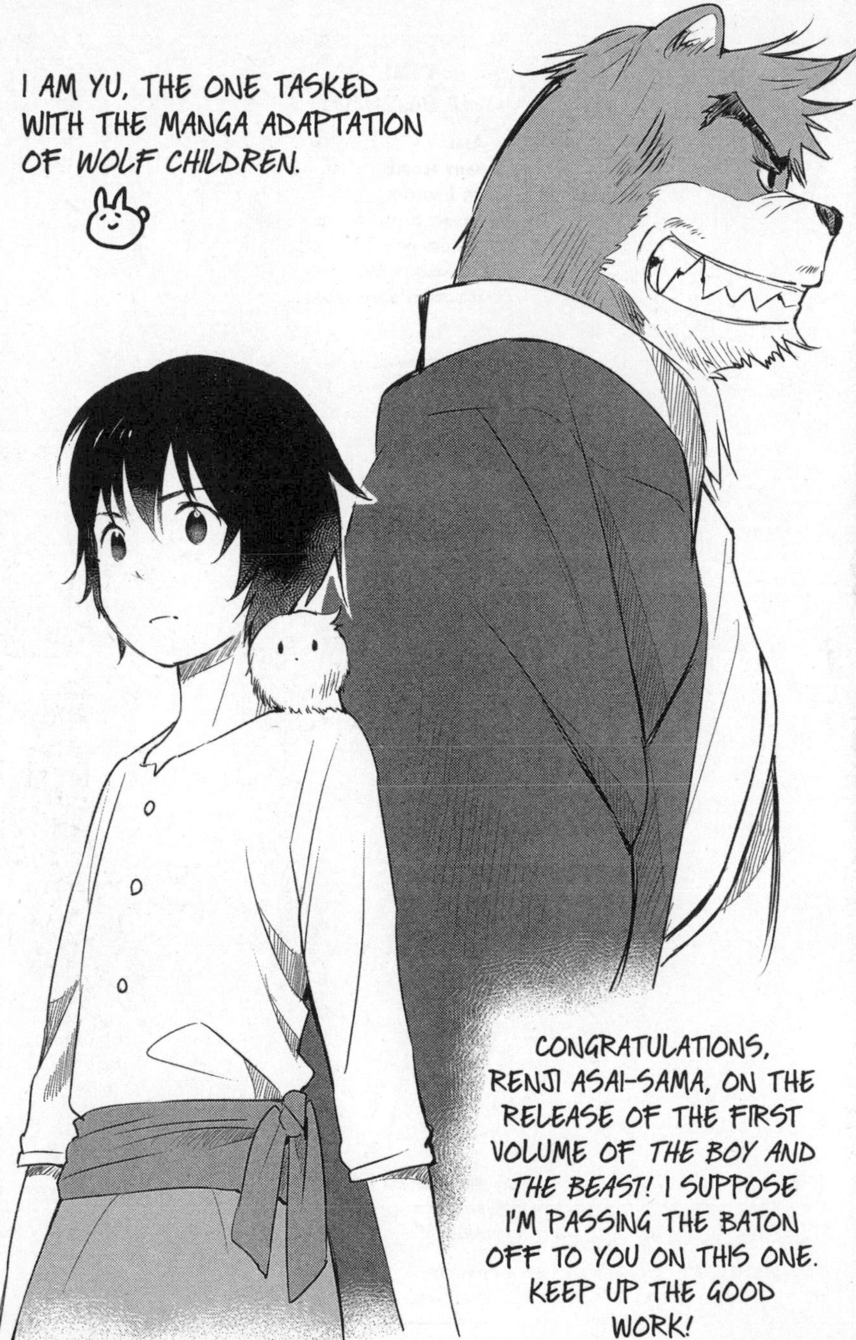
I AM YU, THE ONE TASKED WITH THE MANGA ADAPTATION OF *WOLF CHILDREN*.
CONGRATULATIONS, RENJI ASAI-SAMA, ON THE RELEASE OF THE FIRST VOLUME OF *THE BOY AND THE BEAST*! I SUPPOSE I'M PASSING THE BATON OFF TO YOU ON THIS ONE. KEEP UP THE GOOD WORK!

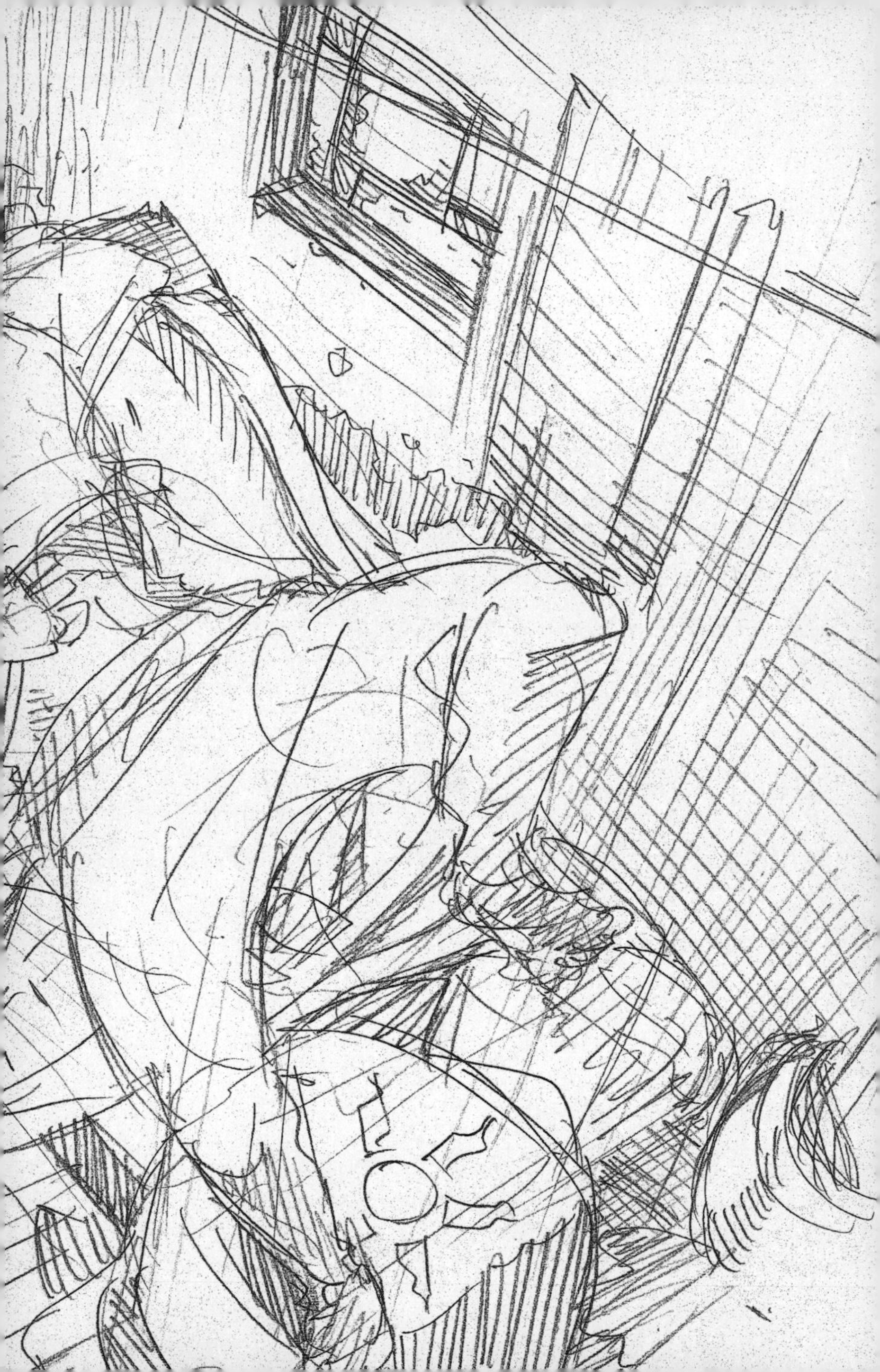

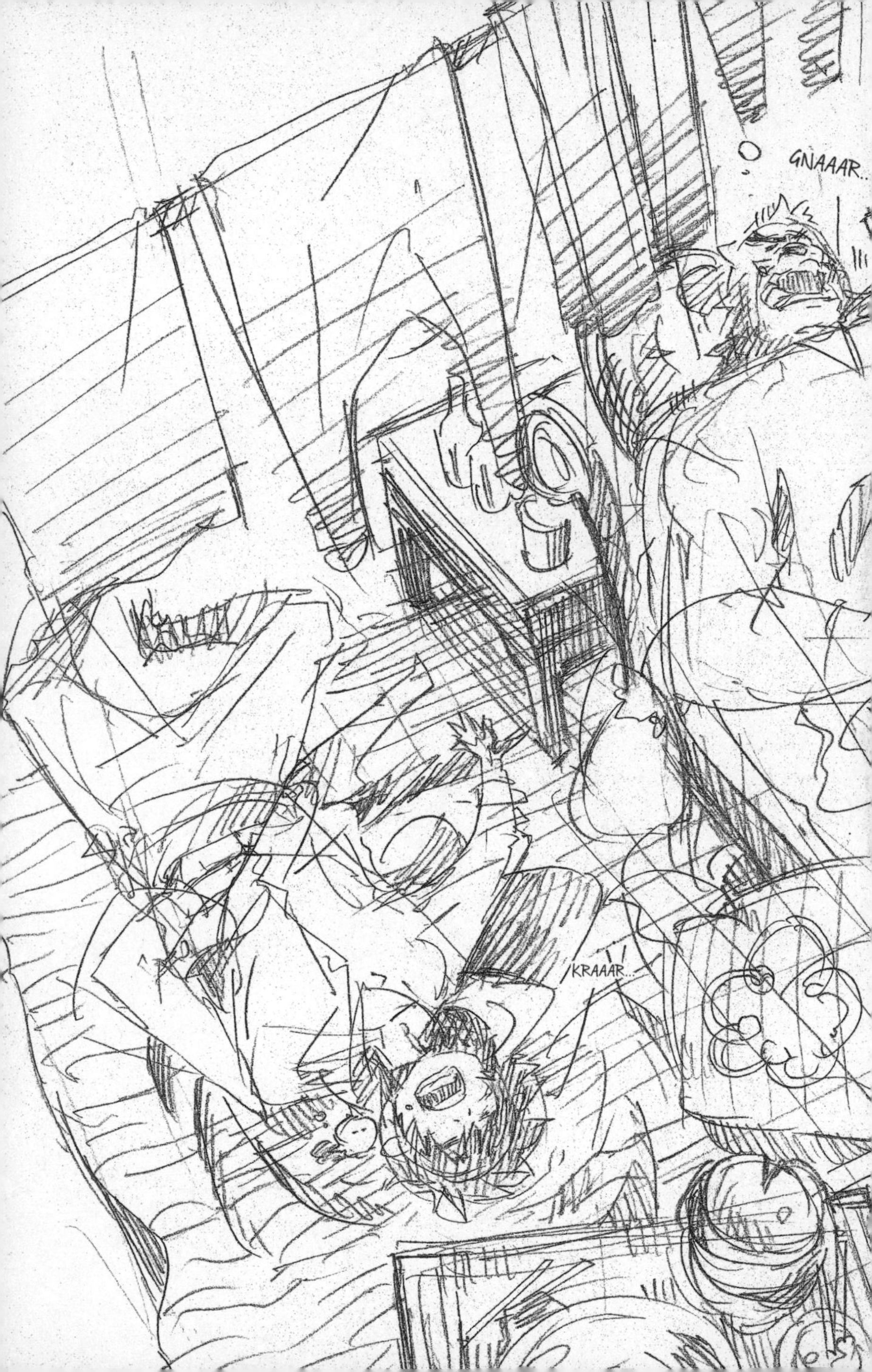
GNAAAR..
KRAAAR...

TRANSLATION NOTES

Many of the character and place names in *The Boy and the Beast* carry special significance.

Jutengai taken literally, means "rough heavens town." However, the Japanese character for *ju* in *jutengai* corresponds to the character for *shibu* in Shibuya, so it is also meant to imply a sort of Shibuya for beasts.

Kumatetsu, appropriately enough, comes from the Japanese characters for "bear" and "strike."

Iozen is derived from "boar," "king," and "mountain." Quite fitting for such a regal mountain of a boar. His two sons, meanwhile, are ***Ichirohiko*** ("first boy") and ***Jiromaru*** ("second boy").

Kyuta means "ninth boy." Kumatetsu gives Kyuta this name upon learning that he is nine years old. Kyuta's name in the human world, ***Ren***, means "lotus," which connotes holiness and enlightenment in the Buddhist tradition.

PAGE 95
A common breakfast in Japan involves cracking a raw egg over steaming hot rice. Kumatetsu, however, takes it to an extreme, which a normal Japanese boy like Kyuta would likely find gross—hence his complaint in the original Japanese is *tamago kusai*—"It smells so eggy!"

**TWO CHILDREN. TWO WOLVES.
TWO LIVES. ONE CHOICE.**

WOLF CHILDREN
AME & YUKI

Mamoru Hosoda, creator of *Summer Wars* and *The Boy and the Beast*, tells a tale of growing up and growing out, of roads taken and abandoned, and of the complicated bonds between a mother and her children. With Ame and Yuki's wolf father dead, Hana must raise her two children alone. But they are both human and wolf. How will they survive in a world with no place for them? Artist Yu brings Hosoda's film to manga form in a book YALSA called one of its top ten graphic novels of 2015!

Available at bookstores everywhere!

Yen Press

YenPress.com

The Boy and the Beast ❶

Original Story Mamoru Hosoda · *Art* Renji Asai

Translation: ZephyrRZ · Lettering: Bianca Pistillo

THE BOY AND THE BEAST
© Mamoru Hosoda 2015
© 2015 THE BOY AND THE BEAST FILM PARTNERS
Edited by KADOKAWA SHOTEN. First published in Japan in 2015 by KADOKAWA CORPORATION, Tokyo. English translation rights arranged with KADOKAWA CORPORATION, Tokyo, through TUTTLE-MORI AGENCY, INC., Tokyo.

Translation © 2016 by Hachette Book Group, Inc.

Yen Press
Hachette Book Group
1290 Avenue of the Americas
New York, NY 10104

www.HachetteBookGroup.com
www.YenPress.com

Yen Press is an imprint of Hachette Book Group, Inc.
The Yen Press name and logo are trademarks of Hachette Book Group, Inc.

The publisher is not responsible for websites (or their content) that are not owned by the publisher.

Library of Congress Control Number: 2015955216

First Yen Press Edition: February 2016

ISBN: 978-0-316-35820-0

10 9 8 7 6 5 4 3 2 1

BVG

Printed in the United States of America